P9-CNB-622

PREPARE TO DIE!

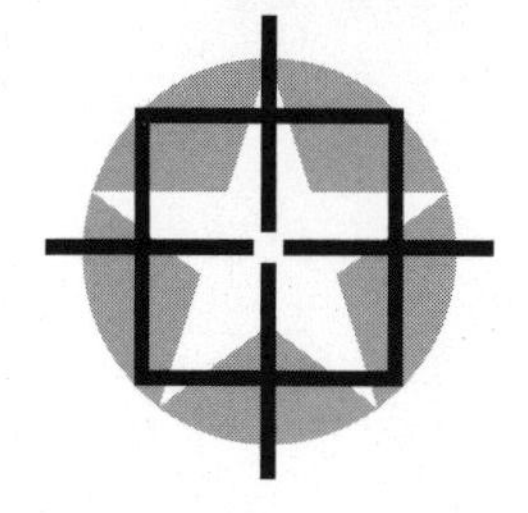

PREPARE TO DIE!

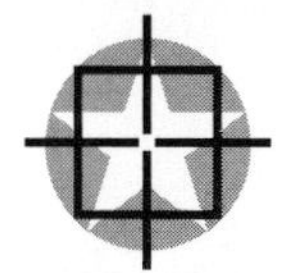

A novel by

Paul Tobin

night shade books
san francisco

Jacket illustration by Anthony Palumbo
Jacket design by Claudia Noble
Interior layout and design by Amy Popovich

Edited by Ross E. Lockhart

First Edition

ISBN: 978-1-59780-420-2

Night Shade Books

www.nightshadebooks.com

For anyone who has ever saved someone else.

And, always, for Colleen.

CHAPTER ONE

I pulled off Interstate 184 into the parking lot of the Minute Marvels convenience store and turned off my iPod. My toes ached from how long I'd been pressing down on the gas pedal. All I wanted was some water, a bathroom break, and of course some caramel crab cakes, but the instant the music was gone I could hear the woman's screams.

Her voice was keening and sharp, like a laser's hiss when it cuts through damp air, or the kiss of metal scraping on metal, and I was out my car door and wishing I could take a piss before dealing with whatever was happening, with whoever's life was being shredded, with whoever was acting the part of the asshole.

I say acting the part of the asshole, but of course for so many people it's not an act. They really are assholes.

The parking lot smelled of gas and confections and soda pop, and my feet stuck a bit to the pavement with each step. The screams were coming from a blonde, too overweight to be considered as pretty, but well dressed. She didn't look like a bad person. She wore a red business skirt with a white top and a dark blazer, and three convicts were in the act of stealing her car, one of them punching her again and again, trying to force her to let go of the steering wheel, which she was clearly holding onto for safety. If someone could have explained the reason she was being hit, she would have let go of the wheel, slid out of the car, and stood aside. Take it from me, though… most people don't have any reasoning abilities during a fight. It leaves them entirely.

I said, "Hey."

Nobody did anything.

I said, "Knock it off. Right now." One of the three convicts stopped what he was doing. I swear to god he was cleaning the windshield, right in the middle of the car-jacking. Another one was topping off the gas while the third man was beating the woman. It was a full-service crime.

All three of the men were in orange jumpers from the Athens Penitentiary. I'd heard a report of the prison break. Two dead guards. Thirteen dead convicts. Three men on the run. Looks like they were tired of being on the *run* and were now trying to be on the *drive.*

The man punching the woman was huge, and clearly a member of some Aryan brotherhood. He was probably the worst threat. The man pumping the gas was a squirrely type, like a Holocaust survivor about halfway through his stay. His jumper was ripped and bloodied near his left calf: he'd taken some damage during his escape. It didn't look too bad, but he wasn't putting much weight on the leg. The man cleaning the windshield, the one looking at me, had a big mustache and a bald head and his mouth was full of beef jerky he'd obviously stolen from inside the Minute Marvels convenience store.

With all the food in that store, he'd stolen *beef jerky*. The criminal mind at work.

"Stay out of this shit," he said. I nodded, and walked closer. All three of the men were now looking at me. The woman was slumped down in the driver's seat, bleeding from a wound on her cheek, mumbling "*Nine One One*" over and over again. The Aryan Brother who had been beating her reached to the top of the car and picked up a Glock. I hadn't noticed it before. It was probably something I should have seen.

He said, "I'm in prison for killin' a man. They goin' execute me. Nothin' to lose by killin' one more." The gun was pointing at me. It was a Glock 19, one of the compact types, and it looked like it'd been dug up from a ditch. I wondered if he'd buried it before going to prison, or if somebody had planted it for him prior to his escape. I could hear sirens from far away. Too far away to make much difference. We were surrounded by cornfields, with corn that was dick height to a midget. Three cows had somehow gotten into one of the fields and were munching on the growth. It was anybody's guess how they'd gotten there. Cows will often go somewhere just because they're too stupid to know they're not welcome.

I told the Aryan, "You're not in prison. You're in a convenience store parking lot, making bad decisions." I tried not to make it sound like a threat, but I've heard people say that everything out of my mouth sounds like a threat… that I could ask someone if they'd like some whipped cream on top of their pumpkin pie, and they'd crap their pants and run off. I do try to smile when I talk to people. That mostly goes wrong, too.

"Just kill him, Bigger." It came from the man pumping gas. He'd topped off the tank and was now purposefully spraying gas onto the pavement. It was running in a stream along a dip in the parking lot. I watched an empty corn chip bag get caught up in the flow. I like the smell of gas, but understand it's not good for you.

I said, "Bigger?" to the man with the Glock. "Your name is *Bigger*?" He straightened to attention, like a dog that's been called by name. The Glock dipped up and down, but the aim remained more or less at my head. He had tattoos of weaponry. White-trash heraldry. Women's names. Hash marks.

"How the fuck you know my name?" he demanded.

"Jesus, Bigger," said the man who had been cleaning the windshield. "The Colonel just said your name. That's how this asshole knows." He was wiping the windshield clean with a paper towel. He threw the towel towards the trash. Missed. Picked it up and put it in place. The woman in the car was still groaning about *Nine One One*.

"Put the gun down," I told Bigger. "Put it down and we can end this."

"Who the fuck are you to tell me anything?" he asked. He fired a shot towards my feet. The woman in the car sat up straight and looked around like she couldn't believe what was happening, and maybe that was true. Her mind was shutting down. Full fetal in the brain. The other two convicts barely flinched when the shot went off. The windshield cleaner pulled at his mustache, as if in thought. The bullet hit less than a foot from the stream of gas that was flowing across the parking lot. There'd been a spark. We'd almost gone to hell. I wondered about the clerk in the convenience store. I hadn't seen anybody moving around in there. A car, parked some thirty feet away, had a man peeking his head up at intervals. Maybe he had a cell phone. Maybe he had called the police. Maybe the sirens I was hearing were coming closer. It didn't seem like they were, but we were in open country and sounds play tricks.

"Who. The fuck. Are. You?" Bigger asked me again. I took a step closer. He didn't like it. He shook the gun, trying to force me to look at it, to acknowledge it, to understand its power. I refused. Looking at a gun just makes these people happy. Instead, I was thinking of Adele. She was still three hundred miles away. That's if she was home. I should have called. I should have told her I was coming. I wondered if her life would change when I knocked on her door, and I wondered if that change would be good or bad, and I, mostly, wondered if I had any right to knock on that door and create that change. I really should have called. I really should have given her the chance to say "*no*." But… without calling, the whole time I was driving, I could pretend that she would be happy to see me. I needed that dream.

"Answer me!" Bigger yelled. He was flexing his muscles. I admit they were big. The day was hot and his muscles were covered in a glistening coat of sweat. His orange clothes were badly stained. If I walked any closer, I'd probably start to smell him, even over the scent of the gas.

"Who am I?" I said. "You don't recognize me, do you?"

Bigger said, "Wha…?" He was thinking about firing another shot. He looked back to his friends, confused about how I wasn't afraid. When he turned, I could see that he had Hitler's face tattooed on the side of his neck.

I said, "I suppose it's true that I'm not in costume, but hell… my face has been everywhere. Though, to be fair, maybe you haven't had a chance to keep up to date. I hear you've been in prison for killing a man." I was getting mad. I usually do at about this time. It always starts calm, but something about the moment when I decide that things have gone too far, it gets my blood raging, and I start to feel like my heart is outside my body, egging me on, pushing me towards these fights.

Bigger said, "Jesus." I think he recognized me, right then. I think my face came back to him. He fired a shot and I'd been right; he'd been aiming at my head. The bullet struck the side of my nose, just below my eye. It ricocheted up and through my hair, tugging at the strands. I stood looking at Bigger. The Glock is a powerful weapon. He'd made me mad.

I said, "I'm Steve Clarke. I'm Reaver."

⌖

Two hundred miles back down the road, the night before, I'd stopped at a motel after spotting signs for it during a ten-mile stretch. The first billboard had no more than the name of the motel, which was, strangely enough, Bates Motel. The next sign had read, "Our showers are safe," which I thought was a nice touch. I was in a mood where I needed some humor. It's a mood I've been in for… let's say a few years, at least.

The next sign just read, "Aren't you tired? You look tired." I'm not sure if I had been tired, or if the sign had talked me into it, but I found myself on the exit and then on a country road waiting for three boys on bicycles to cross ahead of me, with them ambling out of a cornfield where they'd set up a small ramp and had been doing tricks. The corn was trampled and destroyed in that area. I appreciated that. I remember when I was a kid, long before responsibility was a factor in my life. It would have been a wondrous thing to go out and ask those three boys to show me some tricks. There were maybe seven years old, maybe eight, maybe nine, but definitely an age where they wouldn't care if they fell on their asses. I miss that feeling.

When they came out of the field I stopped my car, only about twenty yards past a stop sign, in respect for their youthful arrogance. They took a lingering time going over the road, talking about… something… I couldn't hear. My iPod was blasting Johnny Cash and he was joking with the prisoners at Folsom and making the guards angry. I didn't like what he was doing but at the same time I admired his balls. Still… it was naïve. Most men in prison are there because it's where they belong. Of course, it's equally naïve to think that all of them are there for that reason.

But… the boys' conversations were lost to me. They were probably talking about sports. School. Parents. Food. Maybe even about girls. They weren't at an age where girls were a factor in their lives, but they were at an age where they knew girls were on the horizon, and that in itself needed to be discussed. The girls in their lives would still be lanky, beanpole things. It was hard to believe that Adele had ever been that age, even though I could remember when it was true.

I checked into the Bates Motel, where they had a rubber knife on display behind the counter. The clerk joked a short spiel about the movie, *Psycho*, but didn't want to do it, and was happy when I didn't play along. My room was about twenty feet square, with a bed, a table, a chair, a television that was already on when I went into the room, and a bottle of fifty-cent water with a note that it was complimentary, with an exclamation mark. I walked into the bathroom, faced the mirror, and lifted my lip in order to look at my upper teeth. The left front tooth had been broken in a fight. The tooth was healing. It had the usual green tinge of these things happening. In a few hours the tooth would be whole again. I looked into my eyes and there was nothing wrong with them, but it didn't seem possible that they would ever be whole again.

The shower pressure was surprisingly strong and the water was pleasantly warm and I allowed myself a shower piss, one of man's greatest pleasures. If women could see us pissing in the showers, the way we're not bothered by it running down our legs, I'm not sure they'd ever sleep with us again. Looking at myself in the shower, gleaning what I could from a partially opened shower curtain and a largely steamed-over full-length mirror, I couldn't understand what draws a woman to a man anyways: we're ungainly creatures. My hair was a ragged mop on my head, looking like I was trying for one of those old Tintin haircuts, but my receding hairline couldn't pull off the tuft. I was in good shape, of course; the mirror had no problems with me in that area, though it did reflect the green tinge on several wounds. There were also discolorations. I stand about one inch under six feet, and about thirty percent of me had a bruise of some color. The blows had been deep. I don't usually bruise.

My eyes are green. Just a normal green. Not the healing kind. My hair is black. I sometimes consider dyeing it back to blonde, the way it was before the accident, but it would be vain, and faking a hair color in an attempt to pretend to be real... that was beyond even my own level of melancholy.

I tried to see how the years had changed me, but my thoughts grew philosophical so I turned them off. Snapped them shut. I thought about Adele instead.

Adele, if she would see me, would be nine years older than the last time we'd met. Her hair might be different. Her smile might have grown colder.

It might have even grown brighter. I'm not sure how I'd feel about that last possibility. I mean, I'd be happy, of course. She'd be my age, thirty-one, but it seemed inconceivable that she would be as old.

She might have a husband.

She might have children.

She would definitely have a life.

I should have called.

⌖

Bigger tried to run, of course, but I grabbed the Glock from his hand and crushed it in my grip, catching two of his fingers at the same time. The metal wrapped around them and one of the bullets triggered, trying to shoot from a barrel that was now a condensed lump of metal. There was a small and dramatic explosion. The smell of cordite. Blood. They always seem natural together.

The skinny convict with the leg wound, the one who had been pumping gas, the one they'd called the Colonel, dragged the woman from her car and tossed her onto the pavement. He slammed the door shut and brought the car, a 2009 Prius, into life. Bigger had fallen to the ground and was screaming, with Hitler's face tensing on the side of his neck. The bald man with the mustache was pounding on the passenger side of the car even as it was backing up, staring at me and begging for the Colonel to open the door. My first thought was to disable the car by driving a fist down through the engine, but I decided against that. It was the woman's car. No sense in destroying her property. But… she wouldn't mind a window, I was thinking.

I drove a fist through the driver's window and pulled the Colonel from behind the wheel. He clutched to the wheel for safety, not unlike how the woman had done, but of course I'm a lot stronger than Bigger, and the Colonel's shoulder joints were yanked free, and his grip fell away with his fingers still clawing for purchase. He came out through the window, scratching along the glass and screaming a woman's name. It was Sarah. I tossed him away, with him sailing fifty-some feet over into the cornfield to slam into the side of a cow. The cow went sprawling over. I hadn't meant to do that. I was happy when the cow got back to its feet and the bovines stared at me for a second, trying to digest some thoughts, but that's not what cows are for, and so the whole group of them did their lumpy gallop away across the field, leaving the still form of the Colonel behind.

The car tried to keep going, but I reached inside and turned off the ignition. The last man was still trying to scramble into the passenger door, so I nudged the car a bit in his direction and the impact sent him stumbling. I jumped over the car and landed on his leg. It snapped.

"Reaver!" he screamed, looking up at me.

I didn't say anything. Just kept looking at him.

"You're Reaver!" he said. It took him a scream to get it out. He was terrified. And, with good reason. If he knew who I was, he knew what I could do. A broken leg was the least of his worries. I picked him up by that orange Athens Penitentiary jumpsuit and walked towards the convenience store, carrying him like luggage.

"Don't... don't hit me," he pleaded.

"I have to piss really bad," is all I told him. He could translate that however he wanted. I hadn't decided if I was going to hit him or not, anyway. A lot depended on what I found inside.

What we found inside was a nineteen-year-old clerk named Gloria, which I could read from a nametag that was stained with her blood. She was down, behind the counter, and the store register had been smashed onto the floor. A safe had taken several bullets, but had remained impassive and resolute despite the barrage. I checked for a pulse on Gloria. It was there. I'd left the convict on the counter, sitting on the edge like a man fishing from a dock, after warning him he better not move.

"What happened to her?" I asked him, nodding towards Gloria. She was bleeding from her head.

"S-s-someone pistol-whipped her."

"Someone?"

"M-me."

I hit him. He eyes went wide. His skin, white. Vomit gurgled in his throat. He slumped to one side. I hadn't hit him very hard, but he could feel what had happened.

"It's... it's true?" he asked. He was having trouble with the vomit.

"It's true," I told him. I knew what he meant. Ever since the accident, ever since the crash, ever since the chemicals that nobody understands, something happens when I punch someone. Something about cell degeneration, and bond separation. There isn't anyone who understands *why* it happens, but there are those who do understand exactly *what* is happening, and they've told me, again and again, in reports, at conferences, in newspapers, websites, phone messages, billboards, and so on, and so on. Not everyone condemns me for it. Some people just want to talk about it. To understand it. To understand my feelings about what happens.

I tell them that that I don't understand my own feelings. I tell them that sometimes it feels terrible. I tell them that sometimes it feels great.

They tell me that every time I punch someone, that person loses roughly a year of their life.

Cell degeneration.

If you were going to live to be a hundred, and I punch you, then you're down to ninety-nine. If I get really mad at you (and I admit that I do have problems with my temper) then I might not stop punching with the first punch. Or the second. The third. And so on.

Ninety-nine years of life on the wall.

Punch one down.

Pass it around.

Ninety-eight years of life on the wall.

The man screamed when I punched him the second time. His scream seemed to wake Gloria from her beaten daze. Outside, the other woman was staggering across the parking lot. She'd walked through the stream of gas and was making footprints. I should have gone out to make her stop. I should have been helping Gloria. I should have been calling the police. But I wanted to punch the man with the mustache some more. I really wanted to do that.

"What's happening?" Gloria said. It took her several stutters to get that much out. She was holding herself up on the counter, no more than a yard away from a man with two less years of life. Gloria's hand was next to an empty display box for beef jerky. She moved that hand up, passed it through the space where the cash register had been, again and again, like a blind person searching for it. If she really had gone blind, I wasn't finished punching.

"You were pistol-whipped," I told Gloria. "I interrupted the robbery. You'll be fine. Can you see?"

"Yes. Who are you?"

"I'm…"

"Oh god," she said.

"Right," I told her. "Call the police. Tell them the three men who escaped from Athens Penitentiary are here, that they're under custody, that you need an ambulance. I suppose they do, too."

"Okay," she said. She was moving back from the counter. I noticed that she was closer to the bald man than she was to me, perceiving me to be the more dreadful threat, even over a man who had beat her with the butt end of a Glock.

I'm accustomed to reactions like that.

"Tell the police that Reaver is here," I added, going out the door. I signaled the bald man to follow along with me. He did. He didn't want to. But he did.

He had to shuffle-hop on his one good leg. It looked like it hurt.

⌖

Outside, the Aryan Brother, Bigger, was flicking a plastic lighter. He got the flame going and then stumbled towards the stream of gas, which was now drying in the sun. His plan encapsulated everything wrong about humanity: things had gone wrong for him, so now he wanted to screw it up for everyone. It made me sick.

He saw me coming. He was closer to the gas, by far, than I was. He smiled.

I was faster than him.

No surprise, there, of course. I'm not as fast as some others I know, but I'm maybe three times faster than a normal human, and Bigger barely bent over in preparation for touching the flame to the gas before I had him in my hands again. I snuffed out the flame and wrenched the lighter from his grasp, taking one of his fingers along with me in my haste. Clumsy me. I felt horrible about it.

I tucked the lighter into Bigger's mouth and then punched him in the jaw. He staggered backward, spilling lighter fluid and pieces of plastic from his mouth, and a year older than he was before I struck.

I hit him again, thinking of what he'd been doing to the woman in the car, how his fists had been coming up and down, up and down. I have a very good memory. It might be one of my powers. It might just be that I have a good memory. Either way, I could play out his assault in my head, and I knew that after I'd pulled into the parking lot, after I had turned off my music, I had either seen or heard him hit the woman fourteen times.

Fourteen.

My fist hit him a third time.

He yelled, "Oh shit! No! Reaver! I'm just… NO! Don't do it!"

I hit him a fourth time. Four years of his life were now gone. It was cruel. I hate being cruel. But I hate being forced into being cruel even more. I think that's what feeds me, at times. Feeds me the wrong way, I mean. I get mad at myself for being cruel. And then I get even madder at people who make me that way. Paladin once told me I was strong enough that nobody could make me do anything; if I didn't want to be cruel, I didn't have to be. I wish that I could aspire to beliefs like that. I wish I could. I don't even remember what I told him. Most probably something about there being a reason that I was called Reaver and he was called Paladin. That sort of thing, it doesn't just happen.

I hit Bigger a fifth time. And a sixth.

It was, as I said, cruel. But at the same time I was pulling my punches. I could have killed the man with a single blow. I could have done that. But he had hit the woman fourteen times, and he needed to take fourteen blows.

I spaced them out. And I made him count them.

I suppose making him count them was cruel.

⌖

Afterwards, when the police had arrived, and I'd given three autographs (two police officers, and then a young woman, a paramedic, of the type obviously attracted to danger, and who had mentioned she was single, and free later, and had then whispered something in a voice too low to be heard) I thought briefly about shoplifting some of the caramel crab cakes from the store. Surely I'd earned them, right? But as usual I could hear my moral voice telling me how that wasn't true. For the record, my moral voice always sounds like Paladin. Even now.

I should add that I didn't honestly consider taking any caramel crab cakes, even though I'd been thinking of them for a hundred miles. It's the curse of being the type of person I am, with the things that I can do, that I can't joke about anything anymore without someone thinking I'm serious. A normal man, he can say, "*I'd like to murder my boss, and then toss that blonde secretary over my shoulder*," and people always think he's just blowing off steam. But, me? A statement like that would panic my boss, and the blonde would probably be worried, too. Probably.

Before the police arrived I'd cleaned up the spilled gas to the best of my ability. I didn't have any special way to do it, just grabbed a hose and sprayed the area down. The blonde (her name was Doria Grables) helped me do it, turning on the water while I held the hose. She was astonished that I wasn't doing it in some extraordinary way.

"Can't you fly or something?" she asked. I told her that I couldn't, but didn't ask how she thought flying would help anyway. Once I was sure the gas station wasn't an inch away from a fire or an explosion, I did what I could for the two women. The man who had been in the car, peeking up now and then, pulled away from the convenience store, slowly, as if his car itself was dazed, picking up more speed once he'd made it to the highway, and then more and more speed, barreling away. I thought about stopping him. He was a witness. At the same time, I could understand him not wanting to stay around. I didn't want to, either. All I wanted was to take a piss. Anyway, I let him go.

Doria was nervous as I looked over her wounds. Most people are frightened of me touching them. It's not my touch, though, that drains the years. Only my punch. I told Doria that it was a special power, that it only works when I'm specifically willing it to happen, that it needs to recharge first, so that I couldn't do it right then anyway. It wasn't exactly true. Okay, it's completely false. It's not something I do consciously. I don't have to will it into existence. If I punch something, it decays. Whether I want it to or not. But, it only happens when I punch. A touch doesn't cause the effect.

And it certainly doesn't need to recharge. I can do it all day long. And I have, before.

Doria had a split lip, a couple broken teeth, a split on her cheeks, a lot of bruises. She was still in shock, so the pain wasn't as bad as it was going to be. I took some bandages and a first aid kit from the Minute Marvels store, and a bottle of rum as well. I'm not sure why I didn't consider it to be shoplifting, but I didn't, and I still don't. Gloria, the clerk, watched me take the alcohol, but she didn't say anything. She was talking on her phone. Possibly to a boyfriend. Telling someone she was okay. It looked more accurate than it had ten minutes ago. She'd washed her face and scalp. There wasn't much blood anymore. She was a brunette, with short hair and a few splattered freckles. A long sleek nose. The phone was tucked between her shoulder and her ear. It made her left breast rise up. I felt bad for looking. She nodded at the rum, letting me know it was okay.

I got both women drunk before their pain set in, and bandaged Doria as best as I could, first disinfecting the wound on her cheek. It made her hiss. She looked into my eyes the whole time, scared, but... I think... wanting me to know that she trusted me. Even so, she said the thing that I knew she would say.

"It's... too bad about Paladin," she said. I nodded. He'd had healing powers. He wouldn't have had to disinfect any wounds or wrap any bandages. His touch would have been enough. There were people, I knew, who had prayed to him back when he was alive. Quite a few of them were still at it.

I said, "It's too bad," meaning it to end the conversation. It did. Gloria, the clerk, asked if she could help with Doria, or with what she called *the bad guys*. She wanted to know if we should tie them up.

"Maybe some duct tape?" she asked. "It's not like we have handcuffs here. I mean, there's mine, but..."

"Why do you have handcuffs?"

"Sex things," she said. She didn't seem embarrassed. I liked her for that. I told her that we didn't need to worry about the convicts. Bigger and the Colonel were drained from what I'd done to them. The other man, in the cornfield, would be out for hours. There wasn't a thimble full of fight left in any of them. There were sirens in the distance, definitely coming closer, this time. The residents of Athens Penitentiary would soon be heading home.

Doria helped Gloria with her bandages, and then vice versa. They fell to giggling about their rhyming names, maybe succumbing a bit to the rum, maybe falling a bit to madness, mostly working out their relief that everything had turned out, more or less, okay.

"Are you two good for a couple minutes?" I asked.

"I think so," Gloria said. "Why?"

"Because I have to piss. I have to piss so damn bad."

"You do that?" Doria asked. She was amazed.

"I do that."

"There's a key behind the register," Gloria said. "It's on a paddle. Can't miss it. Or, should I get it for you?"

"I'll find it," I told her. I did. It had been knocked off its hook and was atop a pile of empty cigarette cartons that had been broken down after their contents went on display. There must have been a hundred boxes. It made me think of Paladin's anti-smoking campaign. Tobacco sales had dipped nearly twenty-three percent. After his death, sales had steadily risen back up to previous levels. A sad kind of tribute.

The bathroom had one stall, one sink, several smells, one under-utilized wastebasket and a novel's worth of graffiti on the walls. One notable piece of graffiti was a rough but recognizable drawing of Siren, with arrows pointing out her female attributes, coarsely labeled. A column of comments had been added by successive wits.

"I'd tap that!" was followed by, "Who *wouldn't* tap that, genius?" After that was, "Somebody insane," which was followed by, "Nobody is THAT insane." Following that was, "Pussy. Pussy. Pussy." Next in line was, "Fine. You get the pussy. I'll concentrate on her boobs." Below that was, "This is Siren, speaking. Sorry guys, I'm not sleeping with ANY of you." It wasn't at all in her handwriting. Not even close. After that pretender's line was, "Who said we were all GUYS?"

An assortment of cocks had been drawn over the illustration. A vast and varied selection of cocks. Siren was in her old costume, the one from before Paladin's death, but it was hard to notice that beneath all the floating male genitalia.

I thought about adding a line of my own to the text, but decided that it would have been crass (I'm not sure what I would have written, but it definitely would have been crass) and besides that I didn't have a marker.

By then my piss was ended. I washed my hands, my face, and I looked at my fists, my eyes. From outside, I could hear the sounds of police cars and ambulances screeching to a halt. I started to leave the bathroom and then remembered I hadn't flushed. I turned around and did that, taking one last look at Siren.

When I walked outside, the police were there. They deferred to me, which is always troublesome, because since I have no official standing it makes me go through the routine of softly letting them know that I'd prefer they take charge of the scene, which is always taken as if I'm being humble.

I explained what had happened, what I'd witnessed, what I'd done. Gloria and Doria's stories were the same as mine, as were those of the three convicts, because that type of a man will lie before a judge, but not ever me. There has been internet chatter that my type of person, the powered, exude some sort of mind control that makes normal people tell the truth, or stand aside in deference, or jump into bed with one of us. For the record, for the nine millionth time on the record, that's not true. Normal people tell me the truth because they're scared of me, and they stand aside for much the same reason, because it's more comfortable to do so. And the bed thing... that's a fear, too, but a little fear is good in bed, and most people know that.

Officer Lieber was six feet tall. A little gone to gut. Dark hair. A slight line of a dust tan exposed when he took off his hat and asked me, "So. You hit them?"

"The one with the broken leg, yes. Twice. And then the big man. They called him Bigger. I hit him fourteen times."

"Jesus. Fourteen."

"Fourteen. Yes."

Officer Lieber was silent for a time, puzzling it through. There has been legislation, never passed, but bandied about by certain political figures who wanted to score a few more votes right before elections, that would make it illegal for me to hit anyone. That was probably going through his head, but Doria was only a few feet away, telling her story, showing her bruises, her cuts, and the blood, and Officer Lieber wasn't deaf. He'd already heard Gloria's story.

"Fourteen," he said. I don't think he meant me to hear it.

"Yes. Fourteen years of his life, gone." It was best to have it out in the open.

"You've saved the world, a couple times, I hear." It was his way of saying that he wasn't going to make an issue of anything. His hand came out in a friendly way, going to pat me on my shoulder. Just before contact he suddenly realized what he was doing, and nearly stopped. Instead, he slowed way down and touched my upper arm gingerly, like he was afraid I would break, though of course he was more scared of the other way around.

When nothing happened, he smiled and laughed and the convicts were taken away. Just before Bigger was in the squad car, he bucked away two of his escorts like an enraged horse, knocking one man to the ground and slamming another against the side of the car. Both his hands were wrapped in bloodstained bandages, handcuffed behind him. There were white marks on his skin, even over the tattoos, where I had struck him. It looked like he was trying to escape, but he wasn't; he just wanted one last word.

"Fuck you, Reaver!" he yelled at me. "Fuck the fuck out of you!" The officers had him by the arms and were pinning him down against the car, kicking his legs wide, slamming their elbows into his back. They were wearing plastic gloves, avoiding his blood. He was twisting and screaming.

"Fuck you, Reaver!" he screamed. "Fuck you! You'll get yours!"

"Yes I will," I told him. "In two weeks." He didn't know what to say to that. To him, it was nonsensical, and he had to stop to think, and that stopped him cold. Nobody else asked me what I meant by my comment. The police thrust Bigger into the back of the patrol car, hooking a collar around his neck and attaching it to circle of metal in the back of the seat. Bigger could barely move. He was still staring at me when the door closed on him.

"Sorry about that," Officer Lieber told me, as if something had been his fault. He asked if he could buy me anything and I said yes—some bottled water and some caramel crab cakes. He seemed surprised that I would take him up on the offer. Surprised and pleased. There was a piece of rebar, left behind by a construction crew that had put up a storage shed, and Lieber asked me to twist it into his daughter's name, Beth. Instead, I twisted it into a "B." It wasn't long enough to do anything more.

He said, "This is perfect. Perfect. She's a big fan of… you types. Have time to stop in for a dinner?'

"Love to, but I have to keep going."

"Where are you headed?" he asked, and I almost told him the whole story, but instead I just checked myself and said, "Greenway, Oregon. For a visit."

It was true.

I was going home.

CHAPTER TWO

My costume was shredded as I was flung through the wall, outside the building, and into the street, compliments of a giant black hand that Macabre had conjured from nothing. The bricks burst around me, the sidewalk cracked, and a taxicab, fleeing the scene, caught my hip as I bounced along the pavement and booted me into the side of a panel truck. I barely got to my feet before Laser Beast leapt from a third-story window, shattering the glass as he smashed through, with one of his damn lasers cutting through a light pole and bisecting a parked motorcycle that was only a couple feet behind me. While he was recovering from his landing I picked up the rear half of the motorcycle and threw it at him, accidentally dousing myself with gas when I reared back for the throw.

The half-motorcycle caught Laser Beast in his forehead and he tumbled over backwards, triggering one of his lasers (this time from his eyes) as he went over, sending a beam far into the skies and then, as he continued his sprawl, cutting a line into the Bedelman's Auction Warehouse building.

That's when the lightning hit me.

The skies had been pure blue.

That meant that Tempest was around, and that meant that things were bad for me, because with Macabre, Tempest and Laser Beast, that likely meant that the whole of Eleventh Hour was in on the action. I hadn't played it smart, and I'd walked into a trap, and if Siren was there, I was in trouble.

Hell, even without Siren, I was in a bad way. Tempest's lightning smashed me down into the street and kept at me, not flashing away like normal lightning, but still working on me like a drill. The lightning ignited the gas that was on me, but of course the gas was burning at a far lower temperature than the lightning, so it wasn't anything more than a colorful special effect at that point.

Because I'm largely invulnerable, most people think that I can't be hurt. That isn't true. It was agony, the kind of pain that turns off your brain. I was screaming, bleeding from the ears, half naked because my costume isn't as durable as I am. I hoped it wouldn't peel away and show my damn crotch. I've seen enough of that type of online video. I've saved countless people, the nation, the whole damn world, but sometimes it seems all anyone ever wants to record for posterity is me with my dick hanging out.

I crawled along the street, digging my fingers into the asphalt, like climbing a horizontal mountain, albeit one that was melting from the heat of the ongoing lightning. Finally, I reached a manhole cover, meaning to pull it up, duck inside the sewers, maybe catch my breath. There was a crowd across the street, gathering, filming, gawking. I don't know how many films I've seen of bystanders being killed in situations like this. A fight between the powered is like a locomotive on fire, one that's not restricted to any train tracks, and with a temper, and a bloodthirst. Even so, people still stand around, gaping in awe, literally struck dumb.

"Get the fuck out of here!" I screamed at them. About half of them flinched. Even in the midst of it all, even in the midst of one of This Great Nation's Heroes (I had a goddamn Presidential certificate) being murdered right in front of their eyes, even with four dead already on the street, there were gasps that I'd cursed in public.

Paladin had never done that.

The manhole cover transformed into a giant hairy eyeball. Macabre at work. The eyeball blinked at me and then scuttled away on nine furry legs. Macabre himself came rising out of the open manhole, levitating through a sea of fog. He dresses like an old vaudeville act. Carries a cane. Wears a monocle. I tried to grab his legs but my hand went straight through him.

An illusion, then. Always with the damn illusions. Except when they're not.

The lightning vanished. I was bleeding, bad, from where it had been worrying at me. The wound soon closed, but I knew it would be at least a few days before it really healed. I staggered to my feet, trying to keep on the move, presenting a difficult target, plowing through a sudden wall of ice, shattering it and sending fragments flying all about. Two car alarms were added to the din. There were police on bullhorns screaming for people to evacuate, and one officer screaming, to me, that Laser Beast was back on his feet. There was a crater in the middle of the street from where Macabre had summoned a demon of some sort, some huge red muscled creature with ram horns that had torn out the side of the jewelry exchange and started dropping display cabinets into a huge leather sack hanging at its side. Diamonds and rubies were littering the street, with small creatures running about, gathering them up, rat-like things with vacuum cleaner mouths, compliments of Macabre, I assumed, or… worse… one of Octagon's genetic experiments.

Octagon.

If Siren was around, I was in trouble. But if Octagon was around, I was dead.

Nobody knows if Octagon has powers. It never matters. Somehow, the bastard can always pull the right move at the right time, always a step ahead, and since he has the full powers of Eleventh Hour at his command it matters little if he can talk to animals, or lift a car, or shoot flames from his ass. He wears that entirely black suit, face and all, and a matching cowl, and… I don't know… it must be made of a black hole or something, a void of some sort, because he can reach inside, reach inside anywhere, and pull out of one of his tricks, his traps, his little engines of destruction.

"Reaver!" cried the officer with the bullhorn. "Right behind you! Laser Beast!" I swung around, fists at the ready, to see that Laser Beast was only five feet distant, with his chest glowing. A spear of light shot out and clipped my shoulder. He's so damn hard to second-guess. The lasers can come from anywhere.

Impact spun me to the street. I ripped up a chunk of pavement and tossed it blind. I admit I was panicked. There's only so much that I can withstand. Only so many wounds I can heal. If I could have flown, I'd have taken to the air, and I would have kept going, and everyone else be damned. They should have been gone, anyway.

The pavement hit Laser Beast in his… lower stomach. Okay… maybe a bit lower than his stomach. I hit the bastard in the balls and he doubled over and I scrambled to him and punched him in the jaw, trying to break his goddamn neck.

"Take some time off!" I yelled. The crowd let out a gasp of pleasure. There was even a round of applause. They'd heard me say my catchphrase.

"Damn it!" Laser Beast yelled, knowing that whatever he was, he was one year less of it. His flanks shivered. Back then, he used to dress fairly normal. Pants. Sweaters. Nothing tailored. He always smelled, though. Like a cesspool. These days, he looks like a sadistic werewolf in Victorian clothes and he smells like a sweaty flower. There are fan sites about him. The ladies love him. He's killed hundreds.

What a goddamn world.

⌖

Forgive this interlude. I feel that knowing some background is important. You need to know a man's foundation if you're going to read a story about how it got kicked out from under him.

I grew up in Greenway, Oregon, which has a population of less than one thousand people, and half of them are insane, and the other half are trying hard to catch up. The town's primary export (at the time, you understand) was wool, that being because of the Selood Brother's Sheep Farm, which employed twenty-seven members of Greenway's vast workforce, and sixteen hundred of Greenway's sheep. My father was in charge of the sheepdogs, charged with making sure they were well fed, well exercised, and well adjusted. The last bit is a joke, because sheepdogs are not well adjusted; they have the biggest cases of OCD in the animal kingdom.

Dad would bring the dogs home with him at times, meaning one dog or the other, never the whole kennel. The dog-of-the-moment would rush around the house, barking, trying to get me and Mom and Dad and Tom (my brother) and Judy (Tom's girlfriend) all into the same room. Tom and I would purposefully stray, just to freak out the dogs. Tom always wanted to give one of the dogs some marijuana brownies, just to see if the dogs would mellow out. I never let him, because it could have cost Dad his job, and real jobs were scarce in Greenway.

The town had a small park with a tennis court and some picnic benches. The Masons held a book sale there every summer. Greenway itself held a fair. There was an old log cabin that was on the historic register, empty except for anyone participating in the local custom of girls getting finger-banged as their first sexual experience. There was a succession of names up on one rafter. A list of the inducted. You had to wedge your shoes into the corner and lift yourself up, using the logs like a ladder, clawing for purchase, in order to clamber up to the rafters. Once you'd made it, it was the third rafter from the wall. The list was carved into the wood, forever enshrined by sticky fingers working with penknives. *April and Beth. Lossie. Roberta. Daisy. Ginny. Clio. Georgie. Britney. Paula. Terri. Nora.* A few more. The list was long. That cabin damn well belonged on the historic register. It had earned its place.

There were some streets in Greenway. There were some houses. There were two taverns. Two craft stores. The Selood Yarn Emporium. There was a quarry where a few important dinosaur fossils had been excavated. There was… no… that's about it. That's really all Greenway had to offer.

At least that's what we thought at the time.

⌖

Laser Beast was furious that I'd punched him. Enraged. Growling and snarling and snapping at my arm. It was actually to my benefit. His teeth weren't anywhere strong enough to cut through my arm. It was the lasers I had to worry about.

"Laser Beast! Stand away from him!"

It was Macabre's voice, with him obviously wanting to take a shot at me, do some of his magic shit, but cock-blocked because of Laser Beast being all over me. It was to my benefit to keep the Victorian werewolf pissed off.

"You got a sister?" I yelled into his ear. "I'm asking because I'd like to take a swing at *her*. Knock a few years off her life by pounding away at her. You know what I'm saying?" Without a doubt, this fight would end up online. I wondered if my words would be audible over the swirls of the localized storm (Tempest was whipping up a miniature hurricane between the city streets, all of it centralized on me, but not yet strong enough to put me down) and the howls of the werewolf and the screaming bullhorns and the screech of tires and so on and so on. All the usual audio chaos.

"You don't have to answer," I told Laser Beast. "Just give me her address. I'll pop over and put one in her oven. If you don't have a sister, I'll see what your mom has to offer. She's hot, right? I mean, werewolf hot?" He was clawing at my stomach, trying to rip me open, but it wasn't working. He had a claw clamped on my back, though, just right where the lightning had struck, and that hurt. It hurt pretty bad.

"I don't even know if you're married," I told the werewolf. "Maybe you have a wife? She get lonely when...?" but at the moment I felt his chest heat up and I knew that he was about to fire a laser, which would have cut me in two. I smashed my elbow into his chin and twisted him face-first down onto the street. The laser blast sank into the under city, probably scaring the hell out of the armies of rats and hobos, all those scattered alligators in the sewers, and likely a mad scientist laboratory or two.

I scrambled away from Laser Beast, wary of him firing more of those damn lasers, and was immediately smashed between two vehicles (an emergency ambulance and a taxicab) that Macabre had given life, and had also given rage, with their horns and sirens screaming as they pounded me from opposite sides like linebackers sandwiching a wide receiver. The metal curved and crushed around me, smashing and twisting around my flesh, and I was thrown through the ambulance's engine block, through its cab, passing through the rear of the vehicle (briefly aware of the presence, and deaths, of the two emergency paramedics and the policewoman they'd been attending) and then down onto the street behind them. The taxicab had fared better in the collision, and it stood up on insectoid legs, turned around, settled to the street with its legs transforming to wheels once more, and then it roared into me again. It had only taken a second, or less. The taxi driver was lolling to one side behind the wheel, looking a whole lot of the way to the wrong side of death. The wipers were going, strangely, as if a car that was being guided by a magician still had need of a clean windshield in the driving rain of the growing hurricane.

I was actually grateful to Tempest. It looked like it was me against the whole of Eleventh Hour, and that meant the harder it was to find me, and the more that I could hide in the storm, the better for me.

Someone bumped into my side and I almost tore his head off. It was a random bystander, a young man possibly twenty years old, holding a camera phone and recording me, screaming about how awesome it was to be right there, RIGHT THERE, in the action. Then the hurricane reached its full strength and Tempest cut it free, with me and the guy swept up into the sky, buffeted by the winds. Street debris went along for the ride, gathered by the swirling updraft, newspapers and bits of rubble, a small flock of pigeons, some newspaper boxes. I grabbed the guy and hugged him close, trying to protect him from the worst of the damage. Lightning flashed down past us. I couldn't see straight and couldn't think straight, either. It was chaos.

I watched a Chevy Nova rise reluctantly into the air, like it couldn't believe it was happening, like it was disgusted by having to participate. It soon accelerated, caught in a stronger updraft, and collided into the side of building, smashing through a window twenty stories in the air, missing me and my friend by only a few feet as we sailed higher and higher into the sky.

"How's it feel to be right here?" I yelled at him, but I think he was unconscious. It was hard to breathe; the air was moving too fast for normal lungs to compete.

Ice began forming in the wind. At first it was sleet, then hail, then ice daggers and finally chunks of ice the size of a man. The sleet didn't feel too bad. The hail was like bullets. The ice daggers were like bullets that had been sharpened to a point. A block of ice roughly the size of a CEO's desk caught me in my side and punted me through a window. I fell to the floor of a hallway foyer that opened into a business suite. The man I'd been carrying was gone. I had no memory of just when we were separated. I felt bad about him, but damn fine about my lucky break. Inside the building, I could catch my breath. Inside the building, I could…

"Hello, Reaver."

Ahh.

Ahh, shit.

It was Octagon. He was walking down the hall, heading towards me, and I could barely stand and I knew that being smashed through the window was no longer my lucky break. It was all part of Octagon's plan. The son of a bitch is always ten steps ahead, working the angles. When I'd gotten the call, when I'd heard the screaming voice on the phone, when I'd traced the call, when I'd found the ransom note, when I talked to the parents, when I'd told them I'd do everything I could to find their son, when I'd followed the trail to the Bedelman's Auction Warehouse, when I'd gone inside, when I'd seen the rows of sarcophagi, when Macabre had come out of one of them... it had all been planned.

"Octagon," I said, by way of a greeting. I tried to make my voice sound grim, like I was dangerous, but I didn't at all feel that way. I tried for a smile and said, "You looking for a fight?"

"I'm looking at the results of one. It looks like a mess."

"You should see the other guys."

"I will," he said. "Tonight. There is a gathering. We will discuss the unfortunate death of Reaver. There's not many of your side left, you know. You're effectively the last." It's true. Paladin is gone. Kid Crater was murdered. Mistress Mary is missing.

Octagon was moving down the hall, coming closer and closer, being hard to see, as usual. Something about his ebony costume sucks in light, bends it, refracts it, does all sorts of horrible things to it. Poor ol' light, innocent as a virgin, and Octagon's suit gives it rough play. It isn't right.

The walls seemed to bulge, retract, breathe, as he passed. He was reaching into his costume, pulling out flower petals, spreading them around. He was reaching into his legs and pulling out helium balloons, setting them free.

"Celebrate the end of an era," he told me. "It's a party. The game is over!"

"Fuck you," I said, and I grabbed a fire extinguisher from the wall and tossed it at his head. He'd forgotten how quick I am. They always do. If things get bad, in a fight, I play it slow for a time, let them get used to it, then suddenly speed things up. It catches people off guard, like a batter who's been eyeing fastballs in the low 80's suddenly having to deal with one at around 240.

He warded the blow with his left arm. It broke. The fire extinguisher clipped his head and he went down.

"Fuck!" he said. "Fuck! Fuck! Fuck!" He was dazed. He sounded almost feminine. My body was covered in green lines, green patches, healing me, and I felt better than ever. I felt like I was at the end of the crossroads. I felt lucky that I was inside a building where nobody was going to be filming me, where I could limp to the fallen Octagon and hit him one hundred times. Unless he was immortal, he was about to have a problem.

"Take some time off," I said. I still hadn't reached him. Just wanted him to know what was happening. I think he was trying to reach for something in his leg, something deep in the void of his costume, but he was dazed and his hand was only slapping at the carpet next to his leg.

"Take some time off," I said. Even if there were cameras, even if this was going to be filmed, even if this would lead to a passage of anti-power legislation, even if I went to prison, it would still be worth it.

"Take some time off," I said. I realized I'd gone a bit crazy, saying my catchphrase like a mantra, like a cretin talks about tinfoil and the moon. I still hadn't hit Octagon. Still hadn't quite reached him. There was blood on the carpet beneath his head. His arm was crooked. It would be wrong to say I had an erection. But you'd get half credit.

"Take some time..."

"Reaver."

It wasn't his voice. It was a woman's voice from... from... from the door that was opening down the hall, from the woman who was strutting out of the room, from the woman who was adjusting her costume as if it had, only moments before, been in disarray, or off.

Which was probably true.

"Hello, Siren," I said.

"Fuck you," she said.

She wasn't cursing me.

It was more of an invitation.

I was pinned into place by the oldest of desires, or at least the best of the oldest of desires. That's how Siren is. That's her thing. Her voice, her body, her aroma, it's everything that triggers sex. I've known people who didn't get stiff, or wet, when Siren was nearby... but it's rare enough to warrant a comment.

Let me just go ahead and state outright that Siren and I have a history. I know that she's evil. I know she's done some horrible things. I know that I'm supposed to be a hero, despite how I've done some horrible things. Well, to air it out, Siren is one of those horrible things I've done. Consider it this way, all the internet porn that's ever been shown, all the strippers you've ever seen, all the women you've spied at odd moments, random beauties straightening a garter or twirling a finger through her hair... consider that to be *level one*. Having actual, real sex with one of these women, when you separate the pretenders from what's real, when all of your senses are engaged, when everything is perfectly focused, that's *level two*.

And then there's nasty, *let's-feel-ashamed-about-this-later-but-not-right-now* sex with one of those beautiful women. And that's *level three*.

Just being around Siren is *level five*.

Unless you're a superhuman, you couldn't live through level six or seven. Having sex with Siren is section eight. Wait. ***Level*** eight. I meant *level* eight, of course.

For who she is, she dresses remarkably conservative. She doesn't prance around in a bikini anymore (like she did in the beginning) or the slutty dress (like when she was first teaming up with Eleventh Hour) or the latex outfit (as when she first started sleeping with Octagon) or the Japanese cosplay outfits (which she once changed as often as she cuckolded Octagon) or anything of that type anymore. These days, it's a simple dress in the 1920's "flapper" style. It has a lot of beads. They move with her. They fall off a lot. You can find the individual beads online, scavenged from her appearances, scooped up by an army of amorous vultures. It seems like it would be something that's easy to fake; they're just small glass beads, after all. But, if you've ever held one… you know. Absolutely. The beads retain a sense of her perfume and her scent, and even touching one of the beads is a private affair.

They're not cheap.

"You going to say anything else?" Siren asked me. I wanted to say something else. I really did. Maybe I wanted to say something impressive, or maybe I wanted to say that it wasn't going to work on me this time… that if she came any closer I would turn not into a puddle, but a knife, one that would slice her in half. But with her so near, my voice seemed to be gone, and the walls and everything else were gone as well, or at least far past my range of focus. I wanted to lean on one of the walls, use it to catch my breath, but I couldn't find anything. I wanted to quit sweating. I was aware that I looked ridiculous, with my costume torn and stained. Siren moved protectively in front of Octagon, who was laughing, not with insanity, but pleasure. He reached into that damn costume of his and took out a vial of green fluid. I knew what it was; he'd once distilled an essence of my blood, and could use it to heal. Siren, back in the past when we were having our fling, had told me that the process was incredibly expensive. As Octagon emptied the vial onto his arm, and as the bones began to knit back together, he was spending hundreds of thousands of dollars. Maybe millions. I remembered Siren telling me about the process involved, why the costs were so high, remembered her winding one of her hairs around her finger as she spoke, then plucking the hair from her head (she had long brunette hair, at the time) and wrapping the other end of the hair around her toe. The second smallest toe on her left foot. Around and around and around. Linking her toe and her finger. We'd been in the Philippines, I think. Or maybe Japan? Brazil? It doesn't matter. It was the second smallest toe on her left foot.

Octagon was standing again, watching the interplay between myself and Siren, maybe smiling, maybe not. Behind the costume, whatever was happening behind his mask, it was hard to say. It's interesting to understand that the man is the greatest foe I've ever faced, responsible for some of my worst defeats, my narrowest escapes, but I still don't know his real name, or what he looks like. It's entirely possible that I pass him by on the streets, multiple times, every day of my life. It isn't fair.

"Was the kid even real?" I asked him. "The one that was kidnapped? Was there ever a kid at all?"

"There was," Octagon said. "We set him free the moment you walked into the warehouse. He'd served his part."

"You set him free?"

"Yes." This was from Siren. It proved it, beyond any doubt. Siren never lies to a man. That's how incredibly cruel she can be. Lots of men think that women should tell the truth, explain their feelings. These men should use their wishes more wisely.

A copier came to life in the corner. It spit out paper after paper, each of them an image of a solitary portion of Macabre's body, in the nude, and then also images of his clothing, alone. The images of his body wafted into a small funnel cloud of paper, and when the winds were settled he was standing there, naked, and in the kind of state you'd expect a man to be in whenever Siren was around. It was embarrassing, but he didn't care. He's a magician, accustomed to the stage.

Siren raised an eyebrow to him.

He said, "Duh, lady," and then plucked the images of his clothing from the air, where they'd lined up in order. He merely touched the pages to his body, and then he was wearing that particular piece of clothing. I enjoyed the show, or to be more specific I enjoyed the length of the show. It was giving me a chance to catch my breath, or would have been, if Siren hadn't been stealing it away. She was twirling her toes on the carpet, grabbing at the shag with her toes, pulling the strands left, right, all around.

Octagon said, "Reaver, you've interfered with my plans for the last time. I mean to rule this world, to show them all that I am the only king to beseech, the only power to fear, the only star in the sky."

I said, "Shit." He didn't usually talk that way. He usually talks like a normal guy. This was completely overboard. Laser Beast came in through the same window where I'd arrived. I'd been tossed in by a hurricane, booted by a block of ice. He came in riding Tempest's softest winds, and she came along shortly after. When she's calling on the storms, she tends to go naked. She'd have been the most alluring woman in the room, if she'd been anywhere else on Earth.

"Eleventh Hour," said Octagon, gesturing to me with that little flip of a hand that reminds me of a game show hostess, "… I present to you, Reaver, the last of the heroes of the spill, the last of the hurdles to leap." *The Heroes of the Spill.* I'd heard it said that way before. I tried to remember where. Some website, I think. It referred to how my powers were born. My origin story, if you will.

"Spill this!" I yelled, and I leapt at Octagon, and the dumb son of a bitch still wasn't ready for my speed, wasn't ready for me to be game despite all the beating I'd taken, and because he wanted to gloat, because he wanted to be a showoff, he'd assembled Eleventh Hour in the room along with me, in a space where they would have trouble maneuvering, and I could hit any damn thing and any damn one I wanted, and I knew what was going to happen, knew how they'd react once I started snapping necks, when they found out that just because I have a goddamn Presidential certificate doesn't mean I have to play by any pretty book of rules.

But Siren stepped in the way.

And there's not a man who could punch her.

I'm definitely a man.

And I stopped cold.

Laser Beast shot me in my back. It came out through my chest. Tempest sucked all the air away from my lungs. Siren touched me on my shoulder. Macabre put his fist on that photo-copier and ran off a hundred images of his knuckles, released them into the air, where they swarmed me like bees, punching, punching, a hundred punches, and all I could think of was Siren's touch on my shoulder. I tried to see where she was, needed to know what she was doing, wanted her to touch me again, was screaming at myself for being so dumb, and Laser Beast shot me again even as I was lifting him up, smashing him into somebody's desk, destroying the mahogany, sending pencils and pens flying, ramming a computer monitor down onto his head, racing around the room, getting weaker and weaker, shorter of breath, no damn air, searching for Tempest, finding her near the ceiling, leaping up to grab her, holding her by her left foot, thinking of Siren's left toe, trying to climb the flying naked Tempest, crunching her ankle in my grasp while being shot through my stomach with another laser, this one from Octagon, who was circling my efforts to stay alive, with him holding a futuristic laser pistol and staying at the fringes of the battle, me yelling about Paladin, about Kid Crater, wishing I could catch my breath, nearly encased in ice, shrugging free of the freeze, sending fragments around the room, one of them striking Macabre, who cursed in anger and transformed the various shards of ice into tiny spear-wielding snowmen, sending them against me, stabbing and tripping, and Octagon was circling, firing with his laser pistol, so damn calm, me with no fucking breath and Siren was singing, singing, singing and Laser Beast put another blast through my chest and…

… it

… hurt

… so

… bad.

And I was down. No memory of falling. No memory of giving up. But I had. Eleventh Hour was gathered around. Staring down at me. Siren was handing Tempest that vial of green liquid. She was rubbing it on her ankle… the one I'd crushed. At least I'd cost them a few hundred thousand dollars. Maybe a million.

Octagon put his strange laser pistol to my head.

"Prepare to die!" he said. He added in that laugh. The one we've all heard in the movies.

I said, "How long?"

There was a pause. Octagon's eyes narrowed. I couldn't see it happening, but I could feel that it was true. Of course, I was also feeling my ribs inside my stomach, shards of them inside my lungs, so my mental frame wasn't quite at the top of my game.

"What?" Octagon asked.

"How long are you going to give me to prepare?" I asked. There were things I needed to do. Things I hadn't realized until just that moment.

"I don't… understand," Octagon said. His pistol was wavering. He looked to the others. Siren shrugged. Macabre was inscrutable. Tempest looked mad, frowning, chewing on her hair in that childlike manner of hers. Laser Beast was growling, lowering his head, baring his fangs.

I said, "You win. I want to prepare to die. There are still a few things I need to do. A couple loose ends. Fact is, fuck all this shit. I'm tired of being an asshole that's the last bastion of goodness in this world. I give it all up. I'm exhausted by the dance." I was getting back to my feet. They all made room. Even Laser Beast.

"Give me a month to close the books, and then put that gun back to my head," I told Octagon. "You said I could prepare to die. Give me a month."

I looked into his mask, but his eyes weren't visible. We were about the same height. He smelled like blood. I looked for any sort of emotion past his mask, but there wasn't anything to see. Only blackness. Not even shapes. Still, in that blackness, I could feel his wheels spinning, calculating, deciding. Siren was standing behind him. It didn't look like she cared one way or the other. It hurt to know that she was being honest about it.

Octagon took a deep breath.

His gun went down to his side.

"Two weeks," he said.

CHAPTER THREE

My brother Tom was sixteen years old when he started working at the Mighty Convenient convenience store, a small chain of Oregon stores spawned off the proceeds of a larger chain of auto dealerships. Tom, of course, was besieged by friends to let them buy booze, even though they were underage. Tom never gave in. Not once. Not through all the bribes of money or pussy. They didn't faze him. He even had the Gorner Twins (they always capitalized "Twins," so I'm doing it here as well) say they'd make a three-way sandwich of him. He'd turned them down. They'd walked around in a collective daze for hours, their world turned upside down, until they'd decided that Tom must be gay.

But he wasn't. He was a hero, and he'd told me that he'd made a promise to Vic Davis (the store owner, who died of a heart attack just a year ago, victim of business stress, but I should point out that hoboes can die of stress, too, so if it's going to happen you might as well be a millionaire) that he would never sell alcohol to anyone underage. Tom made that vow, and Tom held to it.

That said, he often shoplifted beer for himself, and for me, and a couple of times for pussy (he once said he'd be gay as soon as he ran out of pussy, but not before) and one day he got me drunk enough to challenge him in a race (Tom was the district's track champion at the time) with a bet involved. If I won the race, he'd have to steal a six-pack a week for me, and I could choose the beer. If he won, he'd get to drive through town in the old Lincoln our Uncle Buzz had sold him, and I'd have to ride on the top of it, with Tom driving slow, and me wearing nothing but my underwear.

So it came to pass that I was on the roof of that Lincoln and Tom was driving through Greenway at a steady pace of fifteen miles per hour. I was wearing whitey tighties, not the underwear I'd wanted to choose (I had a pair of boxers that weren't much different than swim trunks, and I could have claimed them as such to any shocked witnesses) but Tom had pointed out that if he'd lost the bet, then I would have been able to choose the beer, so it was only fair to let him choose the underwear.

That was a reasonable point.

Tom usually had reasonable points.

Tom taught me a lot about doing the right thing, and how sometimes it was hard to do.

I'm not telling this story because I think anyone needs to know about me, age fifteen, in my underwear. I won't go into how the town's only law enforcement, Officer Horwitz, pulling up alongside us, had asked Tom to explain to him "*what the shitting Christ*" was going on, and had then laughed and said, "Carry on, boys. Carry on."

There's no reason to relate how Gus Ferkins, who owned the antique store and was rumored to possess a set of George Washington's dentures, took pictures of me that he put on his website along with close-ups of Boy Scout parades he'd attended over the years.

There's no reason to talk about how Judy, Tom's girlfriend, came out of her house when Tom started honking his horn, and she got into the car for the rest of the trip, laughing her ass off, talking about my chicken legs, and had once poked up her head to say, "Best not peer down here for a bit. I'm gonna give Tom a handjob."

There doesn't need to be a long memoriam of how Trinity, the Claremunns' Rottweiler, had run alongside the car for three blocks, savagely barking, furious for some reason, trying to jump up onto the car and bite my legs while I was screaming for Tom to go faster, and Tom said he wouldn't, that he couldn't, because he'd once promised Dad (I later found out this was true) that he'd never drive faster than ten miles per hour when he was getting a handjob. Trinity, the Rottweiler, was named after the father, the son, and the Holy Ghost. The Claremunns were religious as all hell. Maybe their dog was, too. Maybe he thought my chicken legs and white skin were an abomination in the eyes of the Lord, and his teeth were trying to dish out some saliva-covered penance. Trinity later died during the sixty-seventh annual Greenway Glory Days, a parade and festival held every August 2nd, when he was kicked to death by a horse that hadn't liked him barking. I wish I'd had that option.

Anyway, none of this is important. What's important is that I'd done a damn dumb thing the night before, not only making the bet, but, when drunk as a porn star in a girls' locker room, I'd mentioned the color of Adele Layton's eyes.

So, of course, Tom had to drive the Lincoln straight past her house, honking his horn, circling the block, and eventually she came walking out with a puzzled look on her face, carrying a doll that she'd been mending for her youngest cousin, sewing eyes back into place, but I hadn't known about that at the time, had only known that she was carrying a doll, looking like a child, looking puzzled. Tom parked the Lincoln along the curb. I wondered if that meant the drive was officially over. If so, I could bolt. Of course it was a little late for that.

"Tom?" Adele said, looking in at him. I was hoping the handjob was over and he was zipped up. It was hard to tell how Tom would approach any situation. He has always had a differing sense of propriety.

"Hey, Adele," he said. "I got my brother up on the roof. He's in his underwear."

"I did note that," she told him. She looked up to me and said, "Hi, Steve."

Tom said, "Last night he got drunk and started talking about your eyes. Jesus, you should have heard the poetry. It was plain horrible. I was thinking of punching him unconscious."

"Is that so?" she said. She was looking to me. I was about four inches tall. Shrinking fast.

"I think he wants to get into your pants," Tom said. Adele gave a small jump. I was three inches tall.

"Say that again?" Adele said, frowning to my brother.

He said, "I. Think. Steve. Wants. To. Get." Each word was nearly a shout.

I had to get in there and put an end to it.

I said, "I only said I wanted to go out with her. I like her! I don't need handjobs all the damn time like you do!"

Judy, unseen from below, said, "It's not all the damn time! I'm not a whore! It's like... maybe twice a day!"

Tom said, "Maybe I should keep quiet? Is this one of those times when I should keep quiet? Hey... Steve?" He knocked on the roof of the car. I could feel it in my chest, where my heart couldn't decide between two hundred beats a minute, or none at all. I felt about two inches tall. Dwarfed by my underwear.

"Hey, Steve," Tom said. "Let me know if I should be quiet now."

"You should be quiet, now," Adele told him, then she should looked up to me, met my eyes, and said, "No handjobs, and you'll have to dress a bit more formal, but, yeah... we can go out." She didn't say another word, just walked back into the house, carrying that doll, looking back over her shoulder, smiling, a little.

Tom started up the Lincoln and pulled away from the curb.

I felt about nine feet tall.

⌖

Adele and I had our first date on the day that Warp was revealed to the world. I was picking her up from her house, having borrowed the Lincoln. I was too young to drive, and Greenway was so small that everyone knew that. It was also, however, so small that everyone let it go. The town was small enough to consider everyone as family. It's bigger now, of course, with the tourism, and the SRD Base.

I was wearing blue jeans and a hand-printed shirt that said *Anvil* on it, that being not the later supervillain (who Paladin sent to prison for life) but instead the name of the band that Tom had tried to start, a band that was abandoned on the fifth practice, when he and the drummer had gotten into a fight, rolling around in our garage, breaking Mom's car window, and with Jake Everett (the drummer) ending up with a drumstick almost (by Tom's reckoning) three inches up his ass.

When Adele came down the stairs and met me at the door, she was wearing a dress. A green one. Unlike with my shirt, I didn't know that dress's history. She'd worn it only once before, to my memory, and I had a good memory (even then) and a better memory for anything related to Adele.

Once I had her in the car (her dad had made me promise to drive slow, and to think of his grimacing face when considering what to do during the date) I asked what she wanted to do, where she wanted to go.

"You're the boy," she said. "You're supposed to take charge in situations like this."

"I am?"

"Yes."

"Well, that sucks, because it's a thirty-minute drive to Bolton." Bolton was the nearest town of any size, the only chance of seeing a movie, or just hanging out together at the mall. Dates in Greenway consisted of driving around together, or walking around together, or sitting together at the park, or going to the gravel pit and pawing over each other, and I didn't think we were ready for that last one. I know I wasn't. Besides, I wanted something special. It was our first date. I'd even thought about buying flowers. I chickened out, because Tom had told me that it was old-fashioned, and stupid, and that girls just need to be looked into the eyes and told the truth. I wasn't ready for that, either.

"We don't have to go to Bolton," Adele said. "Maybe the park? Do you like the park?" I immediately thought of those names on the rafters of the log cabin, and just as immediately thought of writing her name down on the list, and while I felt mad at myself for the mere thought, I was boiling with an inner debate on the pros and cons.

"I like the park," I said. I tried not to put any meaning in that.

"Can we have a picnic? You're not a picnic-hater, are you?"

"Picnics are fun. Look, I'm not good at small talk. All I want to do is be with you. We can do whatever else you want." I looked straight into her eyes when I spoke, remembering what Tom had told me, but I wasn't likewise remembering to tell the truth; I was just doing it.

"Me too. Let's get a picnic lunch, and you can tell me why you've been looking at me so much, lately."

"Okay." I wondered if there was a statute of limitations on telling the truth. I hoped so.

We stopped in at the Mighty Convenient convenience store. Tom wasn't working. It was Jake Everett behind the counter. Adele and I stood in the snack aisle while I whispered the story about band practice, and Adele felt sad for Jake, rather than laughing at him, which wasn't something I'd considered. We microwaved two chicken sandwiches and grabbed some chips, some caramel crab cakes (homemade by Grace Shanahan, and fresh from her kitchen just down the block) and a couple of bottled waters. I paid for everything (it was clear that I was supposed to) and Jake didn't give me any change, knowing I couldn't look like a cheapskate while on a date.

We were almost out the door when the news flash came on the televisions. We stopped. The Mighty Convenient store had a small café attached. There was no kitchen… just cold sandwiches and a few places to sit. Some coffee. Cake. And two televisions. It wasn't much at all, but it was still one of Greenway's most popular hangouts. Mostly for the older crowd.

"Jesus Christ!" the newsman said. It was Frank O'Neill… the Channel Five "*On the Spot*" reporter. He was (and is) a calm man, but he was then flustered, listening to an earplug, watching the beginnings of a video in his monitors. Adele and I moved closer to the televisions, wondering what was going on. Usually the news flashes were about crashes on the highway, or robberies, or grain silo explosions. O'Neill always read about such events in a concerned, but calm voice. This time, he was sweating. He messed up his toupee when he rubbed his forehead, and he didn't readjust it afterwards.

"Jesus Christ!" he repeated, and then, "Is this for real?"

A voice, coming from somewhere off camera, yelled out for him to introduce the clip. The entire broadcast was ragged, off-kilter, unprofessional. Frank kept watching the clip in the monitor. He scratched at his chest, breathing deeply.

He said, "Breaking news from Iowa, where, where… a *superhuman* has come forward. His name is Warp. And he moves at a pace… far beyond you and I. Far beyond. Jesus Christ."

Adele and I took one of the small tables. We opened our food. We sat next to each other so that we could both face the television. She had a warmth about her. I made a decision that I truly did want to take her to the quarry. I did want to write her name on the log cabin list. Hell… I wanted to marry her. Her eyes, the way she was looking up at the television, I was able to just watch her, see her when she was unprotected, defenses down. It's a crime that evolution has spent a million years making a woman so wonderful to see, and that society has separately evolved in such a way that we're not supposed to look. No wonder men are angry all the time.

So we watched a show, Adele and I. Except that while I myself was watching the slope of her nose, the sharp angle near the tip, she was watching Warp being timed on a hundred-yard dash. The record, at the time, was a bit over nine and one half seconds. Warp ran the distance, timed by lasers, in .007 seconds. A James Bond number. Seven thousandths of a second. Most people couldn't blink in that time.

Adele watched footage of Warp running across water. I watched the way her fingers worked at the edges of her caramel crab cake, crumbling off small chunks, sometimes eating them, sometimes absently dropping them to the floor, forgotten. Her fingers were long and smooth and I wondered if she masturbated. It was more important to me, then, than that first broadcast with Warp. I was well aware that, on the television, the world was changing. Frankly, it didn't matter much. The world always changes.

"He's so… so fucking fast!" Adele said. I wasn't sure if she was talking to me, or at me, or just talking to herself. It was unimportant. I was just watching her lips. Warp was on the television, giving an interview, wearing a mask from which steam was rising. He was talking about heroism. He was talking about the common man. He was talking about endorsement deals. He was flickering in and out of view, racing here and there, and at one point he was gone for maybe two or three full seconds, long enough for the reporter from Iowa, an achingly attractive blonde almost half as beautiful as Adele, to wonder where he had gone.

He reappeared as if he'd warped into existence only a second after her eyes had begun to narrow. He was holding a slice of deep-dish pizza. His favorite, he said… a slice that he'd just grabbed from a restaurant in Chicago, hundreds of miles away. The blonde reporter started to hyperventilate. People were gathering around us in the Mighty Convenient café, not talking, eyes on the television, just murmuring, almost religious, in fact completely religious, making calls, standing up, sitting down, even passing out.

Warp was the first of the superhumans.

Adele was in a green dress that, up close, was nearly transparent, through which I could almost see her skin beneath.

These two facts were of equal importance.

⌖

I suppose this is as good a place as any to talk about my first meeting with Warp. By the time I met him I wasn't sixteen years old anymore… I was in my early twenties. And I wasn't Steve Clarke, either. At least not right then. I was Reaver, and Laser Beast was violently drunk at a strip club called Sassy's, which had one stage running during the day, two stages running most evenings, and three stages at night on the weekends. The girls would strip entirely naked. The management, thankfully, did not encourage plastic breasts. I'd been there once. Twice. They'd served a California chicken wrap that I'd enjoyed, and there had been boobs, and I like them too. Sassy's is in Portland, Oregon, where I'd been living at the time.

The police had been called. One officer, a hostage negotiator, had ventured inside. He hadn't returned. A laser had pierced the door he went through, shortly after he'd gone inside. I stood next to Lieutenant Cooke, being briefed by him and a civilian, a young woman who gave her name as Onyx and who was wearing bikini bottoms, a pair of knee-high boots, and a police jacket. Nothing else. I tried not to look at her sexually. She didn't return the favor.

"Laser Beast?" I said.

Onyx said, "He came in and started drinking. We didn't know it was him at first. He was just another creepy guy."

"You get many creepy guys?" Lieutenant Cooke asked her. She just looked at him.

"What happened?" I asked her. "No. Fuck that. I don't care. What's happening right now? What's the situation?"

Onyx said, "He has Berlin and Persephone dancing for him. Won't let them quit. I think he might have killed Larry, our bouncer. He wasn't moving. I got out the back way. I hope my leaving didn't make him mad at… you know."

"Berlin and Persephone," I said. "What's the interior layout?" She gave me a description, one that I already knew, but I couldn't explain that without mentioning I'd visited the strip club, and giving away any hints to your secret identity is a slippery slope. Look what happened to Kid Crater.

"I can't let you go in there!" Lieutenant Cooke shouted while I walked across the four lanes of the street, all of which had been blocked off. There were sirens going, cop cars everywhere, SWAT-type vehicles, fire engines, snipers in place, barricades, choppers overhead, even a goddamn jet. I felt like it must feel to be a quarterback walking onto the field for the Superbowl.

"You're not going to stop me," I said over my shoulder to Cooke, because I knew he was just doing his job, saying what needed to be said. He wanted me in there worse than anything on Earth, but since at the time I had no lawful standing, he had to say the words. Legally... he'd tried to stop me.

I opened the door.

In front of me, I could hear the ending strains of the Rolling Stones singing "*Some Girls*," mixed with the beginnings of "*Sister Morphine*." Behind me, I could hear Lieutenant Cooke still telling me not to go in, and also to be careful once I was inside, and to save his hostage negotiator, if possible. I could also hear Onyx calling out that she was single, or at least, as she said, reasonably single.

Inside, it was dark. The lights (as they had been on my previous visits) were down very low. My eyes took some time to adjust, but I kept moving, not wanting to stand still, trying to avoid being an easy target, so I bumped into a table, accidentally knocked over a chair, and then I rounded the corner and there were the two girls, Berlin and Persephone, on stage, dancing, rubbing up against each other, scared out of their wonderful stripper minds, swirling around the dance pole. Laser Beast was sat up against the stage and there were empty whiskey bottles scattered around, some of them smashed, some of them sliced into pieces by lasers, all of them empty. The bartender (meaning the owner, Steph) was behind the bar, holding a towel to the stomach of a man in a police uniform. The hostage negotiator, I supposed. There was a large man on the floor near the stage. Bearded. Muttonchops. Tattoos. Big muscles gone slack. A laser burn through his chest. I assumed it was Larry, the bouncer. Onyx had been right; he was dead. I looked back to Laser Beast, and the girls.

I don't know how the hell strippers can dance in those boots.

Laser Beast was a reasonably handsome man. This was before his body began changing to his current near-werewolf form. There are sites all over the web discussing what he'll be like in a few years, if he's going to keep evolving, or (some argue) devolving. Some say he's going to turn into an ape, then a fish, or a lizard. Some say he's going to turn into god. And of course a lot of women say (or at least hope) that he's going to turn up in their beds. These women have never met him in reality. These women have the tingle of fear mixed up with the itch of lust. Goddamn crazy bitches.

Back then, Laser Beast looked like a man in his early thirties, brown hair, stubble, dressed like Mr. Brady from the Brady Bunch. He had a thick and demanding stink. His clothes had holes where they'd been pierced with lasers. Those damn lasers of his... the way they blast out from anywhere... they make him hard to predict. His mind serves much the same purpose.

He looked to me.

"You're that Reaver guy, ain't you?" he said. His words were slurred. I felt bad about the quiver of pride that went through me. He knew my name.

"Let these women go," I said, gesturing to Berlin and Persephone. I didn't know which one was which. Neither of them looked like a daughter of Zeus or a German city. They both stopped dancing and looked to Laser Beast, to see what he would answer. Then, together, they remembered that they were *Not Supposed To Quit Dancing*, and they began the motions again. It wasn't sexual at all. I don't know how Laser Beast could have fooled himself as such.

"Fuck you," Laser Beast said. "Fuck all these whores. Fuck this place. Fuck this city. Wanna fuck with me?" He didn't actually seem to be talking to me. More to the whiskey bottles, I think. A laser spat out from his shoulder and clipped off the top of a bottle. He picked up the remainder of the bottle and whipped it at the two women. It hit one in her ass. She kept dancing.

"Let these women go," I said again. I put more anger into it, this time. I don't like violence against women. I don't like it... not at all. It goes against nature.

"You can suck my..."

"Run!" I told the women, and I went for Laser Beast, because talking with him was the last thing I wanted to do. I'm not good at talking, and not trained on what to say to maniacs, and the nearest person who was actually trained to do it, well, he was nursing a laser wound through his stomach, so you can see where that got him.

Berlin and Persephone dived out of sight, leaping backstage, like pretty dolphins.

Laser Beast heaved a whiskey bottle at me.

The bartender and the wounded cop dropped below, behind the bar, out of sight.

The outside door, the one I'd come in, burst open.

Mick Jagger's voice was coming through an array of speakers, singing about someone's nineteenth nervous breakdown.

Tables and chairs began flying everywhere, as if caught in winds of *cyclone* levels, smashing against the walls, shattering from some incredible force, with a hum so overpowering that Laser Beast and I were holding our ears from the pain of it, with the debris from the tables and chairs and ketchup bottles and menus and a hundred other things pelting us, with the two of us, hero and villain, wondering what the hell had been unleashed inside the strip joint, what new thing was happening, what the fuck was going on.

Everything settled for a bit.

A dazed man appeared on the floor.

It was Warp.

"Fucking dark in here," he said. "Couldn't see shit at first."

And then he disappeared again. The hum returned. And Laser Beast was lifted into the air. Knocked back down by an invisible force. Caught in a maelstrom of punches from a man who was moving too fast to be seen. I immediately saw that I wasn't needed in the fight... that I couldn't possibly get in on such a fight, that my measly *three-times-normal* speed was best used to escort strippers from the premises. I found Persephone and Berlin huddled in a dressing room chock full of scanty outfits and lists of "*do's and don'ts*" on the walls, along with photos of men to watch out for. They were hiding behind a rack of clothes, regular ones, the clothes they'd come in wearing.

"Let's go!" I told them, and I made a doorway in the wall. I might be only three times as fast as a normal man, but I'm a lot more than three times as strong. The building shuddered. The wall crumbled. I took the girls outside, walking into an assortment of eventual newspaper headlines accompanied by photos of me with the two women (Persephone turned out to be the shorter of the two) coming through the dust and the debris, a front page hero. One paper even made a historical pun, talking about me saving Berlin by knocking down a wall. Many of the newscasts speculated on whether or not I was dating the strippers. Persephone played it up like we were, hoping to coax some free publicity, a book deal, a television series, etc. She backed off when she realized that the girlfriend of a superhero gets unwelcome visits from the bad guys. She eventually made a press release saying she never knew me, and that she was a lesbian anyway. All of that came later.

By the time I'd made it onto the sidewalk, by the time I carried the two strippers out of the club, by the time I'd crossed the street, Warp and an unconscious Laser Beast were miles and miles away, moving towards the SRD base, in Greenway, Oregon.

⌖

I had a list in my pocket. Adele was on it, of course. It was precisely written with a permanent marker and looked to have been done with a confident hand, but that was only because I had practice, having written several earlier versions of the list, trying to decide exactly what I should do with my two weeks grace period before I… how best to put it… *reported back* to Octagon. Anyway, Adele's name was on the list. It appeared on several lines. One of the lines just said, "Be with Adele again." It was a line that could be interpreted in many different ways. Some of those ways had been written on earlier lists, but had been deleted for one reason or another, like fear, or… or I suppose they were all versions of fear. Humility and arrogance and all that… these things are borne from fear. Anyway… I'd shortened the list. Now… the list read.

1: Be with Adele again.
2: Take Adele on a date. (pay)
3: Talk to Greg's parents.
4: See my house. (steal something?)
5: Talk with Judy.
6: Prepare will (Adele, Greg's parents, Judy?, monument to Dad & Mom, Kid Crater Scholarship)
7: Visit SRD (shut them down?)
8: Fight.

I wasn't sure what the final line item meant. *Fight*. What was that doing there? Why had I put it there? I wasn't sure of the answer. It just seemed like it needed to be down on the paper. It hadn't been listed on the first draft, but had appeared on the second, and had then lived through all the subsequent incarnations, most of which were scribbled onto napkins (at two different strip clubs) or advertising flyers (*Colonel Dan's Bulk Grocery Outlet*) or menus from *City Diner*, *Hash Brown's*, and *Vege Tables & Chairs*. Several of the earlier drafts had a question mark next to the word, so that it read as... *fight*? I hadn't put that question mark in the final draft, but it was only because I'd grown accustomed to the word. If something is around long enough, a person tends to forget all about it, and just accept it into their lives.

I'd looked at the list about a million times. Driving home, to Greenway, it had sometimes been on my dash, stuck there with a piece of tape, and it had sometimes been in my wallet, and it had sometimes been in my pocket. It had often been in my hands. It was making me wonder about a lot of things. I wondered how small I would feel when knocking on certain doors. I wondered if my key would still fit in the door to my house. I wondered how SRD would react to my visit, and how I'd react to that reaction. I played out scenarios in my head. I wondered what to call the Kid Crater scholarship. I wondered if it should be for... sports? Arts? Bravery? How does one go about measuring bravery in the average college freshman?

I wondered about all those things.

But mostly I wondered where I would take Adele on a date.

⌖

My second date with Adele was a double date with Tom and Judy. We drove to Bolton to watch a romantic comedy at the Worthington Theater. I can't remember what movie we saw. I'm pretty sure I didn't pay any attention to it. My thoughts were consumed by making sure, during the movie, that Adele didn't notice Judy was giving Tom a handjob. I wasn't sure if she'd feel embarrassed, or pressured to do the same, or disgusted, or what might happen. I didn't want to know. It was tension, but it was a pleasant version of such. I felt alive.

"Enjoying the movie?" Adele asked me. Tom and I were sitting next to each other, with the girls to either side. I was holding Adele's hand. I couldn't have told you if the movie was even running.

"It's good," I said. I was leaned forward, trying to block her view of Tom and Judy, and I was staring her in the eyes because that way I would know where she was looking.

"You're not even watching," she said. "You always just watch me." Someone from behind us kicked at the back of my seat and told us to shut up.

I turned around and glared. I've always been good at glaring. Having an older brother develops that talent. The object of my objection was Travis Gerber, a man who was then in his fifties, a man who lived two blocks from me in Greenway, and whose wife had left him for some Bolton man, a lawyer, I think. If I was him I would have never come to Bolton. I would have blamed the town.

Travis backed away from my glare, a beaten man again. I stared at him for a couple extra seconds, making sure. He had a chocolate ball in his fingers, halfway to his mouth, frozen in time. For some reason, it made me feel a little sorry for him.

"What's changed?" Adele told me when I turned back. I made sure to not wipe the glare right off my face, not right away. I wanted her to see that I was tough. A man.

"Huh?" I asked. Her question didn't make any sense. The question threw me off balance and I immediately wanted popcorn. If we had popcorn, I'd have something to do with my hands. But if I had popcorn then I'd get oil and butter and salt on my fingers and I couldn't touch her as much. I'd be afraid to touch her dress (it was red, this time) for fear of staining it, despite how Tom said there's nothing better than staining a girl's dress. And if I had popcorn, I'd need to get some soda, or a water, or something to douse the thirst that popcorn always gives me, and if I drank too much, or anything at all, then I'd for sure have to go to the bathroom before the movie was over, quickly becoming some huge bloated piss machine, running to the toilet and looking like a fool, and just having Adele so close to me was giving me shivers, and by that I somewhat mean that she was giving me a boner, and if I went to the bathroom I'd end up at a urinal with (this would be for sure) guys to either side of me, asking why I had a boner, demanding to know what was making me hard, and they'd probably be friends of Adele, and they would definitely tell her how I'd been in the bathroom with my buttery/salty fingers holding my *at-least-somewhat-erect* penis, and then…

"What's changed?" Adele asked again, bringing me back to reality.

"I'm still not sure what you're talking about," I admitted. Tom had given me mixed signals on how to deal with girls. He'd said that honesty was always the best policy, and that the paramount thing was to never show any weakness. I was stuck between one or the other. Confusion divides the line.

Adele said, "Steve… we've lived together in Greenway since we were kids. You never cared much about me. Whenever you went bike riding in the quarry, or searching for fossils, or playing tennis in the park, you never wanted me along. I was always around, but you never asked if I wanted to go. You never even really looked at me. Now, lately, these past few weeks, a couple months, you're always looking at me. So… what's changed?"

"Jesus," I said. I felt a little trapped. I wondered how long the movie would still run, if I could stall until the end, or if I should fake having to go to the bathroom. I wondered if I'd have to fake. I truly felt like I needed to piss.

Tom leaned over to me and said, "Don't be mad, but I've been listening in. Don't tell her a damn thing." He didn't whisper. Didn't try to make sure Adele couldn't hear. She reached over and pushed him, slowly, away from me. I was glad that she was pushing him away, but not at all glad that Adele was touching a man who was getting a handjob.

"Don't listen to your brother," Adele told me. "Be the smart one. Tell me what's changed."

"You just look better in a dress," I said. First thing that came to mind. Well, the first thing that had come to mind past my fears and my thoughts of flight.

"That's all?"

"I guess you look better in everything."

"That's as much as you can tell me?" I had a feeling she was decades older than me, or more honestly, decades smarter. She put her hand on my lap, only on my leg, but she had to have known how it scalded. It's amazing how many things a woman knows.

"You make the town seem bigger," I said. "Or maybe smaller. It's just… the whole town is you. I can't… you move so… I think…"

"Just kiss her," Tom said, leaning over again. Judy was smiling up at me from his lap. She'd pretended to drop something on the floor. The handjob had progressed. Most of her head was covered with Tom's coat, shielding her from view, but I could see her eyes. Adele shifted the coat so that Judy was entirely covered, then she pushed Tom away again, this time telling him not to come back, that his brother could handle himself.

Then, to me, she said, "Is that, those things you were saying, is that some sort of poetry?"

"Guess so. Didn't really mean it that way. I don't like poetry. It's just... you make me think of different things."

She looked at me for a long time. I could hear the murmur of surrounding people. Tom saying Judy's name, low. Her giving a soft answering grunt. I was vaguely aware of the actors on the screen (I really do not have any recollection of that movie) and the sound of the humming projector behind us. I was watching Adele move some of her brunette hair away from her eyes. I was seeing how her skin looked in the movie theater, with the lights down so low. I was watching her eyes sparkle, reflecting light. I was watching how her lips were slightly curled up, how her nose turned up at the end, how her shoulders were rising as she wrestled with some decisions, how her breasts were pointed up, her nipples evident in the cool of the theater, how it seemed like every part of her was pushing up, and up.

"Tom was right," she said after a bit. "Just... kiss her."

CHAPTER FOUR

I rolled into Greenway at almost five in the afternoon. It was the first time I'd been home in nearly nine years. The town had undergone an enormous amount of changes. It didn't look like a small town anymore; it looked like a small town with growth cancer. There were quite a few new buildings. Hundreds of them, in fact. Greenway had gone from a thousand residents to sixty thousand, and all in a decade. The main reason, of course, was the SRD base. As much as I wanted to see Adele right away, I knew that the base would have to be my first stop. And, honestly, I was fearing seeing Adele, so it was a convenient detour, one that was completely within reason, one that had nothing to do (I told myself) with being a man who was three times faster than normal, who was hundreds of times stronger, who could heal from almost any wound, who could steal men's lives, a year at a time, with a punch, a man who had put on a costume and stood against the worst villains that the world had ever known, the only supervillains the world had ever known, the murderers of, in some cases, tens of thousands, creatures that could fly, bend steel, transmute their bodies, fire lasers, control the weather, cast magic spells and a hundred other bizarre talents, and I had stepped up to them, and I had stopped them, so it was ridiculous to think that I (Steve Clarke, the Reaver) could have the slightest trepidation of calling a woman on the phone, or knocking on her door, or walking along any street where she might, possibly, see me.

It wasn't that at all.

It was just that SRD had undoubtedly been tracking my journey home… secretly following my progress along the drive. These people, they would get nervous if I didn't check in.

The sign at the gate was obscured by a trio of armored, nearly identical, well-armed guards. Only when they were shifting around, preparing for my oncoming car, stepping out to block my progress, could I read the sign.

Superhuman Research & Development.

And then… in even bigger letters.

***No** trespassing.*

***No** visitors.*

The gate was made of a blend of blurred glass and metal. I'd seen the type. The metal gave it the strength. The glass (it was far past ordinary glass) was designed to crumple and shatter, diverting any impact. There were probably only four people in the world who could have punched through that gate. There are quite a few who could have flown over it. I could have jumped it easily enough.

I rolled down my window as one of the guards tapped on the glass with the business end of an M240 machine gun, a weapon powerful enough to shoot through the entirety of my car, with ease, though not powerful enough to do any more than dent my skin. It didn't make me nervous. It just made me annoyed. This was all about a power play. I'd grown to hate playing.

"Take that weapon away from me," I said. "I already know you're in a position of authority."

"You are attempting to drive an unauthorized vehicle onto restricted premises," he said, using the type of voice normally used when addressing opposing politicians or child murderers. It's a voice I've heard countless times. It's a voice used by men of personal bravado, of intense ego, who have spent their lives training to become the best that they can be (from a standpoint of being turned into a killing machine) and were then issued a weapon that could mow down a house, and also a certificate that says it's okay to pull the trigger. And then they meet me, or one of my type, and the weapon and the training doesn't mean shit to us. These men become nothing but a vast herd of self-aware dominoes, desperate to avoid being the first one to topple.

I said, "You had to have been expecting me. Open the gate." Nobody moved.

"You know who I am," I said. I didn't try to make it threatening, but, then again, I'm the one who said it. That matters.

Another of the guards took position near the left front of my vehicle. His weapon was slightly lowered, ready to do a strafing run that would perforate my engine and my windshield and (normally) anyone behind the wheel. The third guard was talking on a headset, and a low siren was sounding in the distance. I couldn't see anything of the buildings beyond. There were a series of fences and tree lines in place for security, and to block any sight lines. I could hear choppers warming up. By this time, Paladin would have charmed his way into the base and would have been eating croissants with the commander, discussing favorite brands of tea, talking about kids and school plays.

The guards were identical in lightweight armor that was probably designed by Checkmate, the mental wizard who had a short public career before he was carted away to monkey with technologies that most of us couldn't conceive. He'd always worn full armor during his public appearances. Nobody had ever seen his face. It was rumored he was handsome. It was rumored he was hideous. It was rumored he was actually a woman. It was rumored that he had an IQ somewhere around five hundred. It was rumored that he was a virgin. It was rumored that he was provided with a harem. It was rumored he'd built a mechanical harem. It was rumored he did everything with science. It was rumored he did everything with magic. It was rumored that he was dead, too bored to live in a world of imbeciles. It was rumored that all of the rumors were true. Nobody could say. I've met him twice, at SRD. He's still in the armor.

The guard's armor had a shimmer to it. Probably a force field.

"You know who I am," I repeated to the guard. His weapon twitched. He was caught between saluting and firing. The guard who was talking on his headset looked up sharply, listening to someone relaying orders, and he gave a whistle and the others stepped back and told me I could proceed. The gate was opening. The low-level alarm quit sounding. Security cameras were swiveling. By then, the choppers were in the air. Hovering above. Most choppers look like insects. These looked much the same, but more poisonous.

Instead of pulling ahead, instead of driving onto the base, I turned off the car and stepped out. This was met with confusion. I'd been told I could go ahead, but I wasn't. I was screwing up their game plan.

Yes.

Yes I was.

I do not like it when people put guns in my face.

"Park that somewhere," I told the man who had tapped on my window with his M240, and I tossed him my keys. "Don't scratch it. It's a rental."

He held the keys in one hand, just held them out, unmoving, at the point where he'd caught them. He looked to the two others, but they looked away, making him bear the brunt of my asshole-ness all by his lonesome. I walked into the base with the choppers hovering above.

Along either side of the road, as I passed, a series of small gun emplacements perked up, tracking me, rising out of the lawn like yard-high toadstools. They smelled slightly of machine oil, but mostly I could smell nothing but grass. It had been recently mowed.

Occasionally, as I walked, a red dot would appear on my chest, my arms, my legs, and once or twice the light got in my eyes.

The trees were pretty. Well kept.

⌖

Commander Bryant said, "It's changed since you were last here," gesturing to the base, which looked like it had been recently buffed. Spotless. Everywhere. The silos. The holding buildings. The research labs. Everything had a gleam to it. It felt wrong to touch anything, like a single smear of human oil would scramble a hazmat team into action, or perhaps the entire base would simply be considered tarnished beyond all hope, and quickly abandoned.

"Yes," I said. "It's changed." Commander Bryant had met me even before I reached the main compound, surprisingly coming down the road himself, alone, with no guards, not counting the choppers that were hovering above. The choppers themselves were almost ten thousand feet in the air, but I had no doubts that they were well within range of whatever they felt that they needed to do.

Bryant was younger than I would have imagined. Maybe only forty years. He had the lean type of body most often seen in rock guitarists who indulge in cocaine and pussy with equal ferocity. He had a heavy brow and a light suit, business casual, though with the same nearly transparent glow I'd seen around the guards' armor. There was a slight stiffening of his left leg, making it scuff, not all the time, on the pavement as he approached. I wondered what the story there was. Lots of good stories, on that base.

He'd taken my hand and clasped it in both of his, like a preacher.

We'd discussed who I was.

He'd said, "Sorry about this, but I need to prove it," and then he'd reached into his jacket and pulled out a Browning P-35 with a draw so smooth and fast that it would have been too late to do anything, assuming you were a person who didn't move three times faster than most anybody else. As it was, I could have taken it from him, or dodged the shots (three of them, to my chest) without much effort, but it was easier to stand there and take it, to give him a frown, to watch his reaction to me having no real reaction, to keep quiet as he reloaded his clip, stashed it away, and then turned and started back up the road, beckoning me to follow.

"Did it even hurt?" he finally asked.

"I feel the kick. Like being tapped."

"How long before it didn't freak you out?"

"Nine years. So far."

"What would you like to see while you're here?"

"Nothing much," I said. "It's just that… I wanted you people to know I'm in town for a visit. Only just for a visit. Not to mess with anything."

"What happened in your last fight with Eleventh Hour?" he asked. For this question, he stopped in front of me on the road. We were coming up on the base. A line of scientists and a couple of their caped successes had emerged from out of one metal silos to watch our arrival. A larger group of soldiers was instructing them that now wasn't the time.

"I lost," I told Bryant.

⌖

Before we move too far past it, I want to talk about my first kiss with Adele Layton. Once she'd given me the go-ahead, I didn't wait. Even before she gave me that go-ahead, I could see it in her eyes. I leaned in closer and her lips were harder than I'd thought. A woman's lips are so often described as soft and yielding, but hers had a force. The first kiss wasn't much more than the two of us pressing against each other, her leaned over, me twisted in my theater seat, my neck cricked to the right, and she let out a sharp huff of breath into my mouth as we met, and again as we parted, explosions of breath that meant something important was happening, and of course I'd known how it was true, but I'd thought all the importance was from my side, and to feel the warm proof of how she was feeling the same way, that we were both in the role of the aggressor, to think of her thinking of me, not just reacting to me, but gauging me, being alive, no longer some transient creature that existed only in my range of sight, but a person who had wanted this moment, had spent time working this instant into reality, maybe talking with her sister while mending that doll she had carried, the two of them laughing about me on the roof of the Lincoln, with me hugging the car roof, splayed in my white underwear, and Adele wondering what I would be like to kiss, deciding she had to know.

"Oh," I said. She'd kissed me into a realization.

We'd fallen in love.

The second kiss was stronger than the first. Her tongue was there to meet mine and there was another of her explosions of breath, and I was thinking of how glad I was that we hadn't gotten any popcorn, that we hadn't gotten any soda, no chocolates of any kind, because this way her lips didn't taste of salt or butter, not of corn syrup or anything else excepting Adele Layton.

I kissed her for some thirty seconds. Expecting her to tell me to stop. Realizing she wouldn't. Wondering if I would. Only finally interrupted by Tom's laughter, sinking into me somehow, him at the tail end of his far less passionate embrace, and also interrupted by one other thing.

Adele's back was pressed against her theater seat, her lips on mine. Our tongues were shameless. Glorious. Adele had her eyes closed. But mine were open. I wanted to see her.

But in seeing her, I also looked past her, to the seat behind, where Travis Gerber was eating his chocolate drops and staring into my face. He was looking disappointed. Looking like he thought I was doing a very wrong thing.

He didn't understand how Adele and I were in love.

A man like Travis Gerber couldn't know of such things.

Kissing Adele couldn't possibly be wrong.

But of course, he was proved right in the end.

⌖

Let's talk about Paladin.

Saying those four words feels strange. I can't count how many times I've said just the opposite. Microphones surrounding me, reporters with notebooks, e-mails from students who needs quotes for a thesis, women in bars, the nightly news, congressional hearings, people on the streets, Presidential requests, all of them asking (and quite often demanding) for me to talk about Paladin. About how it began, and how it ended.

And I've always told them no.

But…

… what the fuck…

… let's shock the world…

… let's talk about Paladin.

Paladin's real name was Greg Barrows and he was probably my best friend, excepting only my brother Tom. Greg was a boy I'd grown up with and we'd bonded on tales of pirates and Greek gods. We'd made a game in the creek beds, him with his Greek gods (they were actually repurposed He-Man figures) and me with corked wine bottles we pretended were pirate ships, and my pirates and his gods would do battle (we made up new rules every time) and we would then have to, on the spur of the moment, create stories about what had happened, embellish the narrative, so that if a wine bottle ran into Hercules (portrayed, in this instance, by Vikor of Grayskull) it was actually the lead ship of Bloodsword (the king of my imaginary pirates) ramming into Herakles (we spelled it differently, at times) who was on the beachfront of Paris (we weren't bound by history or geography) while they were both vying for the hand (and so much more) of this and that wayward princess. All of our princesses were wayward. On that we were consistent.

Greg and I were on the same baseball team together, not surprisingly, of course, since Greenway could only field one team at the time. He was a pitcher and I was a first baseman. Both were positions of responsibility. We both batted well. He pretended to be a god that was batting quarrelsome meteors. I pretended to be Count Vladbeard (my newest pirate captain, who was also a vampire) knocking back the enemy grenades that had been hurled at my ship by the Sailing Templars.

I could go on with a hundred similar examples of our actions and our childhood fantasies, but in them we didn't vary greatly from any of our friends, from any other of the boys, and we largely abandoned these tales at about the same time as the rest of the boys, and for the exact same reason. The girls were growing up.

Kathy. Allison. Angela. Dylan. Jennifer. Mikla. Adele. Paula and Petra… the Gorner Twins. Clio. Georgie. Nora. We were suddenly consumed by our thoughts of all of them. These thoughts needed urgent discussion. Because of this, most of us ostracized the girls who had been our friends, suddenly unable to face them, though the thoughts of them dominated conversations whenever we were awake, and held sway in our dreams at night.

In my first sex dream, the Gorner Twins and I took off all our clothes and stood simply looking at each other, unsure of what to do.

In my second dream, the night after I'd spent half the day walking around with a porno CD (*Mass-Ass-Blasters Chapter 6*) that I finally watched the second my parents closed their bedroom door (allowing for ten extra "security" minutes) our antics (this time it was me and Georgie and one or the other of the Gorner Twins) were far more athletic and involved, though even in the dream I was screaming, "*Am I doing this right? Am I doing this right?*"

I could go on and on. Every teenage boy, of course, could go on and on. I could tell you about the discovery of every aspect of sex. I could tell you that every time I thought I'd discovered every aspect of sex, some website would reveal to me that I was mistaken, that there were more things under the sun, and under the covers, and often chained to a bench in certain German townships. I could tell you of stained socks, stained towels, stained shirts, embarrassingly whimsical boners, of Tom coming home and telling me to sniff his fingers for a "*nasal glimpse into Judy's Forbidden Valley*," of how the two of us would sit on our porch, after our parents were in bed, and I could talk of Tom giving me a beer stolen from Dad's outside fridge, the two of us discussing girls, about how nothing on the internet ever translated into real life, how movies had it all wrong. I could relate how Tom was sometimes quiet, lost in thoughts, admitting that girls scared him (I'm not sure this was true… it may have been said entirely in order to make me feel better) and the two of us sending each other links to the very best pornographic websites, and also to yoga and strength-training regimens because it was clear, from the online portrayals of sexuality, that it was only those in the very best of condition and the most limber of limbs that could possibly achieve any satisfaction.

You can get these tales from any teenage boy.

And, I assume, from any teenage girl, substituting some elements, such as crusty socks, and replacing them with vegetables suspiciously disappearing from the refrigerator.

What's important is that, by the time Greg Barrows and I were headed to the quarry that day, we were almost finished with the age of telling tales concerning mystical might, and we were succumbing to the tales of the Curvy Ones. It no longer mattered that the princess was being rescued… it mattered somewhat more what she was wearing, and how favorably she'd look upon her savior. But mostly it mattered what each and every girl in school had been wearing that day, and if she had known (did they actually KNOW such things?!!) that we could see her panties (how could she NOT know?!!!) and would it happen again tomorrow?

Reality had interfered with our fantasies, because reality had boobs and, we came to realize, KNEW that it had boobs, and actually wanted to show them to us.

Greg and I were drinking lemonade from cans, riding our bikes, crisscrossing the streets, soaring across yards, up and over the Gerbers' bike ramp (it was only there during the summer months, when their nephew came to stay) and Tom was along with us, trying to ride his bike backwards for a whole block. Greg was riding beside him, asking about Judy, asking if he could borrow her, and Tom was trying to gauge if Greg was serious (he wasn't) and I was trying to gauge if Tom was seriously considering it (he was) and Adele waved at us from her yard (I remember this) and we made it to the quarry without any incident remarkable to a teenage boy. Tom had fallen three times and was skinned along his shin, bleeding somewhat. I'd run into John Molar's red Ford truck when he'd gone through a stop sign (he did it enough that I should have been expecting as such) but had little to show for it except a dent in my forehead that was probably going to get me a scolding from Mom (unfortunate) and some nursing from Adele (fortunate) and Greg had racked his nuts trying to stop his own bike from colliding with the red Ford, and so we were having a good time making fun of him.

We collected several fossils from the quarry that day. I may still have mine around. There was a full ammonite from the Cretaceous period. That was the best find. There were also several plant fossils, I assume from the same age. Greg found something that may have been a bone of some kind. He patiently chipped away at the fossil, brushing loose rock aside, while Tom and I were wrenching what we could from the rocks. We'd finished the last of our cans of lemonade from our backpacks, but we'd expected that, and we were well prepared. We had beers.

We got drunk.

For the first time ever, I heard the rumor (Tom told it) that Warp had grown up in Greenway. That he was a local boy. Tom had read the rumor on some website, along with a thousand other rumors.

I told Tom, "Everybody thinks Warp comes from their hometown. Everyone."

"Petra Gorner says she saw him," Tom countered. "She says she was getting undressed, and her curtains were open, and she heard a noise, and she looked, and it was Warp."

Greg said, "She couldn't have seen him. He'd have run away too quickly."

I said, "She does undress with her curtains open, though." I knew this to be true. Every boy in Greenway knew this to be true.

"But he would have run away. Far too fast to see him!" Greg wasn't making any arguments that Warp wouldn't have been peeking in a window; tales of Warp's hobbies were already beginning to surface. He liked his nightlife. That's one way to put it.

"Maybe he wasn't done looking," Tom said. That gave Greg pause. Petra had indeed reached a point where she needed some looking, and it wasn't something that could be rushed.

"Doesn't mean he lives here, or ever did," I said. "Warp's so fast, he might live in Paris, just run over here for the peep show." Paris was the only foreign city I could think of, back in those days. I've traveled quite a bit, since then. Paris is still a very nice city, of course.

"Why here?" Tom said. He belched. It was a good one. It was a champion. It should have been fossilized and preserved for future generations.

Tom's question gave us all pause (and plus we were silent in awe of that belch, though of course the echoing quarry walls had played not a small part) and we really couldn't think of any reason why someone like Warp would have come to Greenway unless he lived here, or had lived here. Past that, Petra was beautiful enough that her claim of the Warp sighting couldn't entirely be discounted. Being around a beautiful woman is always worth the price of stupidity, and if that woman happens to have a twin sister and also happens to undress with her curtains open, then you've just plain got to believe what she says.

"Online," Tom said, "I found a quote from Warp." He was standing tall, looking knowledgeable, waving a beer can between me and Greg.

"Yeah?" Greg said. There were only about ten million quotes from Warp online.

"He said that he's come a long ways from his days of shearing sheep."

"Shit," I said. "He did not say that."

"He did."

"Dang," Greg said. His mother didn't like him swearing. That curse was a lot, coming from him.

I said, "It's not like the Selood Brother's Sheep Farm is the only place that's ever had sheep, or people that shear them."

"Australia," Greg said.

"Australia," I agreed.

"Australia doesn't have the Gorner Twins and an open window," Tom said. "These things add up."

"Maybe Dad can tell us something?" I said. Dad didn't talk much about work. He mostly liked to talk about politics. He was thinking of running for mayor of Greenway. We didn't have a mayor, but he was thinking about running.

"Maybe we can find out something ourselves," Tom said. He came over and he tapped me on the chest, and he tapped Greg on his chest. We both looked at our chests like we suspected he'd left a mark.

You have to understand that both Greg and I knew Tom. We knew he wasn't talking about going to the Selood Brothers Sheep Farm during the day, talking to people, asking for a tour, or anything like that. He was talking about an expedition. He was talking about being secretive. Of breaking into the sheep farm at night, when all the secrets would be left out in the open, with no one to guard them. Tom was a man (we considered him a man, then, though I'd say a boy, now) who had began our games of hiding action figures on certain rooftops around Greenway, and then he'd send his friends notes about where the figures were hidden, and if you could retrieve the figure, Tom would steal a six-pack of beer for you. It's anybody's guess how many action figures are still hidden up on the rooftops of Greenway, possibly covered in moss, or perhaps adopted and tended to by crows.

"Field trip?" Tom said to us, raising his beer can.

"Field trip," I said. I raised my own beer can.

"Field trip," Greg Barrows agreed, clicking his beer can against mine and helping to set in motion a chain of events that would change the world, and in the eyes of some people, turn him into a god.

⌖

I'm moving too quickly, now. I want to talk more about Adele.

We turned, both of us, sexually shy after the day at the movie theater. It wasn't, though, truly about the sex. I've never been all that shy about sex. I've heard it said that people who grow up in big cities are more blasé about sex, and in some ways that might be true, but on the other hand, you have to understand that we (meaning "*people who grew up in small towns*," not the "*we*" that I usually mean, the one about "*we… who put on the costumes and toss boulders and fly through the air*") didn't have much else to do. There were only so many fossils to be collected or games of tennis we could pretend to play at the one city park. We did a lot of canoeing, outdoor things, but we had the same curiosity about each other's bodies, the same need for each other's bodies, and a world that was a whole lot more open in which to exercise those curiosities. I'm trying to say that sex wasn't a mystery to me or to Adele, which isn't the same as saying it was a known factor, either. We were both virgins, but it wasn't sex that was making us shy (not an ounce of that, really) but instead the fact that we both realized we'd fallen in love.

City people. Country people. Small-town folks. We all fall in love the same exact way. With a happily churning sense of giddy fear.

So Adele and I went for walks together, and we were in love together, and one day we bought three boxes of dog biscuits from Tom when he was working at the Mighty Convenient convenience store (he asked us if we were planning on doing something really kinky, some sexual role-playing, and Adele told him that we certainly were, but declined with a smile when asked who was to portray the role of the dog) and then we went all over Greenway, walking each and every street, and if we saw a dog (and they weren't rare) we would go up onto its yard (happy barks, angry barks) and give it a biscuit, pretending that we were gods descending from on high to bestow wisdom and dog biscuits.

We were, Adele and I, the permanent friends of every dog in Greenway after that… though of course I didn't live there much longer.

But I'm not talking about dog biscuits. I'm talking about phone sex. It occurs to me, now, how much Tom would have loved the transition, but… at the same time, I guess I won't dwell on that. It's a bit strange to talk about your brother and phone sex at the same time. I'll avoid that.

Eight nights after our first kiss in the theater, and subsequently the next fifty or sixty kisses in succession, Adele called me at nearly one in the morning and asked, "Am I your girlfriend?"

"Yes." If anyone wants to know if I hesitated (the tabloids always want to know if I hesitated, no matter what the situation) then the answer is no… I did not.

"Then I'm naked," Adele said.

"What?" I hesitated, here. Put that on record.

"I'm naked and I'm playing with myself."

"What?" I was starting to understand. I'd been thinking about making a similar call, but couldn't believe that Adele had done it. Girls don't do that, do they?

"I'm playing with myself. Do you know how girls play with themselves, or do you need me to describe it to you?"

"You better describe it to me." This wasn't from a stance of ignorance on my part, not anymore. This was from a firm (immediately) stance of knowledge. Whatever Adele was doing, however she was doing it, I wanted it to be described in lingering detail.

Which is what she did. She started from the beginning, from talking about how she had considered making the call when she was taking off her clothes and getting ready for bed. And then she had decided against it and had masturbated. And then she had taken a shower. And when she was in the shower she had masturbated. Adele told me about every drop of water from the shower, about where each drop had hit, and how they had felt. It was wonderful knowledge. Wonderful.

After the shower she had gotten into bed. She described this as well. Talking about her legs sliding into and under the covers, how the cool blankets had touched her (moist) body, and where it felt the coolest, and the warmest, and she had mused on thoughts of certain things that had occurred to her in the shower (she wouldn't tell me what they were, which was genius on her part) and those thoughts had led to another bout of masturbation, and while she was masturbating she was looking at the phone and then she was dialing my number and, well, here we were.

Weren't we?

Yes. Yes we were. And the conversation continued for almost ten minutes, including me going to my door and locking it, because sometimes Tom would come into my bedroom (high, from smoking marijuana) and tell me about visions he'd had, or visions he wished he'd had, or things that Judy had done, and while I actually enjoyed his visits at times, I was right then at that moment having phone sex, and, of course, phone sex and brothers do not mix.

But… apparently, at least once, phone sex and sisters do.

Adele was telling me about my fingers, how she'd taken to noticing them, how she was gauging their length and was instructing me where they should go, and at what speed they should make the trip, and she was talking about certain words she would say that would mean I should stop doing whatever I was doing, and how she would say certain things that would sound like she was telling me to stop, but that I should *By No Means* stop doing whatever I was doing, and then I heard her screech (I thought she'd, you know, peaked) but then she said someone else's name, which is always a bit disappointing during sex of any kind.

She said, "Laura!"

I was wondering why Adele would call out her sister's name during sex (in some ways I wasn't against it, because, you know… I have a penis and everything) but then I heard Laura's actual voice.

She said, "Adele! What the hell? Are you having *phone sex*?"

I heard, "No!" I heard the sound of the phone falling to the ground.

"You were!" Laura's voice.

"Get out! Get out of here!" My girlfriend's voice.

"Who with?" Laura, again.

"Stay the fuck away from my phone! Don't! No! Steve! Steve! Hang up!" That was Adele's voice again, and there was no way in hell I was going to hang up. I wanted to hear all of this.

"Steve?" said a voice on the phone. It was Laura. I was (with a certain amount of pleasure) picturing the scene. Adele was naked; I knew that. She was probably still a little wet from the shower, and there was no way that anything that was happening was my fault, so I didn't have to worry about that.

Laura was one year older than Adele. She was a foot taller. Boyish hips. A small chest. High cheekbones. Dark eyes. Grinning, most of the time, in the manner of someone who already knows the punch line and is just loving spending time with the joke. She was an oddity, having black hair but prominent freckles on her face, big blotches that some of the Greenway boys (myself quite definitely included) thought were interesting and some thought were ugly. She was an oddity in another way, too, in that she didn't give a shit about the Greenway boys; she was all about the Greenway girls.

"Steve?" she said on the phone again. Her breath was huffing, strained, and I realized she was fighting to keep control of the phone.

She said, "Steve! Hurry! Tell me what you guys were talking about! This is awesome! Ahhh! Adele! Quit it! I just want to know! Owww! Jesus! She bit me!" Laura was laughing and I was trying to make up my mind about saying something, because while nothing that had happened so far was my fault, if I said one word, any word at all, then it could be argued that I was complicit.

Laura said, "Steve? You still there? Say something because… Owwww! God! Adele's a biter, Steve! Seems like you'd best keep that in mind. Unless, maybe you *like* that? Hurry up and tell me the dirtiest thing you two were talking about!"

I'd decided that I'd best remain silent, and was continuing on that course of action when I heard a knocking sound from the phone (at first I thought maybe Adele was tossing her sister repeatedly against the wall) and then the sound of Adele's mother, the Layton girls' mother, yelling for the two of them to *keep it the goddamn hell down*. Almost immediately, my phone went dead. I figured it meant that Adele had won the fight. I listened to the dial tone, and it was one of the sweetest things I'd ever heard. I was more excited about being alive that I'd ever been, before.

I put the phone by my bed and sat looking at the ceiling, waiting. I was patient. I was impatient. I was alive, all the way.

Fifteen minutes later, my phone rang again.

Adele said, "Laura is gone. My door is locked. I'm wearing my panties. Go ahead and talk me out of them."

⌖

The sheep were restless, but what were they going to do about it? Sheep are sheep and we moved through the vast flock of them with relative ease, only somewhat bothered by how our shoes were getting layered in sheep shit. It wasn't the shit itself that was bothersome; we grew up in the country and some occasional horse/cow/sheep/dog shit was no big deal. It was like stepping on a dead branch, kind of.

The difference between stepping on a dead branch and a clump of fresh shit is that the branch doesn't adhere to your shoes and come along for the rest of the ride. We were going to have to sneak into the buildings, into the offices, into the secret lairs (we were drunk and had settled on a belief that the farm held government secrets of vast import) and it was going to be harder to do that while leaving an easily traceable line of shit-ridden footprints. We took to wiping our shoes on the sheep themselves. Their wool-covered sides were perfect for such a solution, and they were to blame anyway.

We were wearing entirely white outfits.

It had been the biggest debate of the outing. Should we wear black (as demanded by our presumed ninja ancestry) or white, which was more suitable for sneaking through sixteen hundred sheep? We'd finally settled on white, though I myself was only in a white button shirt with white shoes, and then dark gray pants. I didn't have any white pants. They seemed feminine to me.

"Any one of these sheep could be superhuman," Tom said as we moved through the flock.

"None of them are human," I noted. "So… they can't be superhuman."

"You know what I mean. Warp was born here. In this sheep farm. There has to be some other experiments. Some reason. Sheep must be easy to experiment upon, to breed and create superpowers, to perfect the techniques."

We'd all reached the point where we accepted what Tom was saying was true. We were young and we had been drinking all day. Because of this, we were picturing sheep with super-strength, with flight capabilities, with wool like Medusa's snakes, with singular eyes that could fire lasers, or triple eyes that could see the future. We saw no evidence of any of this, but we were certain these sheep, the ones we had so far encountered, were simply waiting for the experiments, and that we would find the end results of the experiments further on.

The sheep were making their *baaa baaaa* noises, and a couple dogs were sounding in the distance, stuck in their own pens for the night, agitated at their charges for not keeping their goddamned mouths shut. We weren't too worried about the dogs. We didn't have a reason that we weren't too worried about the dogs. We just weren't. We were full of optimism in every respect.

"Getting anywhere with Adele?" Tom asked me. He was pushing a stubborn ewe out of his way so that he could climb a wooden fence into the next pen, steadying himself on a light pole, one that had gone dark for the night, so that the sheep could slumber. We had decided to go through the pens because the roads were probably lined with security cameras and likely mined as well. I should again point out that we were young and had been drinking all day. In fact, I'll just go ahead and admit that Tom had run across some marijuana (John Molar had given it to him in regards for how we hadn't reported him running the stop sign and knocking me flat) and we'd smoked a good deal of that, enough that I was, at the time, wondering if the sheep were actually making sense, speaking in a language that only I could understand, telling me the secrets of the ovine. In such a mental state, believing that a sheep farm has buried land mines along their incoming road isn't such a large leap at all. It's more of a stumbling sprawl, mentally speaking.

The night was wide open and dark. The stars were ancient jewels. I wondered how long it would take Warp to run to one of the stars. I wondered how long it would take him to shear the sheep. If he worked at the farm, he could put everyone out of work. Dad included. I worried about that.

Tom said, "Steve. Numbnuts. Chucklefuck. I asked you a question. Getting anywhere with Adele?" He meant, of course, was I getting laid? It was a private question, and I could feel even the sheep waiting for an answer. I felt like I could ruin Adele's reputation if I said the wrong thing in front of 1602 witnesses, counting Tom, Greg, and the sheep. I felt like I could ruin my own reputation if I told the truth. I decided my reputation was of lesser importance. A girl has one chance at a reputation. A man's chances are infinite.

"We're just kissing," I said. "Sometimes a little more."

"You don't get to be vague," Tom said. He leapt off the fence and down into the other pen, but his focus was on me and he landed partially on a milling sheep and went thudding to the ground. He stood up. Wiped off. The sheep were all running away from their fence-leaping aggressors. There were maybe three hundred of them in the pen. They made a noise like one hundred horses.

"Hand in panties," I said. "Mouth on nipple."

"After three months?" he said. He'd been watching the retreat of the sheep, but he turned back around to face me.

"Two months," I said.

Greg said, "Still makes you a pussy." I could see in his eyes that he didn't believe that, but we were both in the habit of saying things that we thought Tom would like to hear. Greg's own girlfriend lived out of town, and despite how she had three times verified her existence by visiting Greenway, Tom and I still pretended that she didn't exist, that she was a lie Greg had created to hide the fact that he was gay. She was real, though, and her name was Katherine, and she wanted the whole name pronounced. She didn't want to be just Kathy. She said it made her sound too friendly. I hadn't known what to think of a girl that didn't want to be thought of as friendly. Her hair was long and blonde and she had blue eyes and very large breasts. Even then, when I was fifteen, I knew she would have trouble later in life. Back problems. Lechers. Tom had told me that Greg and Katherine hadn't progressed past the handjob level, despite how she wouldn't have minded something more, or a great deal more. He didn't tell me how he knew that. Tom had also said that Katherine's areolas were huge, twice the size of normal. He wouldn't tell me how he knew that, either.

We were coming up on the last of the pens. It had three rams in it, young ones, and Tom decided we should name the three of them after each of us, and then have them fight to the death. That set us to thinking for a long time, the three of us sitting on the top of the fence, watching the three sheep, talking about what in the hell could ever induce sheep to fight to the death.

"We could get them liquored up," Tom suggested. "Then tell them the others have been spreading rumors about them."

"That might work," Greg said.

"What kind of rumors?" I asked.

"Whoa. Yeah," Greg said. "Hadn't thought of that. What kind of rumor would make a sheep mad?"

Tom said, "Maybe that they give bad wool. Or that their mothers appeared in some sort of strange porno film."

"Dang," Greg said. "Harsh." One of the rams lifted his head to regard us. We pretended that he'd heard us talking about his mother. We waited for any of its powers (we were still high, and still positive that the sheep had powers) to manifest. Nothing happened. It just quit looking at us. I wondered if sheep thought that we, all of us humans, had super-powers. We can think almost for ourselves, and we can ride bicycles and change our underwear and, in the animal kingdom, an opposable thumb is more wondrous than the power of flight.

"How about you guys?" Tom said.

"How about… what?" I asked.

"What could make you fight?"

Greg said, "About anything. Injustice. I think maybe I'd like to be a lawyer. Do some good in the world."

Tom said, "Lawyers don't do good in the world. They just *do* the world, period."

"I'd fight for Adele," I said.

Tom said, "Damn? Really? But you haven't even gotten any pussy yet!" Two of the rams looked up. I wondered what the key word had been.

I told Tom, "I guess you'd fight for pussy." He smiled at me, not needing to answer, then jumped down off the fence and grabbed one of the rams by its horns. It didn't like it, and tried to pull away. The dogs were barking again. Still in the distance. But closer. Their pens were right up near the buildings. We weren't far off.

"What would you fight for?" Tom asked the ram. He was looking it in the face and I was hoping it would butt him, but not too bad. If it knocked him out, we'd have to carry him home, and that was a long ways to carry someone with shit on his shoes.

"Baaaaa," the ram said. Or at least that's what Tom pretended it to say, holding its lips open, using his hold on the ram's horns to bob its head up and down. The other two rams looked over at this, interested, annoyed, but still just sheep in the end.

And that's when the flashlight lit up on us.

Scared holy hell out of us.

Came from nowhere.

Came from only ten feet away.

Greg shrieked like a girl (I'm real sorry to use that expression, because it sounds demeaning not only to girls, but also to the man who would become Paladin, but the truth is what it is, and Greg Barrows shrieked like a girl) and he jumped down off the fence he'd been sitting on, down into the pen with Tom, and he immediately turned and tried to run, meaning he ran full into the fence he should have remembered was there, since he'd just jumped off the thing.

I froze into place.

Tom jumped on the ram's back, straddled it like a horse, and started yelling, "Giddy-Yap! Giddy-Yap! Ride, you beautiful bitch! Away we ride!"

I was still frozen in place, trying to see where the light was coming from, but it kept shining in my face whenever I looked at it, blinding me. In my mind I was thinking that if the sheep farm had given birth to someone like Warp, to someone who wasn't merely human anymore, a place where Nazi horrors were assuredly in place, where alien artifacts were twisting the minds of men, where Mayan gods were holding sway over the destiny of mankind (we really had smoked quite a bit of marijuana that night, quite a prodigious amount) then we'd should have known that the premises would have incredibly sophisticated security, such as what appeared to be a sentient beam of light, drawing out my soul.

Again, the marijuana.

"Ride, bitch! Ride!" Tom was yelling to the ram. Instead of galloping away, carrying Tom over the fences with great bounding leaps, the ram settled heavily to the ground and sent him sprawling.

"Tom Clarke," the voice behind the oncoming flashlight said. "That you? Sounds like it's you. What you doing with that sheep, boy?"

"Not sex," Tom said. "Definitely not."

"Thank god for that," Officer Horwitz told him, clicking off his flashlight, climbing halfway into the pen, regarding the three of us.

Tom was simply dusting himself off, unperturbed at the turn of events, because he was unshakeable. A rock. I was a rock, too, but only because I was frozen into place, still, trying to understand how a beam of light had transformed into a man. I thought of Star Trek teleportation, mostly. Greg was holding his bleeding nose, which was broken, having snapped sideways when he ran into the fence.

Yes. He broke that nose when he ran into the fence. I know how many of you have wondered how Paladin, the healer, could have a broken nose. The truth is that it happened before he got his powers, so it was set in stone before he could do much about it. The truth is that Paladin's broken nose had nothing to do with any supervillains (like he would sometimes claim) or any meteors (which was kind of an official story) and instead it was from how, when he was sixteen years old, he'd ran face first into the side of a sheep pen at the Selood Brothers Sheep Farm.

My mind, at the time, a bit late, was suddenly realizing that there were no aliens involved in the night, no superhumans, just Greenway's only law enforcement, Officer Horwitz, who was grinning at the three of us and shaking his head, trying not to laugh, and laughing all at the same time.

"You boys is drunk, ain'tcha?" he said.

Tom said, "We boys is drunk."

"That marijuana I smell?" Horwitz asked. He made the words sound resigned, like a father who understands a boy has got to grow up in his own way, and make his own mistakes.

"The sheep," Tom said.

"Pardon?" Horwitz asked. Mike Horwitz was country beefy, which is different than city beefy. Being *country beefy* means you have some girth to you, born of nights of deep-bottomed stew pots and days of walking long miles and moving occasional trees or rocks or confused bovines. *City beefy* means nights of greasy-bottomed fast food bags, and days of riding elevators, and being a confused bovine.

"The sheep gave us marijuana," Tom said. "They are our guides to the celestial."

"More likely you got it from that Molar son of a bitch," Horwitz said. "He's the only one around here with access to marijuana good enough to reach the stars, which is exactly where it sounds like you boys are tripping. Come up out of that pen. Get out here."

"I think my nose is broke," Greg said, holding it. There was blood coming from between his fingers, and his words were muffled and twisted. "*I finkk muffh noff iff broff.*"

"Might be that it is," Horwitz said. "It won't heal any faster in there, though. Come on, boys."

We came out of the pen, with Horwitz helping Greg the most, but still holding him mostly by the shoulder, trying to avoid the blood on his nose, the blood on his fingers, the shit on his shoes. The three rams were up against the fence nearest us, as if they too believed they were getting out of the pen. A couple times there was one of them that made the *baaa baaaa* noise and of course now it sounded more like laughter. I wondered if it might have been the one that Tom had tried to ride, but I really couldn't tell them apart. Dad would have been able to. I hoped we weren't getting him into any trouble.

When we were assembled, Horwitz made us wait next to his car while he radioed back to headquarters, which was in Bolton, not Greenway. On the radio, sitting half out of his car, staring at us, he said, "Nothing spectacular. Just three boys trying to rile up the sheep. Yes. They're drunk. Greg Barrows, and then the two Clarke boys. They weren't hurting anything. Yes. Very drunk. No. I don't see as how we need to cause any big ruckus. Barrows hurt his nose. He's crying about it."

That wasn't fair. Greg wasn't crying about. He gave a hurtful look to Horwitz, then a look to my brother and I, wanting support. We nodded in outraged sympathy.

Horwitz, still on the radio, said, "Not sure. Let me check. And… we need to know this for official? Okay then, I'll ask." He put down the radio and beckoned to Tom, waving him closer with that two-finger wave that officers learn in their first day of training. Tom took a step closer.

Horwitz said, "Headquarters needs to know if you're wearing condoms when you're scoring on Judy." Tom's eyes went wide.

"You know she's related to Bolton's chief of police, right?"

"No. Sir," Tom said. It was about the only time I'd heard him say *sir*.

"*No*, meaning you're not wearing a condom? Or, *no*, you didn't know that?"

"I didn't know that," Tom said. Greg and I were looking at each other, then back to Tom. Some lights had gone on in one of the nearby buildings. A voice, in the distance, was yelling for the dogs to keep quiet. One of the light poles in the sheep pens had gone on. There were maybe fifty of them, spread out, but only the one had gone on. Horwitz was giving Tom a serious look, and his hand had strayed to his gun, unclicking the strap that held it fast in his holster.

"Holy shit," Tom said.

"Fuck," I said.

Horwitz looked to me, eyes narrowed, and he gestured at me with the radio in his hand, shaking it at me, the cord of it brushing along against his sideburns, but he didn't even blink.

"And, you, Stevie Clarke," he said. "Headquarters needs to know… you getting anywhere with that Layton girl?"

Greg hissed in a breath. I mumbled something. Tom moved protectively in front of me, even though Officer Horwitz's hand was on the butt of his gun. I loved him for that. I loved him anyway, but I loved him for that, too.

Horwitz burst out laughing suddenly, turning around and hooking his radio back into place. "This fucker's been off for two minutes," he said. "God damn and Mother Mary, you two fuckers is oughtta have seen your faces!"

Tom was the first of us to laugh. He said, "You ugly fucker!" but he was laughing so hard he had to lean on the police car in order to support himself. "You ugly *ugly* fucker! You brilliant fucker!"

Horwitz was laughing even louder. Greg started in as well. I still didn't see the humor in it.

Horwitz told Greg, "I was gonna brace you, too, but I heard your girlfriend has got big titties, and even an officer of the law has to respect that."

"The honor of the badge!" Tom laughed. Greg didn't know what to make of other people laughing at his girlfriend's big titties, but he smiled because we weren't getting shot. His face finally made me laugh, just as Conroy Selood, one of the sheep farm's owners, came walking out with a flashlight and a border collie. He asked us what the hell was going on and Horwitz told him about catching us in the sheep pens. Conroy just looked at us for a long time, and then mentioned… to Tom and I… that our father worked there.

He added, "Sheep are so damned dumb. You didn't hurt any of them, did you?"

Tom said, "I tried to ride one. Didn't work. You have any super-powered sheep?"

Conroy said, "Boys. You're drunk. Officer… just take 'em home, if you would."

Horwitz asked us, "You walk out here? Ride bikes? Steal a car? Ride any sheep?"

I said, "Walked." We had thought it would be stealthier.

Horwitz told us, "In the car, boys. In the car." We all three of us started for the car but Horwitz stopped us before we'd even really started.

"Not with those shoes, boys. Not a chance."

So we all had to take off our shoes, and Tom even his pants, and we left them crumpled against the fence at the Selood Brothers Sheep Farm and rode about halfway back to Greenway (it was less than two miles) with Greg and I in the back seat of a patrol car (which smelled of disinfectant) and Tom up front, noting, but not quite complaining about, the cold leather seats, since he was only in his underwear.

Greg was the only one to really see the tanker truck.

I mean, before the accident.

⌖

Horwitz was steering with one hand, staring back to me, not believing that I'd dated for two months without getting any pussy (that's *real* pussy, son, not just *kissing* a girl that *has* one) off of Adele Layton.

Tom was fiddling with Horwitz's handgun, for which Horwitz had given him permission after stripping the gun of its magazine and even firing off one round into the night sky, making sure the weapon was empty.

I was making excuses that would have sounded like poetry to a girl, but like bullshit to a man, and right then I was a man among men (though that was, obviously, being questioned) and wondering if I should make a more ardent move on Adele. I was even considering if it was too late at night, that very night, for tapping on her window and seeing about making some progress. The negatives to this were that it was very late at night, and that her ground floor window was directly beneath her parents' second floor window. Also, I smelled like sheep shit.

The positives were that I might get some pussy. And, anyway… didn't women like the smell of shit? Wasn't there something *primal* about it? Some sort of pheromone in place? I'd read that somewhere. I'd read a lot of things, online.

We were going through the intersection just out of town, the one near the derelict house we all called the *Scooby-Doo house,* abandoned by the Wright family a half century ago and said to be inhabited by ghosts. The place is just past the old airplane hangers from the Wennes airport, a recreational airport that shut down in the air traffic controller strike of 1981, and just never reopened. The airplane hangars were barely visible from the road. We didn't much glance in their direction, though I can remember seeing a light near one hangar, which I thought was odd. Greg started to yell something. We were halfway through the intersection and that was as far as we were going to get.

A tanker truck appeared in front of us. For me, in that split second, it was just a flash of white, an apparition in the road. It was a septic service truck, or at least it was disguised as one. That type of truck is sometimes known as a *bowser*, and they typically carry about 3000 gallons of liquid. This one wasn't quite full. It held a little over two thousand gallons.

We were doing almost a hundred miles per hour when we slammed into the side and cracked that bitch open. Horwitz had been trying (successfully) to impress us with the power of his squad car. He died instantly on impact.

Tom, Greg and I… we all did something else.

CHAPTER FIVE

I sat in the corner of the old log cabin in the park at Greenway, Oregon. Or, more precisely, I sat in the corner of the rafters, there in the historical log cabin (comprised of one room only) situated at the northwest corner of Charles Park, which is in Greenway, Oregon.

Where once I'd had to wedge my shoes into the corner and lift myself up, scrambling up the logs in order to climb up to the rafters, this time I easily leapt the ten feet, landing nimbly on the third rafter, making barely any sound. Time does change things.

What it hadn't changed was the list of girls that had given their all (and by all, I mean a bit of their virtue) in order to earn their place on a very special roster. Or at least time hadn't erased that list. There had indeed been changes. There were a few more inductees, which pleased me. There was still April. Beth. Lossie. Roberta. Daisy. Ginny. Clio. Georgie. Britney. Paula. Terri. Nora. A few others that I remembered. Past that was Clementine (a name I can't read without humming that old miner's song) and Colleen and Annie and Petra (it must have been the Gorner twin, but the incident would have hardly been her first experience), Gladiola and Wendy and Adele and Libby and Fran and a whole host of others. With the Greenway population explosion, the roster had increased exponentially, so much so that I sniffed the air, trying to scent the hundred or so girls who had given that finger-length piece of their virtue here in the log cabin, because surely the smell of teenage sex must have permanently bonded with the oaken logs. Nothing, though. It just smelled like wood.

I've twice stated that the girls gave their virtue, and I should correct that. There's nothing virtuous in not experiencing what life has to offer, and it's a slap in the face that some people count a boy having sex as a triumph, and a girl having sex as a defeat. These girls on the list, they hadn't been defeated; they'd only lived life, and done so with pleasure.

That said, I was heartbroken to see Adele's name on the rafter. I hadn't put it there. Who had? The name didn't, of course, have to refer to Adele Layton. There are other Adeles in the world. It's an uncommon name, but not singular.

Anyway, it wasn't fair that I felt the burn of acids inside my stomach, in my lungs and heart (and, hell yes, soul) when I saw her name there, since after the accident I had been in a coma for nearly three months (Greg was in a coma for five days and Tom, well, more on that later) and by the time I woke I wasn't the way I had been. My own life had assuredly moved on, and hers had to, as well. It's not like she was the one in a coma. It was fine that she had found somebody else. It was fine that she had laughed with him. It was fine that she had gone to movies with him, movies that he maybe even remembered, and it was fine if they looked for fossils together in the quarry. It was absolutely okay if she wore her green dress and they'd walked along Greenway's sidewalks together. I had no issue with how she'd taken her panties off, sliding them down from her legs, maybe with him holding her dress up, watching Adele as she stepped away from her panties, him with a grin that wouldn't quit, and a pen knife in his back pocket, ready to carve her name in a rafter that…

… a rafter that

… that I almost broke with a sudden clasping of my hand, crushing part of the timber in my grip, sending a crack along a rafter that had been in place for nearly one hundred and fifty years.

It wasn't fair to feel that way. Adele had a life of her own. Myself, I was sitting alone in the rafters where only teenagers are supposed to go, and I was sitting with ten days left in my life. I'd given my word of honor to

Octagon, and I meant to keep it.

I am Reaver.

A hero.

Heroes keep their word.

My brother Tom taught me how solidly that was true.

No matter how much it hurts.

I had ten days to make things right in the world. That's not possible, of course. I'd spent years trying to make things right in the world, and I'd done some tidbits of good, but I'd only barely jostled the scales, and for several of those years I had Paladin at my side (I know there are those out there, reading this, who would say it was the other way around) and it was a time when Mistress Mary and Kid Crater and Warp were in their prime. What a golden age. Then, it had seemed possible; it had seemed that…

I found that I had left the park and was running, at three times the speed of a normal man, to Adele's house. Her name was listed in the phone directory as having the same place of residence as back when I'd lived in Greenway. The same house. That was a relief to me. I suppose a psychiatrist would call it an anchor. Ten days from death, I wanted a solid footing in the past. I'd looked up Adele's name on one of Checkmate's computers, at the SRD base, with Commander Bryant typing in a password (he said the password didn't make any real difference… that Checkmate's computers simply used the keys to fingerprint you as you typed, and to retrieve and match a genetic sample from your skin flakes) and then turning discreetly aside while I did my research.

Adele's parents were dead. One quick heart attack. One lingering battle against cancer.

Adele had no marriage certificate on file. Which didn't mean she was single.

She listed her occupation as "self-employed blogger/researcher/author." She had written a number of books on the topic of the superhumans. They had moderate sales. The subject matter was popular, but her approach (according to a brief scouring of her reviews) was too scholarly. People like the sensational.

Continuing to stalk (ahem… research) Adele's file on the computer, I saw that her health record was enviable. There were no listed pregnancies. She had been investigated five times by the Secret Service, four times for intruding on Presidential secure zones during public appearances (each time during press conferences concerning superhumans) and once for hacking into government files in order to access documents about… Reaver.

So, that was interesting.

Commander Bryant had told me that I should ask Adele, myself, in person, if I wanted to know any more. He told me a personal story about stalking a girl online, a girl he'd met in a bar, and by the time he'd slept with her (he clearly wanted to tell me all the details of the encounter, which had happened in a bunker, a quarter mile below the holding pen where Warp is stored these days) she was so frightened by all the intimate knowledge he knew about her, all the things she'd never told him, that it hadn't progressed to any real intimacy, just the fake variety that computers foster.

I'd told Bryant, "I thought you were turned around. Not looking." For once, I'd meant to use the Reaver voice, the one that scares people. He'd only smiled. I suppose that's fitting, as he's the man who, every day, goes and talks to Mindworm, down in the cells, asking him to release his hold on the citizens of Farewell, New Mexico, a town of 2700 people that have been caught in Mindworm's dreams for over seven years. If a man can talk with Mindworm, he's not going to shit himself because I use my nasty voice.

So I'd turned back to the computers (Checkmate's computers were made of glass, or maybe diamonds, and, according to Bryant, a handful of quarks) and I (knowing full well that Bryant was right) intruded even further into Adele's life, accessing the SRD satellite surveillance photos of her house, taken over the past couple of years, showing her house (there was a new porch addition) and, in three of the photos, Adele herself, walking outside the house, going inside the house, and, in the last of them, spilling groceries as she took two bags from her car.

And now, a few hours later, after sulking like a spoiled teenager in the log cabin rafters, I was standing in the street in front of Adele's house.

It would have taken a normal man ten seconds to make it to her front door, and to knock.

It would have taken me one third as long.

Instead, I took out my phone, took a deep breath, took a look up into the sky (where I assumed that at least one of the SRD satellites was tracking me) and I dialed a number.

Adele's number.

I felt worse than when Firehook had once torn out my left lung.

I felt worse than when Laser Beast had once (on purpose, that fucker) shot a hole through my balls.

I felt about the same as when, right after the tanker truck accident, I'd woken up (briefly, and for the last time in months) on the highway, wreckage all around me, and I could see what had happened to Officer Horwitz, and to Greg, and (only somewhat) to Tom.

I felt like I could hear Adele's phone ringing, in the house.

I watched her move past the window on the 2nd floor (she'd apparently taken her parents' old room) and then, after six rings, I heard her, in the phone, saying, "Hello?"

And I felt it.

CHAPTER SIX

The majority of people who read this aren't going to care about my relationship with Adele. My memories and thoughts concerning the boys and girls in the bright-colored underwear is what they're going to find fascinating. I was once offered an embarrassing amount of cash to make a pornographic film with Siren, who had (according to a producer who was later found dead with all his fingers missing) agreed to the film as long as it would air on primetime television. One network had said they wouldn't consider doing so under any circumstances. Three others had said there were, possibly, some circumstances that could be considered.

I'd turned the offer down.

I turned it down just like I'd turned down all the merchandising deals. I'd declined most public appearances (Paladin always seemed able to talk me into them) and various requests for my sperm to be used to fertilize loving couples and even (I'd be lying if I said I didn't consider this, at least from an amusement standpoint) one group of fifty-six (yes, fifty-six) Ukrainian lesbians who had formed a warrior cult and lived in caves. Warp (this was before his breakdown) ran over to check out the premises and said the caves were actually very nice. Like modern homes.

There isn't an awards show I haven't been asked to host. Emmys, Grammys, Oscars, the Nobel prizes, La Liga soccer championships, and so on and so on.

Ugly as I am, I'm one of the beautiful people, and the citizens of the world want to know about beautiful people, demanding to know about any battles with villains, any demeaning secrets about heroes, mystic rites that supposedly exist to allow them (meaning every housewife, weekend sportsman, trailer-park resident, Wal-Mart employee, roadie, carny, frat boy, sorority girl, news anchor, etc. etc.) to become one of us, to soar through the skies and heave cars aside.

People want to know how many times I've been shot (even I don't know that) and how many times I've been dropped from space (twice: fuck you, Stellar) and how many women I've slept with (it's a fair number, and some of the names pop up again in the list of those who have shot me, or dropped me from space) and, of course, people want to know about my punch, and the year of life it smashes aside.

People do not want to know about how I was heaving in something close to fear (it was more like being uncomfortable, but a superhuman size of uncomfortable, a feeling which all regular people need to face, anyway, at times) when I was holding the phone to my cheek, and how my cell phone felt as heavy as the boulder (twice the size of the trailer it had destroyed) that I lifted in order to free Joshua Williams, who had survived an avalanche by the expedient of falling into a hole that had been prepared for installation of a new septic tank.

Adele, on the phone, said, "Hello?"

I said, "Yes," which was nonsensical.

She said, "Steve?"

I said, "Hello." I was getting things backward. If Mindworm hadn't been in his cerebral holding carriage, I would have suspected he was at work.

Adele said, "I was told that you were in town. I'm… I'm… happy. Steve. I'm happy. Where are you?"

"Standing outside the log cabin," I answered. "In Charles Park." I don't know why I lied. I mean, I lied because I was panicked, but I don't know why I was panicked. It was Adele. On the phone. That's why I was panicked. I knew that, of course.

"Do you want me to come there?" she asked.

"I don't think that would be a good idea." She was going to ask why not. I needed to have an answer ready. I was backing away from her house, hunkering down behind a Smart Car that was barely big enough to hide me. I found myself wishing for Tom. He would have kicked me into view. I needed that kick.

"Why wouldn't it be a good idea?" Adele asked. She came to the window, parted the curtain, looking out.

"A fight," I said.

"A fight?"

"With Eleventh Hour. It… didn't go well. I'm beat up pretty bad. Don't think you want to see me like this."

"Steve," she said. "I just want to see you."

She didn't make it sound tearful, or pleading, or false, the way old lovers will sometimes do. Any one of those might have made it easier.

I didn't say anything.

She was still standing between the parted curtains, but she'd turned off the lights in the room, probably so she could see outside better.

"Are you hiding behind the Smart Car?" she asked. Damn. Damn it to hell. I stood up.

"There you are," she said. There was a catch in her voice I would have given anything to understand.

"How'd you know?"

"That's where I would have hidden. Listen, my downstairs door is locked. I'm going to go unlock it. Okay?"

"Okay," I said.

I started walking towards the house.

⌖

Octagon announced his presence to the world, as everyone knows, when he stormed the Churchill, the secret (well, secret at the time) British nuclear submarine then off the coast of Portugal taking part in an underwater mapping exercise.

Octagon appeared in Captain Wilmer Bosley's quarters (beaming a live video feed that piggybacked onto television waves worldwide) and boldly strode throughout the craft (which was then nearly six hundred meters below the surface) disabling the crew members with a device that radiated a disrupting charge (attuned to the human brain, rendering all within the field of effect unconscious within seconds) in a circle that could pass through the bulkheads, and was nearly seventy feet in diameter, which is an epic measurement in an underwater craft.

He robbed them.

That's all Octagon did.

He mugged each and every one of the unconscious crewmembers.

Their wallets. Their rings. Any money they had in their pockets.

A worldwide live broadcast of the oddest mass mugging on record.

He said, "I am Octagon. My eight arms reach everywhere. You have ceased to be safe."

The rings, and all the personal photos from the crewmember's wallets, were later found floating inside a hard rubber balloon (with an attached air horn that was sounding in bursts) about the size of a beach ball, floating in the Thames.

The world wanted to know how Octagon had gotten into (and subsequently, off) the Churchill at such a depth. The world was also curious about how Octagon had, for the time he was aboard (two hours, after the crewmen were rendered inert) managed to pilot and maintain the ship's course completely by himself. The world wanted to know what Octagon's suit was made of… how he could reach into the black void of his costume and bring out all sorts of devices. The world wanted to know this.

The world wanted to know about Octagon.

So they sent me after him.

⌖

The first time the American public became aware of Macabre it was because he'd robbed the First United National Bank in Harrisburg Pennsylvania, later claiming he had chosen this site because of their name. First. United. National. F. U. N. Fun.

That's all it was. It wasn't about money. He just said it sounded like it would be fun. What did a master of magic need with money? He could conjure himself a castle. Servants. Food. Gems. Everything. It was famously said that the only thing Macabre couldn't conjure was a sense of morality, and he was the one who coined the phrase.

Seven men and women died during Macabre's first appearance. Keep in mind they didn't have to die. Macabre could have done anything he wished. This wasn't a man who had a gun in his hands and was firing in panic, out of his mind, trying to preserve his own life, caught in a situation that had gotten out of control, or half out of his mind with fear. This was a man with reality in his hand, twisting it at whim, making no effort to preserve anyone's life, completely out of his mind with arrogance and power.

Greg Lemond: a teller. His body was, during the course of the robbery, turned into coins. It started with pennies dropping from his ears, sliding out from his eyes, heaving out of his choking mouth. Then, quarters and dimes and staters and kruggerands and drachms and rubles, coins from all ages, began flaking away from his entire body like scales, like pieces of his skin, until there was nothing left of him but a memory of a few horrible moments of screaming, and a large pile of assorted coins, many of which were surreptitiously pocketed by onlookers, the police, and a bewildered coroner.

Judith Swan: Another teller. She was four months pregnant. Her fetus burst into flames, burning (according to Macabre himself) at six hundred and sixty-six thousand degrees centigrade for the space of three long seconds. No trace of Ms. Swan was ever recovered, unless you were to count a blackened smear on the nearby walls.

Alfie Breeks: He was there at the bank in order to deposit some winnings from a fine night of poker. He was a small-time crook. Or maybe a medium-time crook. He was devoured by a demon. It came up out of a deposit slip box, or possibly it was a deposit slip box. Witnesses are unclear on this.

Jason Fenel: A customer who was closing his account. Moving to Australia. A new girlfriend had encouraged him to become either a poet, a wilderness adventurer, or a kangaroo farmer. Macabre turned him into a piece of paper and presented him to Judith Swan with a demand for money written on the surface, and a pair of unblinking, terrified eyes on the back of the sheet.

Nathan Offutt and his girlfriend, Lisbeth Zoni: No matter who fired on Macabre, no matter their vantage point, no matter the timing, no matter if it was a bank guard or the police, every bullet had its path diverted. Redirected to either Nathan or Lisbeth. There were hundreds of shots before people understood what was happening.

Jeremy Bond: A bank guard. Still there. Still frozen into position. Unmovable from the spot. Possibly alive. An office has been built around him so that customers can't see him, can't grow uneasy, won't take their business elsewhere. The employees, of course, have learned to live with his presence. Somewhat.

Macabre left the bank with two hundred thousand dollars in cash. Less than thirty thousand dollars per life. Outside, in the street, he scattered more than a million dollars worth of five-dollar bills. He'd never needed the cash at all.

He just wanted to rob.

He just wanted to kill.

So they sent me after him.

⌖

Tempest had been known as Anya Neatridge, but nobody calls her by that name anymore. For all intents and purposes she died when she fell (there is a body of evidence suggesting she was pushed) into the waste containment facility at SRD, at a time when I was three buildings over, being systematically injured so that I and a group of interested onlookers could gauge my healing abilities.

Anya had surfaced only once, (at least when she was still Anya) and even then it was just her foot. Her clothing had dissolved instantly within the radioactive brine. Surveillance tapes (there were no surviving witnesses) suggest there was a bubble of light, as if something of brilliant magnitude was brewing below. In the videos, it's possible to see papers, attached to a clipboard hanging on the wall, begin to ruffle. Soon after, these papers, the clipboard itself, a work safety poster, and a number of safety garments (lead-lined "raincoats," helmets, goggles, a glove with a built-in Geiger counter, etc.) begin to swirl about the room. The footage itself begins to shudder. The walls are shaking. Ice forms in several places. It begins, against all reason, to hail. Lightning streams down from the ceiling as if it were being spouted by the fire containment system.

Three guards rush in from an adjoining door. Two of them are struck instantly by lightning and they fracture into several charred pieces. The remains of these two men (and the third man, who was, at that point, still alive) are swept up into the winds to be battered against the walls amongst the rest of the debris. The vat begins to buckle. Waste begins to spew outwards. One of the cameras is wrenched from the wall. In the remaining camera's view, the walls themselves begin to shred. There is a brief moment of the sky and then, according to some people, Tempest herself rises from the vat and into the air. But the form (whatever it is) is just a rush of color, a quick swath of white, and amidst all the other debris it is no more likely to be Tempest herself than a burnt area on a piece of toast is truly Jesus Christ.

The last of the cameras goes out.

Three days later, Tempest, pure white flesh, pure red hair flowing about her naked body, was floating above Osage, Iowa, held in mid-air by a series of strong updrafts of her own making, and which were absolutely under her control. It was her first official appearance. It was Osage's last.

Tempest's storm blackened the land. Her rains rose the waters of the normally placid Cedar River over twenty-four feet in a matter of minutes, far enough that many of the town's buildings and residents were swept away in the flood. The others were soon encased in ice. Buried in snow.

They found Tempest atop the snowdrifts, sprawled naked, laughing to herself. In this case, "they" were two state troopers on snowmobiles they'd had to haul out of summer storage, and four other officers staggering up and onto the giant white drifts. Along with the entire town of Osage, Tempest killed them, too.

And they sent me after her.

⌖

Adele, when she opened the door, was wearing a red skirt with a white top. The top hadn't been tucked in properly, and she was pulling on a stocking, revealing a glimpse of upper leg as she hopped across her porch, so that the first thing I did, after not having seen the love of my life (please, tabloids… it was never Siren, or Stellar, or Mistress Mary, or any of the models) is burst out laughing.

"Don't laugh at me," she said, but in a tone of voice making clear that it was okay that I was laughing at her.

"Why didn't you get dressed first?" I asked. "I mean, all the way dressed?"

"Didn't want you to run away before I got to the door. I hear you run fast."

"I do. Three times normal."

"What's that mean?" she asked. She was tucking the white top into her skirt, circling her waist with a practiced swoop. "I've heard it said you're three times faster than normal, but what's normal? Most normal people are about sixty pounds overweight and can't run over five miles an hour without breaking into a profuse sweat and costing their insurance company a hundred thousand dollars in hospital bills. So… three times faster than five miles per hour? That's only fifteen miles per hour. It's not all that impressive."

"I thought I would be the one to babble."

"You too? God. Damn. You want a beer?"

"I want a beer," I told her.

"You're still holding your phone," she told me, beckoning me into the kitchen. "Thanks for not being in costume."

"I hate being in costume. I'm… sorry for not calling. I mean, you know, the years." I put away my phone. She pretended she didn't hear me, which was for the best. Her kitchen was medium-sized, well kept, with an assortment of devices that I wouldn't have known what to do with. There were machines that chopped and sliced and liquefied. I mostly call out for food. I don't mind cooking. Or I never used to mind cooking. How long has it been since I cooked? I couldn't remember. I was suddenly consumed with a desire to cook. I wondered if Adele would think it was strange if I came into her house and started making pancakes, seared trout, linguini with a sauce I used to make with Portobello and morel mushrooms. I hadn't made it for, what, three years? The last time was for Siren, so, yes… about three years.

Adele grabbed me a beer from a fridge full of vegetables, leafy greens, fruits, yogurts, and an amazing array of other consumables. I sat at a round walnut table with a flower vase that was nearly invisible beneath a crush of gladiolas. There was a map of the world on the wall, with pins stuck in various places. The map, for certain reasons, reminded me of my brother, Tom. There were no pictures of kids that I could see in Adele's home. Not on the fridge or the walls or on any of the shelves. There was, as far as I could tell, nobody else at home. There was no way to ask without it being obvious, without it sounding like I was attaching too much importance to the question. It really didn't make all that much difference. It was, at the same time, the most important question I could possibly consider.

"What's wrong with being in costume?" I asked. Adele sat across from me at the table. She opened her mouth twice to answer, but backed away each time. A cat (white with brown splotches) came into the kitchen, looked at me, didn't care, left. Adele's long brown hair was touching her shoulders. Her eyes were as wide as they once were. A couple worry lines spread away from them, but they just made her look human, not really any older. Her lips were still her lips. Her nose still had the upthrust tip. It was like she was still Adele, but of course that was impossible.

"I remember waving to you and Greg and... your brother," she said. She sipped a little from her beer. She noticed I hadn't opened mine and she stood and walked to me, opened it, licked away a touch of beer that had gotten onto her index finger, touched me on my shoulder and went and sat back down. She had avoided saying Tom's name, which I understood. She hadn't hesitated when she touched me on the shoulder, which isn't something I'm used to anymore, not these days, and it felt like a damn rainbow. Yeah. Ten minutes into her presence, and I was talking like a poet, again.

"You were going to the quarry," she said. "On your bikes." It was something that had happened plenty enough times, but I knew the day she meant.

"That was the last time I saw you," she said. "At least when you weren't in a coma." She started to drink more of her beer. There were a couple of gulps and then she stood, quickly, scowling, and poured the rest down her sink, washing it away with a three-second cascade of water from her faucet.

"Sorry," she said. "I just... I was an alcoholic for a while, okay? I shouldn't drink beer this late at night." The cat came back in, still didn't see anything it liked, left again. I thought about asking for the cat's name. They say one way to a woman's heart is to let her talk about her pets. It seemed an awful time to intrude on any woman's heart, though. Especially Adele's. It wouldn't have been fair. I was pledged to another. I had another date. It was only ten days away, and it was holding a laser pistol in one hand.

Adele said, "I suppose, what I meant about the costume is... you never came back. You had the accident and I sat next to you in the hospital, before, you know, before." I knew what she meant. When I finally came out of my coma there had been an incident at the hospital. My location was moved. Adele wouldn't have been able to sit anywhere near me. Not after that.

I said, "So, you needed me to come back. Closure for you? And if I came back in costume I wouldn't have been Steve Clarke anymore?"

She said, "I needed you to come back." The cat sauntered into the kitchen, jumped up onto the table and brushed its tail through the flowers. They rustled. The cat looked at me like it expected to be praised for this achievement. I picked it up and sat it on the floor. It walked off. Adele didn't introduce me to the feline. I wondered if that was a good sign or a bad one.

I heard creaking on the stairway.

Someone was coming down the stairs.

Someone.

I froze into position, listening, feeling like the footsteps on the stairway had somehow meshed with my heartbeat.

Adele saw that I went white and tried to divine what was going through my head. It must have been hard for her. The Steve Clarke she'd known, the one she could predict, was years in the past, and had been human. I was something else. At least a little.

"Oh," she said, fluttering, looking back to the stairway (it was in another room, so that when the footsteps ended their creator would soon appear in a living room filled with bright throw pillows, well-tended plants, a long slithering couch suitable for entertaining, etc.) and then to me, then back again, as if piecing together the puzzle of my sudden fear. She actually made it. Maybe she could still predict me. Maybe I was still Steve Clarke. Anyway, Adele understood.

"It's just… no… it's not anyone," she said. Which was, of course, stupid. It was someone.

"I mean," she said. "It's… not." She stared at me. Her lips were pursed. Her brow furrowed. Her fists shook. She looked like a little girl. Acted that way.

"Goddamn you, Steve Clarke," she suddenly blurted. "I'm single!"

My heart felt like it ripped free. Shit… maybe it really had. I heal at a good rate. Maybe my heart had actually torn loose. Maybe it fell into my stomach. Doused itself in acid. It felt like it had. Maybe it had fallen away and a new heart had formed.

"That's..." I said, starting to say something (god knows what... my tongue was another thing that felt like it had ripped free) but at that moment a person came around the corner of the living room, moved some hair out of her sleepy eyes, stretched (providing a nice view, because she was very pretty, and wearing sweat pants, and nothing else) and then flopped onto the long sinuous couch. The cat jumped up onto her lap and she began to pet it, scolding it for always being hungry.

She said, "Wiggles, if I fed you every time you begged, you'd be the fattest fucking cat in the history of..."

She looked up and saw me.

She was Adele's sister, Laura.

Adele said, "Sis. We have company." Laura gaped at me, then glanced all around the house, quickly, as if gauging if other visitors might be lurking.

Finally, returning her gaze to Adele (she was now avoiding looking at me) she said, "I... thought the voices were the tee-vee, but... they're not."

I said, "Hi, Laura."

"Do I know you?" she asked, squinting. I leaned farther away from the table, letting her get a better look at me, wondering if she knew she was topless. She hadn't done anything about it.

Adele said, "Laura... it's..."

"Oh my fucking GOD!" Laura shouted. "Steve? You're here? You came here? Are you two back together?"

"Sis!" Adele screamed. "What the fuck? Could you... not? We haven't seen each other for years!"

"We're not back together," I said. It was what I thought Adele wanted me to say, but I caught a glance from her, and I could see that it had hurt her. I couldn't believe it. I've seen men fly into space... I've seen a man survive an atom bomb... I've seen a woman walk through a wall like a ghost... I've seen Paladin heal wounds that were clearly fatal... I've seen buildings come alive at the whim of a mad magician... I've seen a man pick up a cement truck and beat another man to death with it... I've seen a woman bathing, happily, in a wall of lightning thicker than steel... but I've never seen anything as unexpected as the hurt in Adele's eyes.

"Where's my glasses? Where's my glasses?" Laura screamed, scrambling up from the couch. The cat (Wiggles, apparently) clawed onto her sweat pants, surprised by the sudden tumult. She swept him away with a wave of her hand (he tumbled to the floor and then walked away, unperturbed, because cats are never perturbed) and she darted up the stairs, was gone only long enough for Adele (in the guise of the long-suffering sister) to shrug her shoulders at me, and then Laura sped back down the stairs wearing her glasses, though she was still topless.

"Steve!" she said. She nearly flew into the kitchen and she pulled me (I was frankly in a bit of shock) to a standing position, and she hugged me so tight that it nearly hurt, and I'm a man that can withstand some muscle.

"Laura," Adele said, somehow magically combining a sigh with a shout. "Put. A. Shirt. On."

"I should," she answered. Her freckles had never faded. Nine years and they were standing strong. In fact, they'd spread onto her chest. All over her chest. Maybe they'd been there before, I guess... but I'd never had the pleasure of an introduction.

Laura sat at the table with us (still topless, but now moving the vase and its gladiolas in front of her) and looked me in my eyes, waving me closer, glancing to Adele in a furtive manner, as if we were about to share something she didn't want her sister to hear.

"Get her to make you pancakes," Laura said. "She makes them round. I mean, like, precision round. Also, she likes foreign movies. She hasn't had a boyfriend for six years. Hasn't gotten laid in seven."

Adele said, "Holy fuck! What did you just tell him? Fuck!" She got up from the table, stalked to the fridge, grabbed a beer, looked at it, put it (unopened) in the sink and sat back down. Laura smiled at her.

Laura, putting her hand on my forearm, said, "She likes hiking. Hike with her. If you know anything... anything... in French, say it. Doesn't matter if it's a weather report. Oh... and romance novels make her horny."

"Don't tell him that!" Adele said. Wiggles, the cat, was on the kitchen's boundary line, trying to decide if it should come closer. It sat, considering.

"She likes to go to live music, but, guess what? We live in Greenway. The pickings are lean. Of course, it's bigger here, now. But... fuck all that... the people here aren't musical. It's not a music town. Take her out dancing in Bolton. Do that. Hey... do you dance three times faster?"

She turned to Adele and asked it again. "Sis. Does he dance three times faster?"

"I don't know. Maybe. God, Laura, put a shirt on. Please? For me?"

"It doesn't matter if Steve sees my tits," Laura said. "For fuck's sake, I'm a lesbian."

"How does that make any difference?" Adele asked, and I did too, at the exact same time, and the cat came farther into the kitchen and I, against all expectations, was actually happy to be sitting in a kitchen in Greenway, Oregon.

Home.

CHAPTER SEVEN

Octagon ran between the buildings. At rooftop level. Twenty stories above the street. As if there was some invisible pathway. I even put out a foot, testing the air as I was watching him dart across the open space between the buildings, but there wasn't anything solid. Just… air. I wondered how he was doing it. Flying through the air is just flying, but running across the air is cheating.

He reached the opposite building and turned, apparently ready to gloat or taunt, but by that time I had moved back from the building's edge, had built up some momentum, running as fast as I could, and I had leapt into space.

"Shit!" Octagon yelled, because I was an incoming mortar shell. I was a beautiful barrage. I was a meteor. A comet. A human bullet that was…

… not going to make it.

I fell short of my mark and crashed through the sliding glass door of a balcony one floor below, shattering the glass and sending it into a living room where Mark Blickens was having a threesome. I found out his name later and sent him a card in apology. I didn't catch his name right then because I was busily tumbling across his floor, smashing through a small bookshelf (it had a collection of framed mini-paintings of characters from cereal boxes) and a guitar stand and then into the back of the couch with enough of an impact that a blonde woman (god, she was pretty) went flying from between the legs of another woman and crashed into Mark's own legs. He'd been standing only a few feet off, naked, ithyphallic as can ever be, filming the event on his cell phone.

Some of you have probably seen the footage online.

If so, you've seen me stand up and say, "Fuck! Sorry! I… holy shit. Oh, Christ, I really *am* sorry!" You've seen me look at the brunette on the couch long enough to ascertain that her bondage was consensual, and then you've seen me get the hell out of there, repeating *sorry* again and again.

But you haven't seen me, on the balcony, leap up onto the roof. Octagon was running away by then, but I'm three times faster than him, and though he had a good lead I was quickly closing the gap, darting past lawn chairs on the rooftops, past coolers that had been strewn about, past all the empty beer cans, a bong that had been placed atop an old packing crate, ducking clotheslines (Octagon ran straight into one of them, and the towels and the line itself burst into flames, for some reason) and leaping over alleyways, hoping that Octagon wouldn't run out into space again, eventually wrenching a brick from a stray pile (workman had been repairing a chimney) and thinking about throwing it at him, thinking about my days in Little League, about my work as a first baseman, about how Greg had been a pitcher, about how he'd thrown that baseball through a tire swing for hours on end, hardly ever missing, and I knew that he'd be able to peg Octagon with a brick, easy, even on the run. But at the time he was battling Tempest (this was, for those who are constructing timelines, during her waveringly successful attempt to install herself as a goddess in Ecuador) and I was six thousand miles away in Marseille, trying to capture a madman.

I threw the brick at his back.

But he ducked as it came closer, as if he had eyes on the back of his head. He doesn't, as far as I know, but I've noted that he often knows what's happening all around him, anywhere, in a 360 circle, so there's something strange going on.

Anyway, the brick missed him and scuffed off the top of the roof and then went over the edge. I stopped pursuit long enough to glance to the street (my nuts tightened, as I could just picture the brick zeroing in on some baby carriage) and watched the brick smash into the sidewalk next to some late-night revelers, who shouted in surprise and then held three wine bottles high, giving the fragmented brick a hearty round of *hurrahs*, celebrating it in some way that could only make sense to a drunk.

And then I was after Octagon again.

I'd trailed him for over a week, using SRD surveillance and tracking reports, always a step behind, spending my time in Kinshasa, Muscat, Pondicherry, Banda Aceh, Topeka, Sioux Falls, and then Marseille. Octagon had involved himself in a myriad of activities in these places, encompassing a wide swath of morality. He'd sold illegal weaponry (even some black market knockoffs from Checkmate's original designs, which Paladin and I later recovered) and he'd tried to install a dictator and he'd eliminated a slavery ring and he'd provided aid and comfort in the aftermath of a tsunami. He'd slept with, as far as I could tell, every pretty woman in all of the cities, and there were rumors that he'd skipped across the gender lines on a couple of instances. There were certainly a few willing men waiting with their toes on that line. More than a few. This was still a couple years before his rumored affair with Tattoo (obviously, since Tattoo disappeared during the time of their rumored liaisons, and hasn't been seen or heard from since) and it was still almost three years before he and Siren were shacking up together, whenever she wasn't shacking up (ahem) somewhere else.

I should have been noticing where I was going, of course. Octagon is a criminal mastermind, and while it's easy to be called a criminal, it takes some effort and planning to be called a mastermind, and Octagon's name is forever linked with the word. He looked back to me, saw that I was catching up, swore, and pulled something from that damn void of his costume, a small metal ball that he tossed over his shoulder in my direction.

It landed near me. It didn't roll the way that it should have. Just… landed. Stayed put. I frantically ducked and twisted and did all sorts of things, wondering what the hell was about to happen, wondering what fiendish mechanism the son-of-a-bitch had unleashed on me. I even thought about leaping over the edge of the roof, taking my chances on the fall (I wasn't, then, aware of how durable I really am) or maybe tearing a hole into the rooftop and dropping down below. A few seconds passed, me caught in place, staring at that big metal marble, before I realized it wasn't going to do anything. Anything at all. By then, Octagon was four rooftops over, going through a doorway that led down into the building, which was a church of some kind.

I raced across a rooftop, leapt across an alleyway, did that again, and again, and hurled myself onto the church, smashing through a stained glass window depicting a shepherd. I admit that I did that on purpose. My powers were still relatively new and I was still full of myself, fucking thrilled to be in costume, leaning towards anything dramatic, and my ego-cock and my real cock were both as hard as they could be.

"Jesus!" Octagon yelled as I came smashing through, sending stained glass fragments into the darkness, over the walkway, down onto the pews of the darkened church, several stories below.

"Not Jesus," I said. "It's Reaver." I couldn't resist.

Octagon was running along a circular balcony that looked down upon the church's worship area, forty feet below. He gauged the distance between us, gauged how long it would take me to recover from my entrance (I was slipping on glass fragments) and calculated that I'd have my hands on his ass in about two seconds if he kept running along the walkway. So he jumped.

I jumped, too.

But he'd jumped before I did, and I don't fall three times faster than a man, so he hit the ground first, landing lightly on the back of a pew, and so softly that it was left undisturbed. He started to run towards the front of the church and then I hit ground floor as well, smashing into a pew and crushing it, snapping it in half, sending wooden fragments and prayer booklets scattering about.

"Freeze!" I yelled out, angrily watching the bastard leaving me behind again, and not having anything more quip-like to yell. Octagon didn't freeze. Instead, he moved a device on the wall (I couldn't see what he'd moved, or what button he'd pressed) and then a section of the wall moved slightly outwards, a secret door in a church (I loved that… I truly did) and he slipped through and disappeared down some stone steps before I could reach him.

The doorway slid shut.

I fumbled for some seconds, with the wall, pressing my hands here and there, trying to trigger whatever mechanism Octagon had engaged. There didn't seem to be anything. No torch sconces. No statues. No buttons.

No nothing of any kind. Just a blank wall. It took me almost a minute of fumbling, of being intricately aware of how Octagon was getting away (and childishly aware that Mistress Mary would scold me for letting him escape, and even more annoyed that Paladin would forgive me for the mistake) and then I suddenly realized that I wasn't a police officer or a detective looking for the hidden switch… no… I was Reaver. A superhero.

So I tore the wall down, plunging my hands into the wood (which was lined by thick steel on the opposite side) and wrenching it from the wall. A whole section came loose and I tossed it aside (more property damage, and in a church, forgive me) and then I was running down several flights of stairs that seemed to have been erected by an architect who specialized in monster movies from the 1940's, or cautionary tales from the 1640's.

I'm not sure how many steps I went down. It seemed like thousands, but might only have been hundreds. I'm not sure how many decisions I had to make. There was always another offshoot, other stairway to take, corridors that branched off, sets of open doorways with nothing but darkness in some, torches in others, electric lights in a few, and a couple of them lit by what seemed to be luminous lichens. Always, though, there was the sound of footsteps, or the click of a latch, a hushed exhalation of breath or a soft moan of pain, that made the decision for me. In time, I met the end of a hallway, or the seeming end of a hallway, but there was an illumination coming from behind the stones (the walls had been steel at times, or glass, or wood, or rough stone, or bare earth, or finely cut marble) in the outline of a door, suggesting the stones were false, or could at least be moved aside, and I moved them aside by the simple expedient of running into them at full speed with a lowered shoulder.

They were harder than I would have expected. Maybe only four men (and two women) on Earth could have burst them asunder in the way that I did. My shoulder hurt for a couple seconds, then quit that shit, healing already, and I found myself in a large circular room that had all the trappings of a modern arena, and of course that's just what it was.

Three levels above me, on a circular observation balcony, were crowds of people in seats. How many of them? Hundreds. Most of them were in the dark, impossible to see with the background glare of the floodlights. A few, though, were in positions of prominence… seated in places where they could be seen, and recognized. I quickly spotted, for instance, Laser

Beast and Firehook, and Stellar was there as well, the first time I'd seen her in person.

And of course there was Octagon, up above, in a throne fit for the gaudiest and least color-coordinated of kings, and he waved down at me like an old friend and said, "At last. At last. We were getting restless. But you're here, and I'm pleased, and we'll make a night of this meeting, and, Reaver, Steven Thaddeus Clark, I bid you welcome to my octagon."

The surrounding doors opened and the rats came inside.

⌖

Adele hated rats. I just wanted to throw that in here. It's not by any means a startling revelation. Most girls hate rats. Most people hate rats. There are those who keep rats as pets, and they say they're very loving animals, and these people (the rat-owners) claim themselves as rat-lovers, but it's a very different thing, a pet rat and a wild rat. Nobody loves wild rats. I'm talking about the *mangy-yellow-toothed-gnaw-on-you-alive-or-dead* type of rat. Nobody loves them. Adele and I had seen them twice. Once while biking into the quarry on what amounted to our fifth date. And once when we snuck down into the basement of Bolton High School in order to see what she looked like with her shirt off. A rat had then come out from behind a custodial cart and raced across the floor, making that noise that only the hated rats make. You never hear that noise from the pet rats. Maybe they can actually make the sound, but are smart enough not to do it, because then they'd be out on the street.

⌖

At the time, it wasn't well known that Octagon played with genetics. He was a mystery then, even more so than now. These days, a folder on Octagon would have about twenty pages of real facts, meaning hardly anything at all, really. In those days, a folder on Octagon would've only had five pages, and wouldn't have included how, if you were to fight him in an underground arena, you might suddenly find yourself pitted against an assortment of six-legged rats that were the size of horses.

I was glad that Adele wasn't there.

Here's a moment of honesty, though; I was glad to be there, myself. I was glad because I was still full of my powers, still full of myself, still believing that *good* always triumphs over *evil* instead of getting trounced by it, or more often wandering over to the other side to see what all the shouting's about. It seemed, at the time, that an arena was a good place to prove my moral superiority. I still felt like morals, in a fight, made any difference.

"Come down here, unless you're chicken," I told Octagon, which is the sort of taunt that works on a three-year-old child.

"You're serious?" he said. "Why would I do that? I go to all the trouble of luring you here, almost losing you in Pondicherry, having to wait nearly three hours so that you could accidentally run across me in Sioux Falls, and did you even know that I was the old lady that gave you directions in Muscat?"

"Yes," I said, meaning that everybody there was treated to a front seat view of my lie, which was treated with the derision that it deserved. I decided to keep my mouth shut, because, hell… I was busy. Those rats.

They weren't attacking right away. They'd congregated on the opposite side from me, six of them milling about each other in that overly-friendly way of rats, crawling over each other, sniffing and sniffing, which in this case sounded like horse snorts.

"We haven't trained them to kill, yet," Octagon said, in a sort of apology, and I gauged the distance between us and leapt at him. It was three stories. I could make it easy.

As it turns out… there was a force field. I hadn't known that. I smashed my head into it with the full power of my leap, and was batted back down to the ground. I was dazed and the floor seemed uneven. I could hear rats snorting. I could hear the crowd laughing.

I could hear Octagon saying, "There's a force field."

"Fuck you," I told him. My quips still weren't at their best.

"Ring the bell!" Firehook demanded, and he spat some fire down at me (coming from his mouth and eyes at the same time) which I didn't even bother to dodge because, first of all, I was beneath a force field and, second of all, I'm pretty much immune to flames.

The force field cheated.

The flames did, too.

The flames burnt like holy blistering hell, seeping into my arm.

I screamed.

Octagon rang some sort of bell (I wasn't looking… was desperately trying to wipe the flames away on the sandy floor of the arena) and when the bell went off the rats all suddenly became very focused on me… intently focused on me… murderously focused on me.

Octagon said, "I outright lied to you. The rats are trained to kill."

The first rat was on me before I knew it, moving faster than I'd expected, bounding to me in two driving leaps with an impact that sent me on my ass. The rat's teeth clicked into place around my neck. My skin proved too strong for the rat to break through or else I would have died in that first instant. I would have died wondering why the forces of justice (I still believed in them, actively) had decided that a moral man should fall in battle to a six-legged rat. Then, even though the rat couldn't break my skin, it began to be clear that it could still kill me, could strangle me not with fingers, but with teeth. I began to feel light-headed, heavy in my body, and I knew that it was time to stop playing with the pets.

I punched the rat. Three times in the head. It fell away from me. Dead.

Here's a hint for future madmen: if you're going to attack me with genetically altered creatures, do it with turtles or something. The average life span of a rat is two or three years. To me, that means two or three punches, tops. There's a reason I'm called Reaver.

I heaved the dead rat at the others, leapt across the arena and took advantage of its impact, fists flying, not really caring which rat I hit, only needing to land a few punches. More of the pests dropped dead. Experimentally, I picked one up and heaved it at Octagon, but it struck the force field and exploded like a piñata of vile bones and blood, showering me with the refuse of the dead, which sizzled when Firehook's next blast came down from above, glancing off my back, sending me rolling on the ground in agony. The last two rats pounced on me, with one clamping on my neck and the other shaking my leg like a dog worrying on a… well… on a rat. It wrenched me from the other's grasp and then died as I kicked out at it (I snapped its neck… my kicks don't steal the years in the manner of my fists) and then I rolled beneath it and picked it up, hefting it around my shoulders like the world's very worst fur stole.

The next blast of flame hit the rat.

"He's cheating!" I heard Firehook yell out. Even Octagon had to laugh at that one.

The last rat was keeping back, intelligent enough to know that it was overmatched. Firehook tried to goad it into battle by sending spats of flame behind its ass, and Octagon was ringing and ringing a bell, but nothing was happening. I was covered in rat gore and rat carcass. I had a third-degree burn on one arm, and another on my back. I was grinning like a madman and might well have been one. The rat kept its distance. My burns (glowing a soft green) went from second degree, to first degree, to being slight rashes, to being gone. I wished I could have said the same about the smell of the rats, but it didn't keep me grinning.

"Your rodents are dead," I told Octagon. "Now... try to ring *my* bell."

⌖

Firehook was an arsonist. A super-arsonist, truth be told. He looked like James Dean, if Dean's head and hands were on fire, all the time, constantly, sizzling and cracking. It would have made going to the bathroom uncomfortable, except he was immune to fire and flame and heat and, I guess, dandruff.

He set things on fire. He couldn't help himself. He didn't want to help himself. His first public appearance was when he, on a motorcycle, stopped a busload of students, grades six through nine, outside of Decatur, Illinois. He negotiated with the bus driver at first, and later with police, saying that one student and one student only could leave the bus before he turned it, and everything in it, to ash. The bus driver, Honestia Yoder, an ex-Amish woman, begged on actual bended knees that Firehook would let everyone go, and she was still in the middle of the begging when she suddenly burst into flames, like it was spontaneous human combustion, though of course there wasn't anyone who believed that was true. The police (only four officers managed to reach the scene before the deadline) opened fire on him, but the bullets melted away before they could reach him. One officer went into for a running tackle, and Firehook made his hook (a flaming whip, in one hand, with a large fiery hook on the end of it) and plucked the officer's head from his shoulders. Another officer tried to run him down with his police car, but the engine stalled, understandably, when it was turned to slag. Firehook let the officer live because he wanted someone to narrate the footage he figured (it was true) was being recorded from inside the police car.

I was near Bethel, Alaska, tracking credible reports of a Bigfoot sighting, assigned to determine if it was another appearance of a *super*.

Paladin was meeting with a group of military officers in North Korea, the only man they would agree to meet.

Warp, who would have been our best hope for reaching the scene in time, was in a coma, having previously ingested cocaine snorted off the stomachs of fifty Taiwanese hookers, accomplishing the feat in 2.4 seconds. As an indicator of his mental state during those years, I could add that it was well off his best time.

Mistress Mary was in Saudi Arabia, snuffing out a terrorist cell.

None of the others were anywhere near enough to Illinois to be of any good. It wasn't even close. Firehook's deadline was only five minutes. Five minutes to choose one student who, in a busload of forty-three, would be the only survivor. The students themselves chose who would live. Nobody, of course, knows how it was done.

Thirty seconds before the deadline, Lennie Grakes stepped out of the bus. She was a ninth grader. Red-haired. Lanky. Three days earlier she had won a contest to stand in front of several congressmen and talk about the environment. She was said to be an excellent speaker. After the Firehook incident, she refused all interviews, absolutely too distraught to even think of talking. She, in fact, never spoke another word, slitting her wrists two days after the incident. She was found naked, with flames drawn all over her body in red marker. She'd been crying and didn't leave a note. A note wasn't needed, of course.

Once she stepped from that bus, the metal began to twist and droop, victim of Firehook's will as he superheated the metal, only the metal, hardly any flames at all, just small ones flickering around a white-hot bus that collapsed inward on the students.

Firehook, getting back on his motorcycle, said, "There. A busload of kids. Just wanted to establish what kind of man I am."

There was pursuit, for an hour or so, but none of them survived.

⌖

All in all, when the rats were dead, and when Firehook said, "Fuck this," and leapt over the side of the seating area, jumping down into the arena with me, landing on a rat, getting goo on his shoes and turning the rat to ash in childish retaliation, I had no reason to go easy on him. The man who managed to put that asshole down would be a national hero. An international hero. A man who pulled out Firehook's eyes and spat down into his brain would be doing the right thing.

"Ladies and gentlemen and whores," he shouted to the crowd, holding his hands on high, addressing them, turning so that they could all see him, as if a man with burning hands and a flaming head wouldn't draw their attention. There were answering titters from the crowd. A pair of panties came fluttering down. A following round of applause at that. Octagon's voice came down to us, telling Firehook that his actions were unsanctioned. Firehook, with that, created a big flaming hand, with one big flaming middle finger. He picked up the fallen panties, inspected them for a second, then put them in his back pocket and raised his hands once more.

He said, "Ladies and gentlemen and... especially, the whores. You're about to see a man die. You're about to see Reaver meet the end of his years. Too late, I know, but better late than never."

He stopped to look at me. I was using the time to look over the arena. The sandy floor. The walls. The force field above me. I was wishing I could see some of the faces, those above me, better, because I wanted to remember everyone, and discuss the day with them later.

"Ladies. Whores," he said. "You know this shit excites you. So get ready for what happens afterwards. About half of you aren't going to walk right after tonight."

I'd seen what I needed of the sandy floor, the walls, the force field, and I'd definitely seen enough of Firehook, so I went into action.

About three times faster than he expected.

I'd backed myself up against one of the stone walls and I elbowed it suddenly, shaking the foundations of the entire arena. Cocktail glasses rained down from above, and a stone the size of my torso broke free of the wall. I nabbed that out of the air and heaved it at Firehook. He had the reflexes to get some flame on it, but couldn't melt it away before it took him in the stomach, lifted him into the air, and sent him flying back towards the opposite wall. If he hadn't hit the pile of rats, by chance, that would have been the end of him.

By then I'd repeatedly kicked at the floor, scuffing my foot along the ground four or five times, kicking up a sandstorm that obscured the entire arena. Then I went for him, and I should say that at the time I could have told you, from memory, the names of every kid who had died in the molten metal of the collapsing bus. I can't do that anymore. But I could then. You can guess my state of mind.

I grabbed him by the arm before he knew where I was, hefted him onto my shoulders in the manner of the rat I'd worn before. He was already burning me. It was already agony, but I put that aside and then I jumped up as hard and fast as I could.

There were two possibilities, the way I saw it. Either the force field was keyed to let things down through it, but not up through it, which would mean I was about to crush Firehook between an immovable object (meaning the force field) and an angry and nearly unstoppable force, meaning me. The second possibility was that the force field was keyed for Firehook himself… giving him a free pass, and in that case I wanted to go along for the ride.

As it turned out, the force field let Firehook pass, but then tried to grab onto me. Fortunately, I'd gained enough of a wedge, enough momentum before it could collapse around me, and I made it through. I stumbled a bit on the landing, but stayed upright. I was standing in the balcony seating. I was among them. I was one of the beautiful people.

All of the seats were plush. There was no lack of legroom. Each of the chairs had monitors keyed in on the arena… suitable for close-ups on the action. The chairs were divided into blocks of four, and each block was complete with a table, and each table was laden with wines (whites and reds) and champagnes and other liquors, and with a buffet of fancy dishes in far larger portions than any profitable restaurant could allow. The people in the chairs (aside from shocked/horrified/lurid expressions) were dripping with money, or else they were whores or boy-toys. Rich women always dress their toys in the finest suits. Rich men clothe their women to look like cheap whores.

Waitresses traipsed among the elite, dressed in ways that made it clear they were there to serve every need. There were no waiters. Just the women.

The waitresses were the first to run when I landed amongst the crowd with Firehook on my shoulders. I was glad of that. They were potentially innocent, and I was in a bad mood.

I tossed Firehook at Octagon and screamed something, not even a word, and began plucking men from the seats, upsetting their drinks, upsetting their women, listening to chastisements of "Here, now! No need for this!" and exclamations of "Fuck!" and a few people screamed as I tossed them down into the arena below, and a few screamed when I punched them (holding back on the strength, but taking a year, here and there, nonetheless) and of course a few of them screamed when I did both.

I didn't want to punch any of the women. I was too much of a gentleman for that. More on that in a bit.

"Reaver!" Octagon yelled, trying to scramble up from beneath Firehook, whose head was gathering flames, creating a mass around him, a whirling vortex that was a visual manifestation of his anger. It didn't seem to be affecting Octagon in the least. I wrote that down in a mental notebook. I wondered why he was yelling my name, and was thinking about asking him when I took a shot from Laser Beast (who I'd all but forgotten) that went right through my jaw, barely missing my brain. The closest weapon at hand was a chair, so I tossed that at Laser Beast, barely noticing that a man was in the chair. It wouldn't have mattered much anyway. I was none too pleased with anyone who'd bought tickets to the fights.

"Fuck!" Laser Beast cursed as the chair (and the rather fat man) collided with him, and the two of them (and the chair) went toppling over the side of the arena, falling below amidst the moans and broken bones. I turned back to Firehook in time to see the flames coming.

He had cut loose.

Gone close to atomic, I think.

A ball of flame the size of an Indian elephant washed over me. And it washed over, also, those behind me.

I could hear Octagon yelling, "Dammit! Dammit! God damn it!" I could hear the roar of the flames around me. I could hear the horrified cries of those who had been on the fringes of the flames. The ones who had been within the ball of flame were gone. Just… gone. Not even shadows, like at Hiroshima.

Of those who had been struck by the flames, I was the only one left. My costume was gone. I was hairless. My fingers were nubs. My eyelids had been burnt away. My nose was gone. My face was nearly a flat plane.

I was glowing green.

I toppled forward. Hit the graduated seating floor. Normally, I would probably have bounced down a couple of the steps, but I didn't. I stuck in place. Like goo.

Octagon's voice was garbled. He was saying things about…? About *assholes*? About *paying customers*? About *orders*? About *punishment*? The words were muted, I realized, because I didn't have ears. Only holes. Each time Octagon said something, Firehook would cut in, saying the same thing, over and over again.

"*Fuck off. I killed him.*"

"*That wasn't the purpose of this day.*"

"*Fuck off. I killed him.*"

"*You killed my friends. My customers.*"

"*Fuck off. I killed him.*"

"*I can't let this stand.*"

"*You can fuck off. I killed him.*"

And so on, and so on, and with each sentence the words were becoming more clear, more audible, and I suddenly took a breath through my nose (it was nice to have a nose again) and my fingers (welcome back) were grasping at the front of a chair, making sure I didn't fall down a step and attract too much attention, and there was a woman by my side (I couldn't look at her without giving myself away) who was saying that I was getting better, was reforming, was getting handsome (why did she put THAT in?) but nobody was paying attention to her… everybody was arguing, or screaming, or trying to help people, or had run away, or was dead. Only minutes before, I'd been the center of attraction, but now I was forgotten. Except for one woman who I wished would shut up and let me glow green for a while.

Octagon, unseen, said, "I am in charge."

Firehook, unseen, though I could feel his location from his radiating heat, said, "Maybe you being in charge, maybe that's bullshit."

Then I heard Firehook scream. Why? How? I wanted to look. It would have been dumb to look, dumb to stand up and see what was happening, foolish to give myself away before I was completely returned to normal.

I stood up.

I'm called *Reaver*. Not *Genius*.

"You kids arguing?" I asked. Octagon's head snapped up. His face, behind the void of his mask, registered shock and confusion. I couldn't see it, but I could feel it in just the same way that I'd sensed Firehook's heat.

Octagon was holding what seemed to be a ball bearing to Firehook's chest, maybe the same type of metal marble that he'd thrown at me during our rooftop chase. Firehook was unconscious, slumped over, fallen over backwards, supported only by Octagon's hand in the middle of his back. It looked like a Virgin Mary painting. Or a romance novel cover.

The man destined to be my arch-nemesis was staring at me.

"You… lived?" Octagon said.

"I did. I always will." I tried to sound menacing. It worked. My throat was still raw from almost being melted away. But… I was back. I was whole again. I was exhausted, though… not having ever before known that healing took so much out of me. Too much healing could kill me. That was the first time I ever understood how that was true, and I was only a few minutes away from a refresher course.

For then, though, for that moment, I was whole. Even my hair was pushing back out, returning to how it had been before Firehook's attack. I felt a hand going through my hair and turned to find a woman there… the one who'd been talking by my side, and she was beautiful, some French-African mix, with full lips and small breasts and hair the color of my own, which she proved by holding handfuls of our hair together, comparing them, merging them.

"God. You're so beautiful," she said. Her eyes traveled up and down the length of me, stopping here and there, always pleased. By then I was almost completely restored, with only a few spotted patches of the green glow remaining. Of course I was naked. My costume had been largely burnt away, and what hadn't been incinerated had fallen away. I didn't feel shy. I wasn't in the mood for being shy. The woman's voice had been nice. It had some music in it. Some primal melody from Africa, mixed with the sensuality of France. She even had some of her groin in her voice. I'm sure the meaning of that is clear.

I pushed her over the arena's edge and heard her scream for thirty feet of rapidly declining travel, then the scream was gone, abruptly cut off. Replaced by angry moans. Pained curses.

I turned back to Octagon and he let Firehook fall to the steps. Firehook's flames had been extinguished. He looked like any other normal douche that was about to have his head stomped on like a grape. I took a step forward.

I suppose you note that I'd made a moral decision. It's true. I had. There are people who I consider too dangerous to live, and I've always been a bit simplistic in my problem solving.

"This night has not gone as I had planned?" Octagon said, making a question out of it from sheer disbelief. This changed my focus from Firehook (whose head was then only six feet away from a terminal date with the bottom of my boot) to him. This change of focus, this loss of concentration on the most important facets around me, wasn't the smartest thing I've ever done, and I should've learned my lesson when I'd been distracted earlier. But… I'd been burned before, and was about to get burned again.

I told Octagon, "Your night is only going to get worse. But don't worry… you're about to get some time off." It was the first time I'd ever uttered what is now my catchphrase, and it was only a fetal version of it. Octagon did nothing to acknowledge the perfection of my quip.

He just said, "Stellar. Clean up this mess."

And then she had me from behind, her arms under mine, holding me, embracing me, flying upwards, crashing up through the arena, up through the subterranean passageways, up through the building, through a series of ceilings, again and again, then up above the city, high above the city, high above the clouds, high above the Earth, and finally into the fringes of space.

Stellar's first appearance took place on a rainy Saturday in March. She is a tall woman. Nordic in appearance. Short blonde hair. She has large enough breasts that they have their own fan club. I don't mean that she has a fan club centered around her breasts; I mean that her breasts have an online fan club. The fact that this is true, this churning devotion combined with the type of criminal that Stellar is, says a lot about men. Mistress Mary once said as much to me in a superior way, as if it makes women better than men. I pointed out the multitude of websites devoted to Laser Beast. The wealth of Octagon-related erotic fan fiction. Macabre's dalliances with movie star actresses. The amount of fan mail that serial killers receive in prison. Mary shut up.

Stellar's costume involves a cape and some of what most people would consider lingerie worn over a skintight black body suit. She has stars on a field of black. Her arms often glow with energy and I'm not sure I've even seen her on the ground. From certain angles it might seem like she was standing, but if you look close, there's always an inch or two of separation.

She came to us, as far as anyone knows, from the stars. Most scientists believe she's from Earth, though. It's just too much of a coincidence that she looks so human. Linguists have done endless studies on her vocal patterns, trying to find a dialect, but the electrical hum of her voice (it's not robotic, just... charged with energy) and the fact that whenever she speaks, anywhere, at any time, everyone hears her voice in their own native tongue, makes assigning an origin impossible.

She leaves no fingerprints, skin flakes, or secretions of any kind. There are theories that she is a tangible ghost. Those are up in the air. There are theories that she has no physical form. Those are false. I can well attest to her physical form.

Stellar has never spoken of any incident, any memory, previous to her appearance on that rainy day in March when she landed in the streets of Creely, a small town in Australia, and demanded to be taken to Earth's leader.

An incident had ensued, building up from her being laughed at ("*Take me to your leader*" will get you that) and she soon lost her temper and tossed a car through a building. The laughter had stopped. By then I was already en route, notified by SRD, held in Warp's arms as he raced across the Pacific, taking us to the scene.

In the footage of Stellar's first appearance, a man begins to shoot at her and, after some seconds (she didn't seem to notice at first) she turns to him and tells him, "Jacob, do not shoot at me." He must have wondered how she knew his name. This was, of course, before it was clear that she knows everyone's name. Everyone.

There was little more to the Creely incident. She fired a beam of energy from her eyes, obliterating a house (it had been abandoned anyway, as Creely was on the decline) and then asked each and everyone who had assembled (there were less than fifty) to let "the leader" know that she needed to talk. She called all of the witnesses by name.

By the time Warp and I arrived there was nothing of Stellar left except a contrail, of sorts, from when she had gone back into the air, soared up past Earth's atmosphere, peered in through a porthole of the space station for some moments (sending one astronaut into permanent counseling) and soon after landed on the moon. She stayed on the moon for several weeks, standing almost motionless, brought to focus in some of SRD's most dramatic photography.

She came back once during this time, hovering in downtown London and saying that she understood, now, that Earth has no leader, nor any laws that concerned her.

Hundreds of her fan sites were already up by that point.

⌖

And now Stellar had me in space.

I'd like to talk about the majesty of the view, about how all of humanity's various incarnations seem meaningless when viewed from space, about how the boundless wealth of the open universe reduces a man to his humblest elements. I'd only like to talk about that. I can't, though. Instead, I was fighting for breath, and knowing I was screwed, because I only had one ride home, and that was Stellar, and she was trying to kill me.

"You are Steve Clarke," she told me.

"Yes," I tried to say, but failed. Her voice worked in space. Mine didn't. She plays by entirely different rules.

"Octagon has been my friend," she said.

I was cold beyond imagining (weather rarely affects me) and scared out of my wits and trying to remember that it's not proper to hit a woman. But if I had done so, at the moment when Stellar first grabbed me, if I had simply turned and struck her (three times faster than she might have expected) I might not have taken the ride up through the building, up through the clouds, and up past Earth's universal fence line. The time for being a gentleman had passed, and the time had passed badly.

I punched her. I put everything I had into it, and the blow rocked her. It nearly put her away. She gave me a look that clearly expressed how she couldn't believe she had been hurt, how someone had possessed the muscle to knock her around. Her look was the second clearest expression of disbelief in the universe. Mine was first. Mine was first because the power of my blow had separated Stellar and I, and that separation had sent me aimlessly spinning back towards Earth, which was itself spinning below me. We were both spinning. The only one flying straight was Stellar, who zoomed along with me at my side, looking me in the face (she was just out of reach, and there was nothing I could do about it) and then turning and flying away.

She said, "Have fun, Reaver." Then she was gone.

I began to enter an argumentative atmosphere.

It didn't want me around.

It was burning me. Licking me with flames. Then whipping me with flames. My speed was faster and faster. I tried to surf against the resistance, slow myself down, and I was screaming and then I blacked out and lost some time (and about forty thousand feet of altitude during my blackout) and then I could see a forest below (it turned out to be in Virginia, a long ways from my French point of departure) and it came closer and closer and closer and then I crashed through a few branches, broke a few tree trunks, shattered most of my limbs, traumatized a good number of squirrels and embedded myself almost four feet into the soil of the Shenandoah National Park.

There was blood dripping down onto me from the branches I'd crashed through.

There was blood spreading out from me. Seeping into the loam.

There was a good deal of forest silence. A hush.

There were air force jets overhead.

There was a dark and broken forest, suffused by a localized green glow.

In three hours time, there was Paladin, at my side.

The first time I'd seen him in months.

CHAPTER EIGHT

I spent the night in Adele's house, not really having anywhere else to go. My parents' house had long since been turned into a museum of sorts, a tribute residence to so many of my exploits. It was largely unchanged since the days when I'd lived there, except for one section that had been rebuilt (destroyed by the *Nothing Really Anti-Matters* terrorist organization before Checkmate had arranged the security measures) and a plethora of plaques (citing my achievements) and threadbare carpeting that had endured the footsteps of over a thousand visitors a week.

I'd planned to stay in a hotel and watch some cheap horror movie or some such, but Adele talked me out of it by saying I could do that at her house, making me promise to stay down on the couch, and letting me know that Laura would probably still be walking around topless and, hell… that was something to see, wasn't it? She gave me a look of whimsy, knowing that she'd trapped me because if I left after that it would have been an admission that Laura's breasts weren't beautiful, and that would have hurt her and besides I don't like lying.

We watched monster movies. Creatures of the deep that had arisen, angered over man's interference in the silent depths. Abominations thawed from eons-old glaciers. Technologically advanced monsters from outer space that demanded minerals, obedience, mates. Adele and I were on the couch. There was a large throw pillow between us. Laura, sitting cross-legged on the floor in front of us, constantly adjusting her glasses, would occasionally pull the pillow from between us, and then either Adele or I would wrest it from her and return it in place, staring at the television screen the whole time. It was a wonderful night for thinking of monsters.

Laura (forced into wearing pajama tops) told Adele and I (as a wolf-creature was discarding a scream-laden carriage over the side of a mountain pass) that fear and lust were identical twins, and that if you wanted to make a good impression on a date, never go to a romantic movie. Always create an atmosphere of tension.

"Tingles and shivers," she said. "Gets 'em every time."

"Some people don't need to *get 'em* every time," Adele answered, reaching over her sister's shoulders to button Laura's pajamas, a job that well needed tending.

"Some people are monsters, then," Laura said. "That kind of celibacy terrifies me." Turning to me, she said, "Don't take this the wrong way, Steve, but I want to ask a question of Reaver."

I said, "Okay. We're more or less the same person, you know."

"Of course. But, I'm the same person too. Doesn't mean I can't be a different person at the same time."

Adele gaped in mock (well-practiced) astonishment at her sister and said, "We shouldn't have had vodka and ice cream and popcorn. This was not a good idea." She was holding out a vodka bottle (forbidden to drink any herself, and merely chaperoning it away from her sister and myself) that had a piece of popcorn perched at the top, threatening to tumble within.

Ignoring her sister, Laura asked me, "This *fear* thing, Reaver… what scares *you*?"

I didn't say anything.

"Too personal?" Laura asked. "You can always tell me to shut up."

Adele said, "Laura, shut up."

"See?" her sister said. "Adele tells me to shut up all the time. Doesn't hurt my feelings."

"Kid Crater," I said. "That's what scares me."

Both girls went silent. I knew that I'd been supposed to say things about idiosyncratic fears (such as ostriches, or clouds that look like clowns, or aggressively topless lesbian sisters) or the usual suspects (death, and those letters from the IRS) but I had leapt into the realm of the real, which isn't something that most people see coming. The thing is, after Paladin had pulled me up from the Virginia forest, after he had held my broken form as he soared away into the clouds (giving me, then, shivering flashbacks, because my last trip through the clouds had been a round-trip excursion into space) and outraced fighter jets (piloted by sullen men whose favorite toy now looked to be outdated), he had sat with me for three weeks in a Minnesota cabin on one of that state's famous ten thousand lakes, talking about our lives in the past (as Greg Barrows and Steve Clarke) and our current lives (as Paladin and Reaver) and we'd gone fishing and we'd gone bloodless hunting (merely touching a checklist of animals and birds on their rumps or tail feathers) and we'd discussed how to be heroes, how to best go about the task, and in the second week we'd met Kid Crater. I was the first to meet him. Paladin was holding a press conference at the time (he'd flown to Washington in order to allay any fears that he'd retired) and Kid Crater had discovered the Minnesota cabin and had walked in unannounced, finding me in the middle of the kitchen without any pants, checking on my healing process, me holding my balls to one side, inspecting them to see if there were any remaining hints of green. It had been embarrassing as all hell for both of us, but after he'd joined the team (it was never really a team) and after he became my unofficial sidekick (neither of us were fond of that word, but there it was) we would joke about me and my self-inspection, with him singing a version of that old Jerry Lee Lewis song, except changing it to "Goodness Gracious! Green Balls of Fire!"

"Green Balls of Fire?" Adele laughed. She was balancing popcorn on her nose.

"Because I glow green when I…"

"I got it. I got it," she said.

"Were they… okay?" Laura asked. "Machine still works?"

"We're getting sidetracked," I said. "I meant to talk about the days before Kid Crater showed up. With me and Paladin and the monster movies. We watched a ton of them. Celluloid gems."

It was true. A thousand classics. A thousand monsters. And, I don't know how the game began, but Paladin and I began discussing the movies…

about how we would personally deal with each of the monsters, with each giant clawed hand that was wrapped around a fully-stocked family sedan, each vampire that had mesmerized a semi-compliant fraulein, each alien robot and its cosmically destructive capabilities. Paladin's first stage was always trying to understand where things had gone off track, if there had been some miscommunication, some wrong that could be righted, some bit of folly that could be readdressed. I went right the hell past that stage. Things like that were something that could be considered once the beast had bled out.

"These movies… they reminded you?" Adele asked. She was gesturing to the television. It was wall-mounted, sequestered among a group of paintings (Laura was quite possibly going to be a success as an artist, which clearly confused her) of monster movies with the principal characters reversed, so that a villager was terrifying groups of vampires, and a giant Tokyo businessman was breathing fire on a city populated by lizards. On the television screen right then was a slime creature advancing on an inattentive guard, sliding out from an air duct, which are always sources of terror and assault in the movies.

"They did remind me," I told Adele. "Paladin always thought the monsters were just… misplaced. Considering the way Earth has treated us," here I gestured to myself, and tried to go speedily on, realizing I'd somehow separated myself from Earth as a whole, "he felt that if people just accepted the monsters, they could fit into society."

"What societal role would King Kong play?" Adele asked, protecting the vodka bottle from her sister.

"Center for the Knicks," Laura said. "Or… some sort of athlete, anyway. Maybe a soccer goalie? Hard to score on King Kong." She stopped, a wicked smile teleported into place and her eyes lit up, but before Laura could say anything, Adele, the love of my life, cut in with, "Laura… please don't tell any jokes about scoring on King Kong. Steve is trying to be serious."

"I'm not trying to be serious. I just am."

"We could help with that," Laura said. "I'm an artist and Adele is stupid, so neither one of us is serious. We could teach you of our ways."

I said, "Did either of you know that Greg Barrows was Paladin?"

I suppose I should have had a segue. Some sort of transition. But the question popped into my head and I wanted to know.

The room went silent except for the purring of Wiggles, the cat, on the couch next to Adele, and the screaming of the television guard as the slime cascaded down from the air duct and burnt him to the bone.

⌖

The car was on fire. At some point, it had exploded, and had done so with a noise like the entire Earth had been shoved into my ear. Officer Horwitz had been torn almost in half and my hand was in his stomach. I could feel the warmth of it as I planted my hand, trying to gain my feet. When I understood where my hand was, understood what had happened, his stomach and intestines felt ten times warmer than the flames.

I had been thrown from the car by the collision with the tanker truck, was resting partially in the ditch, somewhat on the road. Greg was staggering around, going nowhere, covered in blood, missing an arm. Tom, of course, was already gone.

The tanker had split open, spilled its contents. About two thousand gallons. The ditch had flooded with an incredible array of foul-smelling liquids, many of them trying to mix, and most of them not willing to do it. They skimmed over each other, sank within each other, separated like boys and girls at the start of a dance. My legs were within the chemicals. And they *were* chemicals. Not just liquids. They'd been separated in the tanker truck, compartmentalized, but a fault line had run its course through the tanker, and the mingling had begun. There was embryonic fluid (from sperm whales, I've been told) and an array of stem cell solutions (chiefly human, but other species as well, including one batch from a resurrected Tasmanian tiger, and a full array of sea life) and the whole mess was radioactive, a tanker full of chemical hell that had been bound for Nevada disposal, having been born/concocted/bombarded in the solution tanks of SRD. They'd been trying to induce mice to regrow their tails/teeth/eyes/sperm count/youth/and maybe a hundred other things.

Back at the SRD base was the first of the Supers. They weren't human. They were rats and mice and, poetically, butterflies. A lot of people don't know that a butterfly's wings are entirely made of protein. When they become damaged, the butterfly looks at its wing and it screams, "FUCK!" It might say it in some lyrical butterfly language... but that's what it means.

Because a butterfly can't regrow its wings. It can't even heal its wings in any manner whatsoever. Butterflies look fragile because they are fragile. But a mile away, hidden beneath the supposedly long-shuttered Wennes airport, was a small SRD laboratory environment (flowers, a petite pond, heightened oxygen, a shitload of sensors) full of super-butterflies, which sounds far more appetizing than the super-rats or the super-mice and of course the super-cockroaches, including one the size of a bus that I hope never gets loose, because I just know I'll be the one that has to fight the disgusting thing.

The tanker had rolled over. The driver (his name was Zach Chu, an aspiring retiree) had been partially thrown from the cab, which had rolled over him once or twice. Once had been enough.

Tom's scream was still in the air. It wasn't echoing. It was… heavy. Lingering. Like an audible fog that had gathered around the crash site.

The shotgun from Horwitz's squad car was on the road ten feet from me. I began crawling for it, heaving myself out of the muck of the ditch, believing that if I could reach the shotgun I could make everything better. I'm aware that this makes no sense. I was not aware of it at the time.

Greg fell into the flooded ditch beside me. Just… toppled and fell in. I watched him go under. Watched the heavy liquid seal the breach. I was aware that he would drown. I was panicked and knew that I needed to do something about it. The shotgun. The shotgun would solve it all.

There were fires. There were sirens. There was a scent that it is not within me to describe. There was the sound of rotors. Of screeching tires. Of machines spraying foam all about the crash site… with a *shoop shoop shoop* chant. There were an array of men in yellow suits, fully encased, like bright yellow ill-fitting anthropomorphic condoms, moving among us, scooping remains into bags, taking the shotgun (NO!) away from me and holding me down, shining lights into my eyes, a breathing tube down my throat, hoses washing away my blood in a trough made of what, at the time, seemed to be sturdy garbage bags.

"This one's alive!" an electronic voice, emerging from within a yellow condom, said to everyone in the area. Other living condoms gathered around me, touching, prodding, looking into my eyes, slapping my cheeks, screaming, "Stay with us! Stay here, cowboy!"

I thought of Greg Barrows. We'd never pretended to be cowboys. It was always pirates. Gods. Gladiators. I began to feel sleepy. More slaps on my cheeks. More demands and admonitions to "*Stay here, cowboy! C'mon, you bastard! Stay here*!"

The lights were in my eyes. The slaps were on my cheeks. The tube was going farther and farther down my throat.

And Paladin came out from the ditch.

⌖

"Paladin was Greg Barrows?" Adele asked. "I thought he died in the accident. There was… there was a body, right?" On the television, a scaled creature was rising from the ocean's depths. Two girls on the beach, wearing bikinis, rubbing lotion on their arms, looked up and screamed. Then they were washed away in a burst of atomic fire from the creature's eyes. Greg and I had watched the same movie. He'd joked that the girls should have used a higher SPF level of sun tan lotion. Then he'd felt bad about saying such a thing.

"The body was a plant," I said. "They wanted to keep Greg's identity secret. He did, too. The corpse was a boy from Michigan. That's all I know about him. They had him on ice. An experimental cadaver."

Adele said, "An experimental cadaver." She made it sound like a horrible thing. I suppose it is. Worthy of its own monster movie.

"A boy from Michigan," Laura said. She frowned. I knew what she meant. Not much of a memorial.

I said, "Greg came out of the ditch with all his powers already in place. He was screaming, and alive. His arm was back. I thought I was hallucinating. He already had the shimmer." Most people know of the shimmer around Paladin. It wasn't a force field, like a lot of people think; it was just some sort of… non-stick surface. Nothing could touch him. I mean, almost anything could touch him, but it would then just slide away.

"What did… how…?" Adele asked. She shook her head. I understood her confusion. Hell... I'd *been* that confusion.

"They had coil guns," I said. "They brought coil guns to the accident scene. Checkmate wasn't with SRD at the time, but they'd hired him to design the guns. They needed him because… there was a cockroach problem." The sisters didn't know about the giant cockroach in the SRD sub-levels.

I waited for them to ask what I meant, but they didn't. I suppose finding out that one of your childhood friends hadn't died in an accident, the way you'd been told, that he'd become Paladin, that he'd died the way Paladin died, meant that talking about cockroaches was something that could wait.

I said, "Everything from the ditch just… shimmered away from him, and Greg was hovering in the air, naked. I really did think I was hallucinating. I think everybody thought they were hallucinating. But… hallucinating or not, a soldier is trained to fire on what they don't understand, to react first and decide later, and that's what they did."

"There were soldiers?" Adele asked. I nodded. At the time I'd thought that all of the men in their hazard suits were emergency personnel, medics, scientists, that sort of thing. But when Paladin (he was still only Greg, I suppose, though the point could be argued) rose up out of the ditch I found out that some of the others were soldiers. Some of them had the coil guns… weapons that emit solid strands of electricity (the science of this has been explained to me, and it hurt my head, and I honestly chose to forget the specifics in regards to my sanity) that come out from the gun in a coiled helix pattern, wrapping around their targets, holding them like the world's strongest rope that just happens to be emitting enough electricity to stun a belligerent mastodon.

One soldier had fired on Greg, wrapping him within the coils, then pulling him away from the ditch. I don't think Greg had noticed it yet. Then another soldier fired. And another, and another, and they were yelling in fear that he wasn't going down and I was ripping the breathing tube from my mouth. I staggered to my feet and began tossing the men around, tearing open their suits and darting among them, trying to reach Greg and feeling… charged… and a soldier fired on me with a coil gun and it hurt. It hurt so bad.

Then Paladin landed next to me. I've been confused here… not really sure what to call the man who came out of the ditch… not sure if he was *Greg Barrows* or *Paladin*. This I do know, though… the man who landed next to me, by that time he was Paladin.

He was wrapped in so many of the coil gun emissions that he looked like the offspring of a mummy and a star. His hand came out and he touched me and all my pain went away. It was the most peaceful thing I'd ever felt. It was a non-sexual orgasm. A full focus of my being.

I said, "Greg? Did we crash?"

And then I passed out.

⌖

"Greg Barrows. Paladin," Adele said. She was putting popcorn into her mouth but forgetting to chew. Just… putting pieces into her mouth. Like a chipmunk storing food in its cheeks.

"Somebody needs to tell his parents," Laura said. "They have a right to know."

"That's why I'm here," I answered. "There's nobody that should tell them except me."

"That's why you came back?" Adele asked. She was chewing. The words were garbled. Her eyes were clear.

"One of the main reasons," I said. "It's… complicated. There are a lot of things I need to do, and I need to do them pretty soon."

"You went to the hospital," Adele said. "Back then. You went to the hospital." She didn't seem to be talking to me. Just about me. She was still chewing. I'm not sure there was any popcorn in her mouth anymore.

"What else are you going to do?" Laura said, and then before I could answer she stood. She glared at me. She looked down at herself and made sure that her pajama tops were buttoned. That's how I knew she was serious. Women have a certain look they give when a man is either in trouble, or is about to be told to change course. Laura Layton had the look. She had my hand in hers. She led me away from Adele, who was watching us, wondering what Laura was doing, who was standing up from the couch to come along with us, was sitting back down when her sister held up her hand and told her to stay.

Laura took me to the stairs. We went up them, making the same sorts of footsteps as when I'd been in the kitchen, when she'd been walking down the stairs, when I'd been afraid she was a man who was coming down from Adele's bed. It hurt to even think about such things. I retreated away from the thoughts and delved into the confusion of what Laura was doing. I wondered if she was seducing me… if she was taking me up to her room. There were framed paintings on the stairwell. Small originals. Small oil paintings of various monsters wearing glasses. More of Laura's work. She was a lesbian. She was Adele's sister. She couldn't possibly be taking me up the stairs to seduce me. Her face was angry, but that meant nothing. Anger is one of sex's best friends.

When we reached the top of the stairs she turned to me and asked, "What else are you going to do? Why else did you come to Greenway? You're going to talk to Greg's parents, right? You're going to tell them about Paladin? Who else are you going to talk to? What else are you going to tell someone?" It all came out of her in a whisper that seemed loud, because she was closer and closer to my face. She wasn't whispering into my ear. It was straight into my face.

I said, "I…"

That's all I could say before Laura said, "Don't be a shit, Reaver. My sister loves you."

I almost fell down the stairs.

⌖

After the accident with the tanker truck, I woke up in the Bolton hospital with an armed guard in riot gear next to my bed. There was a petite brunette wearing a red body suit bending over me, looking me in the eyes. She didn't look like a nurse, a doctor, an orderly, or a guard of any type. She looked like the front page of a fetish website.

She said, "My name is Mary. You are awake." She didn't make it sound like a question. She made it sound like an order.

"Greg?" I asked.

"Elsewhere. He is fine. The truth of this is a secret. You will not tell anyone else. You will tell me how you feel."

"Groggy. But… good. We crashed?"

"You did," she said. "There was a tanker truck. I'm afraid the driver passed away. As did the policeman. You were bathed in certain chemicals. I can provide you with a list, if you wish."

"Why would I want that?" She nodded at me as if I had said something very smart (making me shine with pride, because I wanted very much to please her) and then she tensed when I moved the blankets away from my legs and sat up on the bed. The guard was armed with something that looked like it had been designed for a 1950's science fiction movie. He trained it on me.

"Are you attacking?" Mary asked.

"Attacking?" I said.

"He is not attacking," she told the guard. "You will resume your post outside the room." He left immediately, nodding, backing away, like a child being excused from adult proceedings, or perhaps the other way around.

"Your muscles may be stiff," Mary told me as I stood.

"No," I said. I wasn't stiff at all. It felt like... it felt better than it ever had. My muscles didn't feel like muscles; they felt like *potential.*

"Odd," she said. "You will tell me again how you feel." She reached out and touched my arm. She felt warm. More than that... she felt like... she felt alive. My senses were shining on overload. Everything was information. Everything was accessible. I felt like I was being given secrets.

"I feel like seeing you naked," I said, not believing that it came from my mouth. It hadn't at all *blurted* out. It had been *pulled.* This was the first time that I'd ever met Mistress Mary (and I didn't, at the time, know that I was meeting her) and I had no idea how her powers worked.

Instead of looking shocked, or amused, or anything else at all, she completely ignored the content of my words and said, "No. Physically. You will tell me how you feel. You will tell me what you remember from the crash. You will do this."

I did.

⌖

Mary asked if I'd been sleeping the whole time. If I'd had any dreams. This is the question where it all began to go wrong.

I said, "Nothing. And what do you mean about *the whole time*? How long have I been out? Just... a day, right? A few hours?" I could already see in her eyes that I'd been out for longer than a few hours, or even a day.

"The accident was one month ago," she said. "I can understand if you..." I wasn't listening to her anymore. I was grabbing the television remote from the visitor's chair (noticing some flowers on the table, curious about the card) and flicking on the television, turning to a news channel, not paying any attention to the story the newscasters were discussing (for the record, they were debating if Warp had done the right thing in the Livington Serial Killer case) and only keying in on the date stamp that was running along below.

A month had gone by.

I was a month in the future.

Like magic.

"Calm down," Mary said.

"A month?" I said. "Where's Tom? Where's my brother?" I was shouting.

"You will calm down," Mary said.

"What happened to me?" I asked. "What's going on? Who are you people? Where's my goddamn brother? Why do I have a guard? Why is there an *armed guard*?" I was not calming down. I could see a crease of worry on Mary's face.

"You will calm down," she said. Much louder, this time. It was the first time she'd raised her voice. The armed guard came running back into the room and trained his weapon on me. It irritated me. I went to move the gun aside, but I moved faster than I'd expected. Three times faster. Stumbling with my unexpected speed, I ran into his gun, knocking him aside. He thudded heavily into the wall and I scrambled back to my feet, having myself fallen over a tray cart. Syringes were all over the floor. Mary was reaching for one. I kicked them quickly aside. Too quickly. I fell again. I was aware that things, the other things, were not happening slowly. It was me. I was faster. Something about me had changed. I remembered Warp, and the way the world had become after he appeared, and I remembered Greg coming up from the ditch and I realized I hadn't been hallucinating. After the accident, something had happened to Greg. Something had changed him. And me too. Something had changed me.

The guard on the floor was dazed, but talking into a headpiece, chanting, "Scramble! Scramble! Subject out of control! Scramble! Scramble! Scramble!"

Mary told me, "You will stay!" and it wasn't until then that I realized I was moving towards the door… that I'd decided to leave. I wrenched the door completely away from its hinges, not yet adjusted to my strength. Mary jumped on me from behind, wrapping her arms around my neck and her legs around my waist. She slammed a syringe into my shoulder. It didn't penetrate. Just snapped off. She cursed and began yelling for me to stay but I shrugged her away (I did this very carefully… even then…

as I was beginning to understand that I now lived in a world of extremely fragile creatures) and then I was in the hallway, where several police officers and several soldiers (Fuck! Soldiers?) were running down the hall from both directions. The original guard was at my feet, trying to tackle me, to pin my legs together so that I couldn't run. I swung my leg in a quick arc and he skidded away down the hall, bowling over the oncoming guards.

"Who the fuck are you guys?" I screamed, but even then I was wondering the opposite, was wondering who the fuck I was, because every motion was amplified, everyone else was moving with body language that suggested great speed, fluid movements, but they were so slow... so unbelievably slow... and I ran past them, meaning to leap over the last two men as they sprawled to the hospital corridor floor, but my leap took me higher than I'd expected, so that I gouged along the ceiling and fell tumbling near an elevator. I stabbed at the elevator button with one hand, still on my knees, watching Mary come out of the room I'd been in. She was yelling orders and she was being obeyed. She was telling the others that they were on their own... that they would need to deal with me, that I wasn't responding to her. She sounded frantic about this. And confused. And pleased.

What the fuck was I doing trying to take the *elevator*?

That thought suddenly occurred to me. The men were slow, but the elevator wasn't a goddamn vertical bullet train or anything, and weapons were raising up to point at me and Mary was yelling for people not to fire and I was turning to head for the stairway (Where the hell was it? Why aren't these things MARKED better?) when the first shots went off (the triggers had been pulled before Mary spoke) and a spray of bullets notched divots into the concrete walls and tore holes in my hospital gown.

I barely felt them.

"What the hell *am* I?" I screamed down the hallway at them. "What the fuck happened to me?"

Patients were being moved from the floor, hurriedly evacuated. Doctors and nurses were running about in the slow motion that people have been stuck in, for me, since that day.

I could see past them.

All the way down to the end of the hall.

It was about a hundred feet distant.

A long hall with a window at the end.

Mary began to say something, maybe to talk about what had happened to me, maybe to order me to calm down again, or maybe anything. She told me later that she was confused. She hadn't been confused for a long time. She said it made her feel human. Challenged. She said it made her feel horny as hell. It was years after the hospital incident that she said all of this, and we were walking past the Eiffel Tower and she took my hand and put it on her hip... and then moved it, some, until it was not proper, at all, for me to be touching her there. We hadn't stopped. Soon I was stripping her somewhat naked, and doing things about it. She'd called my name a few times (meaning Reaver, not Steve Clarke) but mostly she had been screaming, "*Do not look! Nobody look! Nobody but Reaver can look! Nobody will look*," and so of course nobody did.

But that was years after.

Right then, in the hallway, I was only sixteen years old and I was scared and I knew that everything was different. And then I watched the window at the end of the hallway explode inward, and there was Greg Barrows flying down the hall, moving at speeds greater than mankind's, moving at speeds equal to my own, and he was in a costume.

You all know Paladin's costume.

The cape. The boots and gloves. The orange colors that would have looked silly on any man but Paladin. The emblem of the sword on his chest. The radiant sun behind it. I once told him that he looked like a gay templar. He had laughed and then flipped me, as far as I knew, the first legitimately super finger in the history of the world.

In the hospital hallway, though, all I knew was that he was in costume, and that he seemed, then, to be fighting for the wrong team.

He flew into me at full speed and we smashed back through the elevator door, tumbled some twenty feet down the shaft and onto the top of the oncoming elevator, and then he put his hand on my chest and pinned me against the wall, both of us rising slowly along with the elevator. He was staring me in the face with those famous eyes. That famous nose, twisted only slightly to one side. Paladin's face. We all know it.

He said, "Steve. It's me. It's Greg. You finally woke up."

And then he hugged me.

The elevator climbed steadily upward, rising to the floor where we'd been, called by my finger on the button at a time that was only seconds in the past. When we arrived, we did so with a horrible screeching, as the elevator cried out in protest against the twisted metal of the ruined door.

It reminded me of our car accident.

⌖

"Booty call," Laura said into her cell phone.

She listened for a bit, winking at Adele, nodding to me, and then said, "Lube it," and then hung up her phone.

"I'm gone," she said, stowing the phone in her purse. "You kids can be alone now."

"Not you, apparently," Adele answered.

"At all," Laura said. "Booty call is... she's nice. Works at the grocery. A stock girl. Apple."

I said, "She stocks apples? Isn't that kind of a... way over-specialized job?"

"Her *name* is Apple. Or... actually it's Ming, but we call her Apple. We've been seeing each other. Off and on, at least. She travels a lot, but tonight she's home and I'm going to travel into her bed."

"Do you know you're a slut?" Adele asked in the pleasant voice of siblings insulting each other. It made me miss Tom. A lot.

"At least I get laid," Laura said. And then she was out the door. She had never bothered to change from her pajamas, but I guess there was little point in taking the time.

That left me alone with Adele, all except for Wiggles, but the cat most likely didn't count, especially since Genus was in Africa, fighting against poachers, meaning the only (known) person in the world who could talk to animals was thousands of miles away.

Adele asked, "How long are you going to be in Greenway? You're welcome to stay here as long as you want. Okay... that came out too forward. But... you know what, that's okay. I'm forward."

"You made me promise to sleep on the couch."

"Fuck that. You're a superhero. You're Reaver. You can break through walls. You can't break through a promise?"

"No."

"Then I could stay on the couch, too. I have a big couch. Did you notice how big the couch is?"

I said, "Did you send Laura away?"

"We're sisters. We have mind reading. Not..." she waved her hand, flustered. "Not super-mind-reading. Damn... this is so hard. You're not even..."

Out of nowhere, she started to cry. Well, I suppose it was out of somewhere. I just didn't know where, or at least didn't understand all the complexities involved. I tried to think of something to say... something to do... some solution I could present. I would rather have been punching walls. I would rather have been fighting Octagon. Maybe even Stellar, or Firehook. Hell... even though he was my nemesis, Octagon was the nicest one of the bunch. The others...? Well, I suppose it goes without saying that super-villains are evil, but... damn.

Anyway, I would have rather have been fighting any of them, instead of fighting a complete inability to do anything about a woman crying. About Adele crying.

"Stay on the fucking couch, then," she said. And she went up the stairs. I listened to her movements, the creaking boards on the stairs, and then on the floor above. There was the sound of something being slammed against the floor. Apparently, it wasn't slammed hard enough the first time, because it sounded again, shortly after. I heard a shower running. I heard Adele come part way down the stairs. A minute passed. She went back up the stairs. I heard her making a phone call... talking with someone... laughing twice. It was good to hear her laugh. It was a relief. I stretched out on the couch after picking through a bookcase with books on nursery rhymes and several treatises on how the Greek gods were similar to Paladin, and to me, and to all of the others of my kind. I've seen several books of the type and had refused (of course) several interviews on the topic. Paladin always gets to be Zeus. I'm often Charon. He's always shining. I'm always a cautionary tale. One of the books listed Adele as a co-author. I thought about picking it up. Did. Her picture was on the back. Her hair was different. It felt like an intrusion to see her that way, at a time when I was avoiding her and her life, so I put the book back on the shelf, noticing, as I did, other books with her name on the spine and pictures of super humans on the cover. There was "*Reaver: One Year at a Time*" and there was "*Molten: Paladin and Reaver's Last Great Day*" and there was "*Warp Speed: The Trial of the World's Fastest Man*" and a few others as well. I touched a couple of their spines, fooling my fingers into thinking I was going to pick one of them up, but eventually grabbed a book about Germany's lack of morals during the Weimar period, profusely illustrated with pictures of women (and men) who were draped in smiles and little else. Having a lack of morals looked like fun. I wondered if it was Adele's book. It was probably Laura's.

I heard music, upstairs. Jazz. Not the new stuff. Classic. I heard Adele talking on the phone again and walked very quietly to the stairs (I am very good at this… as it's a skill a man develops when he has to sneak up on someone like Stellar) and heard her say only one line (*Well… can't you buckle a strap-on and talk at the same time?*) before I became embarrassed over how poorly I was acting as a guest. I went back to the couch. Stretched out. I heard a few cars go by. Something that sounded like a firework. I heard the hum of the refrigerator. Two drunks (one male, one ambiguity) walked past on the sidewalk, loudly singing about a horse with no name. I heard a clock. Then another. I heard Wiggles, mewling in complaint, just outside the door. I opened the door and let her back in, wondering how she'd gotten out, and only then noticing the cat door. She could have come in at any time.

"What's your problem?" I asked. "You had an open door." The cat purred at me, rubbing its head against my shoulder.

"I get it," I told the cat. "You just wanted me to let you in. Makes you feel wanted."

It was only afterwards, laying on the couch, after the fight, that I realized I was smarter about cats than I was about women.

CHAPTER NINE

At almost three in the morning, something came in through the cat door. I was awake (I sleep very little... my body naturally heals even exhaustion/drowsiness) and looking at the cat at the time, because it was on my chest, staring at me, as if confused by my continued attention.

When I heard the cat door flap open, Wiggles looked quickly in that direction, hissed in anger, then sped off into the kitchen. A moment later he came rushing back, hissing in fear, and raced beneath the couch.

A small demon walked into the room. A demon. Two feet tall. Muscled. Flickering with small flames. Cat-like, but on its hind legs, wearing clothes, standing straight, walking easily and confidently. Seeing me, it doffed a bowler hat, taking its head with it. Blood welled out and pooled on the floor.

"Two weeks?" the demon said. "How can I possibly wait?" The words were strained, as if the demon's throat was not built for human speech. The organs were being twisted, destroyed. The demon's head was back on its body, but situated poorly, so that it faced the wrong direction. The eyes were dead. Blood was coming from its nose.

I said, "Macabre."

"Just so," the demon said. "And… impatient. Octagon gave you two weeks, but I am not Octagon. Do you want to come outside, or should I visit the woman upstairs and…?" By then I was moving as quickly as I could without making any noises that would alarm Adele. I was going through the kitchen. The porch. I was opening the outside door, wondering if I would ever make it back again… if I would ever have a chance for Adele to open the door for me, to smile and welcome me into her house. The chances of it weren't good.

Macabre.

Damn it.

Macabre.

There was a trail of bread loaves leading off down the street. Not crumbs, but loaves. They were animated, dancing, jiggling, spinning in place. As I passed each of them by, the previous ones would fall upon each other in a cannibalistic frenzy… devouring themselves while chanting, "Brains. Brains. Loaves of brains."

The trail, at first, led down the middle of the street. At one point it went through a car, with a loaf in the back seat. I walked around the car, trying to pick up the trail on the other side, but it was deemed as cheating. The loaves disappeared. The trail was gone.

"Fuck," I said. "Really?" Then I went back to the other side of the car (the singular bread loaf was still waiting in the back seat) and opened the car door and got inside. The car moved forward some twenty feet while I was crawling through the back seat. I put my hand into something sticky in a child's safety seat, then opened the door on the other side.

I crawled out of the car, and the trail forward had reappeared. A dog ran out from a yard and began barking at the bread loaves.

"Quiet," I told the dog, because Macabre kills things for sport, or whim, or because he feels better when he kills. Who knows? The point is that he's a madman, and a madman thinks it's keen to kill man's best friend.

The dog was a cocker spaniel. It looked at me and then to the trail of bread loaves, trying so hard to understand. I hurried past before the dog could get into any trouble. I hurried past while worrying that Macabre was only drawing me away from Adele's house so that he could do… something… there. There was a lump in my throat. There was a lump in my chest, my brain, everywhere. All I could do was follow the trail.

The demon trotted past me, eating a sandwich. Peanut butter and jelly. He held it up to me, half eaten, and asked, "Last meal?" I shook my head and kept following the trail.

The trail went over houses (I had to climb them, and follow the trail precisely) and the trail went through backyards (dogs would bark, cats would either run away, or pretend to not care, or honestly not care) and the trail went up into a tree that I had to climb, and then went past a woman's third floor window, and then vanished for nearly a minute, leaving me, maybe humanity's greatest remaining hero (meaning there weren't many of us left) crouching on a branch, praying for the resumption of a trail of bread loaves while a woman (I determined her age, but it's best to leave it indeterminate) was not ten feet away, naked, reclined on a bean bag, with her laptop computer recording a webcam show that involved her lower body, and her fingers, and three items normally considered as food. The cat demon was slowly climbing the outside wall, inch by inch, and was no more than a foot from her window when the trail of bread loaves reappeared. I moved on, hoping the demon would come with me, and it did.

The trail led straight through three different houses, an office building, a bakery (*Tarts*… closed for several hours, by that time) and in each of these places I moved through as quietly as I possible, picking locks when I had to (I'm good at this… because the skill is necessary in my line of work) and wondering what my picture would look like if I was arrested for breaking and entering. I wondered if Macabre was just trying to humiliate me. I wondered if Macabre was truly going against Octagon and his *two-week* grace period. If so, I wondered if Macabre was forgetting what had happened to the last member of Eleventh Hour who had gone against Octagon. Brambles, the man who could control plant life, had only been a member of Eleventh Hour for one week before his public rebellion (during the Louvre incident) and had been found only three hours later, in stasis, frozen in time, at least physically, because his eyes were alive and terrified and moving back and forth. His mouth was shaped into a scream, but hasn't moved at all since that time. It's been fifteen months now, more or less. I personally can't sit still for two minutes.

The trail of bread loaves led up to the top of Greenway's original water tower. I climbed the ladder, and as soon as I put my hands on the rungs all of the bread loaves (floating above) succumbed suddenly to gravity, falling down, showering me with bread, bouncing off my shoulders and head. Macabre has a low watermark of amusement.

I found him on the top of the water tower, hovering in place, with the small demon racing about the edge of the tower. It was sixty feet down. The demon didn't seem concerned. I'm not sure it's technically possible for Macabre to fall, and of course I've fallen from somewhat more impressive heights.

I said, "Octagon gave me two weeks."

"Two weeks is..."

Macabre had threatened Adele. I wasn't in a talking mood. My speed (always... always... always) took my opponent by surprise, and I leapt for Macabre's throat. A shield (glimmering like glass, radiant as car headlights, shaped like a Roman's tower shield) appeared in the air a foot in front of him, just before I hit, absorbing almost all of the impact, but I managed to break a fist through and grab Macabre by his arm. I yanked as hard as I could, pulling him forward into the shield and nearly knocking him unconscious. The demon leapt onto my shoulders and tried to bite my face, but my skin was too hard for its teeth to break through. I couldn't see for shit, though, and it stalled me long enough for the dazed Macabre to mumble some words, and then suddenly the water tower developed a blowhole, like a whale's, right beneath me, and an abrupt spout hurled me far into the air. I twisted about during my flight, trying to maintain a sight line on Macabre, because the damn thing about the son of a bitch is that you never know what he's going to do next.

I landed on a car dealership, rebounding off the neon "Quincy's Cars" sign (*Super Deals for a Super Town*) and fell onto the roof of a display station wagon from the 1970's, put in place as a cautionary tale of what you might end up driving if you went anywhere but Quincy's. I smashed through the windshield, crushed part of the hood and would have rolled away if the steering wheel hadn't grown tentacles and pulled me into the driver's seat. Glass had gotten into my left eye... chunks of glass as big as gravel, and I struggled with sight while trying to fend off a car that had been given life by a madman.

"Road trip! Road trip!" the demon yelled in my ear, appearing in the back of the car. "Daddy! Let's go on a road trip!" It leapt over the back seat and started trying, as far as I could tell, to reach down my throat and fish around in my stomach. Its arm was furred and barbed and began choking me. I was aware that Macabre was outside the car, standing in front, directing the chaos with waves of his hand, but I needed the glass out of my eyes and the demon out of my throat before I could deal with anything else. I didn't want to be the first recorded person in the history of the world to choke to death on a demon's arm.

The car began rolling forward.

"Seriously," Macabre called out. "Two weeks? I wouldn't have given you *two minutes*. How much does someone like you need to prepare to die? Who gives a shit if your hair is combed or you're wearing proper funerary underwear? So what if you leave behind a few unpaid parking tickets? Does this shit seriously mean anything to you?

"I'll tell you what," he said, with his head growing so large it was the size of a horse, of an elephant, a building, and was looking into the car like someone peering into a dollhouse. "I'll tell you what, after you're dead, I'll reanimate you as a zombie, and then you can go around and pay those parking fines. Do that last load of laundry. Eat a few brains."

The car was speeding forward.

Macabre was perched on the hood, staring in at me. The steering wheel's tentacles were trying to go up my nose. The demon's entire arm was down my throat, plunged down to his shoulder so that his face was against mine, nuzzling like a cat, like Wiggles, like Adele's cat... a cat that was probably not thinking of me, right then, because cats don't give a shit. But women do. Adele would care if I died. Beyond that concern, I'd been given two weeks, and I was feeling cheated.

I grabbed the demon and ripped it in half, digging my hands into its face and parting it, ripping with a sudden wrench that opened the creature from head to crotch, like a zipper, only bloodier. The bowler hat toppled from the torn head and vanished from existence. The arm down my throat gave a spasm, the hand still clutching at my lungs, but I pulled it out (I remembered the breathing tube at the hospital, and wished to hell that Paladin was on his way to me again, ready to give me an explanation, once more, for how life had turned out, and to give me another hug) and I slammed the dead demon's arm onto the car seat, then thought better of that and picked it up and tossed it as hard as I could at Macabre.

It caught him in the chest. Knocked him off the car. The steering wheel's tentacles flailed briefly, devoid of direction, and the glass finally fell out of my eyes. Things were going my way, suddenly.

Except, now that I could see, I could see that the way we were going was straight to hell. Literally. The car was travelling at a good pace, faster than the old station wagon had ever been able to achieve back when it was powered by gas instead of magic. And we were headed right for a Grand Canyon-sized chasm from which the fires of hell and the stench of sulfur were erupting. Winged demons were circling overhead, poking each other with pitchforks because I guess they had nothing better to do. Demons are like tattoo artists that sit around together all day. Somebody's going to get a shitty tattoo. Somebody's going to get a pitchfork in the dick.

"Road trip!" Macabre laughed. He was in the back seat, now, laughing that laugh of his (it sounds like a clown's, but played at the wrong speed, and injected with cayenne peppers) and as soon as I saw him I planted my feet on the dash and pushed as hard as I could, ripping the front seat from its mooring and sinking my right foot into the glove box, and slamming backwards into the madman.

I think it broke a few of his ribs.

"We're here!" I told him, maybe thinking that I was a father pretending to have reached the destination (though I didn't want to reach our intended destination at all) or maybe trying to make some statement of being at the end of the fight, or maybe not thinking at all. Thinking is way overrated in a fight. Just… act.

The whole car came to life, growing tendrils from the dash and the seats and the windows and grabbing at me, trying to stab through my flesh (sorry… too tough for you) and emitting acids (it burnt like hell, but what seemed to be a real and actual hell was only about three blocks away by then, so I could put up with a skin rash) and soon screaming at me (sound is one hell of a weapon, because it nails you through and through) and not one bit of it stopped me from pinning Macabre beneath my knee, the two of us in the cramped back seat (I'm not going to say anything at all about lovers, here) and me succumbing to media pressure, to the way people want me to be, saying the things that people love to hear, even though nobody else was around.

"Take some time off!" I told Macabre, and I punched him in the face. I punched him. And I punched him. And I punched him.

Again and again.

And again.

Because he was too dangerous to let up on.

Because he had threatened Adele.

I punched him.

Again and again.

The station wagon rolled to a stop only thirty feet before the lip of the dropoff, but it didn't matter much. The Grand Canyon of Sulfur, the Lake of Fire, Hell... at least Macabre's version of it... was fading. Slipping away from existence.

I'd probably punched Macabre twenty or thirty times. Nineteen to twenty-nine of those blows hadn't made any difference. I'd snapped his neck and shattered his skull on the very first punch.

I had to rip myself free of the twisted car. I tore myself free and staggered onto the streets of the small town of Greenway. By then I was in the spotlights of the SRD helicopters, coming down from above.

⌖

Wiggles, the cat, stood atop the kitchen table. He wavered back and forth as I tip-toed across the porch and through the kitchen, with him thinking about running, thinking about coming closer to me, obviously wondering where the hell he and I stood in the new-world post-magician order, but only ultimately mewling once before wandering off, padding up the stairs. I wished that I had Mistress Mary's powers, her ability to go to ghost form, float through walls, turn invisible, that kind of shit. Instead, I was going to have to go upstairs and check on Adele, and I would make accidental noise and almost for sure wake her up. After clearing the battle site with the SRD I'd even thought about not coming back at all, about avoiding this encounter, but between knowing that I would worry that Macabre got to her after all, and knowing she would worry if she woke up in a house without me, I'd opened her front door and gone inside.

I'm one of the strongest heroes there are... but I still struggled with the weight of that door.

I pretended to study the paintings on the stairway. I made noises enough that Adele, if she heard me, could have come out of her room and asked me what I was doing, and I could have then said something about the paintings and nothing at all about sneaking into a woman's bedroom at almost five in the morning.

I coughed.

I shuffled.

I even faked a sneeze and talked out loud to myself about the paintings on the wall ("*Dracula looks less menacing with glasses, I believe*," and, "*A mummy in spectacles looks more studious*!) but all that happened is that Wiggles came out of a small bathroom and looked at me like I was insane. Maybe he was a super cat with amazing powers of deduction, or maybe it was just that patently obvious.

There were four doors in the upstairs hall. One of them, the small bathroom, was wide open. The other three were all partially open, as if to invite someone to take a finger (one that could push into solid steel) and test their strength by moving the door an inch or two inward. One of the doors was Laura's (and I did wonder what her room looked like, what sort of toys might by laying in view) and one was Adele's (I knew which one, because I knew she'd taken her parents' old room) and the last was a mystery. I thought briefly about solving that mystery, but knew it would have only been delaying (avoiding) what I had to do, and also would be that much more of a chance to make some sort of damning noise.

I pushed Adele's bedroom door open, using Wiggles (who wondered what the hell was going on) by holding him around the stomach and pushing his head at the bottom of the door, hoping it would just appear (from the other side) that the cat was coming into the room. It was something that a sixteen-year-old would have thought of, and because of that I was proud.

The door swung far enough in that I could see most of Adele's room, but not her bed. I thought of how the room had once belonged to her parents, how it was possible she'd been conceived in this very room. I pushed the door farther open. There was a slight resistance. The door was pushing something along on the floor. It panicked me. It could have been anything. It wasn't all that heavy, but Macabre had been in the house, and that meant there wasn't anything to rule out. Horrors rushed through my head, and I felt nauseous.

I peered around the door.

It was a book.

It was a book titled, "*Reaver*." One of the many unauthorized biographies with my picture on the cover. Adele was the author. Did that explain the slam I'd earlier heard? Probably. I could picture Adele mad at me, slamming the book onto the floor. Maybe the resulting noise hadn't been loud enough to suit her. Maybe it had landed so she couldn't see my face. Or maybe so she could. Either way, I could picture her picking the book back up, slamming it down again.

I didn't have to picture her in bed because there she was. The night was warm enough that she didn't have much in the way of covers. Just one loyal sheet and one straying blanket. She was dressed in a silken negligee that was doing its usual lackadaisical job of covering up a woman. Wiggles had moved into the middle of the room. Bored.

Adele was sleeping. Breathing. I really hadn't expected it any other way. Macabre would have bragged about it, taunted me, if he'd hurt her.

Finding that Adele was okay… that was all I needed, so I turned to go, but she turned over in bed. Her eyes were open. Not wide open. Just *drowsy* open.

She said, "Steve?" She almost fell back asleep during this monumental speech.

"Yes. I was just…" I felt like I'd had some excuses in case I ran into this situation, but I couldn't remember a single one of the damn things.

"Are you seducing me?"

It was another question where it felt like I should have a definite answer at the ready, but I was caught empty again. I was wishing I'd had a chance to read a whole book about her, the way she'd apparently been reading about me.

"I was just… leaving." This was the best I could come up with. Not romantic. Not witty. Not particularly anything. Legions of my baser fans would have been disappointed. I was the man that had slept with Mistress Mary. With the possibly alien Stellar. With two Oscar winners. With a woman married to a head of state (not claiming that was a good idea, here) and so many famous models that it had taken the Vogue article three consecutive issues to bring the matter to a close, and even then they'd published an online addendum.

I was… in fact… the man that had once made Siren, in public, remark that she hadn't been bored. And now I felt like a rookie again. It felt… amazing in a way. Mistress Mary had once told me that there's nothing more soothing than being humbled. Mistress Mary, of course, is goddamn crazy… but sane people say crazy things at times, so there's no reason the water can't flow both ways.

"Leaving?" Adele mumbled. "You mean leaving the house?"

"Just going downstairs."

"If you're not getting into my bed, why did you come up here?"

"Can I tell you in the morning?" There are few things more awkward than coming into an old lover's bedroom to check if a man that you yourself have just beaten to death has killed her.

"Sleep in the corner," Adele ordered. She tossed a pillow on the floor and mumbled about blankets in the closet. She said a bulletproof man shouldn't have any trouble with being comfortable on a hardwood floor. She said to be quiet and not make any noise. She then thought better of that and told me that noises were fine. I'm not sure she even realized she was awake… that she wasn't dreaming.

In less than a minute, she began a soft, repetitive, wonderful snore.

I sat in the corner for an hour or so. Just watching her sleep. Her phone (on her nightstand, next to a copy of *Bulfinch's Mythology*) beeped once, and a text message from Laura (*The Apple is tasty! She wants to meet Steve. Did he roughly sex you?*) appeared. It glowed softly for fifteen seconds, then the phone went dark.

In time, I snuck back downstairs to my couch. I slept a little bit. I waited for morning. I thought about Macabre being dead. About what the public and the media would say. I thought about how Octagon would take it. How would this affect my *two-week* grace period? Had I cheated by fighting back? Had I negated the bargain? I thought about such things.

And I thought about that message on Adele's phone.

CHAPTER TEN

Octagon cut into a tiny little television broadcast in Italy, and it was soon (as I'm sure he planned and knew) all over the Mediterranean, and from there it spread out until it had made all of the world's major news channels, and all of the minor ones, a million different websites, mentions on a billion different blogs. Whenever Octagon so much as takes a piss, it goes viral.

No camera can capture him very well. The strange qualities of his black costume are too indefinable for any electronic eyes... too elusive for any eyes at all, really. On screen, he takes a curious flat quality... as if he is a shadow.

"Last night there was a mistake," he said. "Some of you might already know that Macabre, a member of my team, Eleventh Hour, sought out and battled Reaver. The battle did not go well for the magician. He is now dead."

In the broadcast, Octagon pauses here. He seems to be lost in thought. Perhaps he is. Perhaps he's lost in drama. Villains are like that. Although, truth be told, villains are only like that because villains are people, and everyone gets caught up in drama.

"Congratulations to Reaver on this victory," Octagon said. There is another pause. In this instance, I knew what the pause meant. I was one of the few who would. The others were Stellar, Laser Beast, and Siren. The surviving members of Eleventh Hour. They would know that Octagon's congratulations meant that Macabre had been condemned and ostracized, even as a corpse, for going against the bargain between myself and Octagon.

"This, of course, leaves a hole in Eleventh Hour. But, please, no applicants need file. No resumes need be sent. The void in Eleventh Hour has, I believe, been most adequately filled." Here, he gestured to someone off screen. You've all seen this, of course, and it's old news now, but none of us could claim that we were, then, ready for what happened next.

Mistress Mary walked into view.

Her hair was somewhat longer than the last time I'd seen her.

Octagon's hand was on her shoulder.

And she was smiling.

CHAPTER ELEVEN

Felix and Greta Barrows were both fifty-eight years old. They had been childhood sweethearts... meeting in the seventh grade (Felix was from Greenway and Greta from Lausanne, Switzerland, by way of Bolton) and (years later) forming a book-reading club together. Greg had told me that the book club had boasted, at one time, of twelve members, but eventually it dwindled to nine, to five, to four, and finally just to two... and after one book club meeting (Oscar Wilde's *Happy Prince & Other Tales*) Greta had asked Felix if she really needed to go home that night, or if he would like her to stay, and on the following day Felix had proposed. Greg was born eleven months after. Felix was an architect who had received offers from big concerns in big cities, but had stayed in Greenway because (according to his son, Greg) he was afraid of any other life but his simple one with Greta. Greta was a children's book artist, drawing fuzzy bears, and old witches and monsters, and (whenever she had the chance) pictures of Greg into the backgrounds. I called ahead and told them that I wanted to talk with them. They were happy to hear from me. We hadn't spoken hardly at all since the night they believed their son had died in a car accident, and I was going into their house to tell them Greg hadn't been dead for twelve years… but instead only three years. That he had, in fact, been Paladin. The greatest hero of them all. I didn't think it would make them happy.

Adele opened my car door for me, not because she was acting the gentleman, but because I'd been sitting in the driver's seat for too long, frozen in place outside the Barrows residence, wondering what to say. Mostly I had come to a resolution that there's never any reason to practice a speech in front of a mirror, because the words stay in the mirror, not in your mouth.

"Do you want me to come in with you?" Adele asked.

"No."

"Good. I don't want to go."

"I love an honest woman," I said, walking up the sidewalk to the house, trying to pretend that I hadn't, in the broadest sense of the conversation, just told Adele Layton that I loved her. To her credit (and a little to my disappointment, I admit) she had nothing to say in answer beyond a statement that she would wait in the car.

The house was split level with an attached garage, a huge yard and a lurking tree of the type that always appears it is only waiting for one strong wind in order to betray the house and family. There was a forty-foot span from sidewalk to front door, but the walk had been artistically complicated by winding paving stones and gardening plots, so much so that there should have been a minotaur to act as a guide. The bottom of the house was red brick. The top was wooden, and white. Greta Barrows was peering at me from a ground floor picture window that was partially obscured by a mesh of willow branches. She waved. There was a child standing next to her. A girl. Maybe seven or eight years old. Curly red hair and great big eyes. Nobody had warned me there would be a kid around. I wasn't sure if it would make it easier or harder. I wasn't sure of anything.

I knocked. Three sharp raps.

If you think I can knock on a door without thinking how my punches steal the years away, if you think that I can ever forget that I'm Reaver, you're wrong. Hell… I felt like the years were running away from me, right then, standing on the porch, perched on the square of an astro-turf mat that read, "*If you're knocking, you're welcome!*"

The door opened. Felix Barrows put out his hand for me to shake.

He hesitated, a bit, on that. But no more than I'm used to.

"Stevie," he said. His head bobbed, like a bird's, then he amended, "Steve."

"Mr. Barrows."

"*Felix* works fine. Come in. Come in." He gestured inside. The young girl I'd seen in the window ran up next to him, but stayed slightly behind his protection. She whispered my name (*Reaver*, the new name, not the old name, *Steve Clarke*) in a voice she didn't think I could hear, but I've got damn fine hearing (just *damn fine* hearing, not *super* damn fine hearing) and besides I can read lips. SRD had taught me. They'd taught Greg, too. Maybe the subject would come up.

The visit went barreling along. Greta Barrows gave me a hug that was as enthusiastic as possible considering there was very little body contact. Most people are afraid of touching me. There are an infinite amount of hugs to give in this world, but a finite amount of years in which to dole them out, so it's best to be careful. Again, I understand.

After the hug and the obligatory statements of how I'd grown, and how they still looked great, I was introduced to the third member of the household. The young girl's name was Chase, short for Chastity. I thought of a joke about that, something to do with the preacher's daughter and how you should never name a kid something they might feel obliged to live *down* to, but I was in the wrong company to tell it.

Chase was adopted. An orphan from a trailer park fire. I was told this last bit with hurried phrasings, before Chase could return with the lemonade and biscuits she'd been sent to retrieve.

There were pictures of Greg on the walls, and more of them on a desktop and also a couple of bookcases. There were no pictures of Paladin in sight. I wondered if that would change, after I was gone.

"What brings you here, today, son?" Felix asked me. He was seated on a couch with a floral pattern. I'd noticed, before he sat, that the pattern was worn dull in two places. One of the places was where he sat, and the other was where Greta settled. People get into their patterns.

"Can't I just visit?" I asked.

Chase said, "In school, people talk about you." She made it sound important.

Greta said, "People talk about him everywhere." Somehow, that made it sound less important.

"Is it true? The papers?" Felix asked. He nodded towards a newspaper on the coffee table, a copy of the *Greater Greenway News*, a paper funded by SRD, which did many charitable acts around town. As far as I knew, there was no *Lesser Greenway News*. It would have been fun to put one out and keep it lowbrow. Full of gossip.

The newspaper had an image of Macabre on the front page, and also a photo of the old station wagon where he'd met his end.

"That's true," I told Felix. "We fought last night."

"You seem okay," Greta said, in concern, staring into me like a looking glass.

I said, "I heal quickly." She blushed, as if it was something she should have remembered, as if she'd been rude not to recall, instantly, that she was watching a superhuman man nibble on a biscuit.

"Anything else to tell about it?" Felix asked. He phrased the question so that it could have been heard (for instance, by an eight-year-old girl) as, "*Can you give us any details*?" In truth, though, I knew that he meant, "*Are there going to be any more problems? Any reason that having you in the house could put us in jeopardy*?"

I said, "Not much to tell. An isolated incident." Felix nodded.

"Horrible thing. Car accidents," Greta said, looking at the paper and the image of the station wagon, as if it had been an accident, and not all of it, from one side or the other, definitely on purpose.

So… a car accident. It was a logical lead-in to what I had to tell them, and before I could stop myself, I was zooming right along, heading for a huge bump in the conversation. An accident waiting to happen.

I said, "I have to tell you some things about Greg." Felix and Greta both went silent and somewhat bloodless, and they leaned back. Chase leaned in closer. She had a blush. Ripe and full and childlike. Her eyes were peering at me over a glass of lemonade. The glass was at her lips, but she was not drinking.

"Maybe…" I said. I let my eyes drift from Felix and towards Chase.

"She's family," Felix said. I evaluated that in my mind, wondering if the two of them (Felix and Greta) could imagine how much I was about to tell them. It's okay to bring your child into the shallow water, but there I was sitting with an ocean on my lips, and I wasn't sure if any girl named Chastity should be around when I began spitting it out.

"Maybe…" I said, again. And I let my eyes drift towards Chase, again.

Greta looked at me, and she heaved a huge breath, the kind that lets the lungs know that some serious shit is about to go down. She looked to Chase's hopeful expression (it was, "*Please don't tell me to go. Please let me hang out with Reaver. Please! Please! Please-don't-tell-me-to-go*!") and then evaluated the look on my face. I tried to look serious. It wasn't hard. I've faced down Firehook when my lung was hanging from the tip of his flaming hook, but I'd never been more serious than when looking at the fifty-eight-year-old housewife... her being the mother of both Greg Barrows, and the adopted orphan from the trailer park fire.

"Chase," she said. "Go to your room."

"Awww, shit," the child said. Neither of the parents even flinched at the language. They both just looked at me. Wondering.

When Chastity was gone, I began. I told them about the day of the crash, with me and Tom and Greg and Officer Horwitz, and what had happened just a short distance from the Wennes Airport. I explained to them just why all of our shoes had been left behind at the Selood Brother's sheep farm. I told them how we had never really seen the tanker truck (Greg actually had, but I thought a small lie was for the best, here) before it struck us.

They listened to all of this. There was little that they hadn't already known. Just bits and pieces of new information, new insights of the son they'd once had. The two of them appreciated, I could tell, these new tidbits... though at the same time they were also irritated that I was stirring up the memories that had been allowed to drift away in exchange for a dulling of the pain.

But... we were about to move into new territory. I was about to blindside them with a truck they couldn't possibly see coming.

"Greg didn't die in the accident," I told them. Their eyes said they were curious. They wondered what I could mean. Of course he had died in the car accident. Anything else I was about to tell them (I could read all of this in their eyes and their postures) was no more than a matter of semantics.

"The body... the one at the funeral... it was a plant. Part of a cover-up." With this, I was the only one in the room still breathing, and I wasn't doing much of it myself.

"Greg was bathed in the same chemicals that made me into Reaver." I tapped my chest, in case they didn't know who I was speaking about. I held up my fist in case they didn't know exactly *what* I speaking about. Greta was now breathing in hurried little gasps, like a goldfish in a shallow bowl. Felix was straightening up with one long breath, forgetting to exhale. Chastity was peering down from the stairwell, only her forehead, her eyes, and a flush of her curly red hair was visible. I should have stopped the story and made her go back upstairs, but the story was a juggernaut that had spent years building momentum, and there was nothing I could do.

"Your son was Paladin," I told them.

⌖

It was Paladin who first took me to the SRD facilities. We were in the back of an armored car, and he encouraged me to test my strength by having me push my finger into the sides of the vehicle. I did this while two armed guards pretended that it was none of their business, and pretended that they weren't driven nearly to nausea by the sight of something that every atom in their bodies insisted was wrong.

My finger sank into that reinforced steel. It wasn't even very hard to do. I admit that I felt somewhat sickened by it, too, that first time. I also admit that my dick got a little bit hard.

"Fuck," I told Paladin. He was grinning.

I dug my fingers into the side of the armored car and pulled out a bit of metal. It took some effort, but only some. The metal was like taffy. Resistant, but manageable. I rolled a bit of the metal around in my fingers until I had a rough sphere about an inch in diameter. I flicked it against the wall. It rebounded around the vehicle's interior walls with sharp reports and then smacked me in the jaw. It was a lucky thing that I was the one to be hit. The two guards wouldn't have seen any humor in being shot that way.

I turned back to the wall. Stuck my finger in it again. I couldn't believe that it could be done. Couldn't believe that Greg was a superhero. It all had to be a joke.

"You keep finger-banging that wall," Paladin said, "and we're going to have to turn this vehicle around and drive to the park. Let you write an armored car's name on a certain rafter."

After he said that (I think the tabloids would shriek if they knew how off-color some of Paladin's jokes could be) the two guards announced we were almost at the SRD labs. I didn't know what they meant. Paladin had to explain it to me.

He told me about the man-made tunnels and caverns beneath the Wennes Airport. He told me about how, during the Cold War, we (meaning… America) had been trying to develop super-powers. Mind reading. Invulnerability. Super Strength. Flight. Laser eyes. All of that stuff. Even weirder powers… such as what Mistress Mary could do… powers that meant everyone would obey any order she gave them. We were getting nowhere on the project when the Russian regime faltered, and the Berlin Wall fell, and everybody seemed to think it was possible that the world was just going to shake hands and call it good.

But… the project hadn't stopped. It had veered into genetic research. Into stem cells. Into pushing the limits of aging past ninety years, a hundred years, two hundred years, five hundred years and more. Now that the world was at peace, everyone wanted to live forever, and they wanted to do it in bodies that were youthful and beautiful, with dicks that would stand up and breasts that wouldn't hang down. And… in exploring these new avenues… SRD stumbled back onto their initial path.

The first of the success stories was Warp. Well, he was the first human. There was a rat in SRD that nobody could catch, because the damn thing was intangible. It's still there, right on the front doorstep, a reminder to be careful during research. It's not alive anymore. The fucker (if it wasn't a rat, I'd call it "*the poor thing*") starved to death, unable to eat any food, and had eventually dropped dead. It was still intangible, though. And it was immune to decay. It has been there (and is still there) in place. At first it had been covered by a table, but after a while it was uncovered and received a plaque that read, "*Think of Marty before making your next move.*" Apparently the rat had been named Marty. Nobody could remember giving it a name, but there it was on the plaque.

After Marty it was the insects. Most of them were born in the furnace room, a room that could be sealed off and brought to over two thousand degrees Fahrenheit, a precaution against crafting some super bug that would escape the lab and hit the streets, impregnating all the natives with its *super bug* penis, causing mankind to succumb to grasshoppers or ladybugs or chiggers.

And the SRD cockroaches. Those damn cockroaches, of course. The giant one didn't have a name. Nobody wanted to name that damn thing. It was just referred to with swear words, or as *Subject Seven* or *that big damn cockroach*. Nobody could believe it was still alive. Something that big, it should be dead. It was keeping on with keeping on, though, and laughing at everyone who predicted, day after day, that it would die. Well… not laughing, but chittering. The noise was like… like… like the sound of getting kneed in the balls played backwards on a scratchy tape. Something like that, anyway.

The tanker truck accident, the one that had killed its driver, that had killed Officer Horwitz, that had done what it did to Tom, it had also bathed Greg Barrows and me in waste waters (mostly waste *chemicals*) from a variety of experiments. A mulligan's stew of various radioactive waters and peculiar chemicals had doused us. We changed.

Now, SRD wanted to make us heroes. To have us stand fast against the darkest forces. To shine a light into the void. *Blah blah blah. Etc. Etc. Etc.*

It didn't take much to convince me.

I was young. I was being told I was invulnerable. I was stronger than anyone (at that time) but Paladin. I was three times faster than almost anyone else around. I was told I could wear a costume. I was told there would be pussy involved.

I was going to be a hero.

⌖

You have to train to be a hero. A lot. That shit sucks.

Weeks went by.

I sparred with an assortment of volunteers. Martial artists. Body builders. Soldiers.

Tests were run. On me, during the sparring sessions. And on my volunteer opponents, afterwards.

The extent of my powers began to be clear. Including the thing with the punch.

I was no longer allowed to spar with volunteers.

I sparred with lions and learned the language of the apes and the creatures of the jungle, as created by Edgar Rice Burroughs for his *Tarzan* adventures. I wasn't actually assigned to learn the language, but Jesus Christ… of course I did.

I was young and I was sparring with lions.

⌖

Felix Barrows asked me, "Why did they keep Paladin's… why did they keep *my son's* identity a secret, but *yours* was known from the start?"

"The SRD wanted to keep everything secret. *Everything*. But the accident itself was too hard to cover up, and it provided an easy reason for Greg to be missing."

"But you…" Greta said. "Why not you?" I noticed she wasn't offering me lemonade or biscuits any more. It could have been that she was too deep into the story, or it could have been that I was no longer a welcome guest. It was too bad. My throat was dry. It would have been easy to reach out and grab the pitcher of lemonade, pour me some. Easy for some people. But… me? Right then, I honestly admit I didn't have the guts.

"My powers were dormant for a bit. They didn't… uhh… manifest at first, the way Greg's did. They still thought I was normal, so they put me in the hospital. I was supposed to wake up, to tell the story of the accident, cementing Greg's cover, and then go on with my life. Instead, I stayed in that coma, and then I did start to test positive for powers, a couple weeks in. By then it was too late. They had to keep me there, but they sent in Mistress Mary to tell me to shut up when…"

"That's not what I meant," Greta said. She was using the voice of a woman who would not be offering me lemonade at any point in the near future. She was using the voice of a woman who was defending the memory of a son who had been dead for nine years… until this conversation had begun, when she discovered he'd only been dead for three.

She said, "I meant… why didn't *you* tell us the truth before now?"

"Greg?" Felix Barrows said. He was sitting on the couch, in his favorite well-worn spot, but it was plain that he felt he was floating away… lost in the world. We both looked at him, Greta and I (perhaps the last team-up we would ever have) and he finally snapped back to attention. He wiped away sweat that wasn't there… or maybe he was just trying to dig down deep to the well… deal with it at the source. He cleared his throat a few times. Obvious practice runs for something he was finding hard to say.

"The hell with *you*," he finally said, to me. "Why didn't *my own boy* tell me he was alive?"

⌖

In one of our very first adventures, Paladin and I were flying across Lake Tanganyika, searching for pirates. A local warlord had somehow acquired a small fleet of PT boats and was terrorizing fishing villages and shipping vessels, doing the sorts of things that these people do, the raping and the pillaging. Paladin and I were sanctioned to find the warlord and his PT boats and make an example of them.

"I wish I could tell my parents," he said.

"You wish you could tell your parents that you're in Africa, hunting down psychopaths that you've been asked to kill?"

"I wish that I could tell them I'm alive."

"And I wish that I could tell my parents it was okay to go home." It had become an ongoing debate between the two of us, a debate concerning which of us had the short end of the straw as regards to our parents. Greg couldn't tell his parents that he was alive because then, sooner or later, everybody would know. And "*everybody*" includes people who would use his family against him. He was arguably the most powerful man in creation, but all of that went to hell if he refused to take action, if he excused himself from a confrontation because Laser Beast (just for instance) had his mother tied up in some room, tearing off her clothes piece by piece, warming up lasers that would emit from the fleshy bits beneath his spiked pieces of fashionable genital wear. I'm not just making up this example. It was told to the both of us as we sat in an SRD briefing room, and a public relations expert/assassin (apparently the jobs were connected?) explained what could happen if the public became aware of Paladin's true identity. There were even charts, illustrated scenarios, photo manipulations of Laser Beast and Greta, Greg's mother, with one of them having the time of his life, and the other having the last moment of her life. Greg nearly needed to be restrained when the "*this could happen*" photos were shown to him. It was lucky for the "expert" that Greg didn't need to be restrained, because there was nobody around who could do it. Not even me.

My own parents, by that time, had been moved. I know where they are. Not even Siren or Mistress Mary could convince me to reveal their location. I don't go there. I haven't seen them in years. I send cards to certain people, who send those cards to certain other people, who do the same, the same, the same, until they reach their destination. I am told that the castle is very nice. I am told they live well. My mother is active in the community. After one more year of residency, Dad can run for political office… can finally be a mayor, like he's always dreamed. Mom helps the staff with the gardens. My father had an affair with two of the maids (a horrible thing, of which I am somewhat horribly proud) and my mother forgave him, because what else could she do? Where else would she go?

Two years after Greg and I undertook our mission to Tanganyika, a group of would-be villains named Neo-Spartacus (they patterned themselves after imperial Roman soldiers, so their name wasn't very historically accurate) publicly executed my high school football coach, Levi Graters. This was their way of calling me out. Of challenging me. It worked. Warp and I (this was before the trials, of course) sped to the site of the killing, and then we made sure the cameras were still rolling and we did a few things (you can't spend your whole life being proud of the things you do) and afterwards nobody has ever bothered anybody from my days in Greenway again.

But that was later, and Tanganyika was then, and Greg was holding me around the waist as he flew (I can't fly, so in the early days, during our team-ups, he always carried me, thereby providing fuel for a cock-driven online maelstrom of homo-erotic fanfics) and Paladin's vision (nobody could ever understand Paladin's vision, not even him… he could… see evil?) soon spotted three of the PT boats even amidst the vastness of one of the world's very largest lakes.

He dropped me aboard one of the pirate's boats and flew on to the others, telling me that the Children of the Spill (meaning, the two of us, of course) were about to prove their worth. I wasn't in the mood to prove my worth. I was in the mood to be Reaver.

There were ten men on my boat… and before even I could react, there were eight. One of the men jumped off the boat (taking his chances in a fight against a lake of nearly 90,000 square miles, rather than one man with two fists) and another was shredded into the water by a burst from a .50 mm machine gun, the spray of which also caught me and nearly flung me into the waters, but I managed to grab onto a railing and stay on the boat, grinning like a madman (any or all of them, take your pick) as the machine gun fire washed over my body.

I pulled myself back onto the deck and started punching. This was a time before I was too deep into the guilt of how I steal years away (I'm still only in shallow waters, there, I admit) and we had seen all the briefing photos and reports of what these men had done. We had met, at an impromptu lakeside briefing, a child, an orphan, who was able to describe one of the massacres. He had told us what the warlord (self-deemed as *Colonel Bapoto*) had done to his sister and their mother, how they died, in other words, and this boy (of eight or nine years) had spoken in a measured and emotionless voice that it was clear he would use for the rest of his life.

So... no... I wasn't worried about punching these men. Not at all.

I felt like I had been born to punch them.

I was a man who had sparred with lions.

And one by one they, fell. Some of them dropped to their knees and they prayed and some of them (two more, past the initial one) leapt from the boat (I would have let them all drown, but Paladin later fished a dog-paddling survivor from the waters) and the others died and I wasn't sorry for that. I wasn't sorry for anything until Colonel Bapoto himself came up from below, and he held a woman hostage (she was in such horrible shape that I wasn't even sure she was alive... wasn't sure if Bapoto was holding a corpse hostage) and before he even made any demands he put a gun to her head and he fired, tearing away part of her jaw.

She was very beautiful, in the places that were left unmarked.

Bapoto's death was not quick, but it was quicker than I wanted. I knew that there was a deadline involved. I had exactly one *Paladin* worth of time... defined by how long it would take my childhood friend Greg Barrows to convince two PT boats full of horrendous men to convert to the side of good. This is not a great span of time. Only a few minutes. By the time Paladin came floating down from above, Bapoto was in pieces. I'd taken his hands. His eyelids. His nose. His genitalia. I'd killed him and thrown him into the water so that Greg wouldn't see what I'd done.

When Paladin came down from the heavens (not just the sky, dammit) he landed near the stricken woman and held her in his hands. He did the glow... the one that's been seen everywhere. It doesn't translate well onto television. Not the light. Or the warmth. And, let me just say... there was always some sort of singing. Not a human singing. But... nature itself singing. It was as close to tangible poetry as can exist, and after the glow faded (moments… only moments) the African woman was entirely whole… completely healed. Paladin even dipped her in the waters of Lake Tanganyika, washing her clean.

I myself stayed bloody.

⌖

"He couldn't tell us," Felix Barrows said. "My own son couldn't tell us he was alive."

"Because he loved you. Don't think of it in any other way. It tore him apart. But it kept him whole, too, knowing that he was fighting for a reason, for people like you, so that other people could be with their sons. He took that burden on himself." Practicing this speech, I'd thought about throwing in some sort of mention of Greg being on the cross, but there was enough of that talk going around that none of it needed to come from me.

"We could have lived somewhere else. Somewhere safe. Where are *your* parents? What happened to *them*?" It was known, worldwide, that my parents were alive. That solitary fact was the extent of the worldwide knowledge. I ignored Felix's questions.

I said, "Could you have kept away from contacting him? From trying to? Fuck… don't even answer. Even if you could have, it doesn't make any difference. Greg had to go cold turkey. If he started by telling you he was alive, he would have wanted to tell you something more, to talk to you more. You can't take off a girl's panties without wanting to get her on her back." That last bit came out before I could stop it. There hadn't been any such analogies when I was planning what to tell Greta and Felix Barrows. Chase, still on the stairway, ducked further out of sight. Only her hair was showing. Just her hair and one ear. I had no doubt she was texting friends. I had no doubt her classmates were gathering outside, accumulating like zombies in the yard, or around the car where Adele was waiting.

The problem was, I was having problems myself. It was a conversation I'd had again and again and again. Ten or fifteen times in the mirror and then, throughout the years before, a hundred times with Greg Barrows himself playing the other side, and once (in one of the very few instances where Paladin was a son of a bitch and a bastard and an asshole, all together) telling me that the desire to visit his parents, combined with how he knew he needed to stay away from them, had so overwhelmed him that he'd gone and visited *my* parents. I hadn't even known that he knew where they were. He asked if I wanted him to tell me all about the visit and it was all I could do not to punch him. I kicked him, instead. He hadn't fought back (probably a lucky thing for me) but had instead nearly, almost, just about cried.

All in all, while Greta and Felix were talking from an aspect of a half hour of shock, I was talking from nearly a decade of accumulated and argumentative weight. I suppose I was a little angry. I suppose I felt they were right. Nothing about the whole situation was fair. Mistress Mary had once told me (not ordered me, just told me) not to ever worry about how our lives were unfair... to just keep on doing what we needed to do. She told me that she could go out, into the world, and order every last person to tell her the truth... asking each person if their own lives were fair. There wouldn't have been too many positive answers. True enough.

"I think that's enough for now," I told the parents of Greg Barrows.

"I wish you'd have told us this years ago," Felix said. He was angry.

"I wish you'd never told us at all," Greta said. "Why would you do this to us?"

"Call me if you want me to tell you anything more," I answered, acutely aware that I would be causing arguments between the two of them. But what the hell else could I do? A hero doesn't fight to make things comfortable. He fights to make things right.

CHAPTER TWELVE

"Tell me what all this is about," Adele said. There was a certain part of her voice that reminded me of Mistress Mary. A *central command center* to her tone.

"You're on a date, sis," Laura interjected. "Not an interrogation. Save the handcuffs and paddleboards for later. Let me know if you need to borrow any… oh shit!" The last part was yelped, as if she'd been pinched. I figured it was because she'd been pinched.

Adele was, as her sister had said, on a date. A double date, in fact. The last double date I'd been on had been with me and Mistress Mary, and Paladin and Taffy. Back then, Mistress Mary and I were pretending to have a relationship that wasn't based on sex. That had lasted until she ordered me to tell the truth if I loved her or not, and while her compulsion power didn't work on me, it seemed the right thing to do to tell the truth, so I had (the answer was, "not in the slightest") and we'd broken up. I soon returned to serial dating, or continued it, or whatever. Paladin did not serial date. It was only Taffy for him. A lot has been said (in the press, and in myriad porno "tribute" movies) that Taffy was the perfect woman with the way she could bend herself into any shape, twist and stretch herself even into another person, stretch her arms (or, as the porno films always highlighted, stretch *whatever*) until they were five feet long, or fifty, or a hundred. Paladin didn't love her for the sexual possibilities, though (not that it wasn't a factor… Paladin's libido was as human as the next guy's) but because she was a lovely person. Even if her laugh could stretch a mile wide.

Paladin is dead, now, of course. Taffy is still in mourning. And I was done with serial dating.

This new double date was myself and Adele, and Laura and Apple, the girl from the grocery store, who was willing to pinch Laura when she got out of line, and who turned about to be a tad under five feet tall and have more energy than almost anyone I've ever met, up to and maybe even including Stellar, who claimed to be able to fly to the stars and possibly wasn't lying.

The park was large and included a lake where turtles sat on logs and there were several expansive and uneven lawns where dogs ran free and people tossed Frisbees and the local burlesque circus practiced how to walk on cords suspended between trees, or on stilts, or in clown shoes, or on the stomachs of two women bent into positions that were considered impossible by most people's standards. There seemed to be little difference between these people (especially one woman who could kiss her own ass) and some of the *powereds* I've known. Maybe we were just in different circuses. I often felt that way.

Apple had brought us several fruits from the grocery store where she worked. There were no apples among them. She told us she was resistant to becoming a cliché. She brought sandwiches and a few other things. Some wines. Some cheeses. She had good taste. She had an invoice that she presented to me, telling me that she figured there was no way I wasn't at least a millionaire, and therefore the most qualified to pay for the picnic. It embarrassed Adele, but nobody else. From my side, it was just plain truth, and from Laura's side, her date's impertinence was clearly a sensual draw. I idly wondered if Laura shut down Apple's impertinence in bed, or if she let it gallop freely about the mattress. I had to quit wondering about it because being a superhuman doesn't mean you're not human, with a human's physical reactions, reactions that the love of your life might notice. And by "might" notice, I mean that she would, because Fate is depraved in her humors.

"What… brings you to town?" Adele asked, mostly rephrasing her question, hoping to sneak it around her sister. I didn't mind. I found it amusing. We'd already talked about art (van Gogh won in an imagined knife battle against Toulouse Lautrec, but we all admitted that Henri was victorious in the end, when Edwin went back to his yellow house and Gaugin, and Henri returned to the Moulin Rouge and the whores) and we'd talked about politics (Why don't any of the *supers* run for office? Why don't *I?*) and we talked about sex (the other conversations had been only interludes within this topic) and all along, at every step, we had avoided the question of, "*Why has Reaver returned to Greenway?*" And the thing was... I'd slept in Adele's house, on Adele's couch, and she had a right to know. It felt... odd to be beholden to someone. Being who I am, I normally feel like I'm responsible for everyone on Earth... that I need to step in and save each life and every dream. I'd thought I'd felt responsible, anyway... but it wasn't until I was with Adele again that I felt the truth of that. Not that I was responsible for Adele... but that I had responsibility. A difference, there.

So I took the note from my pocket.

And I let Adele unfold it.

Laura whispered to Apple how they were maybe about to witness (as Adele's very nervous fingers worked the well-worn note) a marriage proposal. That terrified me. I hadn't thought it could look like that and I considered whisking (at three times normal speed) the note from Adele's hands, but then I thought about how that would look (on the heels of the cursed Laura's not-very-whispered comment) and so I paused for too long (I pause at *one* times normal human speed) because I wanted to see what Adele's reaction to her sister's words would be, and then suddenly the note was open and they were gathering around. And reading.

1: Be with Adele again.
2: Take Adele on a date. (pay)
3: Talk to Greg's parents.
4: See my house. (steal something?)
5: Talk with Judy.
6: Prepare will (Adele, Greg's parents, Judy?, monument to Dad & Mom, Kid Crater Scholarship)
7: Visit SRD (shut them down?)
8: Fight.

They read through the note out loud. One line item at a time. I waited for the comments. They sure as hell were going to have them.

Everyone looked to Adele. Somehow, it had been determined that she had the right to be first to speak.

Accurate, but…

Hell.

"Let's start easy, hero," she said. "Item six. Tell us about Kid Crater."

Easy, she said.

Easy.

The boy could fly. He was fourteen years old and he could fly. And he could land like a feather. Or… if he wanted to… he could land like a meteor that ripped through anything that wasn't metal or rock, and he could even rip through about ten feet of that. Leaving a crater.

After he found me in the Minnesota cabin, back when I was recovering from my arena encounter with Octagon and Firehook and Stellar, I took him under my wing. I didn't mean to. I meant to send him on his way, but I started talking about what Firehook had done to me (the nova-level blast that had erased my features for a time) and I told him about what Stellar had done to me (discarding me from space) and the kid said it all probably made me want to kill Firehook and screw the hell out of Stellar, and for those pinpoints of wisdom (the tabloids will love this) I gave the fourteen-year-old the rest of my bottle of whiskey and grabbed another one for myself. By the time Paladin returned from his Washington press conference I had one new friend and much less whiskey.

In my defense, I'd talked Kid Crater out of flying to town and stealing from a whiskey store (he always, after our time in Minnesota, referred to liquor stores as *whiskey stores*) so I had that going for me, but other than that, Paladin wasn't sure the life of hero was a wise idea for the kid, and the argument (it grew heated) continued until I pointed out that he (meaning Greg) and I hadn't been much older when we strapped on our own badges. I meant hypothetical badges… not real ones… until we received the congressional ones, a brand new type of badge, six months later, after the first Mindworm incident.

Paladin admitted that this was true, and Kid Crater was allowed to stay, so everything else that happened afterwards was my fault.

"Big shoulders," Apple told me, interrupting my talk. Laura gave her a pinch. It seemed they'd already developed a precise methodology for dealing with each other's transgressions.

"Let the man talk," Laura said. "Do you even know how hard it must be for a man to admit a failing during a picnic with three sexually alluring women?"

I said, "Ouch."

Adele said, "It wasn't a failing. Don't make it sound like he failed." I appreciated her defense (though it was somewhat ludicrous, because she was defending something I hadn't yet admitted) and did my best to level Apple with a machismo stare that could have leveled Octagon himself, but it didn't seem to faze her. I suppose she knew she could hide behind Laura, if it came to that, and I was clearly no match for Adele's sister.

I said, "Kid Crater had two brothers. Two sisters."

"Sisters," Adele said, in a tone of sympathy.

"Interruption," Laura said. "Two demerits."

I said, "I honestly don't want to tell this story." The three of them went silent. Looked innocent. Or at least tried to look innocent. I thought about it, and then I thought… what the hell… some stories need to be told… or at least some people need to tell some stories.

Kid Crater had two brothers and two sisters. The sisters were older. The brothers were younger. His father had died while fighting a California wildfire… dropped in from above to eke out a firebreak with six other men. The wind had shifted and they'd been trapped in a canyon. Only one man (and it wasn't Kid Crater's father) survived the fire's speedy descent into their position, though he looked only remotely human after the flames had kicked him around. Paladin, when Kid Crater told the story, wrote the man's name down in a book he sometimes carried, a book listing people that he wanted to search out and heal. I'm not sure if he ever got around to it in this case. We lost track of each other, for a time.

There were rumors that Firehook had started the California wildfire, but of course there are always rumors of that type.

Kid Crater's mother was an insurance saleswoman and, because of that, the father had been insured in twelve different ways and his death had brought in twelve different kinds of money, all of it in large shares. There was enough money that she paid for all of the funerals, for each of the deceased firefighters, herself. There were no flowers for any of them because (as Kid Crater had related) she had broken down when choosing the flowers, looking at a flower display, all the oranges and the reds, and she thought they all looked like flames. A thousand dancing flames. There was no way she could have them so close to the coffins.

Kid Crater was eleven years old when his father died. He spent the next two years studying flames… the science of fire. He loved to talk about the flames, even if it was in a haunted way, speaking of *blackbody radiation* and *spectral band emissions* and other things that sounded somewhat like science and also somewhat like the occult. He was a whiz kid about flames, a true genius, knowing more about fire than almost anyone on Earth. Knowing, in fact, so much, that he created a science fair project centered around flameproof suits, and also possible ways to take down Firehook, presented in a satisfactorily animated science thesis/snuff film.

SRD had gotten word. Had been intrigued. They had brought in Kid Crater (who, of course, wasn't Kid Crater at the time) and had persuaded this thirteen-year-old boy to present his findings to some of the finest minds on Earth, including Checkmate, who had sat silently and seemingly inert in his armor, until finally mentioning (this is actually a compliment) that he was not offended by the child's staggering lack of intelligence.

But Kid Crater was, for all of this, still a teenage boy, and teenage boys are not known for their incredible abilities at staying out of trouble, and so he had wandered into sections of SRD where he was not authorized, and had strayed near a burn chute (SRD had, at the time, used burn chutes to drop hazardous materials into a Checkmate-designed furnace that burned at temperatures most scientists didn't think could exist) that was emitting the gases from a previous burn. Checkmate had designed the chutes to absorb even the gases, but budgetary concerns had nixed all of the safety devices inherent in Checkmate's designs. In SRD's defense, they were fighting a war at the time, as Stellar had declared herself sovereign of the planet, and even the combined forces of SRD (as foot soldiers, of a sort) and myself, and Paladin, and Mistress Mary, and Red Blade, and Warp (on emergency parole) had been fighting a losing battle against her. It was Octagon, of course, who finally took her down. I have the deluxe book/video box set of the event... the one purportedly signed by Octagon himself. It was provided to me in the hopes that I would scrawl some sort of endorsement for the regular edition. I didn't. I don't do those types of things. It was tempting, though; Octagon, whatever his reasons, had saved us all.

Anyway, the point is, Kid Crater (not quite yet Kid Crater) had inhaled a combination of gases that were leaking from the burn chute at SRD, and then, after that, he was Kid Crater.

After that, he came looking for me and Paladin.

After that, he became an unofficial sidekick, and we fought the good fight for a time.

After some of that, he convinced us to search out Firehook, who, at the time, was on a hiatus of sorts, having not appeared for well over a year... not since my battle with him in the arena. I was able to later find out the hiatus was enforced, that Octagon had tossed Firehook into an Eleventh Hour holding cell, a prison for powered criminals who had challenged Octagon's authority. A should-be inmate was running the prison, so to speak. When the prison was finally uncovered (during Leviathan's devastating raid on Seattle) it unleashed a torrent of bad guys who hadn't ever made any public appearances... ones that Octagon had nabbed up as being unwilling to follow the criminal status quo even before the public (or even SRD) had known about them. That said... there were a few white hats in that prison, too. That's where Dark Mercy came from, incidentally... not from the "ebony clamshell" she claims in the press packages released prior to her movies.

Kid Crater was nearly invulnerable when in flight.

He (as far as anyone knew) actually *was* invulnerable during impact from his dive bombs.

He was unrelentingly enthusiastic and had a sense of morality that was (putting aside his changing teenage hormones and their omnipresent demands to *rut*) as keen as Paladin's own.

But he was still a kid, and he still couldn't keep his mouth shut.

I sat him down a hundred times and told him to never... never... NEVER... give any clues about who he was in real life.

I should have sat him down that hundred and first time. I should have. I was caught up in my own problems (which are apparent, and too numerous to list) at the time.

In his post-fight interview after defeating the Blast Brothers, he said, "I've got two brothers, and I dedicate this fight to all the times they gave me wedgies." It was funny. A good line. Not smart, though.

When being questioned about how he would resist Mindworm's abilities if the situation ever arose, he said, "Listen, I have two sisters, and I lived through *their* mental manipulations. Mindworm doesn't stand a chance." Another good line. And now... he'd established he had two brothers and two sisters. Not that big a deal. A lot of people do.

"I have a personal beef against Firehook," he said during a brief interview on the red carpet for some teen music awards ceremony, where he was dating (only for publicity purposes, but he did get a handjob, according to his own not-very-trustworthy report) Lili Queen, that seventeen-year-old singer who had a string of viral videos.

"Why is that?" the reporter had asked.

"My dad was a fireman. He died in a California wildfire. It might have been Firehook that started it. That's really all I should say." Lili, hanging from his arm, gave him the sort of sympathy look that a girl gives when she's considering lending credence to handjob stories. Paladin and I, catching the interview an hour after it was broadcast, just a snippet on the nightly news, scrambled to try to protect the family that our young sidekick had just uncovered.

We were too late.

⌖

"I remember this," Laura said. "I don't want to talk about it. Let's look at the list again. Let's talk about something else on the list."

Adele said, "I researched this. I'm a little embarrassed, sitting here, telling you that I wrote articles and books about you. You sure... you sure this is something you want to talk about?"

"I think he has to," Apple said. "Like... therapy."

Adele said, "Steve?"

I said, "It's okay. Maybe Apple is right. Maybe this is shit I need off my chest. Is there any better way to ruin a picnic?"

"Orgy," Laura said.

Apple said, "Reaver said *ruin* a picnic. *Ruin*."

Adele, in a scolding tone, said, "His name is Steve. Not Reaver."

I said, "It's both. And Kid Crater's name was Nile Brakes. He always wished that he could make it public. He said it was fitting. Nile Brakes. No brakes. Kid Crater."

⌖

Kid Crater's real name was Nile Brakes. His sisters had an apartment together, just a block from their mom, testing out living in the real world. It was close enough that Nile's mom could pop over, from time to time, to make sure there weren't any unauthorized parties or penises on the premises. The visits were frequent. The mother was, in fact, at the apartment when the storm broke.

It wasn't a natural storm.

It was Tempest.

It had already been cloudy. Then it grew cloudier. Then the clouds transformed into a woman's face and some people (some citizens of Winchester, Nevada) stood and looked at this in wonder, and other people (primarily those who had seen the reports of Tempest's "goddess" time in Ecuador) ran for what shelters they could find. They needn't have worried too much. Tempest was there for a specific reason. Because Kid Crater was a hero. And she wasn't.

Tendrils of strong wind, like a sentient tornado's tentacles, came down from the sky. They pierced an apartment building's windows and reached inside, searching out their specific victims. Rachel and Tally Brakes were swept out from the building, along with their mom. Mrs. Brakes collided with the windowsill during her violent exit. Most of the SRD investigators agree that she died there, at that moment, considering the amount of blood she left behind.

The two girls and their *very-probably-dead* mother were carried up into the sky. They were subjected to personal hailstorms, individual lightning strikes, cold that was chilling, and heat beyond measure, but always at a low enough levels that a screaming member of the Brakes family could endure the punishment and plead for their lives in voices that were carried (quite purposefully) to the witnesses below. Those voices even further carried for miles and miles, tens of miles and hundreds of miles, spreading out across the United States, from coast to coast, borne along by strands of wind as thin as telephone lines, heard by bewildered and frightened individuals who happened into these streams. There were hundreds of reports of mysterious calls for help. All across the nation.

By then, the two girls and their mother had been tossed aside by the storm's tentacles, cast away to speed to the streets of Winchester, far below.

They died on impact.

Or maybe they'd died shortly before.

But they were dead just the same.

A hundred miles away the two brothers, Kid Crater's brothers, were on a camping trip with a family friend. They were found (after an extensive search with a base camp erected only a few feet from their bodies) in a tin coffee can that had been roasting over a flame. The brothers and their friend were inside the coffee can. Only inches tall. Finely roasted. Macabre had gotten to them.

It was no damn wonder that Kid Crater went crazy.

⌖

Adele was holding my hand. I didn't even remember her taking it. Apple was crying and saying she was sorry, and Laura was stroking her hair and telling her that I'd probably needed to talk about it anyway… that she hadn't done anything wrong by goading me into talking.

I wasn't very good at picnics.

"Maybe we should look at some of these other items on your list?" Adele prompted, holding my "to do" list up in front of her chest. It flapped in a slight breeze. I wondered if any of the three, Adele or Laura or Apple, were thinking about that breeze. About what might be behind it. The breeze was probably normal… of course… but Macabre had already sought me out, and Tempest was still out there somewhere, and she was far crazier than the magician had ever been.

"I'm glad you killed Macabre," Apple said. "I never heard about that campsite. Never knew about that."

"Not everything makes the news," I said. "SRD tries to keep a clamp down on most of the bad things. Best that way. It avoids a general panic."

Laura said, "I, for one, am panicked right now. Let's look at this list again." She took it from Adele's hands and said, "Number one. *Be with Adele again*. Seriously? That's why you came here? You dated each other for a few months, and that was a decade ago, and you… what… *miss* her?" The questions seemed serious, but Laura's wry smile wasn't treating them as such. Still… they actually were serious questions. No avoiding that.

I said, "Adele, I missed you." I said it to Adele. Not to her sister.

There.

It was out.

As close to an admission of love as the picnic could handle.

It wasn't as gutsy a move as it sounds like. If it all went to hell, I was standing at only nine days before my promised appointment with Octagon. I could make it through those nine days. Hell… I'm bulletproof.

Adele said, "I noticed you went through my bookshelves so I'm assuming you saw some of the articles I've written about you. Even the books. I've done a lot of superhero research. I mean… not just about you," she blushed, here. "I researched a lot of others as well. Because we… we were together… because of that… people will talk to me. Anyway… I mean to say that the topic of Steve Clarke is… well, I missed you too, Steve." A thump hit me around my chest. An internal one.

Laura and Apple had taken the appearance of children at the adults' table. I felt bad for them. They were whispering to each other… looking at us. I hate being on display. I hate it. I was glad that Laura didn't let the separation last for long.

"Aren't you… aren't you worried about us?" she asked. Her finger did a loop that included the whole group. Maybe the whole park.

"He kept away from me for a decade," Adele said. "Of course he was worried about us. About me. That's why he stayed away."

I said, "That's why I stayed away."

"But now you're back?" This was from Laura. "You… umm… horny or something?"

"You always put things so nice, sis," Adele told her.

I said, "The thing is, I'm not going to stay long." Adele made an eye flutter. I all but ignored it (outwardly) and went on with, "And then it's not going to matter much after that."

"Enigmatic," Adele said. "Go on."

"Can't. Not yet. Secret, SRD-related confidential top secret classified information. Suffice to say, in about ten days time, nobody will bother much about my friends or family."

"Holy shit," Adele said. "What's going on?"

But I kept silent. Their faces registered expectation, but I didn't say a word. Laura was amused, thinking I was teasing about something. Apple had a look in her eye that said, maybe, possibly, she was worried. It was nice to think that someone I'd just met could be worried about me... nice to think I was that charming a figure. She looked to the note in Adele's hands. Bit her lip. I noticed her the most because I was adamantly trying *not* to look at Adele, because Adele could have read the truth in my eyes, or at least she could have read the first couple sentences of the truth, and dragged whole story out of me afterwards. So I didn't look at her eyes. I didn't. I didn't want her to know, yet, that I was dying from a disease called Octagon.

⌖

Kid Crater flew into the sky. Then down to the ground. Impact was registering all over the United States... maybe all over the world. He would go up. Come down. Paladin tried to calm him, flying along with him on the way up (arms around him, hugging him, trying to pull him away from his course, to get him to listen to reason) but even Greg had to bow out of Kid Crater's downward strike... the blast into the rocky soil of the Blue Mountains in Oregon, shattering sections of the slope, crawling out from the debris, screaming that he was an idiot (for giving away his family's identity) and that he would kill Tempest and Macabre and everyone else... everyone else... because the world was a horrible place full of sickness and evil, of hate and horror, and he was soaring up into the sky and down again and again, with SRD helicopters and airplanes nearby, including one wasp-y helicopter with a single front-mounted weapon, a pointed lance of Checkmate's unmistakable design. God knows what that thing could have fired. It made me nervous, then, to be so close to something that could probably kill me. I'd grown comfortable with moving through a world that was ultimately harmless.

I yelled, "Whiskey store!" when Kid Crater was going up into the skies.

I was holding a bottle of whiskey. Waving it about.

I yelled, "Whiskey store!" when Kid Crater was coming down onto a ridge, sending boulders the size of mini-vans dancing down the slope. One rolled close enough to me that I could have reached out and touched it as it passed. I didn't. It might have broken the bottle I was holding.

I yelled, "Whiskey store!" as Kid Crater was climbing out of the rubble. This was the best time to approach him, before he'd built up any momentum. Paladin was trying to hold him (and was glowing that healing glow of his... but he couldn't heal the type of sickness that had driven its claws into Kid Crater) but the kid was taking to the skies again, and I threw the bottle after him, hoping he'd grab it, but it just arced into the sky, four or five hundred feet into the air, then came down a quarter mile distant, making a slight puff of near-disintegration when it landed. By then I'd raced to our liquor cache (we'd been prepared for Kid Crater's sorrows, but not as prepared as we'd hoped) at three times the speed of a normal man, and I was holding up a bottle of whiskey in each hand, shaking them at the blurs in the sky and screaming, "Whiskey bottle! Whiskey bottle," and probably sounding like some pet-owner trying to call home an errant dog. It wasn't an apt analogy, but it wasn't so far away from one, either.

This went on for five, ten minutes. Maybe a half hour. The SRD were growing increasingly unsettled, knowing that they could have (could they have?) taken down Kid Crater right then... put a Checkmate-designed bullet in his forehead... and called it good. If they did this, they were assholes. If they didn't do this, then what kind of assholes would they be if Kid Crater got it in his head (after he'd been so long in SRD's gun sights) to whisk over to Seattle and start making craters *there*, all over the city, instead of on the side of a mountain?

There came a time when even I (for which I hated myself) was thinking it might be best for them to pull the trigger. Paladin had gotten too close to one of the impacts and was dazed, was on the ground, on one knee and one hand, glowing, healing. A Humvee troop transport had narrowly avoided being a casualty (the kid had slammed into the base of the mountain, triggering an avalanche that advanced on the Humvee and would have swallowed it if I hadn't gotten there first and given it a push) and I'd broken seven or eight bottles of whiskey by throwing them into the air (I guess I was hoping Kid Crater would fetch them like a dog, but

I'm honestly not sure) and I had downed two other bottles myself, alone, trying to goad the kid into joining me. You've maybe seen the picture of me (the SRD soldier was nearly executed for releasing the photo, incidentally) standing atop one of the fallen boulders, waving one bottle of whiskey while slugging the other in nearly superhuman gulps. I admit it's a funny photo, of sorts, if you don't dwell on the tragedy behind it.

Only five seconds after that photo was taken, Kid Crater came down, landing right next to me, softer this time, so soft that the boulder barely cracked. He took the whiskey from my hand and told me he'd kill everyone, everyone, everyone, but that he was the worst of them all. He had to die first. Some other words followed, but there was nothing intelligible. He drank the whiskey. All of it. A whole bottle. He was seventeen years old. Not even legally able to drink alcohol, not yet. In a few minutes he was fetal at my feet, curled up and crying, nursing the empty bottle. Soon after that, he fell into a coma, and soon after that (five seconds, at most) he slid from the boulder and fell onto the ground, impacting in the usual manner, like a regular seventeen-year-old kid.

My reactions are fast enough that I could have caught him, normally, easily.

But I was awfully, awfully drunk.

CHAPTER THIRTEEN

I was dressed in a costume. It was not my Reaver costume, but it was a costume nonetheless. It was a ninja costume. I was dressed as a ninja and I was not completely sober. I wasn't drunk on alcohol, and I wasn't on any drugs (Siren once encouraged me to do 'shrooms, which I really didn't want to do, but anyone would have, if they'd seen the gymnastic way she'd encouraged me) but I was, regardless, not entirely sober.

I was high on a sense of purpose. And the thrill of the illicit.

I was breaking into a house where a hero had once lived. His name had been Steve Clarke and he was sixteen years old when a tanker truck had blindsided the police car he'd been riding in, killing the drivers of both vehicles and changing Steve Clarke and Greg Barrows (also sixteen years old) and doing something different to Tom Clarke (being Steve's older brother) and thereafter changing the Clarke household (after some time) into a tourist attraction.

My childhood home wasn't like Disneyland or Disney World or Power Paradise... it wasn't a theme park in that manner... it was more like the houses where Oscar Wilde had lived, or Rasputin, or any other similarly famous but also somewhat infamous characters.

Much of the house had been preserved (or reconstructed) in the manner to which it had been on the last day that Tom and I left it… or at least on the last day my parents left. The paintings were still on the walls (Mom had loved any painting with horses as the central subject, and I'd spent days at rummage sales and estate auctions uncovering and pointing out these treasures) and my old toothbrush (a commemorative G. I. Joe toothbrush) and even a bar of soap that I had supposedly, dubiously, used. Many of my old clothes were there, including the ones where Tom and I had used laundry markers to write swear words (*Fuck*, mostly) and "clever" sayings (*You dropped something in my pants. Here, I'll get it for you*) on the interior of the shirts, so that we could wear them out of the house (Mom and Dad none the wiser) and then turn them inside-out once we were walking the streets of Greenway.

All of these things and more were still there in the house. And… added to them were the seemingly hundreds of plaques (such as "*1970's Yosemite Sam drinking glass: Once used by Steve Clarke*") and the roped-off sections (*This bathroom for display only: Please use the outside facilities*) and a bevy of security cameras that I was glad hadn't been in place when I was a child, or else the world could have been subjected to an endless supply of downloadable videos of me sitting in front of my computer, downloading pornographic videos, idly masturbating to each one of them in turn, trying to decide what fetishes (Cosplay? Rear entry? Bondage? Cartoon porn? Lesbian gangbangs?) would be the soup of the day before really getting down to business.

I hadn't been to the house in almost a decade. Now I was back.

To steal something.

And I wasn't alone.

Adele was likewise dressed as a ninja. In the terms of Halloween costumes, she would have been known as "*sexy ninja*." This wasn't so much because her costume was a mixture of black lingeries and a frilly mask (though it was, somewhat) but because a sexy woman looks sexy in pretty much any damn thing she slides into. Also, illicit activities make women look sexy whenever they slide into one of *those*.

Laura was dressed as a topless pirate, having stripped away her fluffy/frilly pirate shirt in the car when we'd parked the car four blocks away. She was… distracting. She did not look anything like how I would expect an historical pirate to appear. Historically, pirates were almost exclusively men, and they were almost exclusively not of immaculate grooming habits. Laura was wearing an eyepatch (with a hole cut out of it, so she could see) beneath her glasses, and she had pirate trousers, and boots, and a belt and sword. Apple was with us, and had used colored markers to draw a parrot onto Laura's shoulder. It was a reasonable illustration… once it had been explained.

Apple herself was dressed as Cleopatra, a woman that had ruled one empire and nearly usurped another, and she was complete with a rubber asp, which Laura kept calling a rubber ass.

We were a gang of sodden thieves. Myself… I was drunk on the thrill of what we were doing. The women were likewise drunk on the adventure, with Laura and Apple being additionally drunk in the more usual manner.

Because of who I am, I have access to some extremely sophisticated equipment. I rarely use it. Being fast and strong and invulnerable tends to be a good plan, so that's what I go with, right up front. This time, though, I used a nifty Checkmate-invented device to override the security system, the whole damn set-up, and create a loop that would replay the previous night's data feed. Meaning… we could go in and raise hell and everything would be fine.

"You girls wanna see my room?" I asked. If the sixteen-year-old me could have seen this part, the part with me luring Adele, and a topless pirate, and Cleopatra into his room, he would have thought everything was worth it. That is… if he hadn't seen some of the other parts. The parts with Kid Crater. And Greg. And Tom, of course.

"Would it be vulgar if I asked to have sex on Reaver's bed?" Laura asked.

"Sex with who?" Adele answered.

"You're complicating this," Laura said. She was moving down the short hallway on the first floor. The house's caretakers had put the display table (with fresh flowers, Mom's collection of interesting beach rocks, some old mail) on the wrong side. We always had it on the right hand side, because if we had it on the left hand side then the sheepdogs (whenever Dad brought any of them home from the Selood Brothers Farm) would inevitably scamper from the kitchen, run into the hallway, and blindly impact the vase and the table. I wondered if the house's current caretakers still brought in those sheepdogs. They would have done wonders at keeping the flow of the tourists in line.

"We just need to find something we can steal," I said. "We shouldn't stay long."

"I'm a pirate," Laura said. "I steal innocence."

"Nobody here has any of that," I said. "Except Adele."

"Hmm. And that particular booty is clearly marked as yours."

"Watch it, sis," Adele said. "And keep it down." I noted that Adele hadn't actually disagreed with Laura's statement. It made me think of the next few days. Of what might happen. It made me happy. It made me sad.

I tried not to look at Tom's room when we walked upstairs. The door was open, and I could see the posters on the wall. I couldn't help but look to see if the world map was still there. It was. There were still thumbtacks on all the places he'd wanted to visit. Sorry, Tom.

Beyond the glance at the map, I moved on. Apple and Laura started to go into the room, but Adele gestured them back, whispering, "Tom's room," in a voice that I wasn't supposed to hear, but I did, of course. I gave them no hint that I had heard them (I have a good poker face) and we moved on down the hall.

My key hadn't fit in the front door. I hadn't thought that it would, after so many years, but faced with the realization of the failure (I'd had to make sure not to twist the key too strongly, because breaking locks and/or keys is child's play for a man of my strength) I'd become momentarily maudlin (it changed the years that I had carried the key away from being utilitarian into some sort of desperate grasping for the past) and then suddenly happy… because when your key doesn't fit in a door, then it feels more like stealing, and I very much wanted to steal.

"This is on your list, right?" Laura asked. "Going through your old house, stealing things? Nice!" She was moving through my bedroom doorway along with me, pressing into my room. Because she was topless, because she was squeezing through a narrow space, and because she was Laura, and because she was a pirate, her breasts moved against me. It made me feel like I'd done something wrong (it's often terrible, the training that men go through in life… the hoops through which nurture forces us to jump, even when nature thinks everything is fine, just fine) and I quickly (at three times normal human speed) looked to Adele. She just rolled her eyes. She'd lived a long time with her sister. Apparently, this wasn't anything new.

There wasn't much that was new in my room, either. My bed was still there. It was the same bed, because it had the same scratches where I had put in the initials of all the girls in town that I'd wanted to date. It was a code that nobody else could have cracked, not even Checkmate himself. Sure, "*AL*" (the largest letters) might be linked with Adele Layton, and "*LL*" might refer to Laura Layton (sorry about that, future Adele) but how could "*TTG*" be linked with anyone? What girl had "*RHT*" for her initials? The answers (*Ticket Taker Girl* & *Red Haired Tourist*) were known only to myself. I wondered if Adele had written about these coded mysteries in any of her blogs, articles, or books. I couldn't possibly ask, though, without giving away all the codes, including GTO (*Gorner Twins, Obviously*) and that damning LL, so I just ignored my (seemingly ancient) bedpost scratchings and fondly ran my fingers along a set of Sherlock Holmes novels, editions from the 1950's that had been my grandfather's. They were still on my bookshelf, still the same books (my grandfather's name, Roger, was written with faded letters on each of their spines) but now arranged with several books that hadn't been mine. Books on science. Medicine. Philosophy.

"Some of these books aren't mine," I told the three women in my childhood bedroom.

"I know," Adele said. "I was the first one to spot it. Of course, I'd been here before." Laura started to say something, but Adele continued, drowning her out with, "And then when I came back, a few years ago, I saw that there were different books. Nobody is willing to admit it, but I think it's because you were supposed to be a shining light, retroactively superhuman and superhero, so SRD planted books that made it look like you were a whole hell of a lot more studious than the average teen boy."

"I was studious, but it was for war stories and how to get girls into bed. Which reminds me..." I trailed off (it was probably a poor moment to trail off, in that situation) and went into my closet. There used to be a folder in there that had a collection of photographs (torn out from the worst/best of my Uncle Buzz's selections of decidedly odd porno magazines) and a paperback copy of *Teenage Time Hero*, an "Erotica House" publication concerning a boy who learned how to stop time, and who then went on to save the world from a nuclear holocaust, meanwhile stripping a good number of girls naked and waking them up from their time freezes when he already had them in compromising positions. The women (sometimes in groups) were always happier about it than I suspected most women would be, but I did love that book. Tom had given it to me. I'd kept it tucked beneath the winter blankets and the board games in my closet.

It was gone. The folder was gone. Was it more of SRD's intervention? It might have been, but at the same time my parents might have done something with the folder and the book; they'd had plenty of time when I was laid up in the hospital, and then afterwards while I was training at SRD.

"Looking for something?" Adele asked.

"Old perverted things. A folder. A book. Somebody threw them out."

"Damn," Laura said. "We never get to hold onto the perversions of our youth. *That's* what's truly perverted."

Adele said, "It would have been weird to break into your old home and steal your teenage porno stash, anyway. Don't you want to take something of value? I mean, personal value?"

"You've never been a teenage boy. That book had immense personal value. But… what I really want is some of my parents' pictures. A horse painting, maybe. Some old photographs. By the way, you look sexy as a ninja."

"Thanks. I feel sensuously sneaky. Should we go to your parents' room?"

"Can Laura and I stay here?" Apple asked. She was spread out on my bed. A pretty Cleopatra was on my bed. She was tugging a pirate to her side.

"No!" Adele answered for me. She could see exactly why her sister and her somewhat-of-a-date wanted to stay, for a bit, in my room.

"Don't destroy my childhood dreams," I told Adele, tugging her from the room. I think if I would have done anything else, my childhood self would have ejected himself from the past and soared into the future to give me a well-deserved bitch slap. That bedpost wasn't covered with initials for nothing. As I pulled Adele from the room (I closed the door, because it would have just been weird, otherwise, or at least it would have been tipping the scales to the much-too-weird, otherwise) I resolved to sometime return (I had a short few days for a window of opportunity) to carve a ":P" behind the "LL" on the bedpost (meaning Laura Layton: Pirate) and then add on an "AQN," meaning *Apple, Queen of the Nile*.

Adele and I, two ninjas who were now alone, crept into my parents' bedroom. It was much as I remembered it. The queen-sized bed. The dresser drawers. The exercise bike. The small table where Dad liked to read the morning paper and have his breakfast on days when my mom was out of town working on video shoots. She'd been the aide to a videographer specializing in political commercials. She hadn't been political herself. She'd once told me that, having met so many politicians, she'd come to a conclusion that they were all just bundles of shit packed in boxes of arrogance.

There weren't as many personal items in my parents' bedroom. There weren't any personal photos at all. I suppose I should have expected that. They'd had time to pack what they wanted, in those initial few weeks of my becoming Reaver, when I was first training at SRD, and before they had moved to the *Mysterious Place That They Moved To*. They would have taken anything that meant a lot to them, although I'd heard they'd been instructed to destroy any pictures of me. There was no way they could take the chance of someone looking at their family pictures and saying, "*How adorable. Your son looks just like a young Steve Clarke, which makes you his parents, which means I should call Octagon right now, or maybe the tabloids, and either way I guess you're royally fucked. And... oh! Steve looks so adorable in those short pants*!" Likewise, they'd taken every photo of themselves or the rest of the family. Couldn't have anybody touring this house and saying, "*What a nice photo of that couple, who are, incidentally, dead ringers for that couple I saw in XXXXXX.*"

Paladin had mentioned to me, several times, that it was lucky, for him, that he'd run into the accident at the sheep farm, busting his nose right before coming into his powers, because that one thing... that one slight disfiguration, was enough that people never really connected the two faces. Well, in his case, it was *that one thing*, and the fact that nobody could believe Paladin had ever been human, or, better put, couldn't believe that there was a time when he *hadn't* been *superhuman*. In my own case, people wanted to believe in scandals, in things that would strip me down to size... to make me level with the masses. Or below. Anyway... the photos were gone.

Besides all the photos, my parents' clothes were gone, which was fine by me, because there are probably men who would want examples of their dad's undershorts or their mother's lingerie as a memento, but I don't number myself among that ilk.

"Here's a good painting," Adele the Ninja said. The painting was one of a horse munching on meadow grass. A mountain in the background. A setting sun. Bright colors. I looked for anything menacing (Mom had told me that the painters of such subjects, the professional ones, would often get bored and therefore subversive) but there were no clouds formed into suspect shapes, or open barn doors from where glowing red eyes were peering from the darkness, or any groups of flowers that had been slyly arranged to form any vulgar words or body parts. I couldn't remember the painting from when I'd lived there, though. The thought of Mom finding it at a garage sale, spotting it all by herself, buying it while I was laid up in the hospital or punching a lion and thereby stealing a year of its life, that was heart-rending for me.

I said, "No. Another one. I can't remember that one." My eyes were already on a simple painting of a peasant woman holding up a bouquet of flowers so that a horse (only its head and front shoulders were depicted) could nibble away at the petals and stems. It was a painting that my mother had loved. She'd wondered about the story. Had the woman picked the flowers for the horse, or had someone given the flowers to her, and she'd afterwards decided to feed them to the horse? If that latter… why?

The painting now had a plaque that read, "Unknown Artist: Circa 1950's." I thought about taking the plaque as well, but decided against it. It belonged to nobody but those who had decided to turn my house into a tourist attraction. I wasn't exactly angry about that, and from a legal standpoint I had every right to be in the house, and every right to take what I wanted, but… there was still a part of me that was very glad that I wasn't asking for what was mine; I was taking it.

The painting had a simple wire hanger, but one that was wound around a screw that was bolted to the wall. It would have taken a normal man a good tug to tear it loose. For me, it wasn't much of a fight.

"This is nice," Adele said. She was inspecting a rock in her hands, moving it around in her fingers. It was a fossil of some sort. I've always loved fossils. The tabloids would probably say that's because I have a desperate desire for the past. The tabloids never let anyone love anything out of love. It's always desperation.

The fossil was a complete ammonite. Looked to be from the Cretaceous period. It was about the size of my hand, with the shell appearing like a tightly curved ram's horn. It was very familiar to me, and when Adele, noting my interest, handed it to me, the memory came flooding back.

It was the fossil I had found on my last (real) day in Greenway. The one I'd pocketed out at the quarry with Tom and Greg. I'd put it in my bedroom before sneaking off to the Selood Brothers Sheep Farm to see if we could find out any secret information concerning Warp living in Greenway. Instead, we'd found sheep shit and that ubiquitous date with destiny that the poets like to talk about. I hate poets, and I hate most dates with destiny. One thing about destiny is that it only ever goes on blind dates.

"We have to take that," I told Adele. I told her what it was, and when I had found it. She nodded, eyes wide, as if it was suddenly an artifact rather than a fossil. The house abruptly became smaller to me, more oppressive, and I realized how many mental land mines were inside, waiting for me to stomp my big fat foot right on them.

"Does your sister usually take long to… do… things?" I asked Adele, losing momentum in the description.

"You mean… do I think her and Apple are done in your bedroom? Probably not. But I can roust them if you need me to. Are you okay?"

"There are a lot of memories here. They're suddenly grabbing at me." Adele was the only person in the world to whom I would have told that truth. No wonder I stayed away from her for nine years. Telling the truth is a difficult thing.

"Let's get you out of here, then," she said, understanding what I was talking about. That helped. Being who I am, being Reaver, it's easy to think that I'm the only one with certain types of problems, as if it takes being doused in radioactive stem cells in order to want to forget the mistakes you've made in life, and the things you've lost.

We moved down the hall (not looking at Tom's room… not looking at Tom's room… not looking at Tom's room) on our way to my oldest sanctuary. We didn't reach its safety before Adele put a hand on my shoulder (it seemed stronger than Paladin's hand had almost ever felt) and, then, without looking at me, she said, "Your list. The will. It's like, you're closing your life down. You better not be coming back to me just so that you can leave again, Steve Clarke. You better not be doing that."

I stood silent.

It played out for a time.

I realized I needed to say something.

I said, "I don't have any idea what I'm doing." It seemed an insufficient answer, but Adele accepted it. In a few moments (that stretched out longer than Taffy's arms) she looked up, did that smile of hers, and then stepped to my bedroom door and raised her hand as if to knock, but her smile transformed her into the exact visage of mischief, were it ever given a face.

"Should we knock first, or barge right in and scare them?" she asked.

"Shit," I said. "I never thought I'd have to knock on my own bedroom door, but this time I think it's best if..." That was as far as I got before Adele, without knocking, threw open the door.

Then she blushed.

And closed it.

Quickly.

And we just waited outside.

CHAPTER FOURTEEN

I suppose I should talk about the death of Kid Crater. It started with me in a bar, getting drunk, which is not something I do three times faster than a normal human. It actually takes me several times longer, because my healing abilities fight against the inebriates. Paladin was the first to notice that whenever I'm really drinking, whenever I'm *really* drinking, there is a soft green glow being emitted from my mouth.

I was at a bar in Idaho, on the outskirts of a small town named after some pioneer of some renown at some time in the past. It would have been nice to live in those frontier days, when you could put up a house and declare the surroundings to be a town and it would be named after you, rather than in today's world where the town would be named after your corporate sponsor, so that *Less Fillingsville* would be twenty-five miles from *Tastes Great City*.

At 7:30 in the evening (I'm going to skip on how long I'd been drinking by that time) the waitress (an attractive brunette who I still hadn't put off) carried something to me, a lump of metal, lugging it with both hands and an expression of confusion blended with a touch of anxiety. She placed it on my table (with a thud that startled those at the nearby tables… all the couples having their early dining dates and who would be gone when the serious drinkers arrived to begin their day) and then just looked to me as if I should have a comment in place for whenever a waitress (in this case one wearing a shirt that read, "*Not Available, but thanks for checking!*") places a lump of twisted metal (about the size of a full-grown cat) onto my table, knocking over an empty glass (I was drinking whiskey from a glass in order to appear civilized) that falls within mere inches of the floor before I grabbed it with a speed that is three times faster than normal, making her raise an eyebrow either in regards to my speed or the fact that I'd still been able to make the grab even after running up a good sized tab.

"Well?" she said.

"Well… what?" I asked. "Why are giving me a clump of metal? Is this some local initiation rite I should know about?"

"A woman said to give it to you. She's outside. Said you'd know what to do with it." That was confusing to me. What woman gives out clumps of metal? I inspected the twisted mass closer. It looked to be engine parts, swirled and smashed and mushed together, as if by someone of great strength.

And there was a piece of paper caught in the middle of it, with one edge sticking out, so that the only way to read the note was to twist all the metal aside and…

I picked up the mass of metal and began twisting it, ripping off some bits of metal, peeling others back. Watching me do this, the waitress's entire body shuddered, like she was resetting the whole works, and she had to lean on the table for support. She'd known that I was Reaver (my face is memorable, and the media keeps it on news reports, television specials, the front page of newspapers, and on every conceivable website) but here was the evidence right in front of her.

She said, "Shit. You… Reaver… you're…"

I said, "I know. I'm strong." Bending the metal took little effort. The difficulty was in twisting the metal in ways that wouldn't tear the paper.

The waitress said, "My name. Do you want my name?" I already knew her name. It was Erica. I also knew what she really meant. That's how some women (and some men) react when they see me do something at a superhuman level. It makes some people (not even exactly a minority) go weak in the knees, and in their morals.

Ignoring the waitress, I took the paper from the peeled-open onion shell of the engine parts. The note was handwritten with penmanship that was feminine, but not flowery. It read, "Outside. We will talk. You and I. This time, I promise I will not drop you from the sky." It wasn't signed, but...

Stellar.

I told the waitress, "Close the bar. Keep everyone inside. There's going to be a fight."

"A... fight?"

"Yes. The woman who gave this to you... what did she look like?"

"Tall. She was wearing a hoodie. I couldn't see much of her face. Definitely not from around here, though. Weird thing was, she knew my name, but..."

"It was Stellar. Keep everybody inside. I'll lead her away from here."

With that said, and with people at the nearby tables standing in fear or excitement, I raced for the door, still carrying Stellar's note for some reason, as if I felt I'd have to present it to her in order to validate my invite.

Outside, it was just a parking lot, surrounded by trees. There were cars. Mostly trucks. Mostly dusty. There was a highway running past. There were two dogs that were tied up to a water faucet that came out from the wall of the bar. There were two women talking about plans to get the local school system to provide better lunches. There was a boy trying to climb a tree, trying to hug around its base and shimmy upwards. There was a posting area for local events... all the dances and rummage sales and farmer's markets and certified yoga instructors. There were birds singing. It didn't seem at all like a super-villain setting.

Until the hoodie came floating down from above.

I looked up. Should have looked up in the first place. Not doing so was as dumb as how people are never ready, no matter how many times they've fought me, for how I can move at three times normal speed.

Stellar was maybe a hundred feet in the air. The sun was behind her. Shining. Glowing. I had a moment to wonder if she was really from the stars... if Sol itself was just a relatively close waypoint for her. I had a moment to note that the two women were looking where I was looking, were trying to understand what was happening, to comprehend what they were seeing, to grasp what was about to happen. One of the women (late thirties, a dress long enough out of style that it was due to come back into fashion, a button nose on an otherwise unphotogenic face) reacted even before I did... yelling for the tree-climbing boy (Johnny! *Jonathan*!) to come back, to come back *at once.*

And then Stellar swept down and had me underneath my arms, clasped in her arms, was shifting her body slightly, arcing her direction away from the ground, away from Shaner's House of Food and Spirits, and up into the sky. The note fell away from my fingers. Fluttered off into the wind. We were travelling at a good speed. Faster than Paladin had ever carried me. I wasn't struggling. I wasn't fighting back. I could have punched Stellar. I could have done something. I *ached* to do something. But I waited. I waited because she was taking me over the woods. Taking me to where we could fight without any collateral damage, or at least human collateral damage, meaning that biding my time was a smart thing to do. It was, in fact, about the last smart thing I would do for the next hour.

Because Stellar took me into the woods.

There was a clearing. A creek engaged in a churning escape from its mountainous point of origin. There were large amounts of flowers being excited about the sunny day.

Stellar placed me lightly (relatively… I only bounced twice) on the ground.

She landed nearby.

And started taking off her clothes.

This wasn't something I expected. There was no preliminary. Nothing with her giving me that smile that women give when they've decided to kick at whatever fences are keeping track of their boundaries.

Stellar is a tall woman. She has that Nordic appearance that makes it seem like she must be from Earth, but there's a vastness to her character (not an expansive vastness, but rather that she's always seemingly light years away) that tends to make me believe her extra-terrestrial claims are valid.

She unhooked her cape, first. For a second I envisioned her as some sort of matador, using her cape to lure me (in the role of the lumbering bovine) closer, so that I might be repeatedly stabbed. Instead of waving the cape about, however, she simply dropped it atop a group of checkermallow flowers, then ran a few fingers through her short blonde hair, smiled for a tenth of a second (what the hell was she up to?) and began peeling off her skintight body suit. Beneath it, her body was colored much the same… stars on a field of black, as if her body were formed of the universe itself.

And she did have big tits.

Though I'm a small breast man myself.

It took me all the time that she was undressing before I was able to come up with, "What the hell are you doing?'

"I dropped you from space."

"Is this some sort of erotic apology?"

"Somewhat. We should breed. We are the dominant species."

"I'm human."

"Humans cannot survive being dropped from space." She was moving closer. I wasn't moving away. I was already making a wrong decision. It's the defense of a drunken man to say he was drunk, but of course you make that decision to *become* drunk, so you're culpable all the same.

I wasn't really all that drunk, anyway.

We said some more words. I said the right words, but didn't live up to them… just kept making good words and bad decisions. Suffice to say that I couldn't help but wonder what it would be like to run my hand along a torso that seemed almost as if were the universe itself. For the record, it felt almost exactly like a woman, but one that would have burned my fingers if I hadn't been, as she said, a man who could be dropped from space.

I had her cape tied around her eyes and was making her hold flowers in her teeth, braced on all fours, me working behind her, when Kid Crater landed in the clearing.

I found out later (investigating the incident, talking with Erica, the waitress from Shaner's House of Food and Spirits) that Kid Crater had come to find me, to meet me where I had said I would be, and he received the news of how Stellar had carried me off, how the nefarious and evil woman named Stellar had swept me into the woods, and he had flown off to my rescue.

And he found me.

He didn't land softly. Just wasn't his style. He crashed into the ground, creating a cavity that forever changed the course of the creek. He stood up from the landing, glared at me with an expression of hate, dripping mud and water, and then took to the skies so quickly so that for one moment there was an afterimage of him in place, a three-dimensional shadow shaped in the form of the mud his speed has left behind.

"The boy is angry," Stellar said. She grunted it out. We were still doing what she'd brought me there to do.

"Shit," I said.

Kid Crater curved through the sky and then slammed into the ground again, this time with a trajectory that sliced through an assortment of ancient white pines on his descent, shearing them into wooden debris and tens of thousands of sliver-like leaves creating a *shussssshhh* sound in the air, a whisper beneath the booming of the trees that were being flung about. One of the trees bounced and rolled against Stellar and me... knocking us apart, and then all the pine needles landed around us, coming down like a swarm of locusts.

"What the hell?" I yelled at the kid, but I should have already known what the hell. The mystery was on my side. The mystery was why someone who was *supposed* to wear a white hat wasn't currently wearing any pants, and was (only moments before) having sex with someone who wore a black hat (meaning that in a metaphorical sense... as the only black that Stellar was currently wearing was the *deep space* coloration of her torso) and was known to associate with those who had viciously killed the entire family of Kid Crater, my friend and my sidekick.

So, yeah. What the hell?

Stellar, mad, grabbed the trunk of one of the fallen trees, shearing the branches from along its length with beams of energy from her eyes, creating a barren trunk that she used as a giant club, swatting Kid Crater from the sky just as he was soaring back up to the clouds. If the blow had been struck when he wasn't in flight, when his invulnerability wasn't fully charged, it would have killed him outright. As it was, he fell heavily to the ground, cursing, and calling out the names of each of his family members, again and again.

Stellar was on him in moments, rearing back for a punch that would have killed him, but I... moving three times faster than a normal man, had her by her arm, still thinking I could settle them down, that I could defuse the situation, still dumb enough to believe that I could calm down a boy who had lost his entire family and had then found his mentor having sex with one of the enemy, and I was likewise still thinking that I could talk common sense into Stellar, whose mind wasn't well-hinged at the best of times, let alone when she was enraged and horny, both.

I tossed her to the ground.

Turned to Kid Crater.

He flew into me. I don't mean that as an overly enthusiastic description of what he did. He didn't just start fighting me; he flew into me. And when he was flying, he was the strongest of any of us.

He had me by my throat, using my head to take us through the trees, all the white pines and the Douglas fir and the white larches… all of them just brittle things to Kid Crater when he was in flight, but not so brittle from my perspective, since he was using my face to batter through them, to reduce them to explosions of flying wooden shards, with me trying to twist free and remembering (a hard task, with trees exploding on my face) that I couldn't hit him (no, no, no, no, no… don't hit him) but at the same time wondering if I *should* hit him, if I should strike him again and again until he was old enough to understand the situation, to calm down.

But of course that's not how my power works. People don't mature when I hit them. They just get older.

And, anyway… I was older than Kid Crater, and my maturity wasn't doing much more than telling me that Kid Crater was the one in the right.

Stellar slammed into him from above, taking the three of us down into the soil of the Idaho forest, a soil that I immediately stained green with the glow coming from my head and shoulders as they clicked into overdrive trying to heal the damage that had been done to me. Just the physical damage, of course. The other damage would never heal.

I was the last to recover from the collision.

When I crawled up and out of the small pit, Stellar and Kid Crater were wrestling on the ground. A still photo of the moment would have seemed erotic. She was naked, and smiling in triumph, and atop him, straddling his writhing form. He was trying to take to the air, arcing upward, attempting to buck her free so that he could soar again, could transition into flight, where his invulnerability was at its strongest. He was looking to me for help, because his rage had stepped aside, just for a moment, to realize that being in the right doesn't always mean you win the fight.

I would've had to move five times faster than a common man to reach them before Stellar's fist came down.

That's beyond me.

I can't do that.

Kid Crater died in Idaho. In the Panhandle National Forest.

In her defense, Stellar hadn't started the fight, and was just protecting herself.

In my defense, I have nothing.

CHAPTER FIFTEEN

I was wearing sunglasses so that nobody could recognize me. I was with Adele. We were occasionally touching hands, but not quite holding them. She was pointing out a house to me. There were children in the yard. Two of them. A boy and a girl. About six years old, each. I was stuck between going into the house, simply walking by, or continuing to stand on the sidewalk and staring at the house and the children for so long that it was beginning to look suspicious.

The boy had a small stack of paper and was making paper airplanes, one after the other, and flying them at the girl. Occasionally one of these constructs would actually make the small flight and bounce off the girl's arm or head, but most of the airplanes would simply curl away from her, or crash straight into the ground. The boy was not a master of aerodynamics. I didn't hold that against him. I can't make a decent paper airplane, either.

The girl was idly digging in the ground with a small spade, and whenever a paper airplane would hit her she would, while barely paying attention otherwise, drive her spade down through the paper airplane, slicing it in half. I thought of something to say to Adele, something in regards to those paper airplanes and how it was only the successful ones that were being punished, how the failures were allowed to go on with their lives, but when I was trying out the conversation in my head I found (mentally, in my scenario) that Adele would eventually (rather quickly, in my scenario) tell me that I was being too god-damned maudlin, and she would be right. So I just kept quiet.

"Those her kids?" I asked Adele, instead.

"The girl is Judy's from her first marriage. The boy is her husband's from *his* first marriage. I can't remember their names."

"How long after Tom… how long after the accident did Judy wait before she got married?"

"That's unfair. Judy was sixteen years old when you and Tom had the accident. She was *sixteen* years old. She had to go on with her life."

"True," I said, leaving it at that, at least out loud. In my head, though, I was feeling that Judy should have gone into eternal mourning, like Taffy had with Paladin. Judy shouldn't have moved on. Tom and Judy should have been together forever. She was the last love of his life. He should have been the last love of hers. It was unfair, and I knew it didn't make any sense, but Tom was my brother and that's how I felt.

Also, in my mind, I was avoiding any mention of how I'd been in that accident, too, and if Judy had possessed all the right in the world to go on with her life afterwards, then why hadn't Adele? Why had she written books about me, studied me, from afar, with me not dead, but never calling, and why had she opened her door the very moment I came back? I began to realize that the tanker truck accident had killed a bit of her life, too. Had stolen away her years, not even giving her any superpowers in exchange.

And here I was… stepping back into her life for one more week before my promised meeting with Octagon and his laser pistol. What was I stealing from Adele this time?

"What do you need to talk to Judy about?" Adele asked. She was wearing a dark green skirt with a single embroidered bird. It shifted with her every move and her sandals made pleasant scuffs on the sidewalk. Across the street were five young teenagers who had been following Adele and me on their bikes. They were having a big day. They were watching Reaver. I didn't mind that. It was something I've grown to accept as normal. But two of the boys had (my hearing is very good) made comments about Adele. About her tits. About what was under her green skirt. I hadn't liked that. I realized I was feeling proprietary. I wasn't liking that, either. It was dumb.

I said, "I wanted to talk to her about Tom. About the accident. About the days when she and Tom were together."

Adele started to say something, but I raised up a hand, stopped her.

I said, "I wanted to talk to her about that, but now that I'm here... that's not fair, is it?"

"That's not fair."

"I still want to see her again. And I have something for her."

"Something of Tom's?" Adele's eyes had narrowed into a "*that's not fair*" face.

"No." Adele's eyes calmed down.

"Then what?" she asked.

I said, "You have to understand. Doing what I do, the money builds up. There are donations from people I've helped. From cities I've saved. From countries, even. It's kind of sad, but nobody knows how to say thanks except with fat wads of cash."

"And... you're going to give some money to Judy?" Adele was already making the connection. Reading, like always, like from the start, my intentions.

"That's what I'm going to do."

"How much?"

"Couple million. Do you think she'll mind?"

"People don't mind when you give them two million dollars. But... aren't you now doing what you just said was sad? I'm guessing... I'm guessing you want to tell Judy *thanks* for making your brother happy, back then, but... like you say... nobody knows how to say thanks except for those fat wads of cash."

"Just because I can bend steel doesn't make me any smarter than anyone else. Besides, I'm going to tell her thanks, too. She really did make my brother happy."

"All those handjobs," Adele said. She made a smile. She made a handjob gesture, then even a blowjob gesture. There were hoots and whistles from across the street, from all five of the teenagers. This time, for some reason, it didn't irritate me.

Adele and I walked up to the house, and I knocked on the door.

⌖

Mistress Mary had been seen in Argentina, in Bahia Blanca. Shortly after this, she was spotted in Fortaleza, Brazil. Then in Medellin, Colombia. Then in Campeche, in the Yucatan. Then in Cabo san Lucas, Mexico. Then in Oakland, California. Then, finally, in my hometown of Greenway, Oregon. I followed each of these reports, fed to me by SRD surveillance teams, and I tracked her progress on a map up until she walked down the middle of Greenway's old main street (the tiny, original one, from before all the expansions) and she was facing me as I stood in front of the Ferkins Antique store. By then, of course, I didn't need the updates.

In Bahia Blanca she had stopped two murders. In the old days, before her recent surprise induction as a member of Eleventh Hour, being brought in as a unexpected replacement for Macabre, Mistress Mary had stopped such crimes by the simple expedient of ordering the prospective murderers not to do it. To instead get honest jobs and lead honest lives. Coming from Mary, that was enough. Her voice had something to it… some quality… some superhuman factor, that made people give in to her every demand. This time, in Bahia Blanca, she told the would-be murderers to kill themselves. They did.

In Brazil she merely lounged on the white sands of Iracema beach, doing very little, committing no crimes except telling the merchants that they shouldn't expect her to pay for anything (so they didn't) and telling the occasional beach-goers to put on some more clothes, or to take them all off, according to her preferences. In Campeche she did nothing but shop at an art gallery. She bought three beach scenes from a local painter. She paid for them. In Cabo san Lucas she stood in the public square with a bullhorn and instructed any nearby pickpockets to return their stolen goods. Three people did as they were told. In Oakland, she walked into a bank and asked for seventy thousand dollars and instructed the tellers and the management that they were not to consider it as a robbery. These people dutifully debated with FBI personnel over the alleged "theft," denying that Mary had done anything wrong.

In Greenway, in Oregon, Mistress Mary was carrying a gun.

She had been travelling for three days.

In those three days I'd managed to grow more comfortable on Adele's couch, and she hadn't invited me upstairs again, not since that first night. I was more comfortable that way, because I already felt that I was setting her up for a fall, and sleeping in her bed would have done nothing more than increasing the height of the plummet.

In those three days I'd been flown (on a Checkmate-designed helicopter that I admit my inner twelve-year-old would not stop raving about) to the Athens Penitentiary to quell problems stemming from the recent escape and riot. There was some media talk that I, me, just myself, constituted cruel and unusual punishment. It's wonderful to be loved.

In those three days I began the process of the legal papers for the scholarship program in Kid Crater's honor. I went with *excellence in academia* as the criteria, and had christened it the "Impact" scholarship. Each year, four students (one nationwide, and one from Minnesota, where Kid Crater and I had met, and one from Nevada, where he was from, and one from Idaho, where he had died) would receive a twenty-five-thousand-dollar scholarship. There was an addendum to the award… one that required recipients to drink a glass of whiskey in Kid Crater's honor… and to at least try to get out and meet people and have a life. It didn't seem like either of my demands would be too onerous on any college student.

In those three days I had been summoned four times to SRD. Adele had come along with me twice. The first time they turned her away at the gate, considering her as a security risk, owing to her books (and the secrets they had spilled) on the topics of the superhumans. The second time, I had insisted that she was allowed to come inside, mentioning that if she needed any superhuman secrets she could certainly get them from me, and also mentioning that I didn't think Checkmate's forcefields (such as the ones on the guards' uniforms) were powerful enough to stop me if I decided to peel someone out of their armor and dunk them in the nearby Willamette River if they continued to be such assholes. The four meetings (all with the head of SRD, meaning Commander Bryant) had concerned Mistress Mary (twice) and then a report that a recent earthquake (near Thailand) might not have been normal seismic activity, and then I was also asked to give advice on how to deal with Mindworm and Warp, because a jury of their peers was decidedly hard to come by.

In those three days Adele and I had, like when we were first dating, repeated our purchase of several boxes of dog biscuits (buying them from a young woman at the Mighty Convenient convenience store, one who had gleefully watched as I, at her request, squeezed a handful of quarters into a solid metal chunk, an act which was a felony-level destruction of U.S. currency) and had gone around the streets of Greenway (mostly the old streets, not within the mushroom-like eruption of the new city) and had further gone into an assortment of yards, giving biscuits to all the dogs, either reinforcing the old friendships (rarely) or making new ones, depending on the ages of the dogs. It was much easier for me, this time, as I didn't have to worry about any of the dogs biting me, excepting for how they might chip their teeth.

In those three days I had masturbated once, in Adele's shower, when I realized that I was holding a bar of soap that she had rubbed all over her body. I felt very guilty about this… excepting during the actual *orgasm* part.

In those three days I had done very little to prepare me for the sight of Mistress Mary holding a gun, even though ongoing surveillance (which she did not seem to mind) had placed her as on the way to Greenway. What did Mary need with a gun? Her mouth was her weapon. We'd played on the same side of the law, together, for several years, and she'd never carried a gun. We'd played on the same side of the bedsheets, together, for several weeks, and she'd never carried a gun. She'd had some other objects, but never a gun.

I told her, "You have a gun." I pointed to it, just in case she wasn't smart enough to know that she was carrying a gun, like she would glance down to it with a look of disgust and surprise in the ways that people do with bugs, when a friend points out that they have an insect crawling on them.

"I'm part of Eleventh Hour, now," she said. "I have a criminal reputation to uphold."

"Why did you…?"

"Join them? Because I couldn't talk Octagon out of it. He wanted to recruit me. He gave me reasons. They seemed reasonable."

"Money? Power?" These weren't things that had ever attracted Mistress Mary in the past. She had always been comfortable (though often somewhat cold, or slightly bitter) with thoughts of saving the world. Never… ruling it.

"I'm not here to fight you," Mary said, going past my words. Then she raised the gun and shot me. The gun was a .50 Desert Eagle, which is the gun of people who want to look like they're holding an imposing weapon, as opposed to someone actually holding an imposing weapon. I suppose I should point out that the weapon is still very effective. If I'd been a normal person, it would have punched a hole through my chest with ease. As it was, the bullet smashed into my chest and then rebounded off down the sidewalk, impacting a mailbox with a sharp echoing twang. The sidewalks and the surrounding street were entirely empty. I'd yelled out warnings when I saw Mistress Mary approaching, and, for once, people had actually moved away from the impending danger. I wasn't sure if it had anything to do with these people living so close to SRD, living day to day with the knowledge of superhumans, or else maybe it was just that small town people are, in some ways, smarter about keeping themselves alive.

I said, "You didn't come to fight me? So, why did you come here? Just to shoot holes in one of my good shirts?" It was a brand new button-down shirt. A blue one. Adele and I had gone shopping for clothes. She'd bought a new dress. Some new shoes. Some underwear she mentioned felt good against her skin. The underwear had been more to the level of lingerie. I'm not sure where the dividing line between *female underwear* and *lingerie* stands, but her purchases were certainly closer to the latter. Myself, I'd bought two dress shirts. It seemed like that would be enough to get me through the rest of my life.

"I'm just a calendar," Mistress Mary said. "Or, rather, I'm here to enforce the calendar. I'm going to be in town in case other members of Eleventh Hour come here, wanting to kill you. Kill you before it's time, I mean."

"Octagon sent you? He's concerned about other members of Eleventh Hour going against his promise? Is there some sort of schism in your team?"

"There's some sort of schism."

She began walking away, yelling loudly, loud enough to be heard for blocks, that there was no reason to be nervous about Mistress Mary being in town. People began appearing from houses. Coming out from locked doors. From closed storefronts. After all, there wasn't any reason to be nervous anymore.

"Why did you bring the gun?" I asked Mary.

She said, "I like them, now."

CHAPTER SIXTEEN

Apple was a competent and confident driver. Laura was a pestilent passenger. The two of them were taking me (according to their claim) to the best coffee shop in town. I was, against all my better instincts, about to do an interview. I hate interviews.

"Why isn't Adele here?" I asked Laura. Adele had said she was coming along. Laura smiled at my question, narrowed her eyes, then decided I might not be getting the full effect of her narrowed eyes with her glasses in the way, and so she moved her glasses down a bit on her nose so that I could bask in the questionable glory of her amusement.

"Suddenly can't live without her?"

"Suddenly wondering why I'm stuck in the middle of the jungle, with all the wild beasts, and my safari guide has vanished."

"He's calling us wild beasts, I think," Apple said, sliding into a turning lane, avoiding a bicyclist who was weaving through traffic in seemingly unpredictable patterns, but she had guessed his intentions perfectly. She was way ahead of him.

"We're all wild beasts at heart," Laura said. "The interesting ones, anyway. Now, Steve, look at *this*. I send these videos to Adele all the time, but she never looks at them. Or, I mean, at least she never talks about looking at them. She blushes when I talk to her about them. Sometimes I wonder if…"

"Show him the videos," Apple said. "You're being a tease."

"That's the first time anybody's ever called me that."

"That's the first time a *girl* has ever called you that," I said. There was a moment of silence in the car, then both of them burst out laughing.

"Suuuh… lammmed," Laura said. "Slammed!" She high-fived me in shared amusement, then handed me her laptop computer. It was decorated with stickers from an SRD-themed gift store (unauthorized, but allowed) that was in the new town square. There were photo-stickers of Paladin, and Mistress Mary, and a couple of me, and one of my, "*Take some time off!*" slogan, but mostly there were stickers of Siren, and Siren, and Siren, and Siren.

"Don't you dare tell me about sleeping with her," Laura said, tapping on one of the Siren stickers. "I mean, I know you did, but don't soil her with any of your penis-oriented stories." I couldn't tell if she was serious, and, anyway, she was hitting "play" on a video.

The video began.

In it, a man dressed as me (as Reaver, I mean) was in combat with a woman dressed as Stellar. I was glad it wasn't one of the films with Taffy. Those always made me feel like I (who had nothing to do with their making, of course) had done something very wrong. This film was Stellar, though, and it was a reasonable likeness. She'd been cast well. Laser beams were coming from her eyes, but I (the actor, I mean) was standing tall against them, laughing them off. In reality, the beams that come from her eyes aren't very much like lasers (more like a concentrated stream of agitated protons) and they hurt like hell. Also, I am not as tall as the actor who was portraying me, while Stellar is taller than the actress who was playing her part.

The two actors were fighting in a motel bedroom setting. That part was close to reality. Stellar and I have certainly done that. We'd fought three times after the Kid Crater incident (which I never really blamed her for, because I was too busy blaming myself) and two of the fights had gone to carnal encounters, and the third had led to me being deposited from space again. I was hoping the porno actors would reenact that at some point, though with special effects, because that shit hurts.

"Take some clothes off!" the Reaver-actor said. He slapped Stellar on her ass, and her cape flew away from her as if by magic.

"Take some clothes off!" the Reaver-actor repeated, giving "Stellar" a kick (a good and powerful one, too) in her butt. More of her clothing magically disappeared.

I told Laura, "First of all… my kicks and my slaps don't do the thing with the years. They don't. Second, why are you showing me this?"

"Because they're funny! I *love* them! Adele watches them, too. I mean, she watched some of them because of her superhuman studies, but I think she, you know, *watches* them, too. There are like, hundreds of them on the internet. Thousands, maybe. Some of them are live action, like this one, but most of them are animated. Did you know about this?"

"Did I know that people create literally thousands of porn videos centered around me? No. I was completely unaware."

Apple, backing the car into a parking spot, parallel parking at a level that was (in my honest opinion) nearly superhuman, said, "I think he means *yes*. In fact, I think he means *duh*."

Laura said, "No sass from my girlfriend, please."

Apple said, "I'm your girlfriend?" On the laptop computer, in the video, a woman (a woman?) dressed as Macabre had run into the scene, waving a magic wand and yelling, "Presto! Presto! Stellar lost her dress, oh!" More girls began appearing, popping into the scene as if by magic (or, in this case, by means of not very convincing special effects) and swarming Reaver, trying to… I'm not sure… defeat him somehow? He fought back by means of a method that did not include his pants. I closed the laptop.

"Can I talk to you about Adele?" I asked Laura.

"Yes," she said. Hopeful. But wary. "Remember my warning, though. If you hurt her, I'll hurt you. I'll… I don't know… find some way to contact Octagon and hire him to do it."

"The first night I was here, Adele said she was an alcoholic. Or had been. Is she okay now? What happened?"

"Shit. I hate being serious. Look… she took your break-up hard."

"We never officially broke up."

"I hope you didn't mean that in your defense, because it means you're even more of a dick."

"You guys want to be alone for this?" Apple asked. She'd turned off the car and was reaching for the door handle, ready to step out if we asked her to, but obviously very much not wanting to leave.

"I accidentally called you my girlfriend," Laura said. "So now it's official or something and I'll have to change all my online statuses."

"Does that mean I can stay?" Apple asked. The two of them looked to me. I shrugged.

"Adele drank because of me?" I asked.

"A little. Somewhat. Mostly," Laura answered. She was stowing her laptop in a duffel bag, avoiding my eyes. Usually she likes to look me right in the eyes. Confrontational. I was happy she wasn't doing it. I was sad, too.

"She went to the hospital, a lot, when you were in the coma. Then… when you were transferred, she asked around, a lot, about where you'd gone. But you were secret, then, for a year at least."

"The training."

"Sure. Adele started dating a boy, then punched him when he tried to kiss her. I said she should date girls so they wouldn't remind her of you. But, nothing worked for her."

"Shit," I said. I'd screwed up Adele's life, apparently. Could I have saved her with a phone call? An email? I'd always been too afraid. I can remember thinking the only reasons for my fears were that my enemies would use her against me. Or that they would simply kill her. I can remember not at all thinking that I was a coward.

Laura said, "She started drinking in college. Not like she was partying. Just drinking. Alone, mostly. There were a couple one-night stands. One-week stands. That sort of thing. You probably don't want to hear about them."

"I don't."

"She bought a Reaver costume at a Halloween store. Kept it in her room. She said… and you can't ever tell her I told you this… that she wanted boys to try it on, see if sex would work for her that way."

"Didn't Steve just say he didn't want to hear things like this?" Apple asked. Laura leaned over and gave her the sort of kiss that means, "*be a good girl and keep quiet.*"

Laura told me, "It never worked for her. I mean, she never tried it. She was actually trying to forget you, but… hey… were you trying to forget her? Seriously. Tell me the fucking truth."

"Yeah, I was. But... not because I wanted to forget her. I just... at first I wanted to come back like a hero, like a superhero, and I was biding my time... caught up in some asshole power fantasy, and then afterwards, after some things happened, I just didn't want her to get mixed up in all this." I made a vague gesture with my fist, waving it a bit. Laura understood what I meant.

"Fuck," she said. "That really sounded like the truth." She went silent for a bit and then added, "Thank you."

"If you guys don't want me to stay...?" Apple said. She was reaching for the door again, but, again... doing it slowly. Laura leaned in and gave her another kiss, making it stand as her answer. Apple smiled, nodded, moved her hand away from the door. A middle-aged man, strolling by, walking with a hot dog in one hand, carrying it like a baton he would pass off to the next hungry man, caught a glimpse of the two girls kissing. From his viewpoint, from him looking into a car and seeing two beautiful women kissing, and a man in the backseat, he probably thought things were going better for me than they actually were.

Laura said, "So, Steve, if you were trying to forget Adele, you probably had the easier time of it. You didn't have to put up with her on the news, day after day, saving people from burning buildings, or kicking a bank robber's ass, or dating some incredibly beautiful woman, or fighting magicians, or battling mysterious men in black... you didn't have to have her pushed into your face a hundred times a day." Laura's eyes gleamed at that last bit, and her serious mood wavered, but she stabilized and remained serious. I felt guilty about it.

Laura said, "So... failed relationships. No life direction. My sister was drinking. She drank a lot. Way too much. I was really worried. I wrote you a whole bunch of times, but you never answered."

"I never knew you wrote." The words came out hard. I wasn't feeling well. Apple met my eyes and I wanted to change places with her. I wanted to be the one that could have stepped out of the car. I hadn't known that Laura had written me. I never look at letters, emails, videos, any of that stuff.

Laura said, "I know that, now. I knew it then, too. But I was desperate to save my sister and I finally realized that she was never going to kick her Steve Clarke addiction, so I told her... why not get her fix anyway she could? So she started writing articles about you, and then the others, you know, the *others*, and pretty soon she was a world-leading superhuman researcher. And she's happy, now. So don't you fuck it up."

"I don't know…"

"None of us knows shit, Steve Clarke. None of us knows *shit*. If there's one thing I do know, though, it's this: Adele isn't fooling. She does love you. And it's not some sick *Reaver* fantasy thing. She knew you long before that, and I was the one who endured her nights of *really* sappy talk about the two of you. So don't think she's playing around. She *loves* you."

"I can't think of anything more wonderful," I said. And I meant it.

What I didn't add, what I didn't say, was that I only had three more days to live. Two days in Greenway. One day of travel in order to keep my promise to Octagon… to meet him and Eleventh Hour wherever he wanted us to meet. So, yes, it was the most wonderful thing in the world to hear that Adele Layton loved me.

And it was also very much the worst.

⌖

The interview in the coffee shop went quickly and efficiently and wasn't all that much of a pain. This is largely because I forbade Frank O'Neill (Channel Five's long-time "*On the Spot*" reporter) to ask any questions having to do with me being Reaver, or any of my exploits in battlefields, or beds, or combinations of the two. This frustrated him, and I admit that I enjoyed his frustration. I'd spent some time in the early days (the early days of me being Reaver, before I began to refuse all interviews) being battered by reporters' questions of morality in terms of who I was fighting, and why I was fighting, and how I *felt* when I was fighting (especially in the moment that I had just punched someone) and why I always (in truth, after a time, very rarely) felt so much superior to everyone else. Paladin had looked upon such interviews as not only a necessary part of being superhuman (he claimed that the more familiar people were with us, the more accepting they would be) and, besides that, he enjoyed talking with people. With anyone. I enjoy talking to people. But not with anyone.

This current interview kept mostly within the bounds I'd established. Laura and Apple sat at one booth over, after promising to control themselves and not disrupt the proceedings. They kept their word by staying behind the camera, but watching (with the sound off) another of Laura's beloved superhuman porno parodies, occasionally holding up her laptop so that I could see what they were watching at any given time. This meant that, on the nightly news, with the camera trained on me, it might seem as if I was looking off into the distance, pondering some question that Frank O'Neill had posed, thinking (with my inscrutable and arguably inhuman mind) on thoughts beyond the ken of the common man, but in reality I was trying not frown at a cartoon video of myself and Leviathan (seriously? Leviathan? The size difference alone would... hell... never mind) engaged in carnal activities, or trying not to look interested when Laura and Adele held up the computer together, in tandem, giving me a thumbs-up as the video depicted a mass scene of myself (an actor, of course) in bed (on a bed that was, for some reason, on a rooftop) having sex with five women that were dressed as Siren, as Mistress Mary, as Dark Mercy, as Stellar, and a female version of Warp. Perhaps my most uncomfortable moment was when, as I was presumed to be thinking of how I felt about Greenway's sudden growth, Laura was signaling for my attention, holding her hands approximately ten inches apart, flicking her eyes towards the laptop computer and the (extremely well and perhaps overly endowed) Reaver actor, and mouthing the word, "Really?"

Despite these interruptions, the interview went well.

What were some of my favorite memories of Greenway? Searching for fossils with my friends. Standing together, one night, with Greg Barrows atop the Mighty Convenient convenience store, throwing rocks down into the parking lot until Tom (who was working that night) came out to investigate, and then Greg and I had tried to pee down onto my brother, which I admitted was gross, and juvenile, and all that, but I noted in my defense that Tom had, the night before, given my parents a complete list (gleaned from my computer's history) of what I'd been masturbating to recently. There was a voice in my head telling me not to say such things (and that voice was Paladin's, as it normally was) but I figured what the hell... I wouldn't be alive much longer anyway. Might as well have some fun and tell the truth for a change.

Would I ever think of living in Greenway, again? Of course I would think about it. There's something about being home that makes a man think in terms of progress. You go away, and you move at your own pace.

You develop. You whittle yourself away until you think you've created the person you want to be. And then, out there on your own, you grow comfortable. There's something about coming home that makes a person take a good hard look at that comfort. Sometimes that jumpstarts another growing process. Sometimes it ditches everything.

Did I have any pets? Kid Crater used to have an eagle that followed him around. Just for a couple weeks. Damndest thing. Sure there are pictures of it, somewhere. He named the eagle Tiny Dynamite. Hell of a name for an eagle. Myself, though… no. No pets.

Had I visited my house again? Of course. Hadn't gone in, though. Wouldn't mind it. I'm sure there are a lot of memories, inside. (There had been no reports of a break-in, and I wasn't about to spill any beans during a coffee shop interview.)

What did I think of Greenway's changes? Too soon to tell. I was just getting used to them. Lot of houses, though. There sure were a lot of houses.

Favorite sport? Soccer. Or… women's beach volleyball. Soccer for the beauty of the game. Women's beach volleyball for the beauty of the players.

Okay then, speaking of beautiful women… was I single?

As he asked this, Frank O'Neill leaned closer, his eyes narrowed. I could feel the camera zeroing in on my face.

It's funny, with all the things that I do and that I've done, with having battled individuals who have leveled city blocks, with me having once single-handedly overthrown the dictator of a small nation, with me being a man who's climbed into the core of a nuclear reactor in order to perform a mechanical operation and avert a complete meltdown, with my long-time battle against the Mexican drug war, with how I've used a barrage of punches to slide an array of superhumans incrementally closer to death, with me being the man who walked into a combined flamethrower and automatic weapon barrage, on live television, to rescue Senator Blykes when he was being held by the Sol Gone Anti-Advent Society, with me having been friends and partners with a man who was the clear and current front-runner for the *Jesus of the Modern Age* … with all of this and a hundred (maybe a thousand) other such peculiarities and incidents… reporters always seem to think the hardest-hitting question they can level at me is, "*Getting any lately*?"

I don't think my answer would've been any different if Laura Layton hadn't been sitting one table over. If her head hadn't snapped up and her eyes hadn't trained on me. If she hadn't closed her laptop (so quickly that she nearly caught Apple's fingers) in order to focus all of her attention on me. I don't think, I honestly don't, that my answer would have been any different if Adele's sister hadn't been there to catch my eyes with hers and silently demand that I tell the truth. I don't think my answer would have been anything different than the one that went out over the airwaves to a waiting world, not two hours later.

"I'm in love, Frank," I said. "But I don't know what to do about it."

CHAPTER SEVENTEEN

The winds, as we began our drive home, were strong. We were going first to the Super Eight Grocery Emporium, where Apple worked, a store with *eight... eight... EIGHT ways to save*, a message that was drilled into my head when I was a kid by means of a constant barrage of commercial ditties played during every prime time television show.

Apple parked in one of the first available parking spots, thankfully not one of those people who will spend fifteen minutes driving around in order to save themselves fifteen seconds of walking time. Laura mentioned that sometimes carrying groceries to the car can be annoying, because they get so heavy, but since *Reaver* was with them, they wouldn't have to worry about that.

"How much can you lift, anyway?" she asked.

"In terms of groceries?"

"Yes. Of course. Olympic athletes are always lifting crates of watermelons and bags of rice. No, idiot... pounds. How many pounds can you lift?"

"I've never really measured it precisely." This was a lie. SRD had made me measure *everything* precisely. One day, on my best day, I'd managed to lift the equivalent of a bit over thirty-two thousand pounds. That's a lot of watermelon.

Apple reached over and felt my bicep, pretended to be thinking, and said, "According to my gypsy upbringing and incredible mental acumen, I'd estimate Steve can lift... oh... thirty-three thousand pounds."

"Close," I said. I tried to remember if the data had ever been published. Of course it had. There's little about me that hasn't been published.

"Are you really a gypsy?" Laura asked. "And... why's it so cold? Let me check if I have a sweater." She rooted around in a couple bags in the back seat of her car, paper bags full of clothes, shoes, toiletries, etc. I wondered why she had them in her car. After some thought, I came to the obvious answer.

"Sweater!" she said, pulling a blue cardigan from the bag. It had the design of an iconic sun embroidered on one side of the chest. It reminded me a little bit of Paladin's design. My mind leaps there a little too often.

"You need something, too?" Laura asked Apple, who shivered a bit, frowned, glancing to the sky and then around the parking lot before saying, "It *is* cold, isn't it?" The two of them fished through the bags, came up with another sweater, one that was a bit too big for Apple... though it only made her look adorable, in the manner of a petite woman in larger clothes.

"Probably nothing in here that's going to fit you, Steve," Laura said. "And, even then, unless you like embroidered kittens...?" She shrugged. She blinked. Dust had gotten into her eyes. The parking lot was dusty, and the wind was flinging the particles here and there, like a suburban sand storm.

I said, "I'm good. Regular temperatures don't affect me."

"Regular temperatures don't affect me," she repeated, in a mocking grade school voice. "Because I'm Steve Clarke and I have..." She stopped when my phone beeped at me. I took it from my pocket and peered at it. Laura tried to peer at it, too... but Apple stayed respectively distant. Of course, she could have been relying on Laura to relay the information.

It was a text message from Adele. It read, "I'm planning such a great surprise for you that you should definitely kiss me."

Laura, reading it (damn... she read it fast) said, "Oh, sis. Dummy. It's not a surprise when you tell people it's a surprise. Where's Mistress Mary when you need her? She's still in town, right? She could order Steve to forget he ever read that message."

Apple said, "Mistress Mary's command powers don't work on Steve."

"Really?" Laura said.

"Really. Don't you read your sister's own writing? She wrote, like, four articles on it."

"Not much of a reader. I mostly sit and paint. Or stand and paint. I have body paint. We could lay down and paint."

I said, "If you two want me to leave...?"

"You have to carry the groceries," Laura said.

"And buy them," Apple added. "You're still the only millionaire here. At least until Laura starts selling her paintings at Sotheby's."

"I'll pencil that in for next Tuesday," Laura answered, trying to tug a shopping cart from about thirty of them in a corral, all of them stuck into each other like a sexual conga line of metal-framed rabbits. I thought about telling the two girls about my shopping cart metaphor, but didn't want to get them started.

We moved down the store aisles. Apple mentioned her substantial employee discount. It made buying foods easier. It's hard to try new foods when the prices are as towering as Leviathan. I noticed, not for the first time, how many store advertisements used superhumans to sell the product. We were assured of Stellar tastes. A Siren's call of savings. It wouldn't take Mistress Mary to convince us that Super Eight is #1 in customer satisfaction. Other signs proclaimed similar messages.

There were other customers in the store who began following us around, trying to stay on the opposite ends of aisles, trying to pretend that they were looking at canned spaghetti, fresh bagels, jars of olives, anything besides what they were really looking at. Four people (a young couple, a plump housewife, and a young man with, "*I'm all for anarchy if that's okay with you*," written on his shirt) all had the guts to ask me for an autograph. Normally I would have turned them down. I didn't. Nothing felt normal anymore. I signed a sketchbook (full of competent drawings of grizzled old faces) for the young couple, and I signed the young man's shirt. The plump housewife (Eva, her name was Eva, mentioned four times) had me sign her arm, and then I posed for a picture with her, which Laura took, and afterwards Laura told me that Eva (Eva... Eva... Eva... Eva) would probably masturbate to it, at some point.

I said, "Not everything has to do with sex." I was a little irritated, frankly. Eva had seemed nice enough, and had said that she appreciated what I do... the parts where I put my life on the line. Her father (she mentioned this twice) had been a police officer. She knew it was a burden on him, and she couldn't see how it would be any different for me.

"Not… everything has to do with… sex?" Laura repeated, as if she were rolling the words around in her mouth, trying them out for sound, trying to understand what the words could possibly mean.

My phone beeped again.

I reached for it, but thought better of it. Laura's eyes were a bit too curious.

"Mind kissing her?" I asked Apple, pointing to Laura.

Apple said, "Huh? Sure! Why? You want to *watch* us, or…? Oh. I get it. Pucker up, girlfriend."

The two of them kissed (Apple took off Laura's glasses, first, with a wink at me) and I took the opportunity of their distraction to look at my phone message. It was another text from Adele. Laura, even while locked to her girlfriend's lips, swiveled her eyes towards me, but I'd been a couple steps ahead of her and there was no way she could read what it had said.

She asked about it.

A lot.

She asked about it when we were buying cake (apparently it was needed for a surprise party for an unnamed superhero they knew… though by that time I could guess).

She asked about it when we were buying stuffing. And bananas. And grapes. We bought red grapes and green grapes because none of us could decide which was best, and then we added in wine because it seemed like we should complete the theme.

Laura asked about the message again (earning her a pinch from Apple) when we were grabbing pasta and shrimp and the makings for a sauce that Apple swore would taste exactly eight times better than Siren's kiss.

Laura asked about the text a few more times, but I kept quiet about the truth of it, dropping red herring hints that it had been from Octagon challenging me to a tennis match, or hints that it had been from Commander Bryant, saying that a 30-foot cockroach was on the loose, and dropping further false hints (or I guess, more accurately, false statements) that it had been from the head of the United Nations, appointing me as ambassador to an incoming alien fleet, and I even dropped hints that it had been from Mistress Mary, ordering me to tell Laura Layton to be quiet.

But what I didn't say was the truth.

It had been from Adele.

And it had said, "*I've been thinking about my earlier text, and... Steve... seriously, I do think you should kiss me. I think you should do that.*"

It was... pleasant to see it, right down in real words, where I could read it, again and again. I kept taking my phone out. Looking at the words. There were still there, every time.

When we paid for the groceries, and went outside, the wind was howling.

Howling.

⌖

The first time I ever met Tempest (which is also the first time I fought her, because the number of times that we have met *exactly* matches the number of times that we have fought) was when Paladin and I, some time after leaving the Minnesota cabin, travelled to Ecuador in order to try to root her out of her growing cult, which was centered near Guayaquil, along the coast, drawing converts from the wealth of banana, cacao, and coffee plantations.

Paladin had been earlier negotiating with Tempest, trying to coax her into surrendering herself for the crimes she'd committed in the United States, but she was not only insane (even Paladin should have realized this) but had done an admirable job of inserting herself as a local goddess, Misevályue herself, reborn. Misevályue had been a mythological weather goddess, and the mother of all dancing and singing. Tempest could easily play the part of a weather goddess (it could even be debated, theologically, that she was one) and the members of her growing cult were taking care of all the *dancing and singing* aspects. There were a few sacrifices involved. Goats. Chickens. Foreigners.

When Paladin received SRD word that I'd been killed (as the initial reports said) by Stellar (and how she had dropped me from space) he'd left Tempest behind and flown to Virginia to find me, to pinpoint the spot where SRD tracking satellites had placed my descent. He'd been astonished to find me alive (I'd been no less astonished) and we'd forgotten all about the feud that had divided our partnership. I'd recovered in the Minnesota cabin, aimlessly hiking, watching wildlife, and swimming beneath the lake

(I can't breathe water, but I can hold my breath for… oh… an hour or so) in order to let the bemused indifference of the fish ease what was already becoming, even then, a somewhat melancholy heart.

Of course, Paladin's departure from Ecuador had been taken as a sign that the old gods (which Tempest was considered) had defeated the new gods (as led by Paladin) and by the time he (now with me tagging along) returned to the jungles near Guayaquil, Tempest's cult had grown considerably. Christian churches had been torn down, or else had their roofs removed (often with less than surgical precision) so that the goddess's flock could be in constant communion with the sky. Tempest (I watched one of the "sermons" while in disguise) would float down from above, and she would (somewhat) talk of the importance of nature, with her pure white naked skin and flowing red hair transporting her adherents to various types of rapture. When her words were finished (the devout found them enigmatic, while in truth she was simply raving) she swept two members of her congregation up into the sky along with her, carrying them away. It was supposed that she was transporting them to heaven, to a better place, but of course the truth is that she was carrying them to a nest (made of nearly solid winds) in the clouds, a place where she would have sex with them, and then kick them out of bed. That last part was problematic for her partners, because the floor of the "bedroom" was a long ways down.

I can't say that it probably mattered much, though. Tempest was about twenty percent lightning, and her own orgasms were nearly always fatal to her partners. Still… some went willingly. Paladin blamed me for standing by and letting her take two of her flock, but I'd told him that if you piss on an electric fence (or, more aptly, stick your dick into a electric socket) then you deserve the shock of what you get in return. He hadn't calmed down until I told him (being only somewhat honest) that I'd had to make a hard choice of letting the two men go… or else endangering the rest of the congregation.

We'd defeated Tempest. Whisked her off into proper custody.

The battle had been fierce, and I'd punched her a few times, and Paladin had done his part… keeping her on the ground and within my range, even with lightning playing all over his body… pushing her to the earth, where I could be Reaver, doing what I do.

It hadn't seemed like she'd aged much (I must have punched her thirty times) but some of us have elongated life spans, now, and that probably played a factor. It had certainly affected her, because she began to scream, and in her screams (witnessed by masses of her worshippers, several of whom died while trying to move closer to the site of our battle in order to help their goddess) she began to pray, and she prayed to the Christian god, the popular one, and his son Jesus, and his Virgin Mary, all of which was heresy according to her cult. Why pray to Miseválybe (meaning, of course, Tempest) when she herself was praying to another god? Nobody likes a second place divinity.

Paladin healed a few of the injured before we left.

That got them started again.

⌖

The second time I met Tempest was very brief. I happened to be at SRD (we were studying if it was possible to reverse the effects of my punch, which it wasn't, for those who keep track of such things) when Tempest broke free from the holding cell where we'd stashed her. It had been thought that she needed to be conscious in order to control her powers. We (even Checkmate, oddly) had been wrong about that.

She'd frozen some of the circuits that held her in stasis, dropping her free from the time field. She'd never hit the floor, only hovered (held up by winds) in the holding center, slowly recovering from the drugs. The whole base had scrambled. Full lockdown. Red alert. Lights and sirens. Two soldiers had gone into the holding cell in order to attempt to administer further drugs (it was a mix of quinine and strychnine and, I believe, prussic acid… a mixture that would have killed a thousand or more normal people) but they had been frozen in blocks of ice (they actually survived, which shows Tempest was off her game) and by the time I reached the facility there was a gaping hole in the roof, the dying remnants of Tempest's laughter, and a cloud formation that even a porn star would have considered vulgar.

She was gone.

Escaped.

Three days after that, she was a member of Eleventh Hour.

⌖

The third time I met Tempest she was teamed with Macabre and they were tearing down satellites from space. We all remember this one. We all remember how Earth's atmosphere, for an hour, expanded nearly to the moon, so that there were suddenly a quarter million miles of storms in what had been the dead of space.

I'd battled her briefly before she soared into the skies (and then into space, and then into space that became the skies) and was out of my range.

Octagon took her down that time. *Unauthorized rampage*... he'd said. *Interference with some of his key investments*, he'd said.

Tempest and Macabre had suddenly fallen from the sky as if a switch had been thrown. I'd have given my left nut to know how Octagon accomplished that. Even if I hadn't known for sure, being who I am, that my left nut would grow back... I'd have served it up on plate to knock Tempest out of the sky.

⌖

The fourth, fifth, sixth and seventh times I met Tempest had all been battles. All of them. Most of them with Eleventh Hour involved. We had each survived the battles, though that particular statistic was dicey from both sides. In fact, it could be argued that the seventh time had been fatal, for me, since it was only by delaying my death, by convincing Octagon to give me a chance to prepare to die, that I'd been allowed to walk away.

⌖

The eighth time I met Tempest she was hovering above the parking lot at the Super Eight Grocery Emporium, watching Laura Layton and Apple, her girlfriend, taking groceries from my hands and putting them in the back seat. The three of us, below, looked up and saw the woman hovering in the winds above, and then cars all around us were being sucked into the skies by the tornadoes.

CHAPTER EIGHTEEN

It's never been made public why Paladin and I had our falling out. The truth of the matter is that it has a lot to do with the creature that the media liked to call Devil Mole. If you remember, the Mole had been one of Octagon's genetic experiments, and had grown beyond what Octagon had planned. Word was (this was from Siren, who was dating Octagon at the time, and sleeping with me at the time) that the Mole had grown into nearly human form. I'd originally (before I fought him) pictured some sort of were-mole (which sounded terrifying and hilarious, both) but in reality, when I finally encountered the creature it was more along the lines of a teenage boy with extensive boils.

What happened (again, according to Siren, who, it must be remembered, never lies to a man) is that Octagon had created the creature, trying to turn the animals of Earth into beings we could all converse with. For what purposes I wasn't sure. An animal army? A vegetarian crusade? Skilled and unobtrusive spies? I have no idea. Octagon's brain operates at levels I don't understand. His reasons are his own.

What Octagon hadn't planned upon was that Devil Mole's abilities to converse went far beyond speech; Octagon had created a telepathic creature... one that could link his conversations directly, mind to mind, and could even control another's thoughts to some extent, and to know what people were thinking, and so on and so forth. We're talking about extensive mental abilities, here.

A hundred thousand moles gathered beneath the lab where Octagon was keeping Devil Mole. This was before the public was aware of his existence. This was before he'd shut down New York, and before the mass destruction in St. Petersburg, or the animal uprisings in Africa and, well... everywhere.

This gathering of moles was even, of course, before Octagon discovered Devil Mole's plan. Discovered them a little too late, as it proved. Siren has told me of Devil Mole's escape... the battle with several of Octagon's other genetic manipulations... the griffins (the ones later dubbed the *Flying Tigers*) and the giant insects and all the others. Siren said (she was difficult to pay attention to, at the time, because she was writing some of the key words on her naked body) that one hallway... the one down which Devil Mole made his escape, was littered a yard deep in thousands of bumblebees the size of a man's fist. That image has always stuck with me, partially because that's a lot of bumblebees, and also because, telling me of all this, Siren wrote the word *bumblebee* on her stomach, with an arrow pointing down.

Devil Mole announced himself to the world, shortly after... maybe a week after his escape. By then half the burrowing animals of the entire world were under his control, or at least on his side. My SRD psychiatrist (we all of us, us superhumans, have our own individual SRD psychiatrist, and I'm not sure if that should make the public feel better, or very much worse) told me that I should understand that all of the moles and voles and earthworms and groundhogs were going to see this as their first ever religion, their first ever god, and to think in those terms when I was dealing with them.

I said, "Are you really going to tell me how to best go about debating theology with an earthworm? That's really why I'm here today? To learn how to best facilitate a groundhog's conversations about its personal beliefs?" My psychiatrist (Eleanor Rackham was/is her name... that's a freebie for the tabloids) had said something else, but by that time I wasn't listening anymore; I was only waiting for a moment to tell her that we were through talking. We were. I haven't spoken to her since. The whole thing was ridiculous.

Most of what happened above the ground is known. Most of what happened below the ground is not. Paladin and I were chosen (and chose ourselves) to go down into the tunnels. Warp guarded the entrances and exits for the first few hours, until he had one of his incidents, and then it was Dark Mercy (grabbing all the headlines) and Tattoo. This was, of course, before Tattoo's disappearance.

The tunnels alternated between rough hewn (and barely passable) tubes, to stone corridors that might have been manmade before Devil Mole was ever around, but mostly it was natural systems of caves and caverns.

And Paladin and I fought every inch of the way through. Thousands of animals. Not just the burrowing ones. Other things. Darker ones that maybe Octagon had created, or maybe they came from somewhere else. That was one of Devil Mole's big messages: *not everything comes from human intervention*. When you tally up the score sheet, in fact, most things don't.

I was using a Checkmate-designed flashlight (of some metal that even I could barely dent) and Paladin was good all by himself, because that shimmer of his emits a glow that's bright enough to make do.

There was so much blood that my flashlight was in need of constant cleaning, and all of the caves and caverns and corridors were tinged red by its light, and green by the glow of my wounds. Paladin, of course, remained as pure as when we'd been jackass enough to enter the tunnels. Nothing stuck to that shimmer of his. Nothing.

I was sliding on the uneven surfaces. At no previous time in my life had I ever considered how damn slippery blood could be. Half the time, down there in the tunnels, I couldn't get any goddamn traction.

Paladin wasn't having any such problems. He was floating through the corridors of stone. Flying, even beneath the Earth's surface. There were several times that I lost my footing and only Paladin's outstretched hand kept me from sliding down some forsaken offshoot tunnel to *who-the-fuck-knows* what fate.

I was lost.

He knew which was to go.

It was that vision of his. He knew which direction had the worst of it… where the nastiest of the evil was at… where the worst of the problems were lying in wait. So… that's the direction we went.

It took days, weeks, years, it seemed, before we reached Devil Mole in what amounted to his underground lair. I was shocked, later, to find out we'd only been down in the tunnels for six hours. I couldn't believe it. Literally couldn't believe it. There's a video, I've seen it, where I'm making a jackass of myself by calling a reporter a liar. He'd said we'd only been gone for six hours. I couldn't believe it.

The media has taken some of my words, the ones relating to what we saw down there, into meaning that we found Devil Mole atop a throne made of thousands of bones. That's not true at all. That's making it all sound too *human*. There wasn't any throne. There wasn't any culture. I've seen tabloid depictions of the underground chamber that made it seem as if Devil Mole's lair was the throne room of some baron or count or a princeling aspiring to the crown. In reality, it was dank, and earthy, and bloody, and caked with feces. It's true about the bones, though. There were thousands of bones. Most of them were human, as far as I could tell. Most of them accounted for the hundreds of *missing person* reports that had come in from all over the globe. Paladin has recounted that all of the bones were stripped bare… that there was no flesh, no stench… just bones.

Paladin was wrong about this.

Paladin always had such focus. From the moment he saw Devil Mole, that was all he saw. He didn't see the side rooms… the adjoining chambers, where there were hundreds of bodies strewn all over the floor, impaled on stalagmites or hanging from stalactites, even fused into them, somehow, as if some of the citizens of New York (in particular, the block that had been pulled under on that dark night of October 3rd) had been in the caverns for tens of thousands of years. It didn't make any sense. Nothing we saw made any sense. Maybe I hallucinated. It could be argued that I'd gone a little mad by that time. In fact, it can't be argued that I hadn't.

And there was a stench.

There was a horrible stench.

Devil Mole was not sitting on a throne made of bones. He was scurrying over a huge pile of them, and his words were thrusting into our minds.

The rats, the moles, the groundhogs and a thousand permutations of monsters related to these creatures, they all fought our entrance into that cavern. Even the lichens were against us, somehow, whispering things to us, warning us away, screeching that we would be killed, that it would be our blood, in the end, that stained the walls. Soon, the screams of the earthworms and the lichens turned from taunts into a chanting sort of pleading. This happened, of course, at a time when it became clear that Paladin and I could not be stopped. That we could, at best, only be injured, and we were both of us men who could heal from any wound.

Devil Mole's creatures died in waves. Like the rats in Octagon's arena, these creatures were short-lived, for the most part, and two or three contacts with my fists would end their show, steal away the lives that they had dedicated to Devil Mole.

And finally, the waves of our foes receded and Paladin and I were standing in front of Devil Mole.

Negotiations for his surrender began.

I was not a part of them.

I could not, in fact, believe these negotiations were even taking place.

This was a creature that had shivered a frightened world into a standstill. That had made each of us, every human in the world, acutely aware that we were on the edge of a mass extinction, an overthrow of the dominant species. The two of us, Paladin and I, were amidst the corpses of a million dead bodies (I'm not positive of the real number, but I'm sure that my perceptions were skewed, as it is still hard to believe we were only in those tunnels for six hours) and it had taken two of the most powerful superhumans to even gain an audience with the creature that had orchestrated the whole show. What happened if, next time, the two of us were gone? What happened if, next time, we were on *his* side? The last bit sounds unthinkable, but, standing so near Devil Mole, the pimply near-human creature, his mind was working on my mind, making me question things that had no question.

Considering this, considering all of this, I was shocked when Paladin began to dictate Devil Mole's terms for surrender.

Surrender?

There couldn't be any surrender.

There could only be death for Devil Mole.

So when Paladin was talking about his negotiations, about the terms of surrender, I moved as quickly as I could (at three times the speed of a normal human, taking even Paladin by surprise) and I slid past my friend and drove a fist though Devil Mole's skull and into his brain.

As Devil Mole's corpse dropped to the ground, sliding against the wall and ending up crumpled against stones caked with blood and bones, Paladin just stared at me.

As the creatures there in the cavern shrieked, as they were suddenly bereft of their communal mind, their collective voice, they began to scatter, to escape, to quiver in panic, to fight amongst themselves, and as all of this was going on around us, Paladin just stared at me.

He stared at me as I closed my eyes (I could feel him watching me, still, because that's who he was) and tried to search through my brain in order to make sure, make positive, that all of the various voices (guilt, accomplishment, disgust, etc.) in my brain were mine and mine alone... no longer spoken or tainted by Devil Mole.

Paladin stood aside, slightly, as I knelt on the ground (brushing aside a mass of earthworms to make room for my knee) in order to make sure that Devil Mole was dead.

Finally, Greg Barrows said, "I was talking to him."

"I wasn't. That's not why I came down here."

We were silent for a time. I could feel him wanting to speak, but not wanting to say whatever words were on his lips. I won't, here, pretend that I knew what he was going to say... that I had any premonition of the upcoming rift. Yes... he had surprised me with the talk of surrender, but I honestly felt, at the time (and even more, now) that I had not only done the proper thing, but the only possible thing.

Finally, Paladin said, "You know I see the world differently, right? Not just... morally... but I see... it's hard to explain... I see *intent.* In simple terms, and this isn't quite right... but in the simplest terms I see *good.* I see *evil.*"

I said, "So?" There was probably a lot more to say, but that's all that I said. The animals, all of the creatures, for the most part, had escaped into tunnels, or ran off down stone corridors, but the stench of the cavern remained. It was a presence. It was immense.

Paladin said, "So... Devil Mole... he *wasn't* evil. He just... wasn't like us. We can't expect him to live, to survive, by our own moral code."

"That's all we can do. That's exactly what we have to do. That's how *we* survive. That's how anyone survives."

It could have stopped right there. That could have been the end of it. Paladin and I were different people, and we already knew that. We could have stopped right there. Instead, we said some more words, and then after that we went up into the open air, and to the media and the crowds, and we pretended we were both friends and we pretended we were both heroes. But we weren't, and we didn't talk for months afterwards. Not until Greg, misinformed, thought I was dead.

Down below, in those caverns, standing next to Devil Mole's corpse, I'd been fool enough to say, "So… you can see evil, then? Really?"

Paladin said, "Yes. Essentially. That's true."

I'd asked, "Then… what do you see when you look at me?"

And Paladin had said, "When?"

⌖

One by one, all around us, all of the cars were sucked into the sky until the parking lot was nearly empty. What remained was only myself and Laura Layton, and her girlfriend Apple, and our car, and all the groceries spilled around. Above us, a hundred cars were whirling in the air. Centered around a woman.

Laura said, "Is that… is that Tempest?" As if there was any doubt.

Apple said, "That bitch!" She picked up an orange and threw it into the sky. It didn't hit anything. It didn't come back down. It wasn't much of an attack, but it was all we had, so I emulated it as best I could, substituting Laura's car in place of the orange.

I can't throw a car very far. A block at the most. They're unwieldy… that's the problem. And a car isn't the most accurate projectile ever devised, either. An arrow is shaped like an arrow for a reason. For the same reason, an arrow is not shaped like a 2011 Lexus. But… it was all I had.

It missed, of course, as I knew that it would. It was just a distraction. I won't pretend that I wasn't hoping it would soar into the air, aided by the very winds that Tempest was creating, and smash into the completely naked near-goddess, knock her from the air, send her crashing to the parking lot pavement where I could once again make my way into the headlines as not the most morally sound of all the heroes, with websites screaming that I could have saved her (she was beautiful, after all) and moreover that I *should* have tried to save Tempest, instead of making her into the Very Big Puddle in the grocery store parking lot, amidst all the cars that had fallen from the sky.

But... none of that mattered. I missed.

I missed, as I knew, in my heart, that I would. The distraction was only so that I could gather up Laura and Apple (tucking them under my arms) and make a play for the safety (ha ha ha) of the grocery store. I can run at maybe seventy miles per hour. Hopefully that would be enough.

Winds, of course, can move a good deal faster than seventy miles per hour.

I hadn't gone very far before I knew that I wasn't going to make it. The winds began tugging at my back, trying to take me into the air and to wrest the two women from my grasp. Laura and Apple were both screaming, but their words were lost in the chaos of the tornadoes that were playing all over the parking lot, and the crashings of the cars within them. Debris was raining down from above, falling from the sky and impacting all around, like a flock of metal birds brought down from the skies. These metal fragments were almost immediately gathered back up by the scouring winds, lifting them into a sky so black and so roiling with motion that it looked as if it were a pit of black lava, one that was above us, one that was erupting, one that we were falling into.

I wasn't going to make it to the grocery store.

I wasn't fast enough.

If I was going to make sure that we weren't sucked into the skies, I was going to have to escape in another direction. I was going to have to go down.

I began stomping on the parking lot's surface, driving my feet down into the pavement, sending concrete shards flying all around us, hating myself for trying to run away when I should have been trying to kill Tempest... when I should have been bringing down the woman who had killed Kid Crater's family.

But being a hero isn't about getting revenge. It's not even about staying alive. It is, and always has been, as seen in countless ballads and stories and movies throughout the ages, all about saving the pretty girls. I did have Kid Crater to think about, but I had Laura and Apple to think about, first. So, I did what I could to *burrow*. It's not something at which I'm overly adept.

I was hoping for an underground parking lot, even a sewer system, anywhere that the three of us could hide... could work out a strategy for the fight. One of my stomps sent soil and concrete tumbling down, rather than being flung aside, and I knew there was some sort of sanctuary below, if only I could reach it. I could hear Tempest laughing above, her voice sounding out even past all the chaos. She did not sound like a woman who would allow an escape.

Two things went wrong. Or, at least, two things happened.

The first was that Apple broke free of my grasp and began running across the parking lot.

The second was that Mistress Mary rose up from below, ghosting up through the ground, through the hole I'd been creating, looking almost as angry as I was.

The woman has a myriad of powers. I'm not sure anyone has ever catalogued them all. The thing with her voice, the one that gives everyone an irresistible compulsion to do as she says, that's the one that gets all the press. But there's the ghost form. Intangibility. Walking through walls. Invisibility. She projects a force field. She doesn't need to eat, drink, breathe, sleep or anything like that… though she does them all, now and then, either for pleasure or to feel more human, whenever she's in that sort of mood. There are other powers as well. Some of them she keeps secret, I think, in case she ever needs a trump card. Her powers are as tricky as Octagon's.

Plus, now she carries a gun.

She floated up out of the hole that I'd been stomping into creation (unaffected, it seemed, by the murderous winds) and looked into the skies, shaking her head, like a mother who's looking at a report card that not only has another line of "F's" in place, but also a scribbled note from the school principal that her child is the educational and social equivalent of gonorrhea.

Into the winds, she yelled, "Tempest! Knock this shit off!" I felt the tug of the command in my own mind… the desire to do as Mistress Mary says… and she wasn't even speaking to me and her powers don't work very well on me anyway. I can't imagine what it's like for a regular person. Paladin always said that was one of my problems… that I couldn't imagine what anything was like for a normal person. He, himself, always kept trying to think of himself as a normal person. Look where that got him.

The winds dipped down. The larger, heavier cars began plummeting from above. They hit the parking lot looking like no more than wadded pieces of paper (albeit metal ones) that had been discarded by a giant. I held Laura protectively underneath me, dodging these cast-off vehicles, all the while scanning the parking lot... looking for an escape… looking for

Apple, hoping I wouldn't see her sticking out from beneath some fallen car like the wicked witch of the east. A couple rays of sunlight began making their way through the clouds. The chaos had lowered to a point where I could understand Laura's screams.

"Apple!" she was screaming. "Where's Apple? God *damn* this! Save her!"

I wanted to save her. I wanted that more than anything. But… I didn't know where she was. I couldn't see her. I hoped she was safe. It didn't seem possible.

The winds began to pick up again.

Mistress Mary was yelling, "No. Don't even think about it! Cut off this storm! Cut it off! Tempest! This is Mistress Mary! I command you to cease this attack!"

It was lightning that answered. Lightning answered with a hundred bolts arcing down from the skies, lancing into the (fortunately very intangible) form of Mistress Mary and the (unfortunately) very tangible form of me, Steve Clarke, Reaver. I was hunched over Laura, having cast her down into the hole, covering her.

The lightning hurt.

I was getting really mad.

I've mentioned that I get mad.

I've mentioned how I feel about the death of Kid Crater.

His death, truthfully, wasn't where it all seemed to go wrong. That particular veering moment was long before his death. But… when he died… it put the lid on things. It made it clear that things were wrong. It made it clear, in particular, that Tempest was wrong, and even if I couldn't make things right… I could make Tempest dead.

That had to count for something, right?

Mistress Mary was still yelling into the skies, screaming about calming down, then about *goddamn ceasing the attack*, and then onto, "I will slit your throat if you don't knock this shit off!" A few years earlier, she'd found it erotic that I didn't obey her commands. I guess times had changed.

I asked Mary, "Can you turn other people intangible?"

"I don't reveal my powers. But, yes, maybe. Why?"

I handed her a screaming writhing Laura Layton and said, "Because she's important to me. Don't let her be hurt. Stay here. I'm going to kill a goddess."

Mary took Laura from me, but all the time she was looking me in the eyes, making calculations, thinking the thoughts of whatever someone like a person who's one step away from having the voice of God thinks of at a time like that. I couldn't tell. I didn't care.

"Just do what I say," I snapped. I didn't have time for minds moving in mysterious ways.

"Yes, sir," she said, making a joke of it, but, I could tell, a little scared, too. Laura, in Mistress Mary's arm, turned a bit milky white, a shade invisible. I knew she was safe. Nothing could harm her.

Unfortunately, it seemed like nothing could harm Tempest, either. At least nothing that I could do. The shit thing about fighting a weather goddess is that they don't commune with the ground all that much, and that's pretty much where I stand. I can't fly, and though I can jump pretty high it wasn't going to do me much good against a woman who could fly much higher than I can jump, and who could make the winds do her bidding.

I scurried across the parking lot, searching for some plan, for some goddamn big ladder, for any way to reach the Bitch Above. By then the hails were coming down on me, chunks of ice that were the size of golf balls, then footballs, then beach balls, and finally just goddamn boulders, all of them smashing into me and leaving smears of a green glow wherever they hit. It was nine stages above irritating and one stage below fatal, and with all the ice accumulating on the ground I couldn't get my goddamn footing, couldn't set my feet beneath me, just kept skidding around the parking lot amongst all the fallen cars. The Super Eight Grocery Emporium sign, the one that stretches all the way up, thirty feet in the air, the one with a billboard at the top of a huge metal pole, the one with a giant molded basket of fruit, it caught a wash of boulder-sized hail and was torn to pieces. The pole crumpled near the bottom, tipped over. I barely dodged the chop of its descent.

It made a fine spear, once I'd shucked off the remains of the billboard. I thought of all the Olympic athletes I've seen, the ones doing that spear toss, the spears that always come down near the judges who (in my opinion) are never paying quite enough attention to the sharpened projectiles zooming down from the skies. I thought of all the adventure movies I've seen, the ones with the brave white explorers in Africa, trespassing the arrogant hell out of vast territories, with their pith-helmeted long-legged *white goddess* women, and the tribesmen running from the trees, and some blue-eyed actor who grew up in Hollywood and never so much as threw a tin can or a baseball is suddenly a better marksman with a spear than the tribesmen who've been pinning snakes to trees from two hundred feet away. I thought of all the times that Greg Barrows and I had played in the creek, or in the quarry, and I'd been a pirate (not known for their spear-hurling techniques) but Greg had been a god, and gods quite often toss lightning bolts (hell, Tempest was certainly playing at the game) and so Greg would find anything that could act as a stand-in for a spear, for anything he could pronounce as a lightning bolt, and he'd be Thor, or he'd be Zeus, and he'd be hurling sticks and weeds while yelling, "BOOM! I smite you!"

I didn't feel the need to yell it. I just whispered it. No one was going to hear me over all the rest of the chaos, anyway. There was no reason to yell.

But I still felt it needed to be said.

I said, "Boom. I smite you."

Then I hurled that monstrous metal billboard shaft as hard as I could, aiming for the mass of white (Tempest's naked skin) beneath the flowing red (that hair… that beautiful hair) and nearly falling forward flat on my face with the strength of the toss, just like one of those Olympic athletes. Just like the ones who end up on the podiums, putting the gold around their necks.

But I missed.

Not really my fault.

Olympic athletes don't have to throw their spears into winds that are, what… category fifty hurricane/tornado combination packs? Tempest saw the incoming spear, had time to laugh about it (her winds were slowing the spear's ascent into a lounging sort of distracted amble) and lightning began playing all over its surface, as if she had chosen to destroy my weapon in that manner, but then she thought better of it (which is amazing, because it was hard to believe she was thinking at all by that point… hard to comprehend that she wasn't just a woman-shaped conglomeration of instinct and hate and batshit insanity) and the metal shaft turned about in the air, still limned by the lightning, now being sharpened by winds that were powerful enough to shape steel.

Looking up at it, it felt like my body should start glowing green just in anticipation of the oncoming hit.

Tempest was laughing, laughing, laughing.

Lightning was hitting all around me, chewing up the parking lot, drawing a target around me. It was too bright to see much of anything. Too bright to run. The noises were driving me to my knees and I thought about praying, I really did. I thought about praying.

Couldn't think of who to pray to, though. The Christian god was never much of my flavor. Buddha doesn't, to my knowledge, do much in the way of answering prayers. Greg was dead (no one can deny he's a legitimate contender for future divinity) and besides, I'd seen him urinate, and once you've seen a god urinate he really doesn't seem viable for any prayer-answering legitimacy.

So I just waited for the big steel spear to come down from the sky, and I wondered what the newspapers would say about my failure, and about my death, and I wondered how that goddamn laugh of Tempest's could sneak through all the roaring winds and dodge all the lightning and overcome the crashing of the thunder to reach my ears. It was cheating. It was cheating, is what it was. That's how normal people, everyday people, common people, real people, that's how they look at us superhumans. As cheaters.

Something happened.

Even before anything visually changed, I could *feel* that something was changing. The way you wake up in the middle of the night, sure that you heard a noise, sure that *Something of Import* is lurking in the shadows, or peering just out from behind Destiny's ass, running a hand up and down the back of her leg.

Tempest's laugh was cut off in midstream.

The lightning quit crashing all around.

The very air seemed charred, but breathable. I took the first breath possible in almost three minutes.

The clouds weren't rolling and roiling anymore, at least not as bad. They seemed like *nature in its fury*, which is far less than *nature in its fury about being fucked with by man*.

I had time to look up in the skies and wonder what was happening.

And then Tempest fell down from above.

She was falling limp. Maybe she was dead already. The winds weren't doing anything but getting out of her way. As if they'd never been friends.

Her body hit with a satisfying (or awful, or awfully satisfying) whump…

the sound of a sack of wet potatoes being hit by a brick.

Without thinking, without checking on the fallen woman, without even knowing that I was doing it, I picked up a car and brought it down on Tempest, and while she's a woman who can command the skies, she's just a human specimen, physically, and humans don't do well when a superhuman smashes a few thousand pounds of twisted metal onto their helpless bodies.

So… I got my red smear in the parking lot after all.

It didn't feel wrong.

It didn't feel right either.

It didn't feel much of anything but over.

"You killed her!" Mistress Mary said. She was becoming visible next to me. Laura was with her, colors and form being filled in by the second, leaving invisibility and intangibility behind.

I said, "I'm… I'm not sure if I did. She fell from the sky. Tempest fell from the sky." We both looked up to the sky. The tornadoes had vanished. The storm was fading away. Winking from existence. Pulling a curtain of blue sky over its misdeeds. The sunlight felt warm.

"You didn't do anything?" Mistress Mary's eyes narrowed, nearly closed. I felt the twitch again, the twitch to tell her everything, to do exactly as she says. It was easy, this time. I didn't even try to fight it. I was telling the truth.

"Tried to do something. Couldn't. I mean, I got her with the car, but only after she was down." Mary seemed as if she was going to say something else, but Laura grabbed me by the arm, pulling at me, pulling me nowhere in particular, pulling in one direction and then another, frantic, saying, "Apple! Where's Apple? What happened to Apple?"

The search for Apple didn't take very long, or it took forever, depending on perspective. I hated myself for doing it, or not that I was doing it, but that I was being forced to look for someone I cared about under ruined cars, hefting them up, seeing what was beneath, was sensing another loss, was sensing that Laura Layton was in her own "Kid Crater" moment. People began slowly coming out of the grocery store, customers and Apple's co-workers, many of these people falling to their knees and praying, some of them snapping photos with their phones, several of them simply running off… heading away from the scene. There were sirens, oncoming, no more than a few blocks away. People were chattering on their cell phones, saying,

"*I'm alive! It's okay! I'm alive*!" or, "*Reaver's here! He killed Tempest! Fucking squashed her!*" or, "*Shit, man! You should have… oh shit! Shit*!" and further variations of all these messages, many of them ending with statements that could be translated as, "*You had better be ready for some rough sex, because I made it through this alive and my groin is going to prove it*!" Because that's what survivors do; they fuck. They live.

Laura was running amongst all these people, cursing each one of them for not knowing where Apple was… cursing each one for not *being* Apple, and she ran off in one direction, and I went in another, and there was a lump in my throat when I finally found Laura's girlfriend, when I finally saw Apple, because how could I tell the sister of the woman I loved that her girlfriend was sprawled, unmoving, on the parking lot's surface, was white, was covered in shards of ice from one of the boulders of hail that had come down from above… how could I tell Laura that her girlfriend wasn't alive, that she had been killed by…

"Reaver?" Apple said, stirring, looking my way. "R-Reaver?"

My chest heaved. Apple was moving. She was… she was… I ran to her at something that must have been four times the speed of a normal man.

I brushed the ice away from her. There was a bruise on her cheek. Another along her arm. The boulder must have barely creased her. We had gone one or two inches from tragedy. In the business that I'm in, we call that a triumph.

I held Apple in my arms and yelled, "Laura! She's here! I found her! She's okay!" I could hear Laura's answering calls from in the distance, her yelling my name, and yelling Apple's, hidden by piles of discarded cars. In time, in only seconds, Laura appeared, wild-eyed, grinning, running for me. Well, in truth she wasn't running for me at all. She was running for Apple. But she was looking at me.

She was looking at me like I was a hero.

CHAPTER NINETEEN

Adele was standing in her yard. We'd had to take a taxi home (there hadn't been any such thing as taxis when I was living in Greenway) because I'd thrown Laura's car at a weather goddess (it had missed, and had then been subjected to tornadoes and lightning and the underrated and overwhelming deprivations of gravity) but luckily Laura hadn't scolded me at all. She'd only told me she would have traded fifteen or twenty or a hundred cars, or anything at all, to be able to sit next to Apple (they weren't sitting next to each other, they were stacked) in the taxi, coming home. Apple had laughed off everything, saying that it was too bad about the groceries (she'd taken especial care when selecting the oranges, claiming it was a skill she'd developed when training with orange-picking monks in Tibet) and then, anyway, such things as being hit by avian icebergs were the kinds of things a girl has to expect when becoming friends with one of the *Children of the Spill.*

After Tempest was down (let's face it… squashed dead like a bug) Laura and Apple were treated to a display of how invasive SRD's "Aftermath Investigators" can be, and then we had called several people, quite a few people, to let them know that we were okay. Laura had called her fellow artists (and had hurriedly discussed a new series of paintings based on the day's events) and Apple had called a number of relatives (her own co-workers had been, of course, on site) and between the two of them the number of phone calls had been in the upper teens, or maybe even the low twenties.

I made one phone call.

I called Adele.

I'd said, "You probably saw some bad weather."

"Are you okay? Is Laura okay? Are you okay? Is my sister okay? What... where... are you okay? Steve fucking Clarke are you okay?" There were more words and the same questions and I was trying to cut in, but, I wasn't trying very hard, because I was enjoying the sound of her voice and feeling, for some reason, like I had *saved* it. Like I had saved *her*. I was feeling very much like a hero. Between Laura's grin (while she came running for Apple, slipping on the ice and falling once, but never changing the focus of her eyes or the breadth of her grin) and the relief in Adele's voice, I was feeling absolutely like a hero. So I didn't cut in, at first, because I wanted to feel that way as long as possible. I wanted to be a hero forever.

When my silence began to make me feel as much a jerk as a hero, I'd calmed Adele down (*I'm fine, Laura's fine, and we have one very slightly bruised Apple*) and she had listened to the details, asked a few questions (out of concern) and then a few more questions (out of, I think, research for one of her books or articles) and we had discussed theories of *why* Tempest had fallen from the sky (SRD investigators, had, at Apple's suggestion, embraced a theory that the weather goddess had been so enraged that she had burnt herself out like a light bulb) and finally Adele asked me how long it had been before Laura spoiled the news about the surprise party. I told her it hadn't been long at all, and she'd told me how that was longer than she would have expected.

By the time the taxi dropped us off at the Layton sisters' residence, Adele was waiting in the yard, and was full of information (some true, some false) on the fight. She'd been checking the internet, and during the short time (it had taken only thirty minutes) I'd been being debriefed by SRD, and then the taxi ride home, the internet had provided a thousand different versions of the fight, an equal number of memorials for Tempest, a multitude of flame wars in various comments sections, articles about how Ecuador was in mourning, and the news of the fight had even made the weather sites, where meteorologists were debating if the size of the hail that had pummeled me could be counted as *official* hail, thereby breaking all previous records for the largest hail ever recorded.

Adele ran to the taxi and nearly pulled me out of it, hugging me before I was even standing, so that I was awkwardly half-perched in the doorway of the taxi, suddenly embracing Adele, all the while trying to grab money (for the fare) out of the rather tattered remnants of my pants pocket.

"God damn it," she said, hugging me, running a hand through my hair. It felt better than anything Siren had ever done. I would have kissed her right then. I would have kissed Adele Layton for the first time in almost a decade, right then, if she would have moved a fraction of an inch away, giving me space to move.

But she didn't, and we didn't kiss, and soon Laura was paying for the cab fare (making me feel guilty that she was paying for the cab, because we were only in the taxi because I had Very Much Broken her car) and then we were in the yard and we talking about what had happened. Laura (and the rest of us, too, of course) was shuddering over how Apple had almost died… how we in fact had almost *all* died, and the *light bulb* theory of Tempest's fall from the skies was again discussed (Laura was *so* proud that Apple, *her* Apple, had come up with the theory that SRD had decided upon) and when I opened the front door (I was told to go first) and walked into the house I had to press through a throng of pink balloons that Adele had taped to the sides of the door, to the top of the door, hanging from above, seemingly a hundred pink balloons tied in bunches, pressing my way through them, delving within.

Laura said, "It's like we're plunging into a big balloon vagina," which earned her a glare from her sister, and then Adele thought better of the glare and started crying and hugged Laura instead. It went on, that way, for a bit.

Apple and I just stared at each other. Wiggles, the cat, came and pawed at a stray balloon that had fallen to the floor. The balloon moved in a way that the cat found interesting (perhaps thinking it was an entirely new type of prey) and batted at it a couple more times, making me wonder how the cat would react if the balloon exploded. It didn't explode, which I found to be disappointing. I'm one of those types who thinks it's funny when a cat gets scared.

There was cake on the kitchen table. A party cake. I wondered who had brought it. Wondered who had carried it carefully from what car, then put it there on the table.

We were alone in the house, but there was evidence of other people having been waiting at the party. A couple discarded sweaters. A camera. A purse. The usual clues that a large group of people had just left the room, but in this case they hadn't just left the room; they'd fled the room, running home, hearing of the fight and its results, fearing for people they knew and perhaps, in a few cases, fearing me, as I was soon due to arrive.

"The party is going to be smaller than I'd originally planned," Adele said, coming up beside me, wiping the remaining tears from her eyes, smearing her makeup, just a little. I thought that it was strange to see her in makeup. I thought of how she so rarely wore makeup. And then I thought of how little I knew if that was true. Maybe she'd spent the last ten years wearing makeup. Maybe I didn't know shit about anything. But then she stood beside me, pressed up against me, and it felt like I did… it felt like I knew some things, at least. It felt like I knew the difference between right and wrong.

"Some of the people left," she said. "Well, all of them. But that's… that's more cake for us." She gestured to the cake. It was large. It had twenty-seven candles. It had a frosting inscription of, "*Here's to a year that you can't take away*," being an obvious reference to my powers. A strangely, possibly offensive reference to my powers. I treasured it. Just like Mistress Mary had loved it (years ago) when someone didn't do exactly as she said, I loved the feeling of someone I cared about being willing to take the chance of offending me. I don't get that much, anymore.

Wiggles loped on by, carrying a party streamer in his mouth, like he'd killed a snake. I looked at the cat. The streamer. The false snake. It put some thoughts into my head. I didn't want thoughts in my head. I wanted a party. I wanted cake.

There's nothing wrong with wanting cake.

Adele said, "I know it's not your birthday."

"I wasn't going to say anything. I was afraid you'd take the cake away."

"I'm not that cruel. And I figured that I've missed so many of your birthdays that I can plan a makeup birthday party whenever I want. Now, can we have a talk?"

I thought about saying, "We are talking," but that wouldn't have been clever, or meaningful, or anything but stalling. I looked over to Laura, and to Apple (Laura was putting balloons into both of their shirts and exclaiming how big their boobs were) and I thought some thoughts, and I decided that it would be okay to have a talk with Adele. Or, at least, I decided it was impossible to avoid having a talk with her.

I said, "Okay. Let's talk. Here? Where?"

Instead of answering my question, Adele told Laura, "Sis, Steve and I are going for a walk. Back soon, okay?"

Apple, surprised, said, "Leaving the party? But look how big our boobs are!"

Laura, covering her girlfriend's mouth with a hand, said, "You two go have fun. If you come back anytime soon, best knock on my bedroom door before you come in. In fact, best knock on the kitchen door before you come in. Frankly, you better yell from the sidewalk or something. And… take condoms with you. And, if you're gone for more than an hour, Apple and I are going to straight up eat this cake."

Adele and I walked out the door. We were holding hands. It felt nice (unbelievable, a miracle) that someone (a *good* someone) would trust her hand in mine.

"What are we going to talk about?" I asked.

"Don't be an ass, Steve Clarke. You're going to stop hiding whatever it is that you're hiding. You're going to kiss me. You're going to tell me your secrets."

She waited for me to say something.

I didn't.

She said, "Let's go to the park."

⌖

On the way to the park, Adele and I stopped off at the Mighty Convenient convenience store. We didn't talk, yet, of anything of any immediate import. We talked of how it had been the two of us, together, at that very store, watching the breaking news of Warp, the first of the superhumans. We talked about how odd it was, the two of us watching that report, not knowing that destiny was standing outside the door, peering inside through the window at me, making its plans. We talked of caramel crab cakes, the local delicacy, made by Grace Shanahan and distributed at stores around the region. We picked up some of those. Some bottled water. When she opened the door to the standing cooler I noticed she glanced at the beer, but it was only a glance, and she didn't grab any of them or look back at them after taking the water, the way an alcoholic would do, always, every time, so it seemed like she was truly and honestly recovered from the problems of her past. It was comforting to know that such things as full recoveries can take place. She handed me the waters and the caramel crab cakes and said (I was still the only millionaire around) that it was my job to buy them. She wouldn't let me buy anything else because it would have spoiled my appetite for birthday cake. I said that nothing spoils my appetite. She asked if that was because I'm superhuman. I said that it was because I like cake. No more than that.

And we walked to the park to have our talk.

⌖

"It hasn't changed much," I said. It was true. It was still the same park. Charles Park. Still the same log cabin. A few added names in the rafters. I'd heard that the annual summer book sale was larger now, and while it was managed in the same way as when I was a kid (there were haywagons full of books, subdivided by genres, with *history*, and *fiction*, and *romance*, and *gardening*, and *science*, and so on) there was now always a stand for new books, books about superhumans, books written by local authors, because several locals had taken advantage of living in the town that gave birth to Warp, that gave birth to Reaver, and that was home to the SRD base. It was a cottage industry of people who lived close to the origins of superhumans. I had no doubt that it would only grow (explode, even) when word got out (which it most assuredly would) that Paladin had been Greg Barrows, another Greenway resident. I had no doubt that, somewhere, close by, probably in several somewheres, there were people writing stories about how Tempest had been born (created, anyway) in Greenway, and she had died (squished, as it were) in a Greenway parking lot.

Adele might write one such book herself. I didn't think, in her case, that such a book would have been living off the luck (good and bad) of the land; she had more right than any of the others. She had made me cake.

Adele led me to a picnic bench. It was only ten feet from the log cabin. I wondered if there was anybody in there, anybody right now, making history or marking it down.

The wind was fluttering at the wax paper that had been wrapped around the caramel crab cakes. I was toying with putting one in my mouth. I was uncommitted.

Adele said, "The list. I need to talk to you about your list." I put a caramel crab cake in my mouth. Felt bad about it.

"Your list sounds like… it sounds… it sounds like you're going to…" She paused. I was chewing very carefully. I felt like I could accidentally break the entire conversation.

She said, "Steve Clarke, do you think you're going to die?"

"We're all going to die." I regretted it the second I said it. What a total ass.

"Don't fuck with me. I've waited a long time. I know you weren't asking me to wait. But I did. I didn't even really know that I was waiting. Laura knew. And she told me. But I didn't believe her. I do now. I waited. Don't fuck with me. Do you think you're going to die?"

The wax paper was still flapping in the wind. I spent some time wondering about the wind. The mystery of the wind. What I can do, is I can heal. I can lift a lot of weight. I can take a lot of damage. I can't do anything of the weird powers. Not the truly strange ones. Not reading minds. Not talking with animals. Not controlling the weather. I always wanted to ask Tempest about the weather. Had she controlled the weather by picking it up, moving it from place to place, the way we all do with objects, with tools? Or had she *asked* the weather to do what she wanted, *commanded* it to do things in the same manner that Mistress Mary makes a person do what she says? How did Tempest control the weather? I always wanted to ask her that. But she was a killer. A cold insanity. The question was unanswered. Unasked. So I didn't know if the breeze that was moving the wax paper was intelligent or not. Didn't know if it meant to do it, or if it was just something that happened. I suddenly felt like I didn't know anything.

While almost looking at Adele, I said, "In the last fight, with Octagon, with Eleventh Hour, they had me down. Octagon had me down and I was going to die. I asked him if I could have a couple weeks to do a last few things. I don't know why I asked him that. But I did. I don't know why he granted the request. But he did. Maybe it amused him. Maybe he's like a cat, loving how he's getting to bat around his favorite mouse for a last couple of weeks. Anyway… I made a promise. So, yes… I'm going to die."

Adele said, "You stupid son of a bitch."

I said, "Yes." I wasn't going to argue that point. I felt differently about it. But I also felt, from her viewpoint, that she was right.

She repeated it. She said, "You stupid son of a bitch." This time, she reached out and tried to slap me. I easily avoided it, because I move at different speeds. So… I made her miss. I made her miss because she would have hurt her hand, not because I didn't deserve the slap. She overbalanced for a moment. Glared at me. Sat back down.

The wind was still moving the wax paper. I decided that there was no intelligence behind it. That it was as dumb as I was.

"Your list," Adele said. The wax paper flapped. I put a finger down on it. Held it in place.

"Your list," Adele repeated, after a time. I hadn't said anything in between. I didn't know what to say. I wanted to have another caramel crab cake, because that would give me an excuse to move my mouth. Maybe that would kick-start things. Maybe I could gain momentum that way. There were two caramel crab cakes left. If I picked up one, it might reduce the weight on the wax paper enough that the wind would carry it away. I considered the ramifications of such an event. They seemed momentous. I knew that my brain wasn't working.

"You brought the list to Greenway," Adele said. "You made it. You brought it. In it, you were supposed to be with me again. And you talked with Greg's parents, and you talked, almost, with Judy. Have you made a will? *Don't* put me in it. Don't do that. Goddamn you; don't put me in it." She was starting to cry. I was the worst villain in all of creation. I was worse than Octagon. I was worse than Macabre. I was the bottom of the barrel. I was sitting with Adele Layton and I was making her cry.

I took a big long breath.

I said, "I have to tell you something. Will you… will you write it down, for afterwards? Can you do that?"

Adele didn't answer. Nothing beyond sniffles and a whisper that I was a son of a bitch. I should have bought tissues at the Mighty Convenient convenience store. I should have done that. Why wasn't I thinking?

There was a rock garden around the log cabin. I stood, picked up a rock about the size of a pineapple, faced away from Adele (to protect her from any flying shards) and snapped the rock in half. It sounded like a gunshot and Adele gasped. I should have warned her what I was doing. I still wasn't thinking. The interior of the rock had sparkly bits, shiny bits, sections of bright gray, the way that gray can be only if it hasn't seen the sun in a few thousand years.

I brought half the rock back to the picnic table, and I sat down across from Adele, and I used the sharp edge of the rock to slice open my arm.

Even though the rock was, of course, as hard as a rock, and even though the edge was sharp from the fresh break, it was still difficult to cut my nearly invulnerable skin. It took a good deal of my considerable strength to get the job done. Adele watched me with the sort of revulsion that a woman would give to a man strangling a dog.

But this was something that someone needed to see.

This was something that needed to be recorded.

This was a memorial.

This was something I'd never told anyone.

Not Paladin. Not Mistress Mary. Not even Siren.

My blood oozed out.

The wound trembled and began to glow with the bright green color.

The wound began to heal. To close.

Adele was trying to look away but I very much needed her to see what was happening. I couldn't die without sharing the knowledge. Without giving the truth. It wouldn't have been right. It would have been selfish.

I said, "Look at this." I pointed to the green glow. Adele wasn't looking, not much. She was trying to look, but was turning away. I suppose I would have done the same thing if she'd grabbed a knife and cut herself open. But I couldn't let her aversion stand. She needed to look.

I yelled, "Look at this!" in a voice that was much louder than I'd meant it to be, but it was fueled by nearly a decade of bottling up the sentence.

Softer, I said, "Adele, please look." She turned her head, and she looked at the green glow around the edges of my rapidly closing wound. She nodded, as if in affirmation that she was looking.

I said, "This green glow," and that was as far as I got before the words stuck in me, a little. I needed to stop, to breathe. Mostly, I needed to look up and see that I was talking to Adele Layton. She made it all seem okay.

I said, "This green glow. This is Tom. This is my brother, Tom."

⌖

The car was in flames. It had been twisted by impact with the tanker, crunched and shattered and compressed. I was frantically trying to push open the door, kicking at it with legs that were being washed by the chemicals pouring from the tanker truck, chemicals that were flowing in through the shattered windshield and cascading through the car, sizzling with exposure to heat and flame, and the door wouldn't give and the door wouldn't give and the door would *not* give because it has been caught in an accordion vise by the compression of the car. I was screaming for Tom. I guess that's important.

I was screaming for Tom.

When the car exploded, Officer Horwitz (half dead already, with the steering column having previously punched into his chest during the collision) had been looking back to me, clinging to life, advising me on the door, not telling me anything useful, but instead saying not to roll down the window until the car had sank beneath the waves. He must have thought we had gone into the river. He must have thought we were sinking. Who knows what the hell he'd been thinking? The explosion tore him in half and he died. The explosion kicked us both clear from the car, popping it open like a sardine can and spilling the little fish onto the road.

I was dead.

Or, no... I was only dying. I was seconds from death, and not long seconds, either. They were short, impatient seconds. I was yelling Tom's name.

Yes. That's important.

My feelings, my thoughts, pieced together later, are that Tom, who had been in the front seat, had been the first to go under the wave of chemicals that came from the ruptured tanker truck. These chemicals began filling the car, quickly spilling out from the police car into the ditch, and during these moments Tom became the first of the children of the spill. He grew power. He grew tremendous power.

He was a healer.

Like Greg Barrows became.

Like people think I am.

But I'm not.

The green glow is Tom. My brother.

The chemicals dissolved him. They killed him. The chemicals took his mind, his life, took what he had been, and in his dying moments he heard me calling his name, and of course Tom, Tom, Tom…

… Tom was my brother.

And he came to me. Even then.

Because I was his kid brother. And Tom was a hero.

He saved me. Healed me. Even as he died.

I felt his life pour into me, into what was, then, my shattered and charred near-carcass, and I felt Tom bonding with me even as he died.

My wounds closed.

He's been here, in me, ever since.

But his life vanished. It's just… what's left, the green glow, it's not Tom, it's only what Tom wanted in his final moments.

He wanted to protect his kid brother.

And he did.

I felt him go away.

I felt him, in a manner of speaking, stay.

The car's explosion had cast me partially in the ditch, somewhat on the road. Greg Barrows was staggering around, going nowhere, covered in blood, missing an arm.

My brother was already gone.

⌖

When I finished with the story, Adele was barely breathing. There was a pause between each breath, a length of time long enough for her lungs to crawl up into her throat, kicking a bit, reminding her of an important job.

Her breaths had longs seconds in between. Then her breaths stretched for long seconds, themselves. She was looking at my arm, where I had cut myself. The wound was completely healed. The green glow was gone. Receded back within me.

Adele reached out and touched my arm where the wound had been. There was an amount of crusted blood. She flaked it away with her fingers.

Some of it got beneath her fingernails. When she was done, there wasn't anything but an unmarked arm.

She said, "Every time you fight… every time you get… hurt. Every time that happens. Every time you heal? That's… Tom?"

"More or less."

"You must feel so guilty."

It felt like I'd been punched. All the tabloids. All the special reports. All the chatter going back and forth between news reporters. Every post in the comments sections of every blog. Everyone thinks they know me. Everyone thinks they have insight. Everyone thinks they can peer into my mind. But Adele was the only one to get it right.

So I started to cry. How the tabloids would have loved to snap a photo of that. Reaver, the man who had killed Tempest. The man who had killed Macabre. Crying. Like a baby.

Adele came around to my side of the picnic table. Sat beside me. Held me. There wasn't another person in the world who could have held me right then. She talked to me about Tom, about memories of him, about the way he ran through every girl in Greenway, every girl of his age, every girl a bit older, a few girls who were much older. She mentioned, hurriedly, that he'd never made any move on her. She mentioned that he'd once punched out a couple Bolton boys (I'd never known this) who had said a few things about her ass, and what might fit in it.

Adele talked about how, one night, she and Laura had smoked some marijuana (she called it *crazy grass*) that Tom had given her in return for having helped tutor him on calculus the day before a test. The crazy grass had been good. It was the night when Laura had first brought home a girl to meet her parents, the last people in Greenway to know that she was a lesbian. The girl had gone home (Laura had fingered her in the upstairs hallway, with Adele reluctantly keeping watch on the stairs) and the two sisters had afterwards smoked the marijuana that Tom had given them, and Adele said that after a time she could see stars on the ceiling of her bedroom.

"They whispered," she said.

I was still leaking tears. Still amazed that someone on Earth knew about Tom. About his final moments. It felt good to know that I'd given him, in some ways, an extension of his life. Or at least his memory.

Adele talked to me about that hallway finger-bang, about how Laura wanted to write the girl's name (Sally, an old-fashioned name, though the girl in question was one of those *teenage emo-lesbians-of-the-moment*) on the rafter of the log cabin.

Adele pointed to the log cabin. I looked up at it. I could visualize the rafter. The whole thing really and truly should have been enshrined.

I asked, "Did she do it?"

"Not at first. She said that the log cabin was heterosexual. Something about *logs* equaling *penises*."

"That's… an interesting take."

"I know, right? Anyway, Laura wanted to start another place. Another list. A listing of the secret pact of lesbians. But she couldn't decide where, so in time she just wrote girls' names on the rafter, like everybody else."

I said, "Your name is on the rafter, in there." I gestured to the log cabin. The statement had just kind of come out of me. I wanted to retract it immediately. I also wanted an answer.

"I wrote it there," she said, looking at me like I was an idiot. I was, of course, but an idiot rarely knows *why* he's an idiot, so I had to keep asking questions.

"You wrote it there?" My voice broke like I was twelve years old.

"For you. I mean, there was the one night when you, you know, you did that thing with your hand, umm, in my panties, and then you were in the hospital."

"I remember. I mean, the panties thing. I remember the panties thing. I don't remember being in the hospital. I remember waking up there. That's all. There were guards. Mistress Mary. Flowers. Paladin, after a bit."

"I brought in the flowers. I used to sit with you every day, and… this is probably the most embarrassing thing ever, but I was young and I was so horny. You could not believe how horny I was. So, I masturbated once."

"Just once?"

"Just once at the hospital."

"Oh."

"Yeah. And then afterwards I was thinking of how your hand had felt, thinking of that time, and I know boys like to look at sex as some kind of stupid triumph."

"Yeah. We do that."

Adele said, "So what I did was I took my dad's pocket knife from his nightstand, and I snuck out here." She gestured to the log cabin. "And I carved my name on the rafter. In tribute. For you."

I thought about that. I thought about all the medals I'd received in the last decade. The commendations. The honorary titles. The actual titles. The Certificates of Saving the Whole Damn World. They all paled in comparison to Adele's gesture. So, yes… we boys look at sex as some sort of stupid triumph.

I said, "Thank you." I honest to god was almost crying again.

Adele said, "And… I guess… this leads me back into talking about your list." Her tone was evasive. The mood was cold again. The talk of names carved into rafters, it seemed, was going to be a momentary ray of warmth. I nodded, trying to look serious, attentive, but all I could think of was the humor (the very… warm… humor) of the young Adele balanced on the rafter, carving her own name.

"Your list," she said. "It talks about being with me again."

"It does." I noticed how the wind was playing at her hair. Moving strands of it. Why had I been, earlier, so focused on how the wind had been fluttering the edges of the wax paper? What a ridiculous focus. Adele's hair was… it seemed like a wind that moved through Adele's hair was far more likely to be intelligent than any wind that was batting away at something as mundane as wax paper.

Adele said, "You've been… I mean, I read things. I study reports. You've been with Mistress Mary. Stellar. A list of models. I mean a huge line of models. That girl that was in all those romantic comedies. Even with Siren." I nodded at this, slowly, and with no other movement. It seemed very unwise to acknowledge what she was saying, just then, but far stupider to disavow what was known the world over. Still… still, beyond my nod, I kept almost motionless. And quiet. I didn't even want the wind to notice me.

Adele, fingers working against each other, eyes focused on the picnic table, said, "This… coming back to me. It's not… just some part of some other list, is it? The girl that got away? One last checkmark? Unfinished business? A way to…?"

"I've loved you since before our first date. Since before I was riding around on the top of that car, in my underwear. After the accident, I stayed away because I loved you and thought it was the right thing to do… didn't want to put you in any danger. But I loved you then. I love you now."

It was a fair amount of words that I spoke. I babbled some of them. Fumbled about. But I didn't choke on any of the words. Not one.

Adele said, "I love you, too."

We let it stand there, for a bit.

It was strong enough to stand on its own.

⌖

Adele had the last of the caramel crab cakes and the wax paper did indeed blow off the picnic table. She screamed, "I'll get it!" and raced after it. I could have gotten it much easier, much faster, but watching Adele dashing around was beyond any pleasure I could have hoped for, and the wax paper dipped and swirled in the wind, extending my enjoyment. She chased after it, trying to chew her crab cake at the same time, laughing, spilling crumbs from her mouth. A young boy (five or six) left his mother's side to help Adele, never merely reaching for the wax paper, instead trying to stomp on it with both feet, nearly causing several collisions with Adele, the two of them laughing at the elusive paper. The boy's mother (they had a picnic spot of their own, and a *bored-of-course* cat on a leash, and a badminton set with no net) watched them for a few seconds, then changed her gaze (and her smile) onto me, still sitting at the picnic table.

Her smile vanished.

She recognized me.

I watched her mental process as she ticked off all the possible meanings/considerations/ramifications of having a picnic in the same park with Reaver. In time (an eternity, of course, as these things often are) she gave a slight nod to me, and then one to herself, in decision. The smile came back. She returned to watching her son (he had retrieved the paper and was handing it to Adele as if it were a holy relic) and did not pack up their belongings. She stayed in place.

A triumph, for me, there.

I watched Adele returning to my table. She swerved towards a trashcan at one point, obviously intent on throwing away the wax paper, but she changed her direction the moment she realized that she couldn't throw away the paper without damaging the young boy's heroics.

When she returned to the table, and as she was tucking the carefully folded wax paper into her purse, I said, "She keeps wax papers. She carves her name into rafters. She is a hero to all the men and boys."

"Let's talk about sex," she said.

I said, "Oof." Just outright said it. Girls are not supposed to bring up such topics. They do, of course, always. But, still. Oof.

She said, "Pretend that I'm just a reporter, someone that's researching articles and books, and that I'm not at all a potentially jealous woman."

"Potentially," I said.

She glared.

I said, "I'm pretending."

"How did you end up with all those women? You weren't… don't take this wrong… you weren't all that forward, before."

"No. I suppose not. So… now that we're done with that particular topic, I believe there's some birthday cake back at…"

"You slept with Siren." Adele had her elbows on the picnic table. Her chin in her hands. She looked innocent. Perhaps it was a super power. An illusion. She was casting an illusion of innocence.

I said, "Am I still supposed to be pretending that you're not potentially jealous?"

She didn't answer. It was the most challenging answer of all. If a woman is going to make a man walk across ice, she could at least say something about it. "*Hey, watch your step*," or, "*It's a bit slippery, there, so be careful.*" But, no… she remained silent. It was clear I was supposed to say some things, even though it was probably best if I stayed quiet.

I said, "My strongest memory of sex with Siren was something that happened, one time, after."

"Don't give me any stories about cuddling."

"Siren doesn't cuddle." I began trying to think of what to say to Adele. What should I explain? What information (as little as possible) should I give? What information (most, if not all) should I censor? Luckily, the strongest memory I have about Siren isn't completely (not entirely, at least) about sex. The strongest memory I have of Siren is the first time with her, afterwards, with her in the shower, me sitting on the toilet lid, watching her, incredibly glad for my photographic memory, incredibly guilty about what had just happened (sex with a criminal, nice job, hero) and incredibly wallowing in the sexual pleasure of that guilt. The name of *Octagon* had come up, with me asking (hating myself for it, because what could be more pitiful, or less worthy of discussion) if I was a better man in bed than Octagon.

"Competitive?" Siren had taunted from the shower. The water was hitting her from all sides, from four different directions, there in one of Octagon's private residences (it was, soon after, back on the market) with the beads of water sticking to the walls, droplets of condensation from the heat, each of these water drops reflecting her image, tainted (that is absolutely the wrong word) with the musk of her scent.

"Competitive," I answered. It was impossible for Siren to lie to a man. In light of recent events, it seemed like I owed her the same consideration.

She thought for a moment. I was swirling in rising lust (most men would have been dead, seriously and literally perished, from just watching her in the shower… but being superhuman has many many benefits) and also swirling in a sort of rising agony, knowing that most women will have the kindness to tell her most recent man that he is the most talented lover she's ever had… but here I was asking the question from a woman who could tell nothing but the truth. It was possible that the most desirable woman in all the world was about to verbally kick me square in the balls.

Instead of lying, she defused the question, saying, "You ask if you're a better man in bed than Octagon?" She didn't wait for me to nod. Instead, she cupped one breast, rose it slightly, and flicked a bit of water from the end of her nipple. It (obeying every law of such a moment in time) hurtled through the air to splash on my cheek, and while it was running down my face, Siren said, "Reaver, look at me. You're asking the wrong sort of question."

⌖

Adele said, "What then?"

"Then… I asked a different question."

"Which was…?"

I said, "Not fair. You're asking all the questions. I want to know something… when you were in college, did you really buy Reaver costumes for your lovers?"

Adele said, "Oh shit, really? I hate Laura so much!"

"You shouldn't. She tries really hard to make you happy. Even if she does tell me incredibly embarrassing things about you."

"She probably even told you about the vibrator, didn't she?"

"No."

Adele sat up straight. Her entire face went so red that I thought maybe she would pass out. I sat, smiling. Feeling alive. She began cycling through subjects, not even settling on anything, just passing over the heads of possible topics, verbally flying at high speeds. There was sports (she obviously cared little for sports, and was just trying to get me started on the topic) and there was whether or not people should wear helmets when bicycling, if the freedom of the wind was more important than the security of the safety, and then she talked about how it was a decision that I myself didn't need to make, since my head was denser than concrete, although (she was quick to point out) she hadn't meant that I was dense, meaning not smart, because she thought I was very smart, and then she moved on to the topic of food (I'd probably eaten a lot of good food, traveling the world, lauded at state dinners) and did I want to talk about that (I didn't, I was very busy smiling) and if I didn't want to talk about that then what did I think about having lunch with Michelle (her cousin) and did I even remember Michelle (not really) because on the day that I was riding nude (she was trying to bait me… I hadn't been nude) on top of the Lincoln, with Tom driving through Greenway, Adele had been carrying a doll that she'd been mending, and the doll was for Michelle, who was now all grown up and was a young woman who had once watched Dark Mercy use that living shroud of hers to devour (simply DEVOUR) a carjacker, and how Michelle had thought the man had been literally eaten (instead of teleported to the Athens Penitentiary, where Dark Mercy likes to drop her enemies) and it gave her a taste for meeting superhumans, and she (meaning Michelle) once stood in line to get Taffy's autograph during a book-signing (it must have been for *A Good Long Stretch*) and now would it be okay if Michelle met us (Adele and I) for a lunch or something and, okay, honestly, we're babbling here, aren't we, I mean *I'm* babbling, and, and…

"So I wrote your name on a vibrator, once," Adele said. "I mean I wrote *Steve*. Not *Reaver*. It's no big deal."

"The vibrator wasn't a big deal?" I had her on the defensive. I've been in combat many times. I know when to press my advantage. "Just how big was it?"

"Eight inches. Made of semi-rigid plastic. Warmed by a battery, on... the... *inside*." Her blunt answer (said while leaning closer, and giving that look that nature only teaches to women) had me instantly on the defensive. I've been in combat many times. I know when to retreat.

"We should get back to my birthday party," I said. "It's my birthday. You know. Sort of."

Adele stood. She stepped up onto the picnic table, looked down at me for a moment (she was still using that look of delicious trouble) and I wondered if she was going to try to seduce me, right there, on a picnic table in Charles Park, not far from a mother who had decided Reaver wouldn't be a bad influence on her young son, with Fifth Street immediately adjacent, with cars going by, with any number of SRD satellites trained on my every move, and it would be a ridiculous setting for any sex. Especially with the log cabin so close. It would have only taken a few steps (and I move at three times the speed of a normal man) to reach the cabin door and...

Adele sat on the top of the picnic table, her feet down on the seat to my side, the outside of her left knee pressed up against my ribs. Her eyes were troubled. Worried. She did not look like she was seducing me. She did not look like she was thinking of undressing me. She looked like she was wondering how to go about stripping me in the other way... the mental way... the intervention way.

She said, "Steve. Tell me why you're giving up. Tell me about Eleventh Hour. This thing with Octagon. This pact about you dying. Tell me what has you so sad."

"It's nothing. I'm not sad."

"I know you, Steve Clarke. It's me. It's Adele. I know you. You've been out fighting for all of us. This is me. This is Adele Layton. I'm fighting for you. I'm going to save your life."

She nudged me with her knee.

She said, "Tell me. Tell me what has you so sad."

CHAPTER TWENTY

Lava can burn at nearly two thousand and five hundred degrees, Fahrenheit. That's hotter than any normal human can stand anywhere close to without eventually (somewhat quickly) bursting into flames. And you better keep the lava upwind. The wrong breeze can ignite you.

Paladin wasn't planning to just stand near the lava. He was going down into the caldera. Down into the volcano itself. Down into the lava. Down to the hole where the lava was being spit up from below, where it was being belched up through a blowhole, thrust up through the cracks.

It wasn't something I could have done. It wasn't something anyone else (not even, I don't think, Stellar) could have done. I could stand next to the lava... could even scoop some of it out from one of the flows, meld the liquefied rock (it feels like extremely warm and heavy clay) in my hands... make a lavaball (like a snowball, but more insane) and toss it at my friend, Greg Barrows, as long as I didn't hold it in my hands for more than a few seconds. After that, it began to sting.

"You can't be serious," I told him.

"No. I mean, yes. I am. I'm the only one that can do this."

He was already inside the lava, inside the lip of the flow, peering out like a man at the edge of a pool. His expression hadn't changed. He wasn't burning alive. He could endure the heat and said that his shimmer (even he called it a shimmer) kept the lava from direct contact, kept it maybe a tenth of an inch away from him. So, the lava wasn't bothering my friend. In this respect, he was unique in the region, because an enormous volume of the lava had already bothered its way down much of the mountain. It had already buried half of the town of Pilipano, a town that doesn't make any maps because of the squalor, and because it lacks any sort of government or organization, but it had a population of nearly twenty thousand before the first of the eruptions, and now a bit less than ten thousand, after a few thousand of its people had left, and a few more thousand had died.

SRD geologists (irrefutably backed by data from Checkmate) claimed another eruption was imminent. How big? Big enough that the remaining townspeople (who simply could not be convinced to leave, no matter how much Paladin pleaded and I cursed) would undoubtedly be… how to put this… *sacrificed* to the volcano that many of them considered to be their god. In short, in a day or so, we'd have almost ten thousand more puffs of ash that had once been human beings.

Was there any way to stop this tragedy?

Certainly. Of course. Nothing could be simpler.

All that was needed was for someone to adventure down into the crater and reach the vent. From there, this person (are there any volunteers?) would need to plunge themselves into the lava, swim down through the throat of that lava (and who doesn't love molten rock?) until such a time that they were basking (a private bath!) in the magma reservoir chamber itself. Far hotter down there than the twenty-five hundred degree surface temperature, of course, so let's keep that in mind, shall we? Then (after a suitable time of lounging in the undoubtedly restorative powers of one of nature's most interesting tubs) our volunteer (I'm still not seeing any hands!) would have to plunge through the weakened rock at the side of the magma chamber, boring his way (is that a hand I see, raised there?) through a few miles of rock in order to create a new conduit where the lava can flow (there are probably natural channels in places, ones that only need further encouragement, so this part of the task, I assure you, should not be overly taxing) and then the pressure of the lava will vent through one of the neighboring volcanoes and the town of Pilipano will be saved.

Voila! And... *yes*, that *is* a hand I see, raised to volunteer.

Thank you very much, Paladin. You are doing humanity a great service.

Now, if you'll just come this way, we'll continue the briefing. Hmmm? Yes, you can bring Reaver along if you'd like, but I do wish he would quit his incessant statements of how dangerous this is. I assure you, there are only any number of things that could go wrong.

But Paladin hadn't listened. Nobody had listened. Everybody had a wonderful assortment of *hero* scenarios in their minds. I was the only one with a *shit* scenario. I was outvoted (not that there was any voting) and in his no-nonsense manner Paladin had told me that the people of Pilipano needed help, and that's what he was going to do. He was going to help them.

In the language native to the region, Pilipano means, "lip of hell." Make of that what you will. Back then, I tried to make a lot of it. I even wondered if the type of people who build houses (every last one of them constructed of the most inflammable items they could find) in a town called *Lip Of Hell* were worth saving. They *were* worth saving, of course, and I was only casting verbiage about, because I had a feeling in my head that the mission would be a disaster.

I bitched all the way through the briefing.

I bitched all the way through the walk to the transports.

I bitched all the way during the flight.

We landed.

Then I got down to business, because there was nothing else to do. The nominal leader of Pilipano held a banquet for us (we didn't have time for that) and presented us with a necklace (one for each of us, made of woven grass and carven wood) and there was a group of young women, nearby, dressed prettily, acting bashful, in fact acting exactly like a group of nervous young girls would act if they were being offered as virgin delights for the soon-to-be-saviors of Pilipano, but we didn't have time for that either.

Paladin said some words to the townspeople. I'm not sure what they were. They were in the local tongue. He had a talent for languages, and he'd been practicing during the short flight (it was a long distance, but we were in a Checkmate-designed plane that gobbled the miles by the hundreds and thousands) by means of an anxious translator who repeated phrases to Paladin while the both of them ignored my mentions that swimming into a volcano's reservoir isn't the smartest thing a man can do.

The townspeople gave nods of delight at Paladin's speech. They were the last words he ever spoke to anyone but me, and I don't even know what he said.

With his mysterious speech concluded, Greg Barrows picked me up by the shoulder grab he always used when we were departing a crowded area, or arriving at one. During actual flights he carried me in both arms… like a man carries a bride. Neither of us thought it would be seemly to do that when people were around. That's another confessional gift to the tabloids.

Paladin set me down on the lip of the volcano. We stared at the very mouth of hell for a time, and then… with hops and skips and short flights, we were soon next to the lava.

"I'm going in," he said. I didn't try to stop him. It was too late to talk him out of it. At this point, we were committed. He took to the air, dipping his toes into the lava, hovering above it, testing it for temperature, and then slowly lowered himself within.

"Warm," he said. "Not too hot. I can live through this."

"Good. How can you move through all the magma, though? You won't be able to see."

"I'm pretty good with directions, and I should be able to feel my way around. I'll have to see what gives to my touch, what resists me, and I'll make my way along the veins of heat within the molten rock. This can be done. I can do this."

I almost said a few things.

I almost talked about the Greek god of fire and volcanoes, because Greg had sometimes pretended to be as such, not all that many years previously, and now he was sinking down into the god's domain. It was a trespass of entirely unprecedented arrogance. Hephaestus might throw a shit fit. I could have said something about that. But I didn't.

I almost talked about how Stellar had spoken of how she wanted to (her word) mate with Greg. How she'd asked me for his phone number, making me think we were in high school. I could have spoken of how she'd asked about what Greg likes to do in bed… how she had said, "*I should do what I can to become his competent lover*," and she seemed to be in earnest. She had called him by name. Greg Barrows. She knows everyone's name, of course. She never spilled Greg's identity, not (at least I believe) because of any pact of secrecy, but because she honestly doesn't understand that not everyone knows everyone else's name. Some types of ignorance are foreign (or, possibly, alien) to her. Anyway… I almost told Paladin of all of this, but I didn't. He wasn't much interested in women except for relationships, and he and Taffy were already together at the time that Stellar was asking.

I almost, as Paladin was going down into the lava, revealed a monstrous amount of other thoughts. I suddenly wanted to say so very much. I opened my mouth but the intense heat dried my throat, and while I was swallowing, trying to recover my voice, Paladin slipped beneath the lava and he was gone.

I stayed next to the lava for several hours. There were hideous minutes piling upon each other, adding up, with time passing, and me waiting to see if Paladin would ever come up out from the lava… if I would ever see the molten rock slide away from his eyes and drip off that stupidly broken nose of his. In the surveillance footage, taken before the helicopters were nearly caught in the eruption, I am standing still for minutes, for an hour, unmoving, waiting for my friend.

My memory is very good. I remember almost nothing of my thoughts at the time.

A few hours after Greg went down into the lava, the volcano erupted, but it was more of a burp than a roar. Jets of lava reached into the sky, forcing the observing helicopters to retreat (Checkmate's unmanned copter was nabbed by an arc of lava, as neatly as any kraken of legend had ever nabbed any seaman from a boat) and covering me with a splash of lava that had me hissing in agony for the five seconds it took the material to cool to a point that I found bearable, and then I soon began scraping the rock away from my costume.

Just as I finished with that, I saw Paladin surface near the center of the molten pool.

Then, miles away… as Greg Barrows rose to the surface of one volcano, one of the neighboring ones (a smaller one, with no nearby population, a volcano named *Aara Trapano*… the Left Tit of Hell) began spewing flame and ash and, finally, lava. Erupting.

The plan had worked.

I gave a cheer. An absolute pure shriek of joy.

It was a joy that died when I saw that Paladin was foundering in the lava. Struggling and spent. Much of his costume had been sheared away by the molten rock, or burnt away by the heat, or destroyed by whatever else waits for a man when he's arrogant enough to dive down into hell.

Lava is molten rock, meaning it's thick enough that I can run across it, if I'm moving at full speed.

I was.

I was running to help my friend. Running an arc along the surface of the lava, an arc that met up with Paladin at the top of the curve. I grabbed him by his hair (no time for niceties) and was surprised to find it matted with lava intermixed with the strands. That just shouldn't be, you understand. The shimmer should have chased it away. Nothing should have been touching him.

I dragged Greg as quickly as I could to the edge of the molten lava. His added weight was slowing me, and because of this I began to sink into the lava myself. I was ankle deep with every step. And then calf deep. Knee deep. My legs were cooking, charring, glowing a furious green that shone even over the hissing red of the molten rock. The lava was contained in a bowl of sorts… a bowl with sloped sides, perhaps ten feet high. An easy jump if my legs hadn't been burning, or if I could have planted on something as solid as real rock… not the unreal surface of liquefied rock, in which Paladin and I were both moments from death.

With Paladin's healing powers it would have taken the work of moments for him to be fully restored. All I had to do to save his life was to give him that moment. All I had to do was to take him from the lava.

I clawed into the sides of the magma bowl, inching us upwards. My friend was charred in places, and in other places he was boiled meat that was pulling away from his bones. The lava had worn him down, badly, over the hours. A lesser man couldn't have healed from such horror. A lesser man would have long since succumbed to the damage that the lava had inflicted. A lesser man wouldn't have been Paladin, though.

A lesser man wouldn't have been my hero.

"Did… did it work?" he asked. I had managed to scale a few feet up the interior of the bowl. Far enough that I could endure the heat. My lower legs, entombed in hardening rock, were reforming, healing, becoming whole again. I found that I was crying. I was very scared. Shivering with fear. I felt like the world was turning over, tumbling away, leaving me behind, and I was holding onto Greg and trying to catch something… the past or the future or anything that wouldn't break away in my grasp.

Climbing was very much harder than it should have been.

"Did... it... work?" Greg asked. I'd tried to answer him the first time, but my breath and words had steamed away when I opened my mouth. I don't know how he was managing to speak. I don't know what rulebook he had been given that allowed him to bypass all the laws, the ones the rest of us live by. I tried to answer him, but all I could manage was a hiss. A crackle. Finally, a nod of my head.

"Yes," my nod said. It had worked.

"Good enough, then," he said.

It was very much harder to pull him from the lava than it should have been. I was thinking, I remember this... I was thinking that the lava was trying to hold him. That it had him by the toes, the feet, the legs, and it was clenching on him. It had been angered by his intrusion, and it wanted him to pay.

He said, "I dove inside. It was... wonderful. No man has ever seen it. Wonderful." He slipped from my grasp. A desperate grab kept him from falling wholly back into the lava. My grab was at about one times the speed of a normal man. That was all I had in me. Every inch of my skin was glowing green.

Paladin, half out of the lava, limp in my grasp, said, "I wish you could have seen. I wish you could have seen. I wish you could have seen the colors. And it worked. It worked. This is a good way. This is a good thing I've done. This is a good way to be remembered."

It was very much harder than it should have been to pull him from the lava. His skin was peeling away. His muscles were sloughing off. His hair was gone. There wasn't a trace of his shimmer. He was revealed to the elements, and the elements were the worst of their kind.

"Good enough, then," he said again. He gave a smile. For one moment I was amazed by that smile. It had joy in it. For one moment, I believed that we were both going to make it.

And then I realized why it was so *hard* to pull him away from the lava.

Paladin was fighting me.

I was struggling against the strongest of our kind.

And he wanted to die.

"Greg?" I said. It was all I had. My lungs sizzled. I must have been green on the inside, too.

"This is going to be hard for you," Paladin said. "But you don't know. You don't understand. That day. Those chemicals. Being in the accident. My arm. Healing. Being Paladin." His words were chopped. His muscles weren't working. He was dying in my hands and I couldn't… pull… him… up… because he was still struggling against me. Still.

"You don't understand," he said. "All these years. I've tried not to let on. I've tried not to let it show. I've tried to keep a smile on my face. But. Since that day, Steve. Since that day. You don't understand. It's never quit. That day has never quit for me. Each day. Each. Day. Agony. It was agony. And it's never quit. It still hurts."

I was looking down at him. He was only at the end of my arm, but it was so very far away.

He said, "It's never quit hurting, Steve. It's never quit."

I could remember him, at times, being distant. Whenever that happened, I (and let's face it, everyone else) thought he was thinking thoughts that were probably above mine, pondering philosophies on a *very-possibly-might-be divine* scale. Looking into his eyes, then, with me suspended just above the lava, I realized he'd only been trying to hold back the pain. Every day. Every time.

"I saved an entire city, Steve," he told me. "Good enough."

There was too much heat. I couldn't speak.

"Let me go," he said.

Greg Barrows was twenty-five years old. He was my hero. He was my friend. He was the one who had taught me that being a hero isn't always about doing a wonderful thing. Sometimes it's about doing a horrible thing. Sometimes it's not about doing what you want. It's always about doing the right thing.

I opened my hand. I sometimes wish I'd saved him. I sometimes wish that I would have been a different type of hero. But I've always felt I did the right thing.

Paladin was Greg Barrows.

Greg Barrows was Paladin.

I was the only one to hear his last words, spoken as he sank beneath the lava and into the lips and mouth of hell.

Greg said, "Good enough."

⌖

I wasn't surprised that Adele was crying when I finished telling her what had happened in the volcano. I wasn't surprised that I was crying, either. The world at large had only known that Paladin succumbed to the volcano, meaning the true story of his death was new to Adele, so it was understandable why she would be so overcome with emotion. And me, from my side, the true story of Paladin's death is something my very reliable memory has replayed for me every day since it happened. It hits a little harder each time.

After the crying was done, we gathered ourselves and walked from the park, hardly looking at each other, not speaking, feeling (at least from my side) like we were at the end result of a very shameful encounter. We'd walked only a quarter of a block before, without looking at me, Adele said, "It's not your fault." The words more or less swirled around me... no different than the pollen in the air, moving aside with the wind of my passing. Then, only a moment later, she said it again, but this time she was looking at me. Adele was looking at me. It made a world of difference.

"It's not your fault," she said. Her eyes were honest. Her eyes were earnest. Her eyes were Adele's.

It made a difference.

I nodded.

It felt like some weight slid away from me with the nod. Some weight that had been anchored with claws. Some weight that had been chased away by Adele's eyes. Not all, of course, of the weight was gone. But there had been progress. For the first time in years.

We were only a half block into our walk, but I felt like we'd stepped ten thousand miles forward. A hell of a leap.

A block into our walk, she asked, "Your list? It... on it you say that you might want to shut down SRD. Why is that?"

"I'm not... sure anymore." A half block ago I would have described SRD as a sewer pipe. You can point a sewer pipe in any direction, but it's still just shit that comes out of it.

I said, "I'm not sure how much good they do. But I know how much bad they do. Tempest, for one."

"And you for another. And Paladin. And Checkmate is moving the world forward. You read about his ozone restoration project?"

"Yes." I was in an argument I felt like I could lose. I was mentally crossing off an item on my list. Adele was changing my perception of the world, and my list would have to change with it.

She said, "Fighting SRD is like failing an enthusiastic student because they miss a few questions on a quiz."

"You just think that up?"

"It's from one of my books."

"Oh."

Adele said, "And… your list. The last item. It just says… fight. What are you wanting to fight?" We were a block and a half into our walk. Not far, really, but already into the hard questions.

"I'll know it when I see it," I told her.

"Not yourself. Don't fight yourself. Nobody wins those fights. Don't fight against anything. Fight *for* something."

"That from your books, too?" It came out a little sarcastic. More than I meant. I really wanted to know.

"From Paladin. A week before he died. When he was talking at Bolton Elementary."

"Oh."

I was thinking of Greg talking to all those kids. All those kids. Talking about the fight. The good fight. Even while he was in agony. How could I have missed his agony all throughout the years? It wasn't until he was in the lava… until I was looking for it… that I could see it in his eyes. He'd hid it for so long. Heroic.

I was thinking of the swirl of the lava. Lava always looks reluctant. Grudgingly forced to flow. As if the rock cannot believe the twists and turns of its life and its fate. Blundering along. Burning things.

Just under three blocks into our walk, Adele took my hand. A half block later she lifted my hand, somewhat, staring at it, as if searching it for some sort of clue. To what? I didn't know. She was holding my right hand. She wasn't holding the hand that had let Paladin slide into the lava. There weren't any marks on it of any kind, despite all the damages it has sustained over the years. It always heals. It never changes. It lets me handle that chore.

"What are you looking for?" I finally asked. Her eyes jerked up to mine, as if I'd caught her in some sort of criminal act.

"I'm not sure," she said. "Some sort of… difference, I suppose." Her hand grabbed tighter on mine. I felt like I should let her go. I felt like I should have never told her what happened to Paladin. I felt like I should tell her everything. I felt like there was nothing else to tell.

I said, "A difference?"

"Everyone keeps telling me about how you're different. I don't see it."

"I can lift tens of thousands of pounds. I can jump almost forty feet in the air. I can take a bullet to my eyes, to my *eyes*, without being overly bothered. I can…"

"Do you kiss any differently?"

I was saying something (it was probably a question, but I'm not sure) when Adele leaned into me, raised up onto her toes, and she touched her lips to mine. It was somewhat tentative, somewhat respectful, somewhat curious, and those aspects lasted for barely long enough to register (even to a man who sees the world at three times faster than the common guy on the street) and then all of the "somewhat" was gone, as was the *tentative* and the *respectful*. Her kiss became demanding. Searching. Furious.

I kissed her back.

She stumbled. Fell away from me.

I'd been too hard on her. Too much strength. It's like that for me, sometimes. I can poke my fingers into solid steel and my lips have the same proportionate power and…

… and Adele recovered from her stumble. There wasn't any chastisement in her eyes. No wonder. No awe. Nothing but a desire to move back against me… this time with a hand on the back of my neck so that she wouldn't fall away. Her tongue slid into my mouth and her whole body was against mine.

It lasted.

In time, in time, after some time, she moved a step back and she blushed.

She said, "Sorry about that."

She said, "No. Actually I'm not."

She said, "Are you sorry about it?"

She said, "No. Don't answer that."

She said, "Answer it."

I said, "Nothing has ever made me happier. Nothing has ever…"

We were kissing again.

I had barely seen her move.

Me.

A man who registers the world three times faster than most anyone else.

Caught flat-footed.

Right on the lips.

CHAPTER TWENTY-ONE

Laura and Apple had eaten half of my birthday cake, but had replaced the slices with wedges of pizza (ordered when we were gone) abutting up against the remaining cake (as if to disguise their misdeed) with candles on the cake and the pizza, both, celebrating how I was still alive.

"You guys kiss?" Laura asked.

"We guys kissed," I answered.

"Tongue like an iron bar?" Laura whispered to Adele in a voice louder than most people's normal conversation.

"No comment," Adele answered.

"Good god," Laura said. "That's worse than any vulgar comment. Now Apple and I will have to assume the worst of you both. And about time, too."

Apple said, "I should probably be going. It's most definitely *all hands on deck* at the store after, you know, after the parking lot."

I said, "I should make an appearance there, too. I'll give you a ride. I've still got my rental."

"Oh. Okay." Something flickered in Apple's eyes. I wondered what her thoughts were. I couldn't read them. I couldn't even read mine. It had been a strange day. For both of us.

I asked her, "You need to stop off at your house beforehand? Change of clothes?" I'd noticed that Apple's clothes were more than a little ruffled. I'd noticed that Laura was wearing a different top than when we'd left. I'd noticed that Wiggles, the cat, was mad at them for some reason. I'd noticed a dollop of cake frosting behind Apple's ear.

"No reason to change clothes. The cleanup's going to be messy. Not much sense in me putting on any dainty clothes."

There were some few comments after that. Adele made some intimations that she wouldn't mind me staying around. Her eyes flickered up to her bedroom. I admit it made a pair of knees (ones that can support a stack of cars) go a bit weak. Her lips wiggled. I had to look away. I had to focus on being a hero. She had given me a kiss. I couldn't forget that I had to be worthy of such things. I had something important to do.

Laura became petulant. I was driving off with her girl. She pretended to be jealous. Over-pretended. She even took me aside and said that I can't kiss everyone. Her emotions were all over the place. I felt bad for her. I would have said something soothing, something that let her know there wasn't anything to worry about, if my own emotions weren't all over the place as well, and if it hadn't been a lie.

There was something to worry about.

When we left the house, I saw Mistress Mary a block away, watching me as I got into the car. I wondered who else might be watching me. SRD, assuredly, but how about the rest of Eleventh Hour? Tempest was dead. Macabre was dead. Where was Laser Beast? Where was Siren? Were they near? I didn't think so. Siren exudes a certain mood, one that permeates the air. In the lawn next to Adele's, Travis Morton was mowing the grass. He wouldn't have been doing that if Siren was anywhere nearby. He would have been standing, breathing, thinking, breathing, swaying, breathing.

And Laser Beast? Laser Beast doesn't have an ounce of subtlety beneath that fur of his. If he was watching, he'd be shooting. Lasering. Whatever.

"Shotgun!" Apple said, as if it was a prize. There was only the two of us.

"I wasn't about to make you ride in the back. I was thinking you'd drive, anyway. You're a better driver than I am."

"True. I should go pro. You happen to own any racecars? I could… hey… is that… is that Mistress Mary?"

"Yes." I looked to Mistress Mary. Gave a short wave. She returned it.

She was sitting in somebody's treehouse, two houses down. The treehouse was in a big oak tree, hanging over the road, a danger to traffic that would have been removed from any major city, and most minor ones. I enjoyed it. There's not enough Norman Rockwell left in the world.

Apple slid behind the wheel. Adjusted the seat. Both mirrors. She reversed onto the street, backing expertly into our lane and then transitioning into a smooth drive. I watched her hands. They were well trained. Doing their job by rote. Muscle memory. I wondered about her and Laura. If it was love or not. I hoped it was love. I hoped it wasn't.

When we were well into traffic, I asked, "Who are you?"

"Huh? What a question! And frankly, it's something I ask myself all the time. I'm not sure how much longer I can work part time at a grocery store. I mean, it's not like the pay is the best. Still… job security. Food, you know? It's the one thing that won't go out of style." We were passing the antique store. Gus Ferkins was sitting outside. He was a million years old. Like an advertisement for his business. He was a corncob pipe short of a snapshot from another age.

I asked Apple, "Who are you?"

"You mean my name? I guess you don't know my last name, do you?" Her smile was infectious. My own smile was honest. I wasn't kidding her with it at all. She was still unexpectedly pleasant to be around.

She said, "So… my name is Ming Greel. I know it's not a sexy name, but, there you are. I think Mom named me after the Chinese Dynasty. I think Dad named me after that evil bald guy in the Flash Gordon movies. I haven't decided which one's better."

"Who are you?"

"That's the question, right? Especially lately. I mean… Laura. She's… she makes me wonder what I'm doing with my life. I can't be a painter, like her, but maybe school or something? You don't know any job opportunities, do you?"

"Who are you?"

We were driving past the Mighty Convenient convenience store. I had a sudden flash of Tom, standing out back, years ago, trying to learn how to work with a yo-yo with Judy laughing about it, and then her smiling in resigned fashion (and resigned pleasure) when Tom finally gave up, held up the yo-yo, and told me, "See this? See this string? I'm going to tie Judy's wrists together with this, later, and she's going to pretend to be a slave girl and I'm going to pretend that I'm pretending to be her master." That was... how many years ago? I couldn't place our ages at the time. I wasn't sure of who we were, in those days. I remember knowing it all, then, though.

Apple hadn't said anything for a couple of blocks.

I asked, "Who are you?"

She looked at me. She still had the smile. Her look was that of a person who isn't at all nervous at being in a vehicle, an enclosed space, with a superhuman. I've come to be able to distinguish that look. I've seen the other kind, the nervous look, for enough years, starting way back with the guards in the armored car that took Greg and me from the hospital, away from my month long coma, and into SRD's facilities.

Apple parked the car alongside the curb. We were a block from where Greg Barrows once lived. I could have thrown a baseball and hit the house.

She said, "How much do you know?"

"During the fight with Tempest, you broke away from me and you ran."

"Yeah?"

"You broke away from me." I couldn't have only just thrown a baseball and hit Greg Barrows's house. I could have thrown an anvil. I could have thrown a car.

"You noticed that."

"Not right at first. Only occurred to me later. Normal people don't just break away from my grip."

"You must have relaxed your grip, then. A lot was going on."

"Children of the Spill."

Apple said, "Excuse me?" I rolled down a window. It was warm, inside. It couldn't have been the temperature. Not just the temperature. I'm good with temperatures.

"Children of the Spill. That was something Paladin and I called ourselves. A few other people named us that way, too. Not the public, though. Not the public. The public never called us that, because most people didn't know about Greg Barrows. I was the Hero of the Spill. I was the Child of the Spill. It took Greg being added into the mix before it was *Heroes*. Before it was *Children*. Most people didn't know about Greg."

"I think I heard you say it that way, once. I was just repeating it." Apple didn't seem to be trying to convince me of anything. She was just saying words. She seemed to think it was amusing she was even speaking, adorable that we were even having the conversation.

She handed me the keys to the car. That seemed to be more meaningful than any words she was saying.

I said, "Tempest didn't simply fall from the sky. She didn't overload, like you suggested. You brought her down, somehow. That's why you broke away from me. Because you didn't want me to see what you were doing."

"This isn't much evidence. I've heard you can jump like... forty feet. You sure you aren't just jumping to a bizarre conclusion that I'm... what... someone else? Who?"

"I'll be honest. I don't have the slightest clue. Maybe you're Siren?"

"Do I look like Siren?"

"You could transform. I don't know. Paladin was always the smart one."

"No."

I looked at Apple. Tried to understand what she meant. No. *No*? Paladin *wasn't* the smart one? Did she mean... did she mean... that *I* was the smart one? Nobody could believe that. I've blundered through every puzzle I've ever blundered into. It's not like I have an amazing brain. It's not like I'm... I'm not...

I said, "Checkmate?" I hadn't meant it to sound like a question. I meant it to sound like a statement from someone who was standing tall on a mountain of knowledge.

Apple said, "When my brain first began to change, when my thoughts began...." I'm not sure if I blacked out at this point. I'm not sure I retained any real sense of consciousness. Apple's words were an admission of who she was. An admission that she was Checkmate, that she, at least these days, was the brains behind SRD, that she was responsible for half the world's truly advanced technologies, and was known to be holding back a wealth of other advances, machines and tools for which Mankind Was Not Yet Ready. I regained my composure (my consciousness?) fairly quickly. She was still on the same sentence. Or maybe she had started again.

Apple said, "When my brain first began to change, when my thoughts began racing, I decided I needed an identity. Not just a secret identity, but a completely unthinkable identity. So I built the suit. The Checkmate suit. I built it male, on the outside. Nobody seemed to think a decidedly male suit of armor could contain a decidedly female sort of woman."

"Seeing is believing."

"Exactly. The suit had the big chest, the male hips, the male voice, so nobody ever thought to wonder if maybe there was a woman inside, that the male hips were a red herring, that a voice modulator was doing its magic, and that the big chest contained an array of targeting and weaponry systems, along with a fairly nice pair of pert little boobs."

"How'd you bring down Tempest?"

"Didn't even distract you with talk of nice pert boobs, then?"

"Not right at this moment."

She sighed. Opened the car door. After a bit, waiting to see if I would react, and seeing that I didn't, she reached in for her small duffel bag (it had a Siren button stuck into its side) and waited to see if I would react to her reaching for that. To be honest, I hadn't thought about it as being problematic, but her hesitation, her glance towards me, her wary caution, put me on alert.

Still, I let her take the bag.

I've done smarter things.

It's not like I'm Checkmate.

She waited for me on the sidewalk. We were only seven blocks from the gravel drive (the one between George Kuchester's house and the "*Welcome to Greenway*!" sign) that leads down into the gravel pit. There was a row of cherry trees waiting expectantly for someone to notice them. I wondered if Adele would like some of the blossoms. I wondered how they would look in her hair. I wondered how Checkmate had brought Tempest down from out of the skies. I wondered how Apple had done that.

She said, "I studied Tempest, of course, when she was in SRD. So much to learn. She was like a Rosetta Stone to unlock the secrets of nature. Haven't you ever wondered how her powers worked? If she was just… moving the weather around like children's blocks, or if the weather could *understand* her somehow? Haven't you ever just wondered that?"

"No." It seemed important to lie.

"Liar." It seemed inconsequential that my lie had been caught.

Apple, seeing only my blank face (we were both walking towards the quarry, with some unspoken acknowledgment involved) went on with, "And when I studied Tempest, I worked with her brain waves. Tracked them. Charted them. All the peaks. Valleys."

"So?"

"So I knew just how to cancel those waves. I could use that knowledge to set up a valley against a peak, and a peak against a valley. Everything cancelling each other. Flattening out the line."

"You shut off her brain?"

"Essentially. Yes."

There were standing puddles next to the road. The air smelled of dank water. Mosquitoes were buzzing around. The day was warm. I thought of the giant cockroach in SRD labs. I would rather face a mosquito than a cockroach. Unless they were giants. Then it's the other way around.

I said, "Apple. Do you remember when Tempest and Macabre were…"

"Are you seriously about to ask me if I remember the time that Tempest and Macabre changed the very fabric of space and extended Earth's atmosphere to the moon?"

"Okay. I suppose it *is* something you remember." There were mosquitoes buzzing around my eyes. One of them landed on my cheek. Tried for a taste of me. It blunted its… what are they? Stingers? Noses? I'm not sure of the term. Anyway… she (all biting mosquitoes are female, I think I've read) broke her blood siphon on my invulnerable flesh.

I said, "Octagon took down Tempest and Macabre, that time. Octagon did that in the same way as you took down Tempest at the grocery store."

Apple said, "Of course." I knew what she meant by it. But I was waiting for her to say it. I was waiting for confirmation. I shouldn't, of course, have been waiting. Being a man who moves three times faster than anyone else can make you complacent. It's easy to forget that moving three times faster can be cancelled out when you're talking to someone who's ten steps ahead. Or even eight.

Apple said, "I'm Checkmate."

There was a buzzing near my ear.

Apple said, "I'm Octagon."

A mosquito bit me on my neck. Something sank into my bloodstream. A nose. A stinger. Whatever. It was the first time I'd been bitten by a bug in almost a decade.

"Take some time off," Octagon said, staring me in the eyes, pulling a laser pistol from her duffel bag. But I barely heard her.

The world was spinning and I was falling to the ground.

CHAPTER TWENTY-TWO

Laser Beast.

Siren.

Firehook.

Octagon.

They were all there when I woke up.

It would probably be more dramatic if I claimed that I was bound by chains of an unknown metal, unbreakable even to *one such as I*, with evil automatons and other advanced instruments of tortuous devastation surrounding me. Beams of destructive light, blades honed as to be immeasurably sharp, the cackling of a madwoman's laughter rebounding from the stone walls, perhaps soaring outward through the lone window, the one that looks out across the battlements, over the edge of the cliff and down to the roaring surf below.

In truth, though, I wasn't bound at all. I was just sprawled in the loose rocks of Greenway's quarry. My neck throbbed where the mosquito (I had no illusions that it had actually been a mosquito) had bitten my neck. My neck had a soft green glow, barely visible from the edges of my vision. My left cheek was against the quarry floor. Perhaps two feet from me was a fossilized snail of some kind. A pair of fossilized leaves. Ten feet past these remnants of the ancient world was Laser Beast, down on his haunches, grinning at me. Firehook was standing next to him, with drops of fire slipping down from his fingers, sizzling onto the rocky surface, creating tiny pools of molten rock.

I couldn't see Siren, but I could feel her nearby. It wasn't exactly morning, but I was lying on morning wood.

And, past Firehook, past Laser Beast... there was Octagon in the black costume with the male shape, a shape I now knew to be as much a lie as Checkmate's armor. I wondered if the rest of Eleventh Hour knew that Octagon was the girl from the grocery store. I wondered if they knew that. I wondered if I had the strength to stand up. It didn't feel like I did, but I wasn't doing anything else, so I gave it a try.

"He lives! Walks! Breathes!" Laser Beast exclaimed like a carnival barker, watching me rise unsteadily to my feet. It wouldn't, of course, take me very long to regain my full health, my full power. The ghost of Tom Clarke was burning within me. I would soon be green to go.

"We shouldn't let him live too long," Firehook said. "We should kill him now. Before he recovers. You know he recovers! You know that!" The last bits were yelled to Octagon, who was sat on a boulder. In my mind, Octagon was sitting in a feminine fashion, but I wasn't sure if my eyes were registering that because it was true, or because my perceptions were now colored by the knowledge of the girl beneath the suit.

I started laughing.

It made them nervous.

I liked having them nervous, but that's not why I was laughing. Something had occurred to me. I searched around for Siren, trying to find where she was standing, using (there's no way this statement can't be vulgar, so I'm not even going to try) my cock like a divining rod, leading me to the source of its interest.

Siren was leaning against a huge and raggedy boulder, a mass conglomerate of rocks that had been cemented together by eons of pressure, a unified boulder that had fallen from the quarry's wall. She was standing in its shade. Direct sunlight can dry out skin, make it leathery. That's something, of course, that Siren avoids.

She asked, "Why are you laughing?" I heard Firehook grunt. I heard

Laser Beast groan. The possibility of Siren's voice is an aphrodisiac. A few actual words goes beyond that. It made its mark on me, too. I kept laughing, though.

I said, "You remember that time that I asked you who was the better man in bed? Me or Octagon?"

Siren's eyes flickered nervously to Laser Beast and Firehook. So… they didn't know. Siren then smiled (jelly… I was jelly) and answered, "You were asking the wrong question."

It… was… important… to quit talking to Siren. It was important to focus on other things. On staying alive. It was important to fight Laser Beast. To kill Firehook. I could do it. I was Reaver. I could beat them in impressive ways. I could show Siren what I was capable of… display myself to her so that she would…

It… was… important to… quit… talking to Siren.

I turned to Octagon and asked, "I thought I had two weeks? Didn't you give me two weeks? Don't I still have a day?"

Octagon stood. Walked a few steps closer. The voice that came to me was masculine in nature. It was the same voice that Octagon had always used. But now I knew better. I had a feeling I knew what Octagon was going to say. Something about curiosity killing the cat.

"That was before you started playing detective," Octagon said. "That was back when Macabre was still alive. When Tempest ruled the skies. That was back then. There has to be some payment for what you've done. A debit, at least, of a few hours."

There was no longer a green glow from my neck. I wasn't hunched over with the pain and the fog of whatever had been injected into me. I had to think. I had to outthink them. I had to do something unexpected. I had to surprise them. Mistress Mary had said there was some sort of schism within Eleventh Hour. It was quite possibly true that I couldn't beat them. Not all of them, together. But maybe I wouldn't have to. Maybe they could do it themselves. Maybe I could make them forget that I was the one who had killed Macabre. That I was the one who had killed Tempest. That I was the one who had cut off so many of their plans at the root. That I was their foil. That I was an asshole. If I could make them fight each other, focus elsewhere, forget that I was the one who…

No.

Come to think of it...

I wasn't the one who had killed Tempest.

Octagon had done that.

Octagon had brought the storm goddess down from the skies.

Why?

From some notion that my two weeks weren't up? From some sense of honor that her word needed to be kept? Or was she just angry that Tempest was attacking her, too? But Tempest couldn't have known that Apple was Octagon. Or... could she have? I'd presumed myself to be the target. What if it had been Octagon?

What if... ?

What if... ?

What if I discarded these lines of thought?

What if I was smart enough to understand who I was? What if I was smart enough to want to live to kiss Adele Layton a few more times? What if I didn't want to die? Spending any more time *thinking* would have been falling into Octagon's game. She was the best at that. I was the best at other things.

I was the best at being Reaver.

Sometimes... that meant punching someone.

Sometimes... that meant being an asshole.

I was okay with that.

They... are... never... ready.

I move at three times the speed of a common man and they are never ready.

The shit thing about Eleventh Hour is that they are all, each of them, the greatest threat. I had to abandon all hope of playing it smart, of taking out the weakest first, or the strongest first, and I had to plan on taking an enormous amount of damage and I had to plan on not having a plan.

I went for Firehook first, because he was the closest, and because I have never forgotten the time he'd ripped out my lung (it had been during his brief team-up with Nemesis, before he'd murdered her for sleeping with Warp) and most of all, of course, like anybody else with an ounce of moral fiber, I've never forgotten his first appearance where he'd melted the children in the school bus.

It doesn't matter where I hit somebody. A punch to their jaw takes away a year of their life. A punch to their shoulder has the same effect. And a punch to the jaw of man composed of a fire hot enough to burn even me, that would be stupid.

A punch to his nuts seemed like it might be satisfying, though.

Turned out, it was.

Laser Beast had just enough time to say, "He's…" and then I was on the two of them. I punched as hard as I could into Firehook's groin, at the same time ducking the swing from Laser Beast's clawed hand. The clawed hand wasn't even on the way, yet… but I knew it would be. I've studied how each of them fights. These were the predictable ones. I never knew how to handle Tempest or Macabre, because their powers (and minds) were too unpredictable. Firehook likes to snatch portions of an enemy's body with his hook, though. That's what he likes to do. And Laser Beast, despite his lasers, likes to lead with those claws. It didn't used to be that way. These days, though, he's more *beast* than *laser*. It helps.

Laser Beast's clawed hand swiped over my head. By then, Firehook was already falling, his groin a mangled mess. I hadn't held back. I wasn't relying on stealing a few years. I was interested in taking them all.

The loose rocks where I'd been standing, the ones that had kicked into the air from beneath my feet with the speed of my assault, hadn't yet fallen to the ground before I was picking up Laser Beast and hurling him towards Octagon. He, I mean she, I mean Octagon, had to duck her incoming teammate, and also divert a blast from her laser pistol that had been intended to cut me in two, but in reality barely missed slicing the beast in half. That would have been a nice bonus. A crackerjack prize.

A roar of flame came up from below.

Firehook, insane with pain, with rage, and with his usual insanity, was cutting loose. The billow was like a small atomic cloud, and with my perception, with the way things move three times slower to my eyes, I could see the creeping flame inching outwards from Firehook's prone body, eating the rocks around him, turning million-year-old fossils into ash, completely dead at last, with the fire burning the rocks, charring the air, turning everything to glass or ash or into nothing at all, and with the flames clawing at my legs.

I leapt.

I'm good at it.

With no time to make an intelligent decision, I had to make the quickest one. I chose to jump away from Octagon, away from the flames. These were good decisions. I chose to jump behind the nearest huge boulder. This was also wise. I chose to jump closer to Siren, who stood next to that boulder.

Looking at her, you'd think this was really smart, but of course it's not.

The flames billowed up around me as I leapt. They were grabbing for me, eager to thwart my escape. If Firehook had kept his senses about him (not an easy task, when a superhuman has belted you in the groin hard enough to shatter your pelvis and make nasty pudding of your hopes for future generations) he could have shot me out of the air. I try not to leap very often during a fight, because once I give myself up to gravity I take away the element of my speed. Firehook couldn't concentrate, though, and his flames were actually giving me an element of cover (two or three hissing bitches of laser beams nearly clipped me) and I landed safely (ha ha ha) next to Siren, immediately grabbing her and pulling her behind the boulder (Firehook's flames were encroaching on the territory) and then nearly succumbing to the throb and the thrum of feeling her naked flesh. I had her by the shoulder. She was wearing a light spring dress that probably couldn't believe its luck.

"Here?" she said, putting a question (and so very much more) into her voice. "You want to have sex here? Now?" I hadn't wanted to. Before. Hadn't been thinking of it (a lie) and had only wanted to save her life. Now, though, I had saved her life, right? Shouldn't there be a reward?

I was reaching beneath her dress when a laser beam pierced the entire boulder and nearly my head as well. It startled me into sanity (not all the way into it, but within yelling range, I'd say) and I remembered that I was in a fight.

So I moved my hand from where it had been touching Siren (my hand argued about this in an almost perceptible voice, and I'd swear the intimate area where I'd been touching Siren complained about the loss of my fingers in an entirely audible voice) and I braced for some super heroics, and I picked up the boulder.

It wasn't that difficult. Couldn't have weighed more than twenty thousand pounds. Well within my range.

It wasn't a wieldy weight, though, and so I wobbled a bit as I moved forward, and I took a laser to my shoulder and worried about the next few shots, because I wasn't exactly moving at full speed. Luckily, behind every good man (and even behind me) there is a good woman, or in this case a beautiful one, which is largely regarded as the same thing.

Siren called out, "Darling. The lasers are nearly hitting me." That was the end of the lasers. No more incoming shots. That gave me time to waddle forward (Siren was moving along with me, whispering into my ear, telling me how big and strong I was, and how her little body was trembling) with the flames soaring up and around and over the boulder, turning it red hot, igniting my uncovered legs, and at one point a fire hook lashed around my foot (Siren jumped over it with a little "Whoop!" of surprise that sounded so sexually adorable that I nearly came in my pants and dropped the boulder in pleasure) and a huge chunk of my foot was snatched away, forcing me to slow myself even further, but I made progress, and I made progress, and I made progress, until I finally nearly stumbled on Firehook's leg, giving me a clear idea where he was.

Which is exactly where I dropped the big rock.

By then, by that time, due to the deprivations of the flames and all the incoming blasts, the boulder had probably lost five thousand pounds. Not a bad weight loss program.

In this case, though, that still left fifteen thousand pounds of weight, which was more than enough to squash a man who well deserved to be treated like a bug. I had no regrets about snuffing out his flame… none past how the method of his execution meant that I hadn't had a chance to see his expression when the rock was coming down.

When the rock hit, the shudder of the impact knocked Siren off balance. The surrounding flames left us with a WHUFFF of an explosion and Siren's dress fluttered as she began to tumble with an unconcerned look… the expression of a woman who knew that men were put on Earth to catch her when she falls.

I did.

I lost a couple seconds doing it.

I lost even more seconds having done it.

She nuzzled against me with a smile of gratitude and asked if there was anything she could do in return. Her face was alluringly lit by the green glow that was coming from my legs, from where they'd been exposed to the flames. I was lowering my lips to hers (and picturing images that would have sent a Satanic porn star to confessional) when Laser Beast leapt onto me from behind.

He bit at my neck. Maybe he'd been driven mad by how I'd just killed his friend (I assumed Firehook and he were friends, since they were teammates and since people like them have no one else in their lives, no one to be close to, no one to pass them beers and to tell vulgar jokes) or maybe he'd transformed, finally, to nothing about lasers and all about the beast. It's even quite possible that the animal in him had seen my lips about to touch Siren's own lips (a moment he had STOLEN from me) and was defending his territory. Siren, of course, is no one's territory… but we all have our dreams.

"Free-grack KILL you!" Laser Beast said. I couldn't entirely understand him. There were more words, or more attempts at words, or something. His teeth were grating on my neck (not strong enough to penetrate) and I was idly wondering if I would turn into a werewolf if he did manage to sink his teeth into me (of course I knew that such stories were myths, but I'd often had lunch with personages of a far more mythological bent) and about half of me was trying to kill him because I needed to pay more attention to Octagon (where the hell was she and what was she doing?) and the rest of me was paying attention to Siren… because I knew (oh hell yes) exactly where she was and what the two of us should be doing.

So I wasn't paying much attention to Laser Beast and I did not feel it when his lasers began to warm up. I'd stupidly (listen… *everyone* is stupid in a fight) assumed that he'd gone so bestial that I didn't have to worry about the lasers, so it took me by ludicrous surprise when the lasers began emitting from his arms (wrapped around my chest from behind) and his stomach (pressed against my back) and even his teeth, which hadn't been able to bite their way into my neck, so they just blew open a hole and kicked in the doors.

Lasers pierced me from every angle.

The world went swim-y.

I dropped to one knee.

Then two knees.

The rocks all around me were being showered by a mad mess of laser beams, ones shooting across the quarry, shooting into the sky, shooting wildly, shooting most definitely into and through me. Siren had taken a few steps back and was simply watching, glowing with some sort of force field, protected from the barrage by means of either her own personal powers, or perhaps some technological marvel that had been constructed and given to her by the girl from the grocery store. To be honest, I've never really understood Siren's powers… the ones besides her appearance and her raw (cosmic, galactic, thrusting) sexuality, because I (and everyone else) have just never been able to pay much attention, otherwise.

She seemed pleased to have a good view of my death, though.

And I was certainly dying. The wounds were trying to heal, but… there… were… so many holes being shot through my body. Blood was spurting from my neck and unidentifiable *somethings* were sliding out from my stomach (the laser that hit my midsection was a good god-damned two inches in diameter) and my spine had been severed, meaning I was flopping to one side.

Siren was clapping.

It was, even then, sensuous.

My hand was clenching. Opening. Clenching. Opening. It was my left hand. The one that had let Paladin fall into the lava. It had done the right thing, then. I was sure that it had. My dying thoughts were that it had done the right thing. My dying thoughts were that I shouldn't have kissed Adele. It wasn't fair. My dying thoughts were that I should have kissed Adele so much more often. My dying thoughts were that it was strange how I could no longer control my hand… that some quirk of my brain was making it open, clench, open, clench. My dying thoughts were that there was suddenly something in the way of my fingers, something that had slid into my grasp, blocking my clench. It made me angry. All I wanted to do was open and clench. Open and clench. Open and clench. Something was taking even that away, and it was all that I had.

I spared enough notice to see that Laser Beast's leg, wrapped around my waist as he clung to me from behind, with the two of us flailing all over the quarry floor in Greenway, Oregon, had fallen into my grasp when my hand had, at one point, opened.

I clenched.

My grasp was just below his calf muscle on his left leg. My grasp was on the muscle and blood and bone beneath a fine pair of sharkskin pants. My grasp can squeeze steel like putty. Sharkskin pants are nice, but they don't protect a leg for shit when it's caught in a superhuman vise.

Laser Beast's scream was partly a howl, and it was right in my ear, and as he fell away from me I meant to turn and continue my attack, but I wasn't ready yet. Not quite. The green spectre of Tom Clarke was still doing its job, healing me. Laser Beast's leg would never heal… not unless I lost the fight… not unless Octagon could give Laser Beast that fucking potion that's distilled from the protective instinct of my dead brother. I wasn't about to let that happen. I crawled. I crawled to Laser Beast (*I'm already healing, you son of a bitch… and how are YOU doing?*) and I brought a fist down on his injured leg (*bam… a year… and how's THAT feel?*) and I inched forward and slammed a fist down on his chest (that's two years of Laser Beast the universe would be spared) and then I was at his face (I'd managed to clamber up onto my knees, and my spine was reforming, providing me support, and clamoring for some justice and a lot of revenge) and I had one moment where the voice of morality, the one that sometimes whispers in my ear, the one that always sounds like Paladin, was telling me that Laser Beast wasn't one of the invulnerable ones… that if I punched him, he'd die.

I told the voice, "Yeah. I know."

I told Laser Beast, "Take some time off!"

And then I punched him in the face.

I didn't hold back.

My fist sank a foot deep into the rocky quarry floor.

There was a moment of silence except for the heaving of my breath, and whatever whispers were coming from my mouth. What I was saying, I have no idea. The moment lasted for one second. Maybe two. I was glowing green from scores of puncture wounds caused by the lasers. It probably looked like polka dots.

I heard someone scream out, "Yes!"

I heard someone, someone enthusiastic, yell, "Reaver!"

There was a huge burst of applause.

Looking up, I could see the edges of the quarry, the tops of the rock walls, were lined with hundreds of people. The citizens of Greenway. I immediately thought of Octagon's arena… how he (I mean *she*, dammit) had set me up as some sort of modern gladiatorial entertainment, and now she was doing it again. She had, apparently, ordered one of her underlings to gather the citizens of Greenway, for Mistress Mary was among them, was moving through them, running to and fro, carrying a bullhorn, exhorting them to do as she wished (which they were all doing, without question) and of course Mistress Mary was now a member of Eleventh Hour. Maybe she even had a badge. A secret handshake. A clock that only went to eleven. That sort of thing.

The bitch used to be one of us.

Now, in Mistress Mary's *post-good-guy* era, I could see her up there, and with a combination of my very good ears (not superhuman, just good) and the simple fact that she was yelling through a bullhorn, I could hear what she was saying to the people of my hometown.

She was saying, "Don't get too close to the edge! You could fall!" This was just good advice; I couldn't blame her for that. The walls were forty or fifty feet tall in some areas, and the rocks were shale, crumbling, and the edges weren't the wisest places to stand.

She was saying, "Applaud! Applaud! This is the apex! You'll never see a better show!" At least I was supposedly a good show. Give me a bit more of a chance and I'll whittle Eleventh Hour down a couple more notches. Just… give me half a chance.

Mistress Mary was yelling, "This is *good* versus *evil*, Greenway! Choose your side!" Yeah. Piss on that. Piss on *you*, Mistress Mary, telling people that they had a choice. You're the only one who had a choice. You chose Eleventh Hour, and everyone falls in line, because your voice is…

Mistress Mary said, "Reaver is a hero. Remember your heroes! Remember the fight! Every morning! Every day! Remember the heroes! If you always remember the heroes, you always remember what you can be!"

Now how the hell was that supposed to help Eleventh Hour?

Mistress Mary said, "Do you love him? Do you love him? Answer me!"

And they did answer. I saw Frank O'Neill and his Channel Five camera crew, reporting. And there was Gus Ferkins. There was the girl who sold me crab cakes at the convenience store, and even Grace Shanahan, the crab cake maker. Greta and Felix Barrows, Greg's parents, were standing with their adopted daughter, Chase. Next to them was Judy, who had once been my brother Tom's handjob queen, and who now stood with the family she'd created after he was gone. There was Tim Grady, the mailman who always joked about the obvious packages of sex toys he'd delivered throughout the years. I saw the Gorner twins, still looking the same, not only identical but as if they hadn't aged. Slightly bigger breasts, that was all, on both of them, of course. I saw John Molar. I wondered if he still had a driver's license… how many stop signs he'd run throughout the years… how many people had been forced to leap out of his way. I saw Brett Turle, who used to come over to our house to play cards with my parents, up until the day he told my mother (he had, by then, drank near to a bottle of wine) that she had "*by far the most sweetest of asses that he probably shouldn't ought to touch.*" And I saw Laura Layton. And I saw Adele. It was only an hour ago that she had kissed me on the lips in what had been, still, the greatest revelation of my day.

She was standing with all of Greenway.

They were all saying that they loved me.

They were all applauding.

There was so much noise that I couldn't hear any one voice in particular. The clapping hands became a single flock of noises, gathered into one.

Then…

"No," I heard.

It was a single voice.

Someone didn't love me.

"No," she said. It was a woman's voice. Not from anyone who was ringing the heights of the Greenway quarry. No. It was coming from just behind me.

The voice said, "No. I have to tell the truth. I don't love you."

It was Siren.

She was moving closer. Slinking closer. The air hummed around her and my senses were flaring. I could feel the healing charging within me; I could feel it racing into overdrive, believing there was new damage to heal, wounds that needed to be closed, physical threats that needed to be addressed, but my senses were confused because there was no threat, no new wounds, nothing but an ocean of restless desire. An ache. A twist.

"This isn't how it goes," Siren said.

"You die here, today," she told me.

"Octagon promised me," she whispered. She was up against my ear. I wasn't sure how. She was still several feet away. How could she be so close to my ear?

"Nobody breaks a promise to me," Siren said. Some part of her nibbled at my ear. It might have been her mouth. I wasn't sure. It might just have been something in the fog. There wasn't a fog. I felt there was a fog. I was in a sauna. I was on a throne.

"Octagon promised me," Siren said. "She promised when I was taking a bite of that... apple." Siren's eyes were looking into mine. There wasn't a fog. There was only her eyes. Her lips quivered with our shared knowledge of Octagon's identity. I quivered in time. I am quite nearly immune to temperatures. I was burning. I was freezing. I needed Siren for warmth. I needed Siren to plunge me deeper into her fire.

"Didn't *you* promise me something?" Siren said. She was holding my arm. Her skin was against mine. She was pressed up against me. She was a sun. She was a galaxy.

"Didn't you promise that you would die?" Siren said. It was true. I had given my promise. I couldn't lie to her. I knew, now, why Siren never lied. Any lie would be disrobed. Siren was all about exposure. Siren was the truth. Siren was the gut feeling. The intuition. The heart. The soul. Her breast was against me. Her nipple was a thickened dart. It was made of hardened steam.

"Steve Clarke," Siren said. "Are you breaking the rules? Aren't you being the wrong kind of naughty? Are you going back on your word? How would you feel, Reaver, if I went back on mine?" Every... single... move that she made was a promise. It was unthinkable that she could be playing unfair. That she would withdraw what she was offering. We should share the truth. We should bask in it. We should embrace it. We should take it down with us. Siren's fingers were tugging at me. They were on my own fingers. They were on my leg. They were on my cheek. In my hair. Along my arm. Across my eyes. Tapping on my chest. Siren's fingers never moved. They were at her sides. They were all over and across me. They were everywhere.

"Let's seal this promise with a kiss," Siren said. Some parts of her moved against me. They were insistent. Demanding.

"Kiss me your promise, dead man," Siren said. Her lips were radiant. Solar. Ten thousand suns. Soft as air. Her tongue was just within, was hiding, but peeking, ready to surrender. Ready to be taken.

I lied, earlier.

A tiny giant of a lie.

I said that the voices of Greenway's residents had all blended together.

That they were a conglomerate roar without one single mark of individuality. That's almost true. That's completely a lie.

I could hear Adele.

Plainly.

Plainly telling me the truth that she loved me.

So…

I told Siren, "Take some time off."

My blow struck her on her cheek. I admit I was holding back. I admit I wasn't trying to hurt her. It wasn't a deathblow. Not even a staggering blow. Or even a particularly hard blow at all. But what it was… it was a punch.

It was a year of beauty.

Siren knew this.

And she screamed.

She ran.

She ran, I knew, because there is only so much beauty in the world, and only so much beauty in a girl, but there seems to be an infinite number of punches, and I had punches that could incrementally strip down Siren's beauty until she would be forced to look in the mirror and admit that she was no longer the fairest of them all.

So she ran.

She ran while she was still easily the most beautiful woman in the world.

She ran while there was still easily enough of her that the act of watching her run away (I'm mostly talking about watching her ass, but also the lithe form of her legs, and the mesmerization of her hair, and a thousand other visual targets my entire body found inviting) nearly put me to my knees. As it was, though there were certainly other things that should have been on my mind, I watched as Siren sped across the quarry, and out along the long drive, a run of perhaps a minute in length, which was time well spent. I even considered gathering each and every one of the stones that she had stepped on. They had become treasures.

When she was gone, when my eyes couldn't see her anymore, I finally registered the sight of something else.

Octagon was standing beside me.

There was a silver tube in her hand and for one second (this isn't too surprising, since I'd just been seeing and was still thinking of Siren) I thought Octagon was holding a vibrator.

She touched it to me.

The resulting discharge (electrical, or atomic, or nuclear… I wasn't sure) flung me seventy feet across the quarry to impact into a side wall, tucking me nearly two feet deep into the loose rocks with the shale exploding into fragments and dust as the hero with the embarrassing bulge in his pants suddenly remembered that he was in a fight.

I slid to the quarry floor, a cascade of loose rocks tumbling around me. Octagon was nowhere in sight. She had moved from where she'd been standing. Where was she? Where was…

She was right next to me, and she touched the silver tube to my side (just under my left arm as I was trying to ward her off) and the explosion sent me tumbling and sprawling along the quarry floor like a particularly well-thrown rock skipping across the surface of a lake.

I came to rest.

My eyes snapped up.

Octagon was nowhere in sight.

I'm not used to that. I've grown accustomed to being the one in the fight who's the fastest, who has the edge in being able to decide what happens next, because the first move is always mine.

This is why I hate Octagon.

He cheats.

He cheats so much that it took me years to find out that, properly, it's *she* cheats.

She cheats.

When I finally found her, this time, she was standing in the air, just above me. I'd visually circled the quarry with a 360 swivel but I hadn't looked up. Had forgotten that Octagon can simply stand in midair.

Because she cheats.

She touched the not-vibrator to me on my shoulder and the resulting impact simply slammed me straight down into a newly created crater, one that wasn't very large and wasn't worthy of all that much notice, unless you happened to be the object that had caused the crater, that had channeled and absorbed all the impact. In that case, the crater seemed enormous and it hurt like shit.

A shockwave rode out across the quarry floor, picking up dust and small bits of rocks, raining horizontal pebbles in a cloud of dust that scaled half the height of the quarry walls.

"God damn you and your silver vibrator!" I yelled at Octagon.

"My... what?" she said, looking at the silver tube. She was standing thirty feet away. I hadn't seen her move.

"Oh," she said. "I see what you mean. Hah! I never really thought of that before! It really does look like a vibrator!" Even with all that I knew, it was hard to picture Apple beneath the black body suit, beneath the... what...? The black-suited exoskeleton? And her voice was Octagon's, not Apple's. Her voice sounded like the worst of a man, an arrogant arms dealer, an oil baron, a spoiled Ivy League degenerate, an enemy.

The crowd above was chanting my name. Not only chanting *Reaver*, but also *Steve Clarke*. It gave me some strength. I scuffed my way out of the small crater. Thought about charging Octagon. She wasn't where I'd just been looking, though. She was fifty feet in another direction. I wondered how she was doing it. I also wondered how I would solve it. I wondered how I would put her down.

"Hear that?" I said, gesturing to the crowds above. "That's my name! They're chanting my name! Bet you didn't think that would happen when you plotted out this day in that fucking mind of yours! Bet you didn't think I could kill Laser Beast! Bet you didn't think I'd smash Firehook like an evil little bug! Bet you didn't think I could stand up to Siren, did you? Well, fuck you! Fuck you! You hear that?" I gestured to the crowd again. I was ranting. A bit. But I was also vying for position and trying to figure out exactly how Octagon was moving. I was looking for a tell. I was looking for a clue to exactly what she was holding in her hands. I was looking for a way to cheat.

Fighting is all about cheating.

"On the contrary," Octagon said. "So far, everything has gone exactly as I planned." She was behind me again. She was cheating. The silver tube touched my ass and I was sent spinning into the air, cartwheeling into the skies, cursing in agony (and some humiliation... smacked in the ass in front of my hometown crowd) and trying to get my feet back under me before I landed. Didn't make it. Crumpled to the ground on my shoulders and then sprang up (three times normal speed, damn it!) flinging rocks towards the spot where Octagon had been. But she wasn't there anymore.

"I wasn't exactly sure how you would take out Laser Beast," Octagon said. She was rising from the ground in front of me, intangible. I kicked through her face, but she was a ghost, and the lack of expected contact overbalanced me and I fell, and the ghost that I could not touch proceeded to touch me with the silver tube.

"Here's that vibrator," she said. The explosion sent me skimming along the rocky quarry surface, glowing a bit greener with each tumble.

The people above us, the residents of Greenway, began picking up rocks, hurling them down from above, aiming for Octagon. Most of them didn't have very good aim. Most of them didn't come close. A few reached the target. None of them did any damage. Some of them simply passed through Octagon. Others bounced off, breaking into pieces with the contact. She glanced up at the crowds. She laughed. It was a manly laugh. I wondered what the real laugh sounded like. I tried to remember Apple's giggle when Laura pinched her, or when I'd told the worst and best of my vulgar jokes, or any of the other times when I'd listened to her laughing while believing that she was my friend.

"Looks like you have a lot of people on your side," Octagon said, gesturing to all those above. "Looks like you have a fan club."

I started to say something (undoubtedly a cock-fueled taunt of some kind) but she disappeared, winked out of view. This time, I was ready for her. This time I knew she would appear directly behind me. I spun around as fast as I could (and I am by no means slow) but she wasn't there. My fist whooshed through nothing but empty air. I probably looked like an idiot. Greenway should have been throwing rocks at me.

I leapt.

I leapt because if she wasn't in front of me, and if she wasn't behind me, that meant that Octagon had gotten a step ahead of me and had known what I would do, meaning she was probably going to come out of the ground, meaning that I needed to…

She was in midair.

Right where the arc of my leap was leading me. She was waiting. She had time to give me a bright wave before she met my oncoming (helplessly flailing) body with an outstretched silver vibrator.

I was being sex-toyed to death.

"Fuck you!" I yelled. I was to the height of the crowd at the quarry walls. They were watching me being systematically killed, my healing abilities overwhelmed. I wasn't even putting on a very good show.

The silver tube touched me on my fist (I was trying to punch something, either it or Octagon) and the impact slammed me down to the quarry. I bounced. Three times.

On the third bounce, I found Octagon waiting for me, her intangible head peeking up from the ground.

She said, "Insects. Some new ones."

I said, "What the fuck are you…?" and at that point the cockroaches came boiling up from below. Maybe ten of them. Then a hundred. A thousand. The quarry floor was soon teeming with them. They were a chittering carpet, with clicking wings. I was jumping as often as I could, not going for height, but instead only trying to stay off the quarry floor, to jump as often as possible, to avoid the cockroaches much in the way that a "dancing" Russian bear avoids the hot plate upon which it has been chained.

The cockroaches that got onto me, the ones that did heroic leaps of their own, they were biting into me, munching their way into my flesh, chewing on legs that could endure a hailstorm of bullets.

The pain overwhelmed me.

Children in the crowd were screaming and crying at what they were watching.

The gathered adults of Greenway were doing the same.

Mistress Mary was ordering them to watch.

The pain finally brought me to my knees, brought me down to the surface of the quarry, and the cockroaches (up close, with them crawling for my face, I could see that they were green, a dull green, with teeth and lips and tongues rather than mandibles, making them infinitely worse) began swarming me, biting and chewing and burrowing and I was screaming and then…

… they were gone.

Octagon was standing over me.

She said, "I made them susceptible to oxygen. Twenty seconds of exposure and they dissipate. Can't have the little bastards getting loose, breeding, you know."

She was close enough to kick.

I wasn't feeling well enough to do any kicking.

But the seconds were ticking away. Tom's green ghost was doing its job.

All I would need is five seconds and then I could pulverize a few of Octagon's skinny little bitch-fueled bones.

Four seconds.

Three seconds.

Two seconds.

One second.

Her outstretched hand spurted fire.

Lightning rained down on me from above.

Octagon was gone.

The fires burnt into my flesh, which normal fire does not. The lightning flickered its attack once, and twice, and three times, visiting long term, which is another thing that is not supposed to happen.

And then Octagon was back. And I was burnt. And bloody. And chewed by insects. My skin, in places, had burst open from the lightning's assault. I was scraped raw by all the various impacts. I looked like a lunar landscape. I looked like a volcano's aftermath. I looked, I'm sure, like I was pissed off. But I didn't look, I'm equally sure, like I could do anything about it.

"It's over!" Octagon yelled. She wasn't yelling to me. She was yelling to the crowd.

"It's over!" she laughed. "Eleventh Hour reigns supreme! Your lives are mine! Reaver was the last of his kind! The last to stand in my way! I applaud his efforts to save you, to preserve his own life, but in the end it was useless! Useless!"

The crowd was huddled together. Was hugging. Was trembling. I was healing. I could still be their hero. If Octagon would… only… keep… flapping her goddamn jaw, I could still go home to Adele.

Octagon yelled, "There are no heroes! There is no future!"

I could go home to Adele.

I could… go… home to Adele.

Would the cat ever grow to accept me? Would Wiggles ever be my friend?

I could go home to Adele.

Give me an opening, Octagon.

You're the smartest person the world has ever known.

Just this once, be dumb enough to give me a chance.

Octagon yelled, "Steve Clarke! Reaver! It is time for you… to die!" She pulled a marble of some sort from within her black costume. Simply reached inside and drew it forth. I had a moment to see it (a black marble, an inch in diameter, devoid of any gleam or glare) and I was racing (I was moving so fast, the fastest I've ever moved, and it still wasn't going to be enough) and then Octagon was dropping the marble at my feet. At our feet.

I was rearing back for a punch.

The world went black.

An utter void.

I could feel the quarry floor beneath my feet.

But couldn't see it.

Couldn't see my fist as it moved through empty air.

Couldn't see anything.

But I heard Octagon.

She said, "Steve. It's time for you to know my plans."

⌖

When I was quite young my parents were very busy and they trusted me to fend for myself, meaning that I was allowed out of the house for as long as I wished. I often spent time with my friends, of course, and I was often getting into trouble, of course, but I was learning things, too. Like, how close to stand to a model rocket for the maximum mix of safety and hilarity. Or… which windows fostered the most educational view (meaning that of either of the Gorner twins, and also the corner window of 756 Beddell Street during the Grand October when Miss Isaacson was in town as a substitute teacher) and I also learned that a cigarette habit isn't all it's cracked up to be and that mouthing off to older kids isn't always the wisest course of action. That was my youth. My youth was also filled with, whenever I needed solitude, going into the woods and pretending to be a survivalist.

I would stay overnight.

Deep in the woods. Wondering about the sounds. The woods have far different sounds at night.

And the woods, away from the city, away from the town, away from any houses, away from the highways, away from it all, deep within the woods… in these places the forest gave my youthful self a true glimpse of how dark a world can be.

A survivalist boy has plenty of time to learn the methods of moving down a deer trail when not even able to see so much as a hand held up in front of his face, and to wonder if the cost of getting himself beaten up again might not be worth it for another handjob, and to keep a sense of the self even though the woods are very large and very lurking and he is very small and very unable to see himself or anything at all including those things that are always, in everyone's mind, prowling through the woods.

The woods were very dark.

I had thought it was complete darkness.

Until Octagon dropped that marble.

Until she was whispering in my ear, saying, "Let's do this. Let's save the world."

⌖

I said, "What the fuck are you talking about?"

A voice, somewhere in the darkness, answered, "I think you're smart enough to know my plans. *That's* what I'm talking about." It wasn't Octagon's voice. It was Apple's. Technically there was no difference between the two. One was the other. Still…

… it was interesting.

"I can't see for shit," I told Apple.

"Wait a bit."

"Wait… and then I'll get used to it?"

"No. I've nullified light. You can't get used to it."

"Then what am I waiting for?" I was keeping her talking. Keeping the sound of her voice in front of me. If I could just draw her in… just get a hold on her, I could end the fight. Immediately.

"I had to make it look good, so I tossed you around pretty bad. Sorry about that. Anyway, you're wounded now. You're healing."

"And?"

"I'll give you some goggles in a bit. They change the, umm… I don't mean to sound pompous, but you wouldn't understand what they do."

"That sounded pompous."

"I know… but I didn't mean that way. I guess… in simple terms, the goggles nullify the nullification."

"Why not just turn the lights back on?" She was somewhere in front of me, but I kept moving forward, and the voice kept being the same distance away. Either she was moving backwards, or else I couldn't trust my senses, or both. It was not at all nice to be in a situation where I was taking blind steps, and trying to find a woman who was always ten steps ahead.

"Because then everyone could see us, and we need some privacy, and I can't give you the goggles yet because the glare of your healing would be way too strong, right now. So... heal a bit, and then you get the goggles."

"You're waiting for me to heal?"

"I know this is going to be hard to believe, Steve, but... I'm not your enemy."

"Girls with vibrators usually aren't. Usually, they're amazing, but, you... you. I'd have to say you're my enemy." I could feel the crunch of the rocks beneath my feet. I had to believe that I was moving. I had to believe that I was moving forward. That I was closing in on Octagon.

"We don't have all that much time," Octagon said. It was important to remember she was Octagon. No matter what voice I was hearing... I was faced off against Octagon.

"Why don't we have much time?"

Apple said, "Because right now Laura is wondering where I'm at. And right now Adele is worried sick that some asshole villain is killing the man she loves."

I said, "Right now the man she loves is worried about that, too." There was a crunch of rocks off to my left. Her voice was ahead of mine. I wasn't sure which one to ignore. One of them was probably a trick. The other one was victory, and...

"Put these on," Octagon said. Something was pressed into my hand. It startled me. I hadn't known she was so close. I took a swing, a big punch, connected with nothing. Almost fell down.

"Look," Octagon said. "Just... put on the goggles, okay?" She sounded five feet away, or maybe fifty, or maybe behind me. I was disoriented. I had nothing to lose. I put on the goggles.

And I could see. I was very nearly centered in the quarry. The green glow of my healing wounds was intense... far more intense than ever before. My wounds were already halfway closed, healing, fading. If I'd put on the goggles when I was healing at full bore... I'd have looked like the sun.

Laser Beast's body was to my left. Past him, a ways, was a large boulder that was acting as a tombstone and an anti-memorial to Firehook. Up on the edges of the quarry were the townspeople of Greenway, staring down into the pit, obviously confused, squinting every which way, rubbing their eyes.

A bit to my right was a beautiful woman wearing nothing but a pair of panties as she slid out of a black body suit. There she was. My deadliest enemy. My nemesis.

Octagon.

Her panties had a rainbow and a leprechaun.

"Never tell Laura you saw me this way, okay?" she said. "It's just... it seemed like we should talk as Apple and Steve... not Octagon and Reaver. Hold on, I've got a shirt in here, somewhere." She was rifling through the interior of the discarded Octagon costume, searching within it. The costume had retained the shape of a man, one who had fallen onto his side. I lifted my goggles for a bit.

Blackness. Nothing but blackness.

When I put the goggles back in place, Apple was putting on a shirt. Her nipples had been as black as coal. I would never tell Laura of this. I would never tell Adele. It would have been like talking about a dream. Nobody ever wants to hear about dreams, no matter how strange they might be.

"Testing the goggles?" Apple said. "You can't see without them." She gestured to everyone who had circled the top of the quarry and added, "They're blind to us, down here. To them, the entire quarry is nothing but a void. A blob of black. Darker than oil."

She waited for me to say something. I pointed to the Octagon suit and asked, "How's that damn thing work?"

"I built it from pocket universes. I mean, seriously... that much should be clear. That's how I can reach in, anywhere. Infinite storage. Well, not infinite... but for all reasonable purposes, yes... infinite."

"You built a costume using universes as a fabric?"

"That I did. And a dress, too. But I can't wear it anywhere. Also a pair of panties, because it seemed like an interesting challenge. And, you know, fetish-y."

"Your panties have infinite storage?"

"That... doesn't sound right. Let's talk about something else. There's something I need to know. I need to know... Steve... do you trust me?"

I was supposed to answer.

I stayed quiet.

I mean… seriously, I wasn't just talking to Apple, or Octagon, I was talking to Checkmate. The smartest person in the world.

She could figure it out.

She did. She nodded, sadly, and said, "Here's the thing. I need you to trust me, so we're going to do something now. I'm going to do something dumb." She was exasperated with herself, I could tell. She was doing the walk of a person who can't believe she's doing what she's doing.

She was walking closer to me.

She was walking within range.

And she kept walking.

And I nearly went for her.

But something held me back. Something kept me from doing anything. Something kept me from attacking the person I considered the world's deadliest threat. I stayed motionless as she approached, motionless as she grasped my hand, motionless as she took a deep breath, and motionless as she wrapped my fingers around her neck.

Apple said, "If you have to, then do it. If you don't have to, then listen to what I have to say." My fingers were trembling around her neck. The words came out of her hard, struggling up past the clench of my hand. I had lifted her up, taken her feet from the ground. Her legs were kicking, a little, but her arms were at her sides. Her face had gone ashen. Her eyes, tinted red by her goggles, said that she wasn't sure she knew what I was going to do. My fingers were tensing. Her neck was soft. There wasn't the tingle of a force field. It was just a young woman's throat. I had Octagon by the neck and her expression was one of confusion and fright. It was everything I'd fantasized about. It was the wet dream of a battle. My fingers can squish through steel. Flesh isn't any obstacle… not at all. My fingers can crack stone. My fingers can be heroes, each and every one of them.

It wasn't that I couldn't do it. I knew that I could. There wasn't anything of any morality holding me back. Nothing past the look on Laura Layton's face when she had raced across the grocery store parking lot to find the woman who she loved, alive, in my arms. That wasn't so long ago. I have a good memory and it wasn't so very long ago. So it wasn't morality that kept me from snapping Apple's neck. It was love. Not my love. But… love still counts.

Besides that, I wanted to hear what she had to say.

I put her down on the quarry floor and took my hand from my neck.

"Next time you do that, you're dead," I told her.

"I feel half dead, now," she said, rubbing her throat, coughing out the words. "Seriously, do you know what your fingers feel like?" I didn't answer. I wasn't the one who needed to do some talking. She nodded, accepting the role. Hell… she'd probably planned for it.

"The world needs heroes," she told me. It wasn't big news.

"That's why I did what I just did. To give you a chance to be a hero. Now what I have to do is convince you that you made the right choice. That *not* snapping my neck was the heroic thing to do." She was looking me in the eyes. Not at all flinching, even though I am Reaver. Lots of people can still look me in the eyes. But they flinch when they realize they're not only talking to Steve Clarke, but to Reaver. People just have those flutters of anxious realization. Paladin's the only one who never flinched. And Adele. And now Apple. And, I guess, Checkmate and Octagon.

"There's something that I know you understand," she said. "Heroes can't always be heroic. Heroes don't always get to play the good guy. Heroes sometimes have to do some very bad, very un-heroic things."

"Are you going to claim you're a hero?" My words came out harsh. Of course. She was Octagon. Paladin had been my friend. I know about heroes.

"You wouldn't snap my neck… but you're willing to bite my head off," Apple said. She bent over, picked up a fossil, traced the outlines of an ancient branch with one finger. Part of the leaf was visible. She held it up to me. She tossed it aside.

"That's the past," she said. "What we need is a future. Moving to the future means making progress. Progress needs a plan… not just random chance. This moment is what I've been working for."

"You've done some shit things," I said. "All part of your plan, right?" To be honest, I was itching to get back to the combat. I was itching to prove I was a hero.

"Don't get high and mighty with me, Reaver," Apple snapped. She moved closer. Pressed her finger into my chest. Surprisingly, it hurt.

"You want to talk about Lake Tanganyika?" she said. "You killed everyone on those boats. Just killed them. You have any idea who they were? You have any idea what they'd done?"

"They were criminals who…"

"They were people. They were people who were a mix of outright scum, and partial scum, and people just caught up in the events. You didn't ask for any report cards, did you? No you didn't. You went in killing. Two of them were my operatives, gone undercover, trying to break down Bapoto's raids from within."

"I…"

"Shut up. One of my operatives dove into the water. You booted the other one in after him. Broke his spine with a kick. He had a daughter. He had a wife. Two wives, actually. They lived together. They're alone, now."

"I…"

"Shut up. When Paladin dropped you on that boat, they couldn't hurt you. Hear that? You understand what I'm saying? You were on a boat where nobody could hurt you, and you still killed them. You killed them."

"I…"

"Shut the hell up. My operative died, flailing around in the water with a broken back because you needed to use your Amazing Hand of Justice. His name was James Grake and you kicked his spine in half because…"

"I think…"

"Seriously. Shut up. You kicked his spine in half because it was the right thing to do. You kicked him in half because of what was happening at the time, and because the world needed to know, everyone needed to know, that *Nobody Gets Away With That Shit*. That's what a hero stands for… the honor-bound contract that nobody gets away with that shit." She stopped. I felt like maybe I could have said something. I didn't. Instead, I was thinking of what being a hero means. There are a lot of definitions. They change from day to day. Situation by situation. Apple's definition was as good as any of them.

Apple said, "In case you're wondering, I send money to Grake's wife and kids. And, about him being dead, let's just say he wasn't a saint. Also, in case you're wondering, my other man was fished from the water. Paladin saved him. He went into the water because of you, and he came out of the water because of Paladin, but the both of you are still heroes. You and Paladin. You're both heroes. You just fight in different ways." Again, I wanted to say something. What I wanted more than anything was to argue with Octagon's words. But… hell… what was I to say? Where was my argument? That Paladin wasn't a hero? He was. That I wasn't a hero? Shakier ground, but… yes… I do believe I fight for the fights that should be fought. All that was left was to argue that Paladin and I weren't different, so I kept silent. I looked up at the people of Greenway. They were milling about, caught in place by Mistress Mary's demands to watch. I was starting to realize that Mary was all part of Octagon's plans.

Apple said, "You want me to list another thousand or so things you've done that really aren't all that heroic? I've got a list in my head. I have a list of everything in my head."

"I don't doubt that."

"Listen… I do some bad things. I do them because the world desperately needs its heroes, and the world can't have its heroes without its villains. Think of villains as the ones who set the pace, and heroes as the ones who strive to run faster, to race in a better way. People need their pacesetters. People need to be guided. Most people do, anyway."

"Why don't you be a hero? Why this… why do you do these things as Octagon?" I was mentally going through her appearances in my head. I have lists, too. I was remembering that her, her alone, wasn't ever all that bad. Robberies. Threats. It was the rest of Eleventh Hour that were the bastards.

She said, "I've saved the world twice that you know of, three times that you don't. And as Checkmate I *am* a hero, but, here's the thing… the world makes progress in two different, but very connected ways. One way is by raising the top, but you should never raise the top without also raising the bottom. There's no reason to raise the top if you don't raise the bottom. Stretch things too thin, and they pop. The world segregates. Divides. Dissolves. We need heroes to raise the top, and villains to raise the bottom. That's the only way this world can make it. You have to be the top. I'll be the bottom." I nodded, solemn, because she was… she was making some sense.

She said, "And all this talk about you being the top and me being the bottom, I'm talking about public perception, here… not sex." She smiled at this. I smiled back, but she didn't see me. She was looking to the top of the quarry… was looking to Laura Layton. She wasn't paying me much attention at all. I could have reached out and done away with Octagon. I no longer had the urge.

I said, "Eleventh Hour."

Apple looked at me.

I said it again, this time making it a question. "Eleventh Hour?"

"I needed them close so I could study them. I did my best to rein them in. To minimize damage. It was… hard. Too many variables. But… and I hate myself for this… I had to learn each of their powers. The world will need their powers. I needed to know how Tempest controlled the weather. How Firehook spontaneously created fire. I needed them alive to study them. I can forge most of Tempest's powers, now. Even Macabre's magics, a little. I can transform the world, as soon as the world is ready for it. It's too soon, now. But in time, the sacrifice will be worth it."

"Tell that to all the dead people. The ones killed by Eleventh Hour. Tell that to all the dead people."

She said, "Don't for one second think that I don't…" It came out through her teeth. There was such hurt in her voice. Such unbelievable pain. I'd heard that level of pain only twice, before. One time from Kid Crater, and another time from a man who I'd let slip back down into the lava.

Apple said, "Maybe you don't want to hear this, but you're my hero. You're the only one I can trust with all this. It's too much burden, for me. Alone. I can't… I thought I was smart enough to do all this by myself, but I can't. Being smart doesn't… I… Reaver. Reaver, I need help. I need help and you're my hero. You always have been."

"Me?"

"The world. We're too young. We're children. The universe is too large for us to bicker the way we do. Don't tell anyone else, but Stellar is an alien. She is."

"Holy shit."

"Right. Holy shit. Somewhere out there, other worlds. Other civilizations. And we're down here bitching about gas prices, fighting over scriptures, about skin color, sexual preferences, television shows."

"Stellar is an alien? Holy shit."

"You're the first verified man to make true alien contact," Apple said. "I'm talking about fucking an alien, here." She smiled. There was such warmth. I already liked Apple. I was… starting to like Octagon.

"Didn't go right," I said.

"Nothing goes right every time. Not even sex."

"Oh, shit. Sex. Siren. I punched your girlfriend. And, uhh, other things.

I'm… sorry I screwed your girlfriend."

"You mean Siren? Please. She cuckolded me like… like… I don't even have an analogy. I used to keep stats, for fun. But not even I have that kind of brainpower. Now, if you were to ever try and kiss that girl," she pointed up to Laura Layton, who was adjusting her glasses, still trying to peer down into the secretive world of the quarry's void. "If you ever try to kiss her… then I'll go all Octagon on you."

"Adele would kill me first." Apple laughed as I said this. I wondered if the laugh would rise up out of the darkness and reach Greenway's ears. I doubted it. Apple would have thought of that.

"Anyway," I added. "Laura's not my type."

"Really? She's… so beautiful. And so much fun. And… oh so damn nasty in bed. How can that not be your type?"

"She's not Adele."

We were walking past Laser Beast's body. It wasn't pretty. Apple just shrugged. She said, "It was time for Eleventh Hour to go. I have all the data, now. I can replicate most of their powers. It was time to put them down. It's what I wanted you to do. It's what I needed you to do. People need to see you being a hero."

"A couple weeks back, you almost shot me through the head with a laser pistol."

"A couple weeks back, there was going to be a failure in my pistol, one that would have sent an explosive discharge throughout the whole room, stunning Eleventh Hour, letting you make your escape."

"I screwed up your plan?"

"You made it better. Accelerated it. I should have thought of Greenway. It has more theater. More drama. I should have thought of all this from the start." We had walked past Laser Beast, moved past Firehook, and I was looking at Octagon. At the suit, I mean, anyway. I nodded to it. Not wanting to touch it. The suit was still my enemy.

Apple said, "Don't break it. You wouldn't believe how expensive it was to make. Also, it has a failsafe if it's broken. A tiny black hole. It's there to dispose of my body if I'm ever killed during a fight. To compact my remains to sub-atomic levels. It will just look like I've whisked myself away. Forever to be thought of as a *Menace that Might Return*."

"Harsh."

"It's not a pretty job... this thing we do. But... it's what the world needs. It's what I have to do. I can't stop doing it... but it never stops hurting. It just doesn't." She was sniffling, a little. I thought of her words and how similar they were to what Paladin had told me. *Pain that never ended.* I put my arm around Octagon's shoulders. She moved closer. It was the same arm that had given Paladin to the lava. Maybe this was retribution. Maybe this was just something that was happening. I didn't know. I didn't have any grand scheme, no plan. I was just doing what I felt was needed.

I said, "This... all this that you're telling me. Before I can decide, I need to know something. Do you love Laura?"

"Huh?" Apple was wiping her eyes on my sleeve. It seemed so very human. I had thought of Stellar as human but had never truly thought of Octagon in that way. Wrong on both counts.

"Laura. Do you love her?"

"Yes."

I was glad she hadn't said more. I was glad that she thought adding anything else would have been superfluous. Or even a masking agent. I was glad for a simple truth.

I said, "What happened to Tattoo? You were dating him. He disappeared. What happened to him?"

"Nothing, really. He just retired. I've kept his secret. He didn't like the pressure. Wanted to just... paint. He has a cottage, now. Only a couple hundred miles from where your parents live."

"You know where my parents live?"

"No. I mean, maybe. I mean... yes. I'm the one that runs security for them."

"So... you could have gotten to them at any time?"

"Only if I was a total bitch, which I'm not, remember?" I did remember, actually. I'd tensed up a little, but...

... Apple was...

... Apple, I suppose. Not Octagon or Checkmate. And that forced me into some serious decisions. Decisions that a part of my mind was arguing were already made. I'd made them earlier when I was deciding how to fight Octagon. The same logic now applied to *not* fighting her. Because part of my mind was saying, pointing out once again, that I am a man who can lift thirty thousand pounds. I was focused on that. I was telling myself I needed to focus on how I can lift thirty thousand pounds. It would be ridiculous to think that a normal person could out-lift me. Absolutely ridiculous.

I was focusing on that.

I was being smart enough to realize that.

I was being smart enough to realize that it was equally ridiculous for my mind to work at the level of Apple's. Smart enough to realize that I cannot out-think her.

It just wasn't possible.

People can readily admit they're shorter than someone, or maybe not as good-looking, or not as fast, or as strong, or anything excepting being inferior in the category of brainpower.

We always think we're as smart as the next guy.

But, regardless, I had to do something. It was heroic, though it should be commonplace.

What I had to do was admit I wasn't as smart as Octagon. Or Checkmate. Or Apple.

I could do that.

I could.

Because I'm not as smart as Checkmate.

But I'm not dumb.

I said, "Now what?"

Apple looked to me. She saw what I wanted her to see. She saw the truth. She saw that Reaver was entering a new phase of his ongoing life. His second team-up with a fellow superhero. My arm around her shoulders turned into a hug, not brief, and I could smell the sweat in her hair. For some reason, that felt important. That felt *human*. Hell… I even felt human. That felt important, too.

Apple began putting on her suit, again, sliding into another persona, another hero. Becoming Octagon.

She said, "What's next is you fight me. Fight me every chance you get. Show the world that you *Will Not Fall* to someone like Octagon. Teach them how to fight. Lead them. Give them an example. Raise them up. Be a hero."

"I can do that."

"And marry Adele for fuck's sake."

"Jesus."

"But *sleep* with her first! Sleep with her *a lot*! Laura and I were talking with Adele yesterday and she is just *so* damn horny! *Give* her something! I mean, pound her!"

"Holy shit."

"I know, right? But you better get used to me. I'm going to marry Laura, if she'll have me. And then you and I will be family."

I said, "Holy fuck," not for only what she was saying, but for how she was saying it. She was back in the suit. She was Octagon, again, with Octagon's voice.

Octagon said, "In just a second, I'm going to drop the black field, and they'll be able to see us. Afterwards, when you're talking to the media, and you *will* talk to the media, I'm sure that Frank O'Neill will ask what happened down here in all the blackness."

"Yeah. He probably will."

"I want you to tell him that we were in a pocket universe. That we were fighting in a contest of willpower."

"Okay." It was her plan. She's smarter than me. I'd give it a shot.

"Then, when he asks you who won, you look at him and say, '*I'm alive, aren't I*?'"

"I can do that." I could do that. And it would be true. I felt alive. Truly alive.

Octagon was rising into the air. The blackness was fading. She said, "And smile for the cameras. You need to smile more! Smile!" I was smiling. I was a hero. For the first time in years I was feeling purely like a hero. I had defeated Eleventh Hour. I had defeated Octagon. I had defeated, at long last, Reaver.

Octagon and I took off our goggles and let them fall to the ground.

The blackness was gone.

We were revealed to the world.

I saw Adele at the same moment she saw me. We made eye contact. She saw how I was still alive. Was crying in relief. Laura was hugging her. I'd see them, quite soon. I'd be with them. Maybe Apple would come over, later.

Octagon, rising into the air, beginning to speed off into the skies, let out a scream that stunned the gathered citizens of Greenway, Oregon. The scream was anguish. It was horror. It was despair. It was defeat. It was damn good acting.

As she vanished, Octagon screamed, “Damn you, Reaver! *Damn you*! This round goes to you! But I’ll be back! You’ll never beat me! You’ll never stop me! You will *never* stop me!”

I screamed something heroic in return.

Something impressive.

I did that for the crowd, of course.

Because in my mind I was thinking, “No, Octagon. I won’t stop you.”

I never will.

ACKNOWLEDGEMENTS

Thanks are first due to Jack Kirby, who was instrumental in creating the world of comics and superheroes, carrying mythic traditions into a new and vibrantly illustrated age. And of course to all the other comic book creators who toil at their tables... the writers, pencillers, inkers, colorists, letterers, editors and everyone else who brings nobility to life.

And I'm very thankful to my first readers: Colleen Coover, Jeremy Barlow, Graeme McMillan, Josh Williamson, and especially Chris Roberson. You all helped keep my nose to the grindstone. Consider this an IOU certificate for a free drink.

Thanks to Allison Baker, who helped shepherd this project to Night Shade, and thanks to Jeremy and Ross and the rest of the Night Shade crew for giving me a home.

I'd also like to extend my thanks to the staff at Three Friends Coffee House, and the girls and staff at Sassy's. Thanks for letting me sit quietly in the corners, crafting another world.